Edited by Sara Johnson

Staccato Publishing
Zimmerman, MN

First US Edition: December 2010
Second Edition: May 2012
Third Edition: June 2013

ISBN: 978-0-940202-50-1

Empath

by HK Savage

Bree—
We will always
have Nashville. ♡

Ch. 1

My head felt like it was going to burst. "It's part of the whole college experience Mom," I fell back on the same argument I'd given a thousand times as I wandered around my room. Packing my things, I tried to ignore the sense of failure accompanying the stabbing pains in my head and wrenching in my stomach, reminding myself none of them were mine.

"Claire, I just don't know why you can't stay here with us while you ease into college life. There's no need to rush. So much is going to be changing for you and I want you to do well. You know how hard it is for you to make friends." Jeanette, my mother, was overreacting as usual as she sat on my bed playing idly with a loose string on my comforter looking like she was going to cry. Again. Great. My eyes welled up.

She was right. It *was* hard for me to make friends but not for the reasons she thought. She was under the impression I was a loner by choice not out of necessity. But it was that necessity that was giving me a headache right now and making me feel like I wanted to cry. *I* didn't want to cry, *she* did. That was my problem; empathy and too much of it.

I can feel what others are feeling so strongly that it's not just a "feeling" it's a real *feeling*. I can feel it like it's mine, which makes being around other people really hard for me. I would describe it as being at an incredibly loud 3-D movie that is turned up so loud you can't hear yourself think and everything seems like it's all around, so there isn't any sort of break or relief from all of it. What I have is not a choice but an affliction and I have been this way ever since I can remember. The only way I've ever found that I can limit the effect on me is to avoid being close to people. Proximity is difficult, but touching is terrible and that is yet another reason my mother was so upset with me at the moment. She thought I didn't want to touch her or hug her. I wanted to; I just couldn't.

And here she was about to cry. That's always one of the worst things I have to deal with, it's so raw and painful especially when it's because of me. To stay was to keep the cycle going and leaving made me insensitive. Either way we both lose. It has been slowly driving me insane for the past nineteen years and most of my family thinks I'm socially retarded. Now, I had my chance to escape right here in front of me and I was taking it whether she was okay with it or not; it was the only hope either of us had for a somewhat normal relationship.

"Mom, you can't cry about this," I tried gently to disparage her fear while I wiped at my nose now running just like hers. "I will be fine and you know it. You've always said you wished *you* could have gone off to school and now, here you are, trying to keep *me* from doing it. If I stay here while I go, it's no different than the last twelve years of school." As expected I felt the stab of guilt and knew I'd hit home.

My mother grew up in Iowa with parents too busy with farm life and duties to see their daughter needed their attention and love. As soon as my father, a relatively handsome and gentle man with plans to enlist in the army after school had shown some interest, she had latched on and they had eloped at seventeen.

The life of an Army wife suited my mother quite well. My father was usually relocated every few years and she got to try on all sorts of lives for herself in different towns. She was always searching for something that would make her feel complete; whether it was new friends, running, reading circles, quilting groups, anything to take over her attentions and make up for the fact that her family was not what she had hoped. She had grown up dreaming of a big, happy family with lots of kids and their friends always at the house; filling it with their noise and energy. She was made for that kind of thing, with the chasing after and busyness of it all. Instead she got me, a socially limited kid who didn't go out much except for the few outings to movies and dinner a few times a semester I could muster with the relatively small group of girls who were not completely weirded out by my odd behavior.

Because I have never found anyone else with a curse like mine; I have never been able to talk about it or figure out if there's any way to shut it off. My only defense has been to keep my own emotions wrapped up tight and keep a safe distance from everyone else. Oh, and I hold my breath a lot. It seems to help when physical contact is unavoidable.

Not understanding the phenomenon myself, I can't explain it. But the whole, "it's not you, it's me" argument didn't carry a lot of weight when I tried to have it out with her a few years ago. I saw how her perceived failures were eating her from the inside and adding to her growing substance abuse problems. How could I not feel responsible? Since that discovery, I've actually had to withdraw almost entirely from her if I am to keep even a small part of my sanity and I have no idea how to heal the rift that now stands between us.

The best thing I can do now, for both of us, is to get away. I've been waiting for this day my whole life although my enthusiasm is, of course, tempered by a few of the hurdles I can see standing readily before me. School has never been very hard for me. Little social time leads to lots of study time. However, living in a dorm with a pack of overly emotional girls who are finally getting a chance to be relatively unsupervised with a pack of overly hormonal boys. Oh, the joy that is going to be. The difference is that I am better able to insulate myself from strangers' emotions. I can feel anyone, but I've noticed that it takes some exposure and personal connection for me to feel them intensely. Once I have their feel, I can't even lose it in a crowded room. It's just there, on my periphery until I put some actual distance

9

between us. Thus, the need for my own room on campus. A roommate would be a nightmare.

Now, here I am about to head off to Augsburg College, a small, private school in Minneapolis. As much as I would like to move far away, I just couldn't do that to Mom. She needed me to come home on weekends and holidays and I am terrified (probably because she is) of going away to some strange state; it would be too risky if I completely fall apart. I chose a private school not because of the prestige but because of the small classes. As one could imagine, crowds are pretty hard for me to handle.

"Any more boxes? I don't know how much more will fit in the van," my father, Doug's, voice drifted up the stairs and with it, a welcome sense of calm I eagerly tapped into it, feeling my nose and eyes clear at once. A life of barking orders had never transferred to his volume in the house, thank goodness. Dad came through the doorway to the bed where Mom was still sitting. He rested a hand lightly on her shoulder with a nervous glance at her face. Poor Dad. Mom was going to be difficult for a while if her current state was any indication. Her despair was increasing by the minute. I could taste it and feel the air being squeezed from my lungs as I suffocated on her need to keep me close.

"Just one more bag, Dad, and I think we can go."

"Okay, I'll meet you down at the car. " He pulled away gently from my mother with a last lingering pat on her shoulder, which she did not acknowledge, grabbed the bag from the bed and gave me a slight, tight lipped smile that didn't reach his eyes. His anxiety was growing in direct response to Mom's grief and I was relieved when he went downstairs before both of them were a wreck.

I needed to leave this sick cycle before I officially went nuts!

On the surface, they looked like such a normal couple. Dad was balding a little on top through his crew cut brown hair but always had a strength in his hazel eyes that I relied on for stability in my darkest times. Mom was a brunette like me with her hair just past her shoulders in a typical mom bob. Her eyes, light brown, were always a little pinched at the edges, too tight for genuine warmth.

Dad was great at locking down his emotions. It made us work pretty well together. The bummer was that I didn't really know what he was thinking unless I tried. It must be what normal people have to put up with when interacting with others. It wasn't a bad thing, just different. Dad had been shutting down emotionally for years, and with a bit of an emotionally crippled wife and distant daughter, who could blame him. Then there was a lifetime of military training. Not really a breeding ground for warm and fuzzy behavior. I did feel bad for him, though; now that he was retired, he had nothing to do with himself except for woodworking. It was no wonder he spent so much time in his workshop.

We live in Richfield, Minnesota. Minnesota is a state with a surprisingly lively boutique furniture trade. Dad had always found woodworking comforting and constant in his perpetual job transfers over the years. He'd developed quite a knack for furniture design as well. A crib for a friend, new chair for a co-worker; he was always working on something. It surprised us when it turned out the local boutiques were able to sell his designs for a pretty penny; this let him supplement their retirement income and help send his only daughter to a nice school with minimum need for student loans. I would also be working on campus in the library but that was okay with me. My first love was books and I felt perfectly at home in a library.

I made an inspection of the now relatively bare room I had spent the last few years in and looked at Mom. I couldn't think of anything new or comforting to say to her. Whether she knew it or not this was the best thing for all of us.

11

Hurriedly I held my breath and touched her shoulder. She closed her eyes as the tears started and I walked quickly out the door.

Things just have to be better away from here; at least they'll change.

****

It was Sunday evening. Dad left a few hours ago after helping me unload the few boxes of "must haves" that I brought with me to start my college adventure. He'd be more than happy to help set up my confusing electronics for me in a very dad-like way. Stereo, microwave and mini fridge were now all set up and, being a good daughter, I pledged that the fridge would never hold an alcoholic beverage. No worries there, I had yet to sample alcohol beyond a sip or two. The lowering of inhibitions made my curse all the more difficult to bear so I pretty much shied away from it or anyone under the influence.

So, here I sat on my new bed which was perched on a very sturdily, and stylishly built, wooden loft by my dad. From this vantage point, not only could I look all around my ten by ten room, but I could also see out my rather large window on the far wall. The easily four-foot wide opening overlooked the freeway on the far edge of campus but was so high up, I kind of liked it. It made me feel like I was removed from it all. My own little penthouse suite, I smiled to myself.

With classes starting tomorrow, it probably wasn't a bad idea to get the lay of the land before I would have to perform under pressure. I figured now was as good a time as any to find the cafeteria. I could vaguely remember from orientation this summer that it was in the main building which seemed to house everything such as the bookstore, student services, and of course, food. The self-guided tour would give me an excuse to wander around and give this experiment a test run. What would it be like to be around

12

this many strangers in an anonymous setting? And, could I really hope to be saner away from home or was I going to crack up before I turned twenty?

****

Dinner hadn't been extraordinary. There were a number of students getting food when I reached the cafeteria at seven. They mostly looked like freshmen also trying to get their bearings.

I wasn't very hungry; I've never been able to eat when my stress level is up. Instead of a real meal, I grabbed a yogurt and an apple. The apple was portable and could easily accompany me to my room for later. The yogurt gave me something to do with my hands while I watched as all of the lost and scared came in, tightly bunched groups, not unlike sheep. They milled about together as they grabbed trays, filled them and then shuffled over to the tables.

The good news was I discovered that by sitting a few feet away and ignoring eye contact, I was able to ignore most of the emotional output around me. Because I didn't know any of these people, their emotions remained at a relatively low hum. My optimism grew.

Ch. 2

Freshmen 101 classes. My biggest fear. Large, auditorium type setting with way too many people all crammed together and not caring enough about the class to sit quietly and focus. When people focused on their note taking in class, obviously, their ability to emote was greatly reduced. For this reason, I wished all of my classes could be Calculus.

First up on the menu for the day was Psychology 106. This class was going to be a challenge. Not only were we going to sit in an auditorium once a week for over an hour, but according to the syllabus I'd gotten with my class assignment, we would also be expected to break into smaller groups to discuss emotional subject matter.

Girls were usually more honest about how they felt on their feelings, but make no mistake, the guys were equal parts trouble for me. I once threw up in tenth grade Psychology when Todd Adams, my seat partner, had a strong response to our discussion on the effects of violent crime. We were too close together and I couldn't get away quite in time to avoid his strong flashback. The first gut-wrenching wave had taken my breath away and hearing it, he had put his hand on my arm pulling me into his emotional memory with him. I felt his terror tied up in his memory of being held at gunpoint with his mother when he'd been young. Knees weak and unable to stand, I had thrown up right there in the aisle. Thank goodness I had turned my head at least and avoided hitting anyone though the damage to my reputation had been permanent.

I was hopeful that by college my peers would be better able to control themselves. I hoped I was as well. As class was released, I took my time gathering my books, giving me the opportunity to avoid the crush of a mass exodus. Plus, I had a few hours before my next class and I was in no particular hurry. When I did leave the lecture hall just a few minutes later, the hallway was nearly empty with just a few lost underclassmen jogging to make it to their next class on time. I wandered down the hall and turned to go down some short stairs toward the doors leading out into the quad, the open park like square in the center of the main cluster of buildings. University Center was my goal, it was the main building housing the bookstore where I had seen some books I might want to kill some time with over the next few weeks in my anticipated free time and it was only a few yards across the quad from me.

I was pretty well in my own head and at peace due to the crowd control and stranger factor allowing me some much needed quiet time. Actually, I was reveling in it. It had been a long time since I'd enjoyed such a reprieve from the typical static of my curse.

So, it was like a shockwave hitting me in the chest as I came around the corner at the bottom of the stairs and felt the terror and fury clashing before I could hear it. They were speaking so quietly I'm sure no one just walking past would think it was more than a minor disagreement and not even worth a second glance. However, given my sensitivities, I felt the underlying intensity and it took my breath away.

There was a slight, borderline delicate looking student with honey colored hair holding his books in front of his chest like a shield. His huge hazel eyes were staring impossibly wide at his antagonist.

Sturdily built with a muscular frame that had to come in over five foot seven and no visible fat on her; she was a formidable woman. Her thick mane of honey colored hair was the same shade as the boy's but long enough to be pulled into a sloppy bun. She was clad basically, wearing a pair of jeans, and a baggy black t-shirt that did absolutely nothing for her light coloring and large size. But it wasn't only her size that made her frightening. It was the rage and threat of violence in her hushed tone, undetectable to an outsider. Her upper lip curled over her teeth in a snarl as she pointed at him from about two feet away and spoke low and intense.

The two were similar enough in coloring that I thought they must be related and maybe it was a dust up between brother and sister, but even if they were family, this felt like it was getting scary and I was being tossed about between her fury and his terror; it beat against me like an ocean's undercurrents. It was completely disorienting.

Maybe that was why, in an entirely uncharacteristic move, I stepped up to the boy and interposed myself with my back to the girl and asked with concern, "Can I help?" The boy looked at me suddenly and tried to hide his worry by looking down and shuffling his feet. He was embarrassed. With my ability to feel his turmoil, anything he said wouldn't hide what I really saw. What I felt. This kind of emotional intensity cut right through my precarious armor of anonymity.

"It's alright, I'm alright," he mumbled quickly as he pushed an invisible pebble with the toe of his black Converse.

"Move along, this is not your affair," the bully spoke tightly through clenched teeth.

I turned to look at her, thrown temporarily by her odd manner of speech given the heat of the moment. When I looked at her, she was in perfect control of herself and her face had gone completely neutral. A passerby would think I was asking about something as mundane as directions

Returning my eyes to the boy, I saw that he was peeking at me through his shaggy hair, eyes still enormous, but his own features otherwise calm as well. It appeared his eyes were always that big, maybe that was what made him seem so young and vulnerable. "We're having a family discussion.

16

I'll thank you to mind your own affairs," continued the woman.

Given the extra sense my curse provides, I'm usually the first to know when someone is going to do something like hit a classmate or trip someone on the bus. That's why it was so surprising that the woman's push caught me unaware.

One minute I was looking at the boy's face, feeling his apprehension ebbing, which made me feel like I had done the right thing. The next minute, I felt an incredibly powerful thrust to the middle of my back right below the shoulder blades that sent me spinning into the boy. All I had time to think was that I was going to squish the poor little guy. That, and the fact that this woman had issues.

Instinctively bracing for the fall I was sure he and I both had coming, I put both hands out. I try to avoid touching, but I didn't want to break my nose on his face by falling on top of him. *Please don't let this hurt too much.* Ran through my mind on my way down.

Several things happened very quickly, almost too quickly to process. My hands went out to his shoulders and after dropping his books, his arms came out to my sides, grabbing me around the waist. We touched each other at the same time and this boy, no bigger than me, stopped my momentum, he felt very solid. And warm. Hot even.

The heat took me by surprise, but even more shocking was what I *didn't* feel. The boy's terror, the woman's rage, the cacophony of the myriad hummings emanating from the several small groups of students nearby, all of these things stopped. Just stopped. It was like I was in a bubble. It was fabulous. And terrifying. What just happened? Also strange, was the fact that even though I hadn't registered any sort of pain, when we touched, I distinctively had the thought "ouch" pop into my head.

17

The boy seemed to have felt something as well as his eyes focused on my face and his mouth formed a little "o."

But the first one to speak was the woman behind us as we stood in each other's arms. "What the hell?" she hissed. "Stephen, back away from her." She tried to reach for his arm on my waist.

The boy whipped his face up to hers and without tearing his gaze from mine spoke softly to her. "Tara, no. You know we have a duty. I'll meet up with you later." At this last, he broke our eye contact to look at Tara. She dropped her hand and, still staring, turned on her heel and left. Although she still seemed angry, I honestly couldn't feel anything coming from her direction as she strode away.

After Tara stalked off, I was left holding on to a complete stranger, but I didn't let go right away. "Ah, are you okay?" The boy dropped his arms and I mimicked him so that we were standing about a foot apart with our hands at our sides staring at each other nearly at eye level.

As soon as our physical contact ended, the low grade "noise" crept back into my consciousness. As an experiment I didn't even realize I was conducting, I reached tentatively to the boy and touched his hand with my own. Just as before, when we made contact, the buzzing of others' emotions were gone. He just stared back and a slow smile spread across his face.

"Hi, I'm Stephen Andrews. Do you drink coffee?"

Shaking my head dumbly I heard myself answer, "I prefer tea."

Ch. 3

Stephen suggested the bagel place just a few blocks up the street from campus. It was a quiet walk with Stephen striding confidently ahead of me, his arms swinging freely, appearing completely at ease. Hadn't he just been terrified as Tara berated him only five minutes before? And now he was showing absolutely no traces of that fear. Was I missing something?

While we walked, I looked over and it struck me again how little this guy was. He seemed so young. I was 5'2" and he couldn't have been more than a few inches taller than me. Plus his wide face, freckles and large eyes made him seem like he was barely past puberty.

"I'm Claire Martin, I'm a freshman." My voice was loud in the midmorning quiet.

"Hi Claire." He looked over again through his shaggy mop of hair and gave me an easy smile. He didn't seem old enough to be at college. He was so small and childlike; it was hard to think of him as my peer or even my superior. Maybe that was why I had felt compelled to try to protect him earlier; it was maternal or something.

We continued on without speaking for about five more minutes before reaching our destination and upon arriving, ordered our drinks. I felt like something soothing, so got a Tazo mint tea and Stephen ordered black coffee. After getting our drinks, we took our seats below the front windows. I unwrapped my tea bag and began to dunk it rapidly in my apprehensiveness, letting the scent rising to my nostrils work its magic and slowly unwind my nerves while waiting for him to talk.

Stephen took his time. He seemed unconcerned with the whole strange scenario and settled into his chair with a slight slouch over his cup before looking back from the window and meeting my eyes.

I looked down at my tea again and noticed that I could feel the murmurings of the others in the store, I couldn't feel *anything* coming from my companion. I was equal parts intrigued and frightened as to what was different about Stephen than anyone else I'd ever known.

He took a sip of his coffee and examining the side of his mug asked casually, "Have you ever been to the basement of the library?"

Uncertain where he was going, I tried to follow. "I just got here yesterday so I haven't had a chance yet. Why, should I?"

"There is a book there I think you would find very interesting. This author, Roger Jenkins, he wrote a book about the paranormal and ESP and stuff. It might be something someone like you would find interesting." He continued to study his mug.

Considering the fact that I had tried my entire known existence to keep my curse a secret for fear I would either be committed or experimented on, I was more than startled that Stephen would have me pegged so quickly. I had to swallow to make my voice sound remotely normal. "I don't know what you mean. I don't buy into that sort of goofy stuff. See," I said leaning back and waving a hand over my scant makeup and orange shirt for his examination. "See, not goth. I don't buy into that sixth sense stuff." I added with a laugh that was too high to my ears.

With a hint of a smile, Stephen looked at me and ran his finger around the lip of his steaming coffee mug. "Are you sure you wouldn't be interested to find out how to shield yourself a little better? I mean, doesn't all the noise get to you?"

It was all I could manage to keep my jaw from falling into my teacup. "How...?"

"Well, for one, you just about blasted me when you touched me." He was watching my face, only the unblinking intensity of his hazel eyes belied his otherwise casual demeanor.

"Blasted?" I had no idea what he was talking about, my astonishment plain on my face. My curse was receiving. It had never occurred to me that I too might be projecting something.

"Yeah, energy is just flying off of you. You're like one of those static orbs in a science lab." For such a crazy conversation, Stephen was maintaining an enviable mien of near boredom. I was tempted to look around for a camera crew; was I being punked? Or any minute were the orderlies, who were certainly not far behind, coming to pick me up and throw me in the looney bin.

"I don't know what you're talking about with all of this hocus pocus stuff but I'm not interested. I should probably get back to my dorm anyway. I promised my Dad I'd call after class. Checking in and all, I have to do it a lot. My parents are very overprotective and keep a close watch on me. They'll worry if they don't hear from me soon." Let this guy think I have people who would miss me right away if he kidnapped me and put me in his trunk. He just seemed so creepily calm and it spooked me that I couldn't feel him in the slightest, I couldn't gauge his sincerity and it had me panicked.

"You'd better get going then." Stephen looked down at his cup and back out the window. "Check the book out though. It's the real deal, not hokey like a lot of those books can be."

I got up to leave before this could get any more surreal.

21

"Nice meeting you Claire," he said quietly, watching me stand and turn away.

"Umm, yeah, you too," I mumbled as I grabbed my bag off the back of my chair and walked out the door too quickly. It was a strange walk back and I looked over my shoulder several times as I hurried back to my dorm, arguing with the voice in my head telling me to run. I was shaken to my core by Stephen's words. He'd seemed so unassuming discussing the curse I'd disguised with relative success the majority of my life. Yet, he had me pegged within five minutes of meeting me. And he was so cool about it, like he knew something the rest of the world didn't. Plus, factor in the slight detail that was throwing me for a loop. I couldn't feel him even when I *tried*. I resolved to go the other way if I saw him again.

Ch. 4

Tuesday morning broke too early for my taste. I'd been tossing and turning all night trying to wrap my head around my conversation with the confusing boy I'd met yesterday.

The sky was overcast with the first hint that fall was on its way out. I took a long look as I opened my curtains seeing the first of the crimson leaves blow past on their way to carpet the ground below. Minnesota weather is its own entity. In some places people talk about the weather as a time filler, but not so in Minnesota. Here we talked about the weather because it's like an unpredictable member of the family. It was always affecting everything you did but impossible to plan for or around. Everything you tried to do in the outdoors had to have a contingency plan, should the weather decide to be uncooperative.

I decided on jeans and a thermal top under a button up short-sleeved camp shirt. I was beginning my on-campus job today at the library and wanted to make a good impression but stay warm in a big space like that. Up until my coffee date yesterday when Stephen rattled me, I was really looking forward to working at the library for the serenity it would surely offer.

Libraries were like a second home to me, not really a shocker given my lack of much of a social life, and I'd noticed Augsburg's library was fantastic, falling in love with it on my campus tour last summer. Big, new and full of books I had never read before, it was tantalizing. City libraries are dicey unless you get into a bigger city, but college libraries are great. They're full of so much research material, I couldn't wait to get my hands on all of it. I'd actually been looking forward to searching for more information on my condition now that I had access to a new wealth of information. It had occurred to me sometime in the night that this boy had given me a direction as to where to start.

Grabbing a jacket in case the weather turned and locking my door behind me, I headed out to check in for my first day on the job. It was a short walk across the campus to get to the library. It was a large, angular, modern building with lots of glass in the entrance and shiny metal framing the exterior of the dome before it angled back into the more traditional red brick. It looked like a cheerful place; not like some of those old dingy libraries where everything smells like mold and you have to take an allergy pill just to read a magazine. I was definitely going to like it here, thoughts of the quirky Stephen temporarily set aside.

Upon entering the bright and airy entryway, I walked up to the smiling brunette with short, orange tipped hair working at the counter.

"Hi, I'm Claire Martin. I'm supposed to start work here today." I threw in a big smile for good measure. You can never be too cheerful when meeting your new coworkers. "I think I'm supposed to talk to a Mr. Campbell?"

She smiled back brightly and I saw a small diamond glint from her nostril, "You mean Henry. I can take you to him." She got up and called back into the stacks behind the desk, "Ben, can you watch the front?" I heard a muffled "sure" from one of the aisles behind her and she came out from behind the desk motioning for me to follow.

We walked straight to the back of the building and down the staircase that split giving us the option of going up to the top floor as well. "I think he was back in religious texts last I heard. The Seminary students have some big project already and are messing everything up." She rolled her eyes looking back at me as we walked. I smiled politely not wanting to jump the gun making comments on people I had no idea about. She seemed very friendly and I instantly liked her

24

feeling that sense of loss when I met someone I know I *should* have been able to be friends with if I were normal.

"I almost forgot I'm Heidi Johnson, Junior year, still no idea on my major. But don't tell my parents, they think I'm a business major." She winked, "You're going to like it here. This new library is great. They just finished it in the middle of last year. There's so much more space; we're still getting new books in all the time, so feel free to put in an order for anything special you might want." She added a conspiratorial wink. "Us book slaves get preferential treatment on orders so make sure you give us a heads up on what you order so we hold it for you." We continued on to the end of the lower shelves and then came to some bigger racks where Heidi slowed and started peeking around them as we walked past; we had to be in the right area.

"There you are." Her head disappeared down the aisle and I arrived at her side only seconds later. "Henry, we have a new book slave." She smiled as she spoke to someone I still couldn't see. Something rustled from behind a rolling book cart stuffed full of texts in all shapes and sizes midway down the aisle.

"Hi, I'm Claire. Financial Aid arranged for me to work here first semester," I said brightly to the rolling rack wondering about the bookworm who was to be my boss for the next nine months.

A warm voice, silky smooth and promising something dark and pleasant in ways I didn't fully understand that tugged at my insides chuckled from behind the rack where a moment later, a thick brown head of short, combed back hair rose smoothly from where he'd been crouching behind the rack. Below the mane was the pale, handsome face of a man in his early thirties; much younger than I would have expected for a head librarian. His brown eyes were dark enough to look black in the fluorescent lights. He was Hollywood's version of what a librarian should look like, Indiana Jones doubling

25

as a college professor. Similarly, I could easily picture Henry adventuring in the Amazon for ancient artifacts on his weekends away from campus, his lean, hard build certainly hinted at a physical hobby in his off-time.

"Hello Claire," his serene voice flowed over me and acted as a tranquilizer, calming me while at the same time holding me transfixed. "I'm Henry Campbell, Head Librarian." He extended his hand over the top of the cart.

Shaken from my stupor, I politely stepped forward to shake his hand in my typically brisk manner, expecting the tingle and bracing myself accordingly. Only when my hand slid into his, I had an undeniable sense of déjà vu. Henry's palm was cold and exceptionally firm but also "quiet," like Stephen's. It was different in some way just beyond my grasp, but it blocked out Heidi's mumbling emotions that were beginning to do more than hum on my periphery and all of the other vague "chatter" of the other students interspersed throughout the nearby tables.

I couldn't tell if he'd sensed something from me. Having been distracted and eyeing our interlocked hands, I couldn't tell if he'd sensed something from me. Stunned, he was eyeing me curiously. Both of us lingered a few seconds longer than was customary. His mouth curved up kindly while his eyes remained cool and I realized I was staring, still holding on to him; I released my grip, feeling the heat creep up my neck.

"Why don't you follow Heidi and she will get you set up and show you around. I'll check in with you after I finish up here." He nodded to me and kept his steady dark eyes on me as I said something I don't quite recall and followed Heidi back out of the racks and down to the front counter.

What was going on here? I've never had a moment's peace in *anyone's* presence. *Ever.* Touching people has always brought on an intense swell of emotions that I've sought to avoid my whole life. Now, here I had met not one but *two* people in 24 hours who had the opposite effect and I wasn't sure if it was a good thing. I wasn't sure exactly what happened the rest of my shift as my thoughts whirled around me, but I didn't speak to Henry again for the remainder of my shift. He was in the library and I saw him several times, however, he didn't come check on me and I didn't seek him out. The way that he moved about so smoothly was surreal. Here I was thinking that word again. This was an odd place.

It wasn't until I was nodding off to sleep that night that I realized I hadn't done any of my personal research. Nor had I looked for the author Stephen had mentioned. I was supposed to work again on Thursday, it would have to wait until then.

****

Wednesday was jam-packed. I had Calculus in the morning, Early European History right after, broke for lunch and then it was an afternoon of French. By the time I finished dinner- a bowl of cereal in my room- I had to sit down and begin outlining some ideas for a huge project my Biology professor had assigned. We would need to memorize the classification systems for over 100 animals from North America for our final test at the end of the semester. My time spent hiking and observing our birds at the feeder in the backyard didn't seem like it was going to be enough preparation so I figured this was going to be a rather time consuming prospect which would take all of my fortitude and then some.

It was ten o' clock before I finally slogged my exhausted self to the shower. It was the best part of my day feeling the hot water run over the top of my head and steam clouding my vision beyond the length of my arm. I couldn't help the wistful memory that came with the steam of when I was a little girl and I used to pretend that I lived on a cloud I created during my long baths and that nothing could reach

27

my cloud if I didn't want it to. I pretended that I would float on my cloud all over the world seeing all of the amazing places Dad used to talk about going before coming back stateside. The water had long since turned my body from summer tan to pink and on to red before I finally shut it off and headed back to my room.

Ch. 5

Ah, September in Minnesota. It was seventy-five degrees, sticky and not even lunch time when I walked into the overly air-conditioned library the next day for my shift. I wasn't supposed to start until one, but I'd planned some time to wander around doing some digging. The question was where to start. Do I go to the occult and paranormal or try to find the book Stephen suggested?

Heidi wasn't working, so I slid past the front counters unnoticed. I had met some other student workers the last time I was in, but no one who really wanted to chat like Heidi. She was so cool. Just as the tiny bubble of excitement began to fill my breast I felt it fizzle as I reminded myself of the painful reality of that scenario. No, just like everywhere else I'd gone to school before, I would have to endure the reputation of being cold and stuck up or weird. That was okay, I tried to reassure myself, I wanted a few hours to myself anyway. Just the books and me.

My first stop was the computer area to find out what we had for cataloged books. After a few minutes of searching our library records, I printed off some promising titles. Fortunately, with my newfound knowledge of our fine library's organizational system, finding my selections was pretty easy.

I had followed Stephen's suggestion and looked first for the Jenkins book. My curiosity had been working on me for several days now and I couldn't get it out of my mind, but considering the guy who'd recommended it, a part of me had already written it off as a joke. Of course, when I went to find the book, it was checked out. I wrote a note on the sheet I'd printed out to reserve the book when it was returned. Much to my surprise, as I wrote a note, a small flash of disappointment reached my consciousness; I rolled my eyes at my silliness. On to my next book idea; it had

29

come up below Jenkins and it was a religious text from the Italian Renaissance on the subject of detection of spirits residing in unsuspecting human hosts. Not quite as heart fluttering, but one never knew when a nugget of truth could be found while wading through the bizarre and outdated. Book found, I wandered over to a work cubby under some bright lights. There were no windows here in the basement, making it completely dependent upon the fluorescents for light despite the sun outside. Upstairs, the floor plan was open, airy, and full of windows, but down here, where the old books were, the sunlight had been banned. Heidi had explained that it was for the protection of the books; too much light would damage them. It made sense although it was a bummer since too many hours in the artificially bright lighting made my head hurt.

The book took some sorting to get through due to the fact that it was translated well over three hundred years ago. Although it was in English, the sentence structure and wording was old and it always seemed to take my brain some time to get into the flow of older translations. When I was reading classical literature, I usually had to set aside at least an hour so that my brain could get itself into the rhythm of the book. I always felt like that gave me a better flavor for what the author was really saying and I wouldn't miss anything.

It seemed like no time at all had passed when I looked at my watch to see I had only about four minutes to get upstairs to the front counters and make my presence known. I stowed the book under my arm to check out before I started my shift.

My shift again passed quickly and I worked without seeing Henry or Heidi, which was just as well because I had quite a few messes to clean up. It seemed some Media class was teaching their students how to locate periodicals by looking them up in our systems. Unfortunately, they didn't seem so concerned about putting them back according to our system.

It took me over an hour to untangle the mess before I was able to head back downstairs to help Ben, the shy but nice enough Sophomore Heidi and I had worked with the last time. He was dealing with more Seminary student cleanup.

We worked in Religious texts another few hours and before I knew it, it was time to head home. I wasn't really hungry and didn't have anyone expecting me so I returned to my friend, the Italian book, who was telling me some interesting facts about inner demons and our turmoil, which could be handled with some prayer and leeches. Nothing like a little blood loss to clear up one's soul or liver, or whatever else ails you. Thank goodness for modern medicine. I don't think I would have had the stomach for the old ways. And with a glass of water on my nightstand I settled in with the old clerics' superstitions for a few more hours before sleep finally won me for the night.

Ch. 6

Friday. No class, no work; nothing. I wasn't going home this weekend. When I spoke to my mom earlier in the week, I'd used the excuse that school just started and I wanted to "get into the swing of things" so I would be staying on campus this weekend to try to meet people and hang out with some of my new friends. Mom and Dad were genuinely pleased to hear about my first week of college. I had to admit, too, that just talking to them on the phone was far less intense and I remembered how much I actually enjoyed speaking to Mom and telling her about things. She, too, sounded lighter and happier than I'd heard her in a while. Reading the direction of my thoughts, perhaps, she commented in the same vein about me and I realized she was right.

I seemed to be made for this life. I could easily limit my interactions with people, surround myself with books and spend as much time studying as I wanted to. I had entire days without classes or parents or other distractions and could spend my time at my own discretion. Sure, there were the usual limitations to that kind of isolation but I consoled myself with the academics. For the first time in forever, my classes were genuinely interesting. In high school, I was able to choose some electives but the pool from which we chose was so much shallower than this one. At college the requirements said to choose a history, then gave about twenty choices. It was great! This was the perfect place for an isolationist bookworm such as myself.

I couldn't help but feel happy taking in the large oaks transitioning to yellow for the season and the flowers in the gardens. The splashes of color lining the path and fronts of the buildings were giving their last good efforts at color before going back to sleep for another six months.

I wandered into the library, signed the book back in and walked it back myself, intent upon keeping it from the generally curious. My attentions turned inward, considering the thin bit of useful information I'd been able to pick from its yellowed pages. I was completely caught off guard as I turned at the top of the stack to head down the row and replace the book.

"Hey, try to find Jenkins yet?" Stephen was sitting on the floor cross-legged, looking at a much abused leather bound book opened to its halfway point. His shaggy hair hung just slightly over his eyes, which were looking up at me with a playful glint to them.

I was so surprised that I jumped up about a foot and my hand not holding my book bag flew up to my face to halt a screech, though an unimpressive squeak still found its way out.
"Oh my gosh! Seriously, I could have had a heart attack." I gasped as my heart tried to find its place in my chest. I reached out to steady myself, dropping my bag to brace against the rack.

He smiled and shook his head to get his hair out of his eyes. "That's the wrong book." He aimed his nose at the one now clutched to my chest.

I couldn't help but glare at him. "Someone else must have it, I haven't been able to find it." I was still trying to recover my breathing now coming in short jagged gulps.

He winked playfully at me. "I wanted to give you a chance to really want it. You know, it's the anticipation that's half the fun." He said looking down at the book in his hand, snapping it shut. "Here." He stood up while handing me the book. "Enjoy."

I took it from his hand and looked at the spine, rolling my eyes. "Huh, well that figures." He liked to mess with people. That explained a lot. "Did you have it when you told me about it or did you check it out afterward just to

33

mess with me?" I didn't like the idea that he'd manipulated me. Or that he'd succeeded in doing exactly what he'd said he wanted to do.

"No, I was being nice. I marked the spots I thought you would find most helpful." He started to point at the book. "It's one of the older books so I was careful to just put paper in the pages you might want to look at first. Post-it's tend to tear the paper fiber you know. Henry's really protective about the older stuff."

Eyeing him, I decided against asking how he came to be on a first name basis with the head librarian. I didn't want to know more about the manipulative character, I told myself; instead concentrating on the text now in my hands. Gingerly, I opened the book and sure enough, it fell open to a spot where a small scrap of paper was wedged in toward the spine, avoiding the need to handle the page. It was actually quite thoughtful of him. I started reading about "shielding." It instantly grabbed my attention and I forgot about him entirely until he spoke again.

"That's what I thought. You might want to read that section twice. It would be useful for someone such as yourself." I heard the satisfaction in his voice and glanced up, ready to defend myself lest he go around starting rumors.

"What do you mean, someone like me? That is not the first time you've said that and might I point out that you don't even know me." I was getting my back up pretty fast but given how much he was guessing about me he could really cause some damage. Plus, I had to admit, as much as I didn't like my curse, I used it a lot when I dealt with people. Knowing how someone was feeling was almost as good as knowing what that person was thinking. It was kind of like hearing their tone without the words. I always came prepared to handle whichever way the conversation would go. In short snippets it wasn't even horribly painful, only mildly so.

Just like last time, I couldn't tell anything about how he was feeling so I wasn't sure if he was teasing me, if he was being a jerk or just trying to get my goat. Regardless, I was out of my depth in speaking to him, and I didn't know how to handle him. I had lost one of my senses. One I hadn't realized I used as much as I did, it was like waking up blind and being told to drive.

"Don't worry, I come in peace," he said as he held his hands out in front, palms out as if to calm a frightened animal. I might not have been so irritated at the gesture if it weren't for his slightly patronizing smile.

"You know, you can really irritate a girl. I can't imagine you have much luck dating."

There was just the slightest break in his smile and then he laughed. It was a pleasant, genuine laugh and it made me smile in spite of my anger.

"Don't worry about me. Just look at the book and maybe we can talk later." With that, Stephen glided away.

Jenkins was exactly what I'd been looking for all my life. I was fascinated by what he had to say about shielding and empathy. Other books shared what he did about the empathy thing, however, Jenkins pointed out that it could take several different forms and that was new.

Some people's abilities were limited to a strong understanding of how others felt when they talked to them or hung around them. Kind of like a super counselor, able to read the emotion behind the words. Other people could feel the emotions of others before they even saw them, it was like they had a wider range of "hearing." And then there were folks like me who could sense the emotions without having to see the person, but also could be altered themselves by the those emotions. It was called channeling. Although I had seen some limited information on channeling before, it

35

hadn't been so thorough. It was like this book was written just for me. I breathed a sigh of relief. It felt so good to know I wasn't the only one and I wasn't crazy. Correcting myself, I thought, at least if I was, I wasn't alone in my insanity.

I hustled downstairs to check the book out at the front desk and couldn't wait to get to my room to learn more from my new greatest resource, Richard Jenkins, who had known me apparently several hundred years before I was born. How many others had this "talent" as he called it?

It hit me all of a sudden as I was walking back to my dorm. I couldn't believe how dense I was sometimes; maybe my family was right and I was socially slow. Was Stephen an empath like me? Is that how he had recognized me? Had he learned how to shield and that was why I couldn't feel him? He became very interesting to me all of a sudden and I couldn't wait to see him again to discuss the possibilities.

Ch. 7

For the hundredth time this week, I thanked my lucky stars for my lack of a roommate as I looked again to make sure that my door was locked and curtains drawn. I felt like a total ass, but was hopeful something good would come of my endeavors.

Jenkins' book devoted a number of pages to blocking oneself from outside energies, something he referred to as shielding. I was trying like mad to put what I was reading into practice, only I had a slight complication. I didn't have a willing participant to test my skills with. So, ever the improviser, I thought of a way to practice in secret.

My room was halfway down the hall on the rather busy twelfth floor. Normally, I had pretty steady foot traffic passing by; usually there was someone at least every half an hour. However, this was Sunday and it was too early for much pedestrian traffic. Those who had stayed at campus for the weekend were sleeping one off, whether from too much alcohol or just too many hours studying and philosophizing with friends. The others who had gone home were not yet coming back to settle in for the week ahead.

So I found myself sitting on the floor, cross-legged and trying to relax, yet remain alert enough to feel anyone who might happen to come down the hallway. The thought was that I would feel them and then try to shield from them without them knowing what I was doing. It was not going well. So far, I had only had two participants and I was so busy trying to remember the process that I didn't focus on them until they were pretty well gone.

Frustrated, I was about to give up when I felt one of the girls come down the hallway. It was probably Lindsey. She was the stereotypical cheerleader who came from a small town in Wisconsin and was, and I quote, "super excited to be here."

I had the impression that she was always "super excited" no matter what she was doing.

Before I could lose my chance, I refocused on her and tried to open up to it so that I would really feel her. It worked. She was giddy about a guy who had just kissed her, at *least* kissed her, if the sexual feeling behind it was at all indicative. Now I tried to picture a door closing between Lindsey and me. It took tremendous focus but I saw the door and was mentally closing it. The giddiness started to fade.

"Oh!" I gasped, jumping a little as my eyes flew open. Oh my gosh! It was amazing. It was possible to block off someone else's feelings! The possibilities were mind-boggling. Depending how good I got at this there was a possibility I could lead a relatively normal life, although touching was probably still out but even so, that was better than I *had* been thinking. It was with overwhelming gratitude that I thought of Stephen. Because of him I might gain some control over myself and my life, and for that I owed him.

Ch. 8

The next few weeks passed in a blur. As September moved into October, I studied hard for my classes which were fascinating but way more challenging than high school had been. I worked in the library three to four times a week and as the classes were picking up, so was the reorganizing of the shelves. I gained a new appreciation for moms who followed their children around all day picking up after them even though the children knew full well how to clean up their own messes but chose not to.

Whenever I wasn't working or studying, I practiced my shielding. It was proving to be a lot harder than I first thought, but it was coming along. I had gotten myself to where I still felt people, but I could dull the buzzing down to white noise, almost losing it in the background. Touching, as predicted, was still too much. Last week I had "accidentally" brushed against Heidi's arm when pushing a rolling cart. I felt the jolt race up my arm like I'd been electrocuted, fortunately I'd still been in motion and going the opposite way so there hadn't been any giveaways. So far my coworkers thought I was private but not weird, it was an improvement.

Today I was on my way to work and was so wrapped up in my thoughts that I didn't see the slight figure standing outside the front doors until I started to open the door and his hand took the handle from my grasp.

"Excuse me," I startled looking over my left shoulder to see Stephen standing next to me, now taking the door. I should have known, no one else could sneak up on me, shielding practice or no. "Hey, what are you doing here?" His book suggestion, the first bit of guidance I had received on the subject had endeared him to me. The smile on my lips was heartfelt.

"How's your homework going?" He asked as he smiled back and we stepped inside together.

"Fine, thanks for the heads up on the book. It isn't easy, but overall it's going pretty well." He was easy to talk to. And even though if anyone overheard what we were talking about we would probably both be certified as nutballs, I found his presence calming. *Peace* was the word that popped into my mind when I looked over at him.

Stephen shifted nervously as he stopped just inside the doors, forcing me to stop with him. "Do you remember the day we met?" I paused as I thought I saw a brief shadow cross behind his eyes.

"Of course, you were fighting with your sister." I'd thought about that incident often as I found myself thinking about Stephen these last few weeks. He'd been so self-assured every other time I had seen him, but that first impression stuck with me, seemingly out of character from what I thought I knew of him otherwise.

Stephen gave a short laugh. "Yeah, my sister. Well, she was worried about something that could be a problem for all of us. Anyway, we have this, ah, thing we are working on and I would like it if you could come and meet with some friends of ours since we are all going to be together tonight for this other thing anyway. I think that we could help you with your gift."

I felt the smile fading from my lips. "Is this what your interest in me has been about? Am I supposed to be some sort of entertainment? Party tricks aren't my thing. I'm not going to do that no matter what books you show me." The disappointment stung. I had hoped that I was making a friend and had met a kindred spirit who could give me some ideas on how to handle my "gift" as he called it. *He* seemed happy, I had entertained brief visions of having some of that

40

for myself. Now it looked like he was just cultivating me for some sort of freak show. My heart sank.

Stephen put up his hands to as if he were going to grab my arms. "Don't touch me!" I lowered my voice seeing we had drawn the attention of the front counter folks and some of the students in the main entry. Now I was going to make a scene. Oh wonderful, just the kind of impression I wanted to give my co-workers. I hoped Henry was nowhere nearby to witness this.

He put his hands down immediately jamming them in his pockets. Then, so softly that I had to strain to hear, he tried to mollify me. "Look Claire, I respect your gift. I recognized your talent right when I first met you. That's why I pointed you to the book I did. You have to have a specific skillset to be able to manage that on your own. Now that you've had some time to work on it, I just thought maybe you could use some help to move your shielding to the next level. I know you don't know me very well. I'm willing to tell you anything you want, but please trust me when I say that I can teach you what you need to know." He lowered his head, bringing our eyes very close. "Wouldn't it be nice to be able to touch someone without being terrified what you were going to pick up?" He didn't try to embarrass me yet I could still feel my neck heating up at having my weaknesses so exposed to him.

I moved beyond the knee jerk reaction and considered his offer. He did seem sincere. He really hadn't given me any other indication that he wanted to take advantage of my curse, or "gift." He *had* helped me to get the best control over myself that I'd ever had and he was promising more. Maybe I owed him a little trust instead of jumping to conclusions.

Deciding to give him a chance, I looked directly at him, hoping to appear sure of myself. "Okay, I'll go but I have to work until close tonight."

"We're going to meet at my sister's house off campus. She lives over by Selby and Dale in St. Paul."

That was a rough part of town and too far to walk even if I wouldn't be raped and killed on the way there. "I don't have a car; I guess I could take a cab."

"Don't worry about it, I'll pick you up here after work. When are you done? Ten?"

"10:15 I'm usually walking out. If you wait outside here, I can meet you."

He grinned and looked genuinely relieved to have me on board. "It's a date! See you at quarter after." And he turned to leave, cocking his head and half turning to look somewhere behind me.

"It is not a date," I was quick to blurt out.

Attention drawn back to me with only a moment's delay, he was confused for a second before he burst out laughing. "It's just an expression."

As he walked away from me and I headed over to sign in, I had something new to worry about. Had I missed the signs? Did Stephen have a crush on me? I hoped not. Dating was not my thing. I had actually never been on a date, but considering how my few friends felt when dating and worrying, I couldn't imagine wanting to go through that. It would be nice to have someone close who I could talk to and share things with, but I couldn't see how it would work with my "gift." I saw no way of keeping a man's feelings off of me in a relationship or intimate situation. There wouldn't be any sort of line between where I ended and he started. It would never work. That and things could get out of hand pretty fast if he were to get it in his mind that he wanted to get physical. His wants would become my own pretty fast and we'd be over the line in a heartbeat. Maybe Stephen

42

could help me in that department as well. If he didn't want to be "that guy" that is.

Fantastic, I thought coming back to the problem at hand. I was going to have to part ways with my only real friend I had made here, unless I could clearly define the boundary before any real damage was done. There was so much to mull over; my shift was over before I realized it. As the lights went out and we locked up, I started to feel my stomach jumping with nerves.

I had decided that I would tell Stephen I had a boyfriend at home. That had worked for another girl I heard talking in French class a few weeks ago. She had a study partner that wanted to do more than study and she didn't want to lose him if she hurt his feelings, so she lied about having a boyfriend. It sounded like it turned out all right. Maybe it would work for me too.

"Hey," came a bright voice from just outside the doors as I was locking up. Ben had already gone past since I had the keys. I jumped, nearly dropping them. Ben and I both had missed him? That is a feat considering all of the glass in that entranceway.

"Hey Stephen." My voice sounded tight. Kicking myself mentally, I tried to breathe deeply and calm down. Turning as I pocketed the keys, I waved to Ben, who had turned and was watching us curiously until he waved back and resumed his path to the parking lot.

Even though I was nervous about letting Stephen down easy, I couldn't help but smile and feel real warmth toward him. Walking easily my way, he looked so sweet when he smiled. He seemed like one of those few people who were genuinely happy. At the moment his shaggy hair hung over the top of one eye, taking years away and again I felt that protective tug. A long sleeved grey t-shirt with some Abercrombie graphics on it and faded jeans that hung over the backs of his

43

black Converse completed Stephen's wardrobe for the evening. It was a casual look that worked for him. Again I was struck by his ease with himself. I would have thought a guy his size and stature would have tons of identity issues, but he didn't give that impression at all. I wondered for about the millionth time what could have had him so worried that first time I saw him when he was arguing with his sister. It must be something very bad, maybe his parents were sick or something. It had never occurred to me to ask. Social niceties were beyond me and I felt terrible. But before I could try to make up for it by asking at this late juncture, Stephen took over.

"Are you ready to meet the clan?" He fell in step beside me, our shoulders almost touching. I could feel the heat coming off of him. It felt good on this brisk fall night.

"You know, I was talking to my boyfriend and he said to thank you for driving me. It's really nice of you considering how late it is." I smiled stiffly at him.

Stephen turned his face toward me, a quizzical look in his eyes. "Boyfriend? Really?"

"Yeah, didn't I tell you about him? We've been together for a while. It's pretty solid." Boy, I hoped that didn't sound as fake to Stephen as it did to me.

"That's funny. You don't strike me as the boyfriend type."

"What do you mean, 'boyfriend type'?" Offended? Oh yeah. I know I'm no super hot long legged gorgeous underwear model, but I could catch someone if I tried. Couldn't I? The reality was I had never tried and with my reputation, no one dared pursue me. My questionable self-esteem took another hit. Maybe all this worry was for naught and even Stephen couldn't think of me that way.

He snorted lightly and smiled again as he looked straight ahead. "I just remembered the way you looked when Tara shoved you into me and you thought you were going to land on top of me. You were terrified. I figured you had never been that close to one of *my* fair sex before."

"I didn't know you! I've touched plenty of guys before you. Wait, that's not what I meant." My neck heated up.

"Relax Claire, you and I are friends and that is all I am interested in. You don't have to tell me anything more about your romances, torrid as I am sure they *all* are." He was having a good laugh at my expense yet I couldn't help but smile in spite of myself. He was interested in being my friend after all and there would be no awkwardness. Yay me, my first friend! Like a kindergartner, my joy knew no shame.

We got to the street and the lights shone on a small red car parked on the curb. I looked over at Stephen and he had the key fob in his hand. Pushing the button, I saw the lights flash as he nodded, "Yep, our chariot for the evening."

We got closer and I saw that it was a newer Toyota coupe, one he could put the top down on in warmer months. "Nice car, is it yours?" I didn't know if Stephen came from money or what but Augsburg was a private college and I had never heard him mention a job or anything and this car was pretty decent for our age group.

"Yeah, it's been in the family for a while." Why did he always smile like he had some secret I wasn't in on? It sort of irked me while at the same time drew me in.

We rode the short distance in relative silence. I spent some time looking at his cd's. "What no ipod? Aren't these a bit old fashioned these days?" I joked shaking a Depeche Mode cd at him.

45

He laughed again, that nice easy chuckle that immediately put me at ease, "I like the feel of them. They are supposed to be this whole packaged experience the artist has planned out for you. The MP3's are so sterile and machine like. Where is the connection to the artist through the cover art and the bonus hidden tracks?"

My return grin was genuine as I realized how much I really liked him. We had an easy time teasing each other and had so much in common. That and, his control over himself allowed me to let down my guard just a little bit and not fear being lost to his emotions. It was a relief to have that for the first time in my life and the realization took me aback. Tears sprang to my eyes.

"Are you all right, Claire?" He was concerned. Uh oh, he was observant too.

"Yeah, just thinking." I blinked the tears back in before any could spill over.

"Are you sad about the rise of the evil MP3's? I certainly didn't mean to upset you with my lament over technology," he kidded.

"No, I think I can handle the decline of my cd's." Here they came again, prickling the backs of my eyelids. I blinked hard for a minute. It was while my eyes were closed that the word *safe* just popped into my head and calm washed over me. When I opened my eyes, they were dry and I was back to feeling contented as I often did while I was with him. My mind was so peculiar lately, it must be all of this messing with my ability I was doing. It was shifting things around. I intended to ask him about it later when I knew I wouldn't be a mess doing it.

Ch. 9

Within about fifteen minutes of leaving campus, we arrived at Tara's house. It was a small Cape Cod common to that area. The houses here were all pretty similar, most of them having been built in the 1920's with two bedrooms on the main floor and an attic upstairs. Small but homey, I had always liked them. We'd lived in one in South Carolina. They were not so large and sterile as a lot of the big houses being built out in the suburbs. The lights were on inside giving it a warm and welcoming glow.

The lighting also made it easier to see that the color was light blue or grey with darker shutters and a red door behind a full length glass front storm door. The yard was landscaped with overgrown lilacs and hostas with some mulched wildflowers thrown into a kidney shaped garden just to the left of the sidewalk. A cottage getaway was not what I was expecting from Tara. Maybe I had misjudged the girl I'd only met once.

With Stephen leading, we walked right in without knocking. The décor took me by surprise, it was not what one would expect for a college student, nor was the house for that matter. The front room was bright with a floor lamp and two matched table lamps illuminating the light hardwood floor and fluffy pale cream area rug. Two small, camel-colored corduroy love seats were on opposing walls with a large window taking up the majority of the front wall next to the door.

The queen of the castle, Tara was sitting on the one loveseat to the left of a tall, thin man sitting next to her with his arms crossed loosely in front of him. He had hair the same color as Tara and Stephen, only his was a little longer, pulled back into a short ponytail. He was dressed in khakis and a blue Henley with a peek of tawny chest hair showing through the opening. When he looked up at me, I saw the same eye and face shape as Stephen and Tara. The resemblance was uncanny. He had to be an older brother, maybe in his early twenties.

Continuing with my scan, I saw another woman lounging on the other loveseat who could have been the tall man's twin. She had long, honey colored hair, and dressed in hip hugging jeans that covered legs that went on forever and a jewel green satin top that ended just above her belly button. I had to admit that if I could make it look like that, I would wear that kind of thing to the grocery store. She lay on the loveseat with her head resting on one hand, elbow on the arm of the couch and legs casually thrown over the other arm. She had to be about six feet, not much shorter than her brother.

All of the Andrews looked up at us when we walked in. The conversation stopped, but didn't feel hostile. The group appeared to be politely waiting for an introduction.

"Tara, you've already met Claire." Tara nodded, not entirely unpleasant, her lips were tight as she dipped her head. "Claire, let me introduce my older brother and sister, Troy and Tonya." They were both reserved but kind as they nodded and Troy said, "Pleased to meet you finally. Stephen has spoken highly of you."

My stomach fluttered nervously and I looked over at Stephen who shrugged. "We're a close family. We talk about everything." He saw my shoulders tighten as I realized what he must have shared with them.

He smiled gently. "Yes, they know about your gift, but don't worry. You are safe here." In my head, I thought *calm and safe*, though I would normally be freaking out with complete strangers learning all about my secret, even if they did call it a gift.

48

It was also then that I noticed I couldn't feel any of them. I guess I got used to my minor shielding working to reduce the "buzz" of people near me to just background, but this was even less, nonexistent. What I could feel was different than anything I had ever felt around people. I couldn't quite put my finger on it. "Are you doing this?" I whispered to Stephen thinking maybe he was helping me out.

He met my hesitant gaze serenely, "We all are."

"What?" I looked at them and they were all so relaxed, like a pride of lions lounging in their den. It was hard to imagine they were putting forth the kind of effort it took me to shield the little bit I had managed so far. I was getting better, but still I had to concentrate so that I always looked like I was deep in thought, sometimes in pain.

"You aren't the only one around here with a gift, you know," Stephen said with no small amount of pride and raised his chin, grinning smugly. I had figured as much, but I didn't understand the feeling I was getting from all of them. There had always been something different about Stephen, only it was more pronounced when he was here with his family.

Troy spoke up without changing his position next to Tara or looking at me, "Why you have invited her, Stephen? You know that tonight we have a meeting."

"I have asked Claire to come here because of her gift. I've advised her that we can help her to develop it. That, and I know we have a meeting which is why I've chosen tonight to invite her."

"I'm not certain about her ability to control herself," the lioness purred from her perch across the room. Tonya swung her legs down and, smooth as a cat, stood in one fluid motion. She was the tallest woman I had ever seen in person. "She feels wild and out of control, yet you say she has been working by herself for weeks. I have to wonder if she is worth the training if this is any indication of her potential."

This was getting trippy. I couldn't follow what they were talking about. I thought of the tea party in *Alice in Wonderland* and wondered if Stephen was the Mad Hatter or if it was Troy who was running things. That, combined with the formality, it was not indicative of what I knew of Stephen at all. Wait, what did I know about this family *or* Stephen? Maybe his family had gone to boarding school somewhere in Europe or something. I had seen that sort of thing in the movies, those people always seemed so much more elegant and formal. Real people didn't talk like this though. And I was getting very nervous of them talking about me as though I was not really human or here.

"Stephen, maybe you should just bring me home if I'm unwelcome." This situation had crossed over from strange to downright bizarre. Oddly enough, though, I wasn't panicking at all.

"Claire, I told you that we could help you to develop your talent, but in order to do so, there are some things you need to know. Things about how the world really looks, not how we're taught to see it. Do you remember the first time we met? Have you wondered how I knew that you were special?" Hazel eyes burned into mine with such intensity, I found myself leaning in and I nodded assent, not even thinking to snort at his use of the word "special."

He sighed, "I need you to hear me out. As strange as some of this is going to sound, I want you to remember that I am your friend and I won't lie to you."

Taking a deep breath, I tried to sound calm, "Okay, I'll try." I felt some anxiety leaking through. Were my newfound shielding abilities keeping me from feeling the full range of my own emotions? Were their abilities lulling me into a false sense of security? I should be running away.

"Let's sit down. Tonya, do you mind?" He asked her breaking his gaze from mine only briefly.

She gave up her claim on the seat, spun and glided into the kitchen without a word.

Stephen and I sat down next to each other, our knees mere inches away from each other. Years of practice made me cautious not to touch and I automatically scooted backward. "My family and I are gifted, like you. We all have special abilities and use these abilities to train others like you to better handle their gifts. However, your talent is stronger than any I have worked with before." At this, there was an odd rumbling from the kitchen. "I'm pretty sure it's stronger than any of us have worked with, which is why I've called you here tonight."

"I don't understand, Stephen, you said that you could help me. I'm sure you can work with mine, even if it is different." Hearing how I was different, even among others like me, only served to solidify for me how freakish I really was.

Stephen ran his hand through his hair, leaving it sticking up in some funny ways. It gave me something else to look at other than his eyes and I was grateful. "It isn't that simple. You see we are able through a special talent that we share as a family, to absorb most of the outside influences and essentially block you from outside stimuli as you learn to manage your own shields in a sort of safety bubble. But yours work differently, they go back and forth instead of just one direction. I haven't seen their equal before. We might need to call in a favor from another family more capable, but that would put us in debt to them." Something definitely growled in the kitchen. Not a dog, though. It sounded like a pissed off cat. I hoped it was locked up; cats hated me.

"Who is this family? Are they cousins or something?" I was definitely missing part of the puzzle; I didn't understand why owing a favor was such a big deal. Stephen wasn't telling me something. "I can repay them, I'm sure. You don't need to owe anyone anything on my behalf."

Tara stood up and was surprisingly graceful for her farm girl build. "I told you she wouldn't understand. This is beyond the understanding of her kind."

"Oh? My kind? What kind would that be?" First impressions definitely served here. Tara *was* a jerk and she was an easy target for the anxious flare up I felt coming on.

Troy put his hand on Tara's wrist to stop her, and she turned to face him. "Let's put it out there and see what she does." That kind of control meant he had to be the leader here. It was good to have him stop Tara's attitude, except I wasn't sure I liked where this was going. It was getting a bit too intense here for me. I started to think about how I could get Stephen to take me home.

A sigh from the couch next to me brought me back. "Claire, what do you believe about the paranormal?"

If he didn't look so serious, I would have laughed right in his face. Paranormal? My life seemed to be constantly going round this theme, but I was the daughter of a man who did not give a lot of time to fairy tales and ghost stories. I was raised to see things as they were and nothing more. My curse was the only hiccup in Dad's rational theories on life but that didn't mean *everything* was real. Out of respect though, I tried to make my point in a non-offensive way. "Books and movies are my only exposure and I'm not certain that those are based in reality. After all, look at what the books say about things like ESP. They aren't all in agreement. Not even close. I think if there was any truth to them, they would be more in sync with each other."

"What about your gift? Doesn't that make you believe there's something else out there? Jenkins' book?" This was from Troy again, who was sitting forward in his seat, elbows on his thighs looking directly at my face.

I was really hoping we were just having a philosophical discussion, but I was careful not to offend, regardless. I was in the minority here and didn't want to test Stephen's loyalties if I could avoid it. "My gift, as you guys call it, is a weird fluke that is just an overly emphasized, but perfectly normal, thing. Everyone understands other people's emotions to a point, I just get them in more detail." That was something I had tried to convince myself of before; I was just really observant.

Troy cocked his head to the side, staring right into my eyes. "First off, you can feel people's emotions not just understand them and Stephen says you can channel people's emotions as well. That is definitely beyond the norm. That makes it para normal." He said this last as two words to emphasize the point.

The little detail that had been nagging gently at the back of my mind kicked me then, Troy knew something even Stephen shouldn't have known. No one should have known because I had never told anyone. My fury swelled in my chest. "How do you know I can channel? I know I have never said that to you. Ever." I stood up. I was pretty sure that I could walk back a block to the gas station we'd passed on the corner and wait for a cab there. I was about two seconds from walking out the door. I didn't understand what was happening, but I didn't want to be here anymore; that much I knew for certain.

Stephen touched my arm, very lightly. His touch was just a whisper, but there was a flash of something. I didn't know how to describe it. In my head flashed my terrified face when I was falling into him, then my fear of feeling him. I tried to remember what he had said that day in the coffee shop after I first met him. He'd said that I "blasted him" when I touched him. I had thought the word "ouch" but had

53

not felt any pain myself. Since then, I had admitted to him that I feel people but never the most frightening part of my talent, the fact that I could lose myself completely in someone else and channel them. That was also the part that I had yet to master control of, the part I wasn't sure I *could* control.

My breathing was speeding up; I was starting to hyperventilate. "How do you know that? Can you read my mind?" I sat back down, my mind going numb with shock. The phrase, "*You have to listen*," running through my head brought me back to the present, and I tried to focus on what Stephen was saying, my heart began to slow back down.

"No, but you and I have more in common than you think. I kind of figured things out when you landed on me. I felt a lot of power there." He sat back into the cushions behind him with a sigh, "You can feel other people's emotions rather strongly, yes?" I nodded. "If someone is having a strong feeling and they touch you, you can't help but feel what they are feeling, right?" Slowly, wide eyed, I nodded the tiniest bit. "Well, I have a similar ability. You feel people by their emotions, I see them by their intentions."

"I don't understand." I was totally confused now and was thinking very strongly about running outside right now despite the compulsion I felt to listen.

"How do I explain?" Stephen looked up at the ceiling and put his hands on his head, mussing his hair again. He looked about twelve years old. He stared right at me, appearing decided. "Think about your parents," he instructed me.

"Why?" I had no idea what was going to happen but I didn't want to give him any information about my family that could be used to harm them or me.

"I'm going to show you what I do." He waited for me to process all of it and gave no more than a slight muscle twitch of the eye when he saw me cave.

"Okay." For some reason beyond my comprehension, I followed his instructions and closed my eyes, thinking about Mom. She was probably worried about me by now, I thought, I should take them up on their offer to come take me to lunch. It was just so easy to get lost in my new life. When I got back to the dorm, I would have to call and invite them down for the afternoon. I could try out my new shielding on them.

"So when are you going to have them over?" Stephen asked, breaking into my thoughts.

Rolling my eyes at him, I answered sarcastically, "That isn't hard to figure out. It's like a phony magician. All you have to do is read me. Here I am, a college student away from home and you have me think about my parents. It is going to either be 'I'm happy I'm away' or 'gee I sure miss them,' you have a fifty-fifty shot at being right."

He patiently tried to explain his point, "Well, as you explained about your gift being one that is just a normal human response heightened to a special level, so is mine. I can go downtown and show you who is going to commit a crime, when a girl decides to go home with a guy from a bar, anything like that. I read emotions like you do, but I can't tell much until the person makes up their mind. That is when I can see what they are going to do."

"So can you tell the future?" My eyes widened in disbelief. No wonder he was so calm all the time, nothing surprised him.

"No, but if the President decided to go to war, I could tell. That doesn't mean it will happen because it isn't that simple to go to war, but I could tell that is what he decided to do. I can see his intentions. It has come in handy a few times when we've needed to figure out if someone is telling the truth."

"Like a human lie detector?"

He seemed pleased. "Yes, that is one way we can use it. I can also see if someone is able to handle strange information." He looked meaningfully at me and I smiled a bit shyly. "My gift compliments yours very well. That is why we," he gestured to his family still in the room. I had forgotten about them, "Have called you here. We have someone who specializes in helping people like you. I brought you in because your gift is so strong, I worry for you if you don't get it under control."

Tonya stuck her head out from the kitchen. "You are forgetting the most important part, dear brother. Or don't you want to tell her what you've been doing to her all this time?" Her expression was smug, and cruelty lit her eyes.

I looked quickly back to Stephen, my own eyes narrowed in suspicion, voice just above a whisper, "What have you been doing to me?"

Stephen looked guilty and rubbed the back of his neck with his hand as he looked up at me and said, "There's more to what I can do."

"More? How much more?" No longer scared, now I was angry with him. Having my legs cut out from under me every few seconds was keeping my fuse short.

"Once I touch someone, I get a feel for them. After that, I can make suggestions to them."

"Everyone can make suggestions, why do you need to touch someone? Get a feel for what?" I was struggling to make the connection that was once again just beyond my reach.

"We all have an energy feel. You feel it when you touch someone, right? You get their specific feel and can pick them out of a crowd later?" Seeing my reaction, he knew he was right and went on. "Once I touch someone, I get a feel for them and can find them if I'm within a certain range. I can make suggestions to them." He saw that I still wasn't making the leap. *"In their head."* And that was where he said it, I watched his mouth remain closed but the words appeared in my head in the same tone as several others had that evening.

My sudden intake of air helped to lift me up off the couch and move quickly toward the door. Stephen jumped up too. I was so furious at him, at all of them, for bringing me here to toy with for their own amusement. When I jumped up, I lost focus and my weak shields slid, allowing the disorienting chaos of their unique chatter to slam into me and I wobbled on my feet.

Stephen reached to grab me, but when he touched me, I skittered back, this time falling into the loveseat. "You bastard!" I shrieked at him. I'd gotten a flash of peace at his touch. He was trying to do it again. "How dare you try to control my thoughts, you have no right! People's heads are private. And what about the rest of you? What do you do? Do you go into people's heads too? Or is that just Stephen's special *gift*?" I spat this last bitterly. It was vulgar, what he was doing. He had been telling me to be calm, to listen, he had been manipulating me this whole time and I was angry with myself for having trusted him.

"Wait, Claire," Stephen reasoned quietly. He started to put his hands out to me, but saw my fury and slowly put them back down. "Think for a minute about what you have heard me say to you. I've asked you to be calm when you were scared and asked you to listen when you were not sure if you should. I promise you that I didn't ever try to sway you or do anything unethical. I apologize that I ever went into your thoughts, but this situation called for it. You need to get yourself under control before you get yourself or someone else in trouble. With our abilities being so closely related, I thought I would be able to help you. When I saw how strong yours was, I even hoped that some day you could work *with* us; you would be a great asset to us." He once again sounded so sincere.

My blocking was not fully back up and I could feel that his intentions were honest and he truly believed what he was saying, making me want to believe him, regardless of how utterly insane this was.

I looked around at his family and saw that they were all very still, watching me for my reaction. Even Tonya had her forehead resting on the kitchen doorjamb with one eye hidden behind the wall, and the other one focused on me. The one I could see looked very worried, it was the only hint of real emotions I'd seen from her.

Taking a deep breath, I looked back and met Stephen's gaze. Moving to touch his knee in front of me, I retracted my hand at the last minute. Instead, I pleaded with a word. "Sit." Seeing his hesitation, I added gently, "Please." He sat wordlessly and closed his eyes, relieved.

Unable to bear the image of him so still and unlike the Stephen I knew, I glanced away and found Troy's gaze, which wasn't hard seeing as it was leveled directly at me while he studied my reaction. "What do you need me to do to get this started?"

Troy's eyebrows ticked up as he considered me. "Claire, there is more that you need to know before committing to this. Not all is as it seems here."

"My friend has offered to find help for me; I need to be responsible for any resulting obligations, what else is there?" Trying to lighten the mood, I added, "We are talking about an entirely different reality than the one I normally operate

58

in, I think I'm being perfectly reasonable." Besides, I really didn't see any other options. If I could get help with this cursed gift of mine and keep his family free of an obligation they clearly did not want, then I just didn't see any question in the matter. And if someday they needed me to help them out with something. I could do that. The idea that something good could come of this curse; now that would be an interesting twist.

It was Tara's turn to speak and she appeared to be reconsidering me very cautiously. "Ours is not a family like any you have known before. Because we have not introduced an outsider to our clan in a long time, I am not sure how to do so." She appeared to be deep in thought and had gotten up to walk to where Tonya stood at the doorway of the kitchen.

I could see that there were some pictures arranged on the wall in a circle surrounding a large oval shaped mirror. Tara motioned for me to join her in front of them. Taking a moment to look first at Stephen, who nodded that it was okay, I rose and walked to stand with her.

We stood looking at the pictures, and judging by the cars, clothes and general condition of the photos, I could see that some went back a few generations. The unmistakable family resemblance was uncanny.

"Is this your dad?" I asked, pointing at a picture of a smaller, slightly built man smiling at me from under a fedora. The suit and car said 1930's. "He looks just like Stephen."

In a cautious voice, Tara answered, "No, that *is* Stephen."

I kept my eyes on the pictures, not certain what she was saying. My head was whirling. How could Stephen be that man? That would make him over seventy years old. What about the rest of them? Did they want me to believe that they were all ageless? Immortal? My brain stuttered on the word.

"Here I am", she pointed to a larger woman standing in a WAV uniform, next to a battleship and a tall, thin man in an army uniform circa World War II. "And that is Troy with me. This is a great one of Tonya," she smiled as she pointed to a flapper in a glittering dress and feather headband complete with beads and cigarette between her fingers, her head thrown back laughing. She was a lot less intimidating when she laughed. Tara raised her voice a hair as she half turned toward the kitchen, "Do you remember that one, Tonya?"

A soft, warm chuckle came from the kitchen doorway behind me. "Those were possibly my favorite years. The roaring 20's, indeed."

Stephen came up beside me and mouthed, "I can help." Operating in a fog, I nodded my acceptance and felt the languid comfort of *calm* flow through me. Right now I was okay with a little help handling this. He was my friend and I knew that he was trying to help his family and had not done anything wrong with my head, only enough to keep me here to listen so that I could make up my mind with all of the information I needed. Maybe I was crazy or getting caught up in whatever this whole charade was, but I still trusted him no matter what weirdness I was hearing. Whatever the reason, he had genuine concerns for his family should he have to make a deal with this other family, making my obligation clear. Any price associated with this deal would have to be handled by me. I didn't have a lot of money but I was honest and I would find a way to make it up.

Immortality. The word slid through my mind while I continued to follow the march of the family through the decades. Well, maybe it was possible. If ESP and paranormal were real, then why not agelessness? What made people immortal though? My heart skipped a beat and

I caught my breath. "Are you," I squeaked out the word, "vampires or something?"

"Or something," Stephen replied softly. "Troy, I'm not certain how to proceed. Do you think I should just *show* her?" Stephen and Troy looked at each other for a minute, Troy gave an almost imperceptible nod and Stephen moved away from me.

I looked up at him, watching him back away until he gave me a last wink, turned and glided into the kitchen. From behind the wall, I heard his voice call out, "It's better that I show you what we are, it's sort of hard to understand any other way." Then I heard a ripping noise, like he was tearing a dishtowel or something in there. At the same time, I felt a prickling along my skin. I glanced down at my arm to see the hair standing up, when a movement coming from the kitchen caught my eye. It was the biggest cat I'd ever seen; it was a mountain lion.

"Stephen!" I called in a panic. Was this the pet I had been hearing in the kitchen earlier? My mind tried to make sense of it. Looking at the cat now, my disbelief grew. Somehow I knew it was him. I just didn't believe it, but he felt the same. This was like one of those late night movies where everyone wore skimpy clothes and the werewolves ate everyone. I wondered if I was going to be lunch. Was this why they felt so strange? I had thought they felt similar to animals but not quite the same, something in between.

The mountain lion walked over to me, purring deep in his throat. Maybe he was trying to make me feel more at ease; unfortunately, it wasn't working so far. I felt him say *Stephen* in my head. Fighting my fear, I reached out my hand to him and he padded forward softly on his large paws before he rubbed his cheek on my fingers and looked up at me, still purring. This was Stephen yet when he touched me I felt nothing more than if I were touching an animal. My

61

lips curved pleasantly while I regarded his hazel eyes with wonder.

Before I could think whether it might offend him, I asked aloud, "Can I pet you?"

He rumbled low and came over to rub on my legs as if he was just an ordinary housecat, only this one liked me. His rippling fur was beautiful under the soft lights in the room. Golden brown with a chocolate tipped tail, he was the epitome of grace and beauty. "Do you have the claws and the teeth? Are you like a *real* mountain lion?"

He raised a front paw in a completely human gesture and spread his digits to show me his extended claws, before moving his face to within inches of my own and smiling at me to show me the largest fangs I had ever seen outside a museum so close they could kill me. Somehow I couldn't be afraid though; it could have been the very human hint of amusement I saw in his eyes. If he was in his human form, I knew he would be smiling and laughing right now.

Remembering the rest of the family was there with us, I looked up at Tara. "Can all of you do that?"

"Yes." Tara narrowed her eyes suspiciously. "Are you not afraid of us?"

"Not of Stephen. *He* wouldn't touch me." I put the emphasis on the 'he', not being so sure of the others. Stephen had said they all had gifts, he wasn't kidding.

Tonya giggled, a totally girlie giggle and added, "She's got that right."

I shot her a look. Not everyone could look like her but she didn't have to be rude. But then got distracted when I caught sight of the pictures out of the corner of my eye. "Is that why you guys don't age?"

Troy spoke up from the couch, still sitting very calmly at his original perch, "We do age, just at a much slower rate than humans. Our change brings our bodies to physical maturity, and then we slow our aging significantly. It is not uncommon to live several human lifetimes without significant changes in our appearance."

There it was, 'humans.' They were not human. Even though I was looking at real purring proof of that, knowing that my only friend was the biggest cat I'd ever seen outside of a zoo, it was fairly hair-raising to hear him referred to as a non-human.

"What are you guys? I know you aren't werewolves since you aren't wolves. What are you called if you turn into cats?"

Their patriarch answered patiently, "We are werecats; there are a number of different kinds of wereanimals. Werewolves are just the kind Hollywood decided to exploit." Troy sounded almost offended, as if *he* wanted to have been in the group made popular. Odd, I hadn't pegged him as a glory hound. Or glory cat?

He must have seen what I was thinking in my expression because he went on to clarify, "The werewolves are fine, but they have gotten progressively more difficult to handle since becoming celebrities. They were quite proud to have been singled out by the movie and book industries. Now, they are impossible to work with when the situation demands."

Funny, I had a picture in my head of a party and the werewolves strutting around, noses in the air, snubbing all of the other groups. I couldn't resist a giggle.

As this new knowledge filed itself into my consciousness, I had more questions. "So, since you guys are giant cats, what could you possibly be afraid of from this other family? Are they werecats too or are they some other animal?"

63

Troy and Tonya exchanged a glance and Tara suddenly had an urge to straighten the pictures on the wall, taking all of her concentration. Stephen walked into the kitchen again and I felt the tingle on my skin again as I heard a small popping sound. I watched the doorway expectantly. Within about a minute, Stephen came back through the doorway behind Tonya, running his hand through his hair and tugging his shirt down. Wow, rapid dressing; another one of his talents. He was the one to answer me.

"The wereanimals are not an issue. We are ruled by a council, which disallows clans from fighting amongst themselves. All grievances are brought before the Council which rules on what actions must be taken to resolve the issue in the best interest of the community."

This just got weirder by the minute. Wereanimals, snobby werewolves, a Council to handle fighting; it was so civilized. "You guys have your own little world."

Tara bristled, "It is not a *little* world, thank you. We have existed for as long as humans. And since the inception of the Council a thousand years ago, we have lived a far more civilized existence than you people have managed, I might add."

"She means no harm," Troy shot a cautionary glance at Tara on my behalf. I had one more ally it seemed.

Trying to placate her, I apologized, "I'm sorry, Tara, I didn't mean any offense."

She shrugged, obviously still huffy.   Turning back to Stephen, I asked again, "So who is the problem with, if not weres?" This was so unreal to be sitting in a normal house, in a normal living room, and to be discussing the social problems of supernatural creatures previously believed to be mythical up until about a half an hour ago.

"Vampires." Stephen said it in a dull tone.

My heart skipped a beat and I shuddered despite myself. "Vampires?" I whispered. That was a word that inspired a true sense of fear down to my very core. Undead, unkillable, blood sucking machines that hated people for some unknown reason. Strike that, they loved people. They loved to drink our blood. I had seen the movies, and now I knew they were real. In an instant, nighttime got a whole lot scarier. My arms wrapped around my middle.

Stephen waved me back to the loveseat. "Claire, let's sit. This is a lot to take in," his tone changed from gentle to something I hadn't heard from him yet, defensive. As we were halfway to the loveseat, Stephen's whole demeanor had changed. He lifted his nose, sniffing the air. "And we aren't done yet. They're right on time."

Looking around at the rest of the family, I saw that Troy, Tonya and Tara had come into the middle of the room, gathering together, forming ranks to greet the midnight visitors. All of this was still registering when I heard the doorbell ring, making it real.

"Why did you have to invite them here to *my* house?" Tara hissed, her eyes narrowing. I could picture her tail switching. It was so easy to see her as a cat; that would explain the moodiness.

Troy diplomatically held up his hand to quiet her. "You know the late hour draws attention on my street. They have come to discuss matters. Nothing more."

I understood then that the other family, the one we had been discussing handling my training, was here now and they were vampires. There were vampires at the door! And in my fear, I felt the shock of disbelief, "They use the doorbell?" How odd that they would do something so absolutely ordinary.

65

"Claire, you do not have to be afraid here." Stephen's tone was somber. His was not just a statement meant to reassure, he was making a promise. For the second time that night, I took a leap and believed my friend. My hands were like ice as my nerves took hold of my body, I forced my arms to my sides to at least appear less petrified than I was.

Troy walked forward to open the door and I realized I was holding my breath. He looked back at me just as he was about to open the door. "You are protected here as a guest of our clan. You have nothing to fear for your safety." He smiled briefly at me as he opened the door to the most frightening thing I could ever conceive to be walking the earth.

Ch. 10

The door opened and I felt my jaw drop. There were two beings standing there at the door when it opened. One of them, I had met before.

"Henry?" I squeaked. I had never fainted before, but thought I might now. Lights danced at the edges of my vision.

He didn't show any outward signs that he was surprised to see me. "Hello Claire," He turned back to Troy standing by the open door then.

Completely normal, no Nosferatu claws or long fangs, not even the haunted black eyes. He was not what I was expecting for my first vampire.

"Troy, I apologize for the short notice, but this issue is serious. " He glanced over at the man beside him. "My associate, James, has come by some information that I felt could not wait for a later meeting."

Troy must have answered but my eyes were locked on Henry's pale associate, James as they stepped in and Troy shut the door behind them. He was about 5'10" with a lean muscular build and in his early twenties. His wavy, light brown hair was pushed back from his face, brushing his collar as he turned his head, taking in all in attendance. But what caught and held me completely captivated were his steady, smoky blue eyes. Was that just the hint of freckles splashed across the tops of his cheeks? I had never heard of freckles on a vampire. Granted, maybe Ann Rice missed that part.

"By all means, Henry," Troy looked over, "James, good to see you again. I hadn't realized you were back in the country. Please, come in." Stepping back to allow them to enter, Troy looked nonplussed to be welcoming the two vampires into the house. Henry must be a good vampire. Was there such a thing? It seemed that the two groups got along well enough to visit each other's homes. It struck me that my world was a much different place this evening than it had been just a few hours ago. And to think, I had been worried that tonight would be complicated by Stephen's romantic interest in me. Huh, if only.

Henry strode inside to stand in front of the large window at the front of the room. James stood a few feet to his left, nearest the door. The Andrews resumed their previous positions on the loveseats. Not certain what to do, I hovered next to Stephen's end of the loveseat, putting as much distance as politely possible between myself and the vampires. It didn't matter that Henry was just a librarian. He didn't look like one right now, I didn't know if he would ever look like *just* anything again.

Henry looked at each member of the family, nodding slightly at them individually. Lastly, he looked briefly at me and nodded deliberately, almost a bow. Not knowing what to do, I bobbed my head back, still holding his chocolate eyes with mine.
Troy spoke first. "Claire has come tonight to visit with our family. I am sure she is finding her visit enormously educational. Isn't that right, Claire? You can speak freely in front of her." He looked at me then, "Yes?"

Again, my assent was silent, eyes drifting between Henry and Troy, relieved when no one mentioned my "gift."

"As you know, James has certain," he paused, "connections in the area. This evening, one of these connections has come to him with some news. The rumors of another coven moving into our territory are true. They are believed to be former military and of a most violent disposition." Henry paused and looked at Stephen. "We are uncertain of their intentions; we merely know they are coming to this area and have been rather flamboyant with their hunting in the past."

Hunting; was that what they called it when they killed people? I felt a cold shiver run down my spine. It was hard to picture Henry or this handsome James sucking the life out of some poor human. Someone like me, I thought. I felt sick and my eyes went to the floor.

"Claire, why don't you sit down?" Henry was looking at me.

Stephen twisted his neck back to where I was standing. "Claire you look a little green." He was worried.

It took a couple of swallows and I licked my lips to speak. It didn't work. I just shook my head and stumbled over to sit next to Stephen on the arm of the couch.

Henry continued, "We prefer not to have any issues in this area that might bring unwanted attention to our own local population. I have come to ask your clan to help us in our efforts to dissuade them from entering our area and continue moving beyond our boundaries. Stephen, would you be willing to assist us?"

Though I didn't know what talents the other members of his family might have, I could see how Stephen's lie detector trick or ability to insert thoughts into people's heads could help to influence the unwanted visitors to stay away. So, the vampires here in this area were quiet about their, er, hunting. That was good. I wasn't sure how good, but I did consider it a good thing that they wanted to avoid a bloodbath. Or whatever it was the other group did that was considered "flamboyant." My imagination was working overtime on that one and my hands had begun to tremble.

While I was thinking, I realized my eyes kept wandering back to James. His face, his body; was it really the conversation that was making it so hard to breathe and focus? Dressed in black trousers and a white dress shirt with the neck open and sleeves rolled up to show nicely muscled

69

forearms, and black dress shoes with a high polish, he looked irresistible from head to toe. Only it wasn't something so obvious that was pulling at me; it was something else, something I'd never felt before but it was making it hard to function. Not that it mattered, the drooling, staring, shaking mess I'd turned into was undoubtedly impressing all of them.

It was during my hormonal internal monologue that I vaguely heard Henry and Troy discussing the minutia of how to go about handling the crisis at their door. I realized with not a minor amount of embarrassment what had drawn my attention back to the conversation. Troy had said James' name.

Henry was answering, "Yes Troy, I agree that it might not be necessary, however, we need to know that if it becomes necessary, we will be able to rely upon your clan as we have before." He looked at James. "Please James, if you could advise Troy of what you shared with me in the car?"

They rang doorbells *and* drove cars? How terribly mundane that seemed for such notoriously scary, otherworldly beings. Maybe there were some other things I had wrong. Maybe the books and movies had painted a gorier picture of these creatures than was deserved.

Again, in my own head, I was shocked back to the conversation when I heard a deep, silky voice come from Henry's guest. More than his physical presence, his voice tugged at my being and I heard myself gasp. Clearing my throat, I tried to mask my reaction.

"My informant has alerted me that the coven is moving up from Chicago and will be here in about a week. Their story is that they are searching for a missing member of their coven and that they will be looking in Milwaukee. He guesses it will take some time before they turn toward us. We may have a few weeks if they have any trouble. That

70

population is more scattered than our own, but they will be upon us roughly before the end of November, regardless."

I wondered if he could see me staring at him; I was utterly captivated. It was as if his entire being changed as he spoke and his voice went straight through to the center of my being. In the same way I could hear my mother's specific tone in a crowd, I knew that I would be able to find his as well without question.

With a jolt, I realized that I heard Troy saying my name. "We were speaking to Claire tonight, initiating her into the clan, so to speak, in preparation of training her."

Then I became very aware of each person then looking curiously at me. At first, I had to stare very hard at the stitching on my brown trainers, until I realized that they were all waiting for something. I looked up, for the first time, meeting James' eyes head on as they looked directly at me. Something in me shifted, that tugging from within and that connection I had felt clicked and I was completely and utterly entranced. His eyes, as he beheld the human in the room, reminded me exactly of the ocean when I had seen it in California during a winter storm. It had been grey and foreboding. James' eyes now appeared equally severe, but I felt them drawing me, regardless. I was afraid I would not be able to speak with him here; it was hard enough to breathe somewhat regularly. Fortunately, Stephen seemed to notice. He cleared his throat and, that failing to get my attention, decided to speak for me.

"Henry, James, please excuse Claire. She's had a lot thrown at her tonight. She had no idea any of us existed a few hours ago." His tone grew severe, "James, could you tone down the Glamour a bit? You don't need it here and it's unfair to use on her. She's human and as you can see, she can't even function."

71

James broke eye contact with me and smiled in embarrassment, which only served to make him all the more enticing. He slid his hands in his pockets and flicked his eyes up at Stephen. "I am sorry for any disruption I've caused, however, I am not using Glamour." He looked back up at me. He was trying to hide a smile, but I thought I had seen something else flash behind his eyes.

Stephen glanced from me to James. He was seeing something in our faces that disturbed him. I heard a new, harsher undercurrent in his voice when he demanded my attention, "Claire, look at me."

I did as he asked and reluctantly broke away again from James to look at Stephen. When I did, the connection I'd felt faded and my cheeks heated up as I realized I'd been staring and everyone had noticed. Even the object of my fascination had noticed my blatantly pitiful ogling. Great, I was blushing and staring. What was I some silly little schoolgirl with a crush? Actually, yes, yes I was. How mortifying.

Stephen considered me for a moment longer and shook his head, tossing aside an unwanted thought. It made his hair go all moppish again and I thought even though I now knew he was a mountain lion, I still loved that he looked like a little brother. I smiled. He smiled back sarcastically, "Glad you are still with us." Jerk. "Claire, if it is all right with you, I would like to share with these two what exactly your gift is and how it might be of use to us in a situation such as this one."

Again, I had to look at my shoes, my self-doubt rising exponentially while I compared myself to these supernatural heavyweights. "Um, I'm not sure it would be helpful at all. Like I told you, I wouldn't consider it much use. It's never helped me."

"Let us decide, hmm?" He said not unkindly.

72

"I guess. Stephen, could I get a drink of water or something?" I needed to get out of the room while they talked about me, and my stupid *gift*.

"Sure, glasses are to the right of the sink. Help yourself to anything in there."

Jumping up, I wobbled on my feet for a stride before steadying myself. 'Way to look like an idiot,' I thought to myself. As I walked to the kitchen to get a drink, I heard Stephen begin, "Henry, you know what I can do."

Henry sounded like he was not surprised by this information, he must be aware of all of the clan's abilities. "Yes Stephen. It has been very helpful in our assessing of situations in the past and I hope that you will help us with it again very soon."

There was a pause, presumably some nodding then Stephen continued. "I'm sure you're aware of Claire's paranormal sensitivity."

"Yes, I felt it when I met her."

He'd known? Of course he had. I felt like the last one to get the answer to a problem.

"Claire is an empath as well. She also has a talent I haven't seen in a long time and one I think would be greatly beneficial when added to our current arsenal."

He paused and I was frozen in place listening, wondering what he knew about my abilities that I didn't. Not for a long time? He'd known others with this capability? Maybe he could help me shield all of it, or even shut it down. I dared to hope for normalcy in my life while I stood in the kitchen of my werecat friend who was talking to vampires. Normalcy. Right. Perspective.

Stephen continued, "She can channel."

No one said anything. I was dying to see how that little tidbit was being received. Did he think that was good?

"How well does she channel? Have you tested the distance to which she can reach?"

Wandering back in, sipping my water from a glass, I refused to look up at them. I just walked right in and sat on the arm of the loveseat again. It was so quiet. I imagined them all looking at me like a puzzle, deciding if they wanted to take the time to figure it out to see if it was worth it. Even if they could use my abilities, I couldn't let go of the idea that they were amusing themselves with me. Holding my breath, I waited to hear which way my future would go.

"Claire, could you help me to explain or even show our friends what you can do?" Stephen prodded gently, knowing I was in a fragile place.

Without looking up, I mumbled, "Everything I know about it is accidental. I feel what others around me feel, the closer they are, the clearer I feel them. If I touch them, I can channel them. That's it. It really isn't a gift or anything. More like a curse." Speaking it aloud, admitting all of it burned but I had to be honest and put my own opinion on things out there whether they cared to consider them or not; this was all beginning to feel like I wasn't going to have a say in it soon anyway.

That alluring voice spoke again, going directly to the same spot where he'd gotten into my head from the start and I let my eyes be drawn to where he stood frowning at me. "I hear what you're saying Stephen, but she is raw. Do we have time to develop her ability before we would need it? Stephen, can your clan work with her? It seems you two are, ah, close." He had obviously mistaken Stephen's protective attitude as jealousy. Great. Like it mattered; it wasn't going to happen between an average looking human and a gorgeous vampire. That I knew.

Hearing Stephen laugh out loud, I looked up at him, slighted. "Yes, I can help her with her sensing, but you know I have never worked with channeling. That is kind of your forte. And you know better than that." He wiggled a finger between us, smirking, "Claire and I are just friends."

Even though we had just discussed it and just that very night I had dreaded it, hearing Stephen laugh at the thought that we were dating stung. I was tired of being talked about like I wasn't in the room. "You don't have to jump all over that one Stephen; I'm not *that* bad." I tried to keep the bitterness out of my voice.

He looked at me, kindness in his eyes as he prepared to soften the blow. I heard Tara belly laugh. I shot her a look but she had her eyes closed, laughing. Hard.

"It's not that funny. Just because I am some dumb human doesn't mean I'm inferior or not worth the time or effort unless it can benefit your cause." I stood up to leave. I didn't have to take this. Human out.

Troy silenced Tara with a quick word. "Stephen, I think you owe Claire an explanation."

I looked at Stephen who now appeared a bit sheepish. "What? Is that it, are your kind not into humans?"

Stephen smiled gently. "My kind likes humans just fine, and I specifically like human males quite a bit."

Now our conversations made sense. Of course he just wanted to be friends, I was a girl, totally not his type. "You're gay?" Was my smile as big as it felt? How perfect! It wasn't because I was just some dumb human. Awesome! "Stephen, that's great!"

75

His eyes hardened in offense, "I'm glad you think so."

Backpedaling quickly, I moved to put my hand by his shoulder, my version of a pat or hug. "I'm sorry Stephen. I have no problem with you being gay, it has nothing to do with that. I'm just glad you don't think it's laughable for someone to want to go out with me."

Stephen, my new best friend, grabbed me into an impulsive and unexpected hug and I couldn't shield from his touch fast enough. In an instant I was filled with his warmth. It surprised me with its intensity and I gasped, eyes and mouth flying open with the shock of it, but feeling his affection taking hold of me, I wrapped my own arms tightly around his body, hugging him to me. Stephen immediately leaned back, pushing me away, and dropped his arms. He slammed up his own blockade system and I took a step back wrapping my arms around my middle, wishing I could disappear.

"I'm sorry, Claire. I should have known to block that. I forgot about that for a sec." He was actually blushing. Maybe I wasn't supposed to know how much he liked me. I didn't care. I was happy to have felt the depth of his affection, only that joy was tempered by the shame of the display I'd just put on for them. I was indeed a weak human just like they all thought.

James spoke my name this time yanking me back to the present, "Claire."

My own name had never made me want to shudder before. "Yes." It wasn't a question. Whatever he wanted, I knew I would try to do it. I wondered how it was that I was having such an intense reaction to him. It wasn't just an attraction, something I didn't understand was happening. I was too embarrassed to ask Stephen though. I'd have to sort it out myself. Maybe it was a vampire thing. Stephen had called it Glamour.

His deep voice tickled my skin. "Claire, if that display was any indication of your ability and lack of control, I think that we should work with you to develop both. Even if you cannot help us, we can't leave you so vulnerable to others. It is only a matter of time before someone figures that out and uses you for their own means. I have experience with channeling; I would like to work with you. Would that be acceptable?"

I tried not to swallow my tongue. "Yes, that would be fine. When should we start?"

"If Henry could help us with the scheduling, I have time to meet every evening for now. We can use my home. If we can get you ready before the unwelcome company we're expecting, your gift could help us to determine threat level. And if you show any proficiency at distance, it could help us tremendously in determining our risks. I can only guess until I have more experience with your talent."

"Your house?" My voice sounded flat and dull. What was wrong with me? "That would be fine."

James dipped his head, and he and Henry turned to leave. Henry looked to Troy, who rose to walk them out. "I will call you to arrange our next meeting. This gives me hope that we can avoid damage to our own position and those close to us. Thank you for that." He turned to me, "Don't worry about your shift tomorrow. We'll move your schedule around to accommodate your work with James." He turned to James, concern lining his brow. "Would you be ready to start as soon as tomorrow?"

He was clearly more concerned about this situation than I thought if he was putting any amount of faith in me to help.

James answered in the affirmative and that seemed to be all everyone needed. The vampires said their good-bye's and took their leave. James turned to me as he was walking out.

"Henry will give you my address. Can you make it tomorrow at six?"

My heart sank. "I don't have a car."

"Hmm. If you prefer, I can pick you up at a quarter till in front of the library."

"Yes, that would work."

"You might want to eat before I pick you up." He flashed me a smile and my stomach tightened, "I will make sure that I do. This sort of work can be exhausting and use up your reserves quickly."

My smile faded as they walked out and, thankfully, my senses returned as soon as the door was closed. Was I an idiot? Hot or not, I had just agreed to spend a lot of time with a *vampire*. I couldn't control myself around a group of "friends." Now I was going to meet with him all by myself. Did I want to die? Oh, but what a way to go! Feeling myself blush again, I had to change tracks quickly before I completely humiliated myself in front of Stephen's family tonight.

After the door closed, I sank back down on the loveseat behind me where Stephen had just been sitting and I welcomed the residual warmth from his body into mine. My head sank back on the cushions and I yawned, exhausted mentally and physically. What time was it?

Stephen noticed. "We'd better get you back before you pass out. You've had a big night," he teased.

Nodding, I agreed and struggled to my feet. Troy stopped me with his hand out as I walked to the door. "Claire, I am pleased to have met you and look forward to working with you. You are a friend to us. We will protect you as a member of our clan, I swear it." His words were formal and heavy with meaning. I found them reassuring, even if I didn't fully understand what was behind them.

"Thanks Troy. I just hope I can help." They already felt like more of a family than mine at home. Immediately I felt guilty, but it was true. It was just that I could be myself and be open with these people. That was something I couldn't see doing with my parents. And my grandparents? No way. Grandma would probably try to send in an exorcist.

Stephen walked out beside me; his shields were back up so all I felt was his body heat. We walked shoulder to shoulder out the door and he opened the car door for me at the curb. I turned to wave from the passenger seat after buckling up and I saw Troy hold up a hand in salute from the window. The girls had gone back to the interior. I wasn't sure their level of excitement about my involvement, but they certainly hadn't been as openly hostile by the end of the evening. That had to be worth something.

"So what was that I saw between you and James?" Stephen was on me as soon as he turned the key in the ignition. I groaned, "It was that obvious, was it? I'm such a dork. I've never had that happen to me before." I put my face in my hands, humiliated.

He laughed, "Can't say as I blame you, he *is* hot. You got his attention though, too. I've never seen him offer up his help so easily." His face grew serious. "You should be careful with him Claire. Getting mixed up with them can be, ah, life altering. I wouldn't have done this if I thought I could have taken you on myself."

Suddenly uncomfortable, I abruptly changed the subject. I was sure the only reason James was showing interest in me was due to my talent and obvious lack of control of it. They were hoping I would be able to help them, or at least not be used against them if I read things right. There was something Stephen had said earlier that had peaked my

79

interest, "Stephen, what is Glamour? You said James was using it on me."

"Glamour is a vampire thing. They can make you go gaga over them if they want. It makes it easier for them to hunt, like deer in the headlights." He was looking ahead at the road, face eerily green in the glow of the dashboard lights. It seemed fitting for the creepy conversation.

"Speaking of which, am I nuts to go to his house alone?" I was genuinely concerned now that I had my wits back.

"Why? Are you afraid you won't be able to keep your hands off him?" Stephen laughed.

Waving him off, I answered slightly annoyed that he was having so much fun with my obvious infatuation, "No, I'm worried he won't be able to keep his hands off *me*."

His eyebrows went up as he looked over at me. "Pretty sure of yourself, huh?"

"Ahh." I groaned in frustration, rolling my head against the seat back. "Are you thick? He is a *vampire*. I am a *human*. Is he going to drink my blood or something?"

Stephen got it then. "Actually, Henry and James both refrain from hunting humans directly and they encourage it among the rest of the Minneapolis coven. It helps them blend more effectively in society. They have a connection with the local blood bank and get what they need that way."

"Really? They drink donor blood? Isn't that supposed to be used to save lives of people who need it? It would piss me off if I knew some vampire was sucking on my donation." Of all the things to seem wrong tonight, somehow that seemed like a betrayal to the populace.

"*Doesn't* it save lives, Claire?" He spared me a sideways glance.

"Oh. I suppose you've got a point there." I hadn't thought of it that way.

We rode the rest of the way in a comfortable silence, each lost in our own thoughts until we got back to my dorm.

"Hey, how did you know which dorm I lived in? I've never told you where I lived."

He ducked his head shamefaced. "I followed your smell before so I knew you lived in this one." He saw the distraught look on my face. "I don't know what floor or anything. It isn't like I've been spying."

"My smell?" This new life was going to take some adjusting. My best friend could follow my smell and my soon to be tutor could drink my blood. College was proving to be a very different experience than I had expected. Not frightening though, strangely enough, just different. There was definitely something wrong with me if I wasn't scared yet. Worse yet, if this wasn't enough, then what was it going to take to scare me smart?

Ch. 11

The next day I felt out of sorts all day. It was fortunate that I had three classes and was able to keep my mind busy in increments. I vacillated between giddy, butterflies in the stomach excited to nausea, gloom and doom fear all day. I was starting to wonder if I would even make it to tonight's big date without having a breakdown. Correction, study session. Best not to even let my mind wander that direction. I couldn't handle a human relationship much less one with an even more complicated creature who far outpaced me on the social scale.

Upon booting up my laptop in my room during lunch break, I saw that Henry had emailed my new work schedule and, true to his word, I was off evenings for the next few weeks bringing us to Thanksgiving break and the time James anticipated the new coven's arrival. Hopefully, no one noticed my boon of day shifts and got upset. Although I wasn't friends with her, I hoped that my sort of friendship with Heidi wouldn't suffer.

Last night on the way home I had gleaned what I could from Stephen about James, aka James Thomas. He worked for the Star Tribune, the main Minneapolis newspaper as a travel writer, which gave him a valid cover story for his travels keeping up on vampire "business" all over the world. He wouldn't tell me more than that, saying James' story was his own, and anything more personal would have to come from him. Most of the supernatural crowd was like that, he said, there were some unwritten guidelines that everyone followed. Though a bit put off, I had to admit the idea of hearing his story in that melodic voice of his had a strong draw to it. Giggling to myself, I wondered if he had ever done one of those phone sex lines. He could make a fortune at it.

Eventually classes were through and, after trying unsuccessfully for about two hours to study, the clock finally reached four. James had advised me to eat before going to his house. My guess was he probably didn't have any people food if I did get hungry. I wasn't sure if I could get or keep anything down though, so I figured it was safest to try my favorite snack, peanut butter toast and a cup of tea with cream and sugar. That would hold me and wouldn't make me sick if my nervous stomach decided to rear its ugly head.

As I tried to figure out when it would be decent to head over to meet James at the library, I looked at myself in the mirror. Blech! It wasn't looking good. My dark, wavy brown hair was sticking up from being in and out of the wind all day, I had circles under my eyes from not sleeping well last night and my clothes were rumpled from being sat in. There was no way I was going to be taken seriously by anyone looking like this.

My closet was not stocked with much for me to work with. Clearly I was not a Cosmo girl, nor did my lifestyle have much call for party attire. While I was washing my hair in the bathroom down the hall, I was clicking through fashion ideas. I finally settled on my favorite jeans and a cream v-neck sweater that accentuated my dark French features and lighter brown eyes. The clothes fit my petite athletic build well, but having heard that my eyes were my best feature, I decided to draw attention to them and throw a touch of dark eyeliner on. My hair was proving difficult, so I gave up and pulled my shoulder length hair back into a loose ponytail. Functional and hopefully reasonably attractive, that was the best it was going to get tonight.

Five thirty. I could leave now and be justifiably early without appearing eager. It would only take about ten minutes to get to the front of the library. But he might be early so that would be reasonable, I justified to myself as I shrugged into my light green down coat. It was dark early now and with the wind up it was downright chilly. Winter was already bearing down on us. Every Minnesotan has at least three coats for all of the different flavors of fall and winter. This one was my favorite. I almost looked forward to colder weather so that I could add my fluffy cream scarf, hat and gloves that looked so good with it. I sighed, only here in the frozen north.

Zipping up, locking my door, and putting my keys in my pocket had never felt so final. What if things went wrong and I died tonight? How long would it be before someone knew I was missing? Stephen would probably be the only one who would even notice my absence here on campus. My stomach gave a turn. Stephen wouldn't let me go if I was in danger, he'd told me as much as had Troy when he'd offered clan protection. That extended to their allies, right? That was where the undeniably strong draw to James kicked in. I *had* to see him again. The idea of he and I together, alone, was both terrifying and irresistible all at once. Maybe I was one of those girls drawn to "bad boys." No, there had been plenty of bad kids at my high school that did nothing for me. It was just this one. The sane part of my brain hoped for my safety that his allure would wear off as I spent more time with him. It looked like I would find out very soon.

He was early. As I walked up to the library's front doors from my side of campus, I looked to the curb just beyond and saw a sleek black car under the streetlight. Silhouetted in the foreground against the bushes across the road behind it, the car caught my attention, but that wasn't what held it. There he stood, arms crossed and leaning against his car. He wore a light blue sweater, a glimpse of white undershirt visible at the open neck and dark blue trousers. How did he do that with his hair? He was pale, but not as pale as last night. Curious. Upon seeing me, he stepped forward a few feet and spoke to me without a readable expression on his face.

84

"Claire, are you ready to come with me?" His voice sounded even better than I remembered. It was husky, as if he had lowered it for privacy; not that he needed to, this edge of campus was deserted this time of night. Everyone was either at dinner or evening classes.

All of my breath left my body. Heart racing, stomach flipping, I nodded a "yes" as I stepped forward to meet him. James uncrossed his arms and turned gracefully to open the passenger door for me. I stepped in and buckled up. As I clicked my seatbelt, he was already in on his side and turning the key in the ignition. He was so quick it was unsettling. The movies had gotten that part right. What else had they been right about? I felt my stomach lurch.

We drove quickly off campus and reached the freeway in less than a minute. His A6 was the nicest car I'd ever been in and it was hard not to relax into the butter soft leather of my seat as the engine growled its way out of the city. It didn't take long, and before I'd gotten too comfortable, we were getting off the freeway at the Penn Avenue exit. I was relieved when we turned off and headed into the nicer area. Though I wouldn't usually care if he lived in a nice neighborhood, I'd lived in some dicey military housing along the way, this was already a stressful situation and I felt just that little bit better knowing we would not be in a tough part of town should I need to make a run for it. He surprised me again by turning into a driveway just off the main drive in the upscale Kenwood neighborhood.

The driveway was short, as they were in this older neighborhood. It was herringbone paving stones with a low stone retaining wall between his house and the neighbor to the right, which was the side the garage touched on and we now pulled into. The house itself was a Tudor style with a sweeping roofline and a higher peak over two stories. The stonework on the front made it look very storybook. It was hard to see the landscaping given the darkness, but I could see that he had a purple leaf sand cherry surrounded by roses

85

in the front garden, uplit for effect. This was my kind of house, complete with a round topped wooden door.

I must have sat too long, because by the time I took a breath and unbuckled my seatbelt, he was at my door opening it for me again. Not usually one for chivalry, I found myself a tiny bit pleased with his gentlemanly manner. Shaking my head, I tried to ignore the small voice in my head suggesting maybe that meant he wouldn't eat me.

When I looked out to stand up, he was just inches away, waiting. His effect on me was a repeat of the night before. It was going to be a challenge not to act like a total goober around him and convince him I was worth his time.

James held out his hand to me, his eyes so intense I found it hard to breathe. "Are you coming?"

Breathe you moron, I told myself. "Yes, just give me a minute, I'm a little nervous. This is kind of new to me."

"What, going to a strange man's house?" His lips twisted into an uneven grin, teasing me.

"No, a vampire's," came blurting out before I could think.

His features hardened and his eyes went dark. "Let's go inside so that we can speak freely."

I wished the floor would open and swallow me whole. Vampires were real; why couldn't people-swallowing-vortices be too? Why would I say such a thing on a public street in his neighborhood? I was guessing he didn't want to be outed right here or he would have posted a sign.

Deciding it was best to just keep my big mouth shut, I hung my head and followed him dutifully into the house.

86

Ch. 12

Inside, the house was as welcoming as it had felt from the outside. Just like Tara's house, the front room had no TV. Did supernatural folk not watch TV? But he did have a low, sleek Havana brown leather sofa flanked by warm mahogany end tables. There was a soft looking camel colored blanket tossed casually over the back of the couch. I reached out to touch it. Cashmere; I loved the feel of cashmere.

The room was painted a grey blue not unlike his eyes, with curtains cut from cream silk. The living room was clean and masculine, opening up into the dining room with a small square table and four high backed wooden chairs pulled up tight in matching mahogany. The décor was simple, but obviously of good quality. I could tell that the wood was hand crafted by the dovetailing and metal accent pieces instead of being machine milled.

Running my hand along the top of the end table nearest me I was curious, "Is this Amish crafted? These are mission style, but not the new way. They're really high quality pieces."

James had led the way into the dining room without giving me a backward glance but turned slowly with a curious look on his face. "Are you are a furniture expert?"

Why did I open my big mouth? I sounded like a know it all, "No, my dad makes furniture in his spare time so I know a little." Awkwardly, I brought my hand back to my side and looked around the room again, wishing I had spent more time learning to make small talk. *Social idiot* kept running through my mind like a schoolyard taunt. Now all I could think of were vampire questions and to ask what Henry meant by flamboyant kills or what he thought my chances might be for learning to master my gift, but all of that seemed like overkill after my flub in the driveway. I shifted from one foot to the other, nervously uncertain what to do.

James raised his eyebrows curiously. "How interesting," was all he said as he moved into the kitchen while I was having my defeatist self-talk. His voice floated out of the kitchen, "Could I get you anything to drink? I have water, coffee and tea."

"I'd take a tea. What kind do you have?" A man who had tea; I was impressed.

He poked his face back into the kitchen doorway. "I apologize but I only have black tea. Not many of my guests take more than that, but I remember enjoying it a long time ago. It was always my preference over coffee, not so bitter smelling either."

I walked up toward the kitchen, "My grandmother was French and brought up in Canada kind of old school. When we would go visit, we would have tea."

He smiled strangely. "I will get the cream and sugar as well."

I felt myself grinning back, relaxing a little for the first time with him. "Good guess."

Following him into the kitchen, I took in the details. Again with the dark wood, mission styled cabinets, lots of glass fronts and deep green and black granite counter tops. The dark colors didn't make the house seem small like they sometimes can; instead, it felt cozy and lived in. It was easy to picture myself cuddled up on the couch with the blanket, reading a book in the winter or cooking in this kitchen. It felt like home, odd for a girl who'd always grown up without a sense of what that meant.

"Did you design this kitchen or have someone do it for you?"

"I designed the entire house, why? Do you like it?" He asked over his shoulder as he filled up the teakettle with his back to me, giving me a long look at his broad shoulders.

"Just curious. Especially with the kitchen since you probably don't use it much." There, I did it again. Pointing out his being different when here he'd been polite enough not to have done the same to me yet.

He stopped filling the teakettle, set it down and turned around, crossing his arms as he leaned against the counter. I swallowed hard.

"Do you have a problem with what I am? You knew it before we agreed to this arrangement." It was hard to read his face, he'd wiped any traces of feeling from it.

There was a spot on the floor that I gave all my attention as I answered, "No, I have just never met a... one of you before. Last night was the first I had even heard that you really existed. I guess I don't know how to go about all of this." My manners finally surfaced and I looked up at him, "I'm sorry if I have offended you. I would never do that on purpose." My remorse was genuine and I hoped he could tell that. I really didn't want to make him angry or hurt his feelings. It wasn't just because he was attractive, well there was that, and then the whole I've-never-known-one-of-them-before thing so it was understandable how I was tripping all over myself. At least as far as I was concerned.

He considered my rationale before slowly dipping his chin once. "I guess that makes sense." With that, he finished putting the kettle on and turned back to indicate with one hand that we were returning to the living room. "Shall we, then?"

James followed my lead and waited patiently while I picked a perch on the far side of the couch. He sat in the matching leather side chair opposite me. Apparently I was supposed to start only I was a blank.

"So, um, what do we do first?" My voice quavered and I cleared my throat. I hoped my tentative shielding would at least hold enough for me to make a decent showing for whatever it was I was supposed to do here.

"What we do first is teach you how to protect yourself. Anything else would be wonderful, but is entirely optional." Growing more severe, he leaned in toward me and I stared into his eyes, deeper blue than before. "I saw how Stephen's touch affected you. Can you touch people without that happening?"

It was hard, this confession. I'd never told anyone all of this. It was too hard to admit. But, if there was anyone who could help me, it was James.

Picking a spot on the wall just over his head and pretending I was talking about someone else, I began, "Since I was little, it's hurt to touch people. It feels like all of my nerves are exposed and the other person's skin is electrocuting me, my whole body all at the same time. My whole self is swallowed up by the other person's emotions. I know what's happening, I don't lose consciousness or anything, I'm still," I paused to pick the right word, "I'm still watching but I can't do anything or say anything to stop my body from going through the same things as theirs. I lose myself in their joy or pain." Even lust, I remembered privately. I shuddered and closed my eyes as I remembered hugging my cousin Roger at our Aunt Olivia's wedding. Roger was fifteen at the time, I was thirteen and he'd had some champagne, which made him feel his hormones running. If it weren't for Mom's intuition kicking in at that moment, making her follow me down the hallway into that alcove, something probably would have happened right there, with my own cousin.

I could hear every beat of my heart as I sat there in the silence, eyes closed with my shame laid bare before a total stranger. It was worse than being naked. My gift left me at the mercy of anyone who might lay a hand on me. Or, I would live without the human element of touch my whole life. That was the true cost of my curse. It could not feel like a gift to me.

In the gentlest of voices, my confessor broke the silence, "Claire, I have known others like you. It will be a challenge, but if you are willing I think I can help you."

For the first time, I wondered if it could be a reality for me to hug my parents and enjoy it. Maybe even hold someone's hand, it wasn't much but it was more than I'd ever dared hope. It would be difficult he said, but I was a good student. I could do this.

I sat up straight in my seat and looked directly into his blue eyes. They were so open that I couldn't help but trust him; maybe it was a vampire thing. More Glamour; it didn't matter, I was going for it. Yet there was something else there I couldn't put my finger on; curiosity? Maybe I was as much a mystery to him as he was to me. Again, I stopped my thinking from going down that road. I was here to learn, that was it.

He shifted his weight forward and put his hands on his knees. It was such a human action that it was easy to forget what he was. "Claire, you are an empath with a remarkably strong ability to channel. This leaves you open to all sorts of attacks, whether through accident or malice. Before we add to the lessons Stephen has taught you I need to understand what you know about shielding."
"Well, he pointed me to the Jenkins book and I've been working on it through my door." I was proud of my progress.

He looked quizzically at me. "Your door?"

I felt my cheeks coloring again. "Well, yeah. I can't just walk up to people and ask them to stand still while I practice blocking them out. They would lock me up in a heartbeat. So, I sit at my door and when I feel someone coming I imagine a door and see myself closing it."

"Tell me more about how you feel them. Is it a general sense or is it more specific? Can you tell if they are human, male or female? How much information can you get from them without seeing them?"

"I can tell their gender, men feel differently than women and age is approximate. Mostly I can tell if someone is older or younger by feel. Younger people feel more strongly. Older and mature people tend to be milder in their emotions. I can tell how someone is feeling and what they are feeling it about, but only as they experience it. Memories fade unless someone is literally having it while I'm listening." How old was he, I wondered. And how many people like me had he known?

He waited motionless for me so I kept going.

"Blocking is easier to do if I am farther away from someone and if I don't know them very well. You know how Stephen needs to have touched you to get a connection he can find later, whenever he wants?"

He nodded.

"Well, that's how mine is, sort of. If I know someone or they have ever touched me, I can't block them as easily. It has been pretty easy here at school because I don't know anyone very well and no one has touched me but Stephen, and that was only the once."

His face clouded with what I took for anger with me for weakness. "I remember how that ended."

I ducked my eyes embarrassed. "Yeah, that's kind of how it can be. He felt affectionate toward me and I picked it up, throwing it right back at him. It can act like a magnifier sometimes because of the looping effect." A thought struck me and I hoped I wasn't being too bold. "Why is his kind so much warmer than yours or mine?"

My request gave him barely a pause. "Stephen is a wereanimal, and they are warmer than your kind because their animal is always with them, a potential change always right there below the surface. Mine is cool unless we've recently fed and have warm blood coursing through our systems, then, by its proximity, we are temporarily warm. Knowing those few subtleties between our species could save your life one day."

"That's all right, *I'll* never need to worry about that stuff. If I'm helping you guys out I'll have Stephen with me and he'll tell me what's what." I waved off his warning.

All signs of gentleness dropped from his face and his demeanor instantly shifted to one of intense gravity. "Claire, you cannot forget that I am a vampire and although I have sworn an oath to protect you, I must be very careful around you. My hands are strong enough to crush your bones, my thirst can overtake me; my desires can be too much for me if I am weak for even a moment or forget myself." His eyes had gone black and hard, his hands were clutching his knees tightly and I saw the cording of his muscles standing out on his forearms as he spoke with passion, leaning in toward me.

Fear was strong but curiosity was stronger, and distracting. I waited long enough to figure out that he wasn't going to kill me on the spot and then asked, "What oath did you swear and to whom?"

He looked baffled at my inquiry, blinking the human back into his features. "Did you believe that your friends would give you over so easily to such a dangerous creature with no

93

promise of protection? I have sworn to keep you safe while you are in my custody.

The last bit of tension that I hadn't realized I was holding dropped out of my shoulders and I sagged from the relief of it. I was safe here. Troy had meant it when he'd offered the protection of the clan.

He smiled though I heard a taste of bitterness on his tongue, "I thought you weren't afraid of me."

"Being afraid and being uncertain are two different things, James." It was the first time I had said his name and I liked it.

James stood and put his right hand into the air separating our bodies. I looked at it and snapped back up in alarm. "What do you want me to do with *that*?" My heart started to race. We couldn't touch. What if he could sense how he affected me? He could do whatever he wanted then and he could just tell Troy and Stephen I'd gone willingly to the slaughter. It would be easy to get me to mirror his thirst.

"I will shield you myself and take it down a little at a time as you learn to pick it up on your own. But I will need to know how your ability functions to better work with it. I sense people's talents, but need to touch you in order to do so. Each person's is different. I cannot help you to contain or manipulate yours if I don't know the peculiarities of it." He held his hand out palm up and wiggled his fingers playfully at me, a grin crept back into his eyes. "You will have to trust me."

I stood too, wiping my now sweating palms on my pants, glad I had picked the jeans. They hid the marks so much better than khakis. I raised my right hand and held it palm down a few inches from his. Our bodies were little over a foot apart and my heart started hammering in my chest. My stomach was fluttering and I felt the sweat beading on my back and under my arms. I thought I was having an anxiety attack.

His face was calmly watching mine like this was the most normal thing. "You must learn to settle yourself, we haven't even tried our first experiment yet."

"Give me a moment." I closed my eyes so that I couldn't see him, then I concentrated on my breathing. With all of my issues I had spent a good amount of time practicing deep breathing and meditation. Taking this moment to "find my breath" as my books had instructed, I found my heart rate coming down and my body responding to my wishes. I reopened my eyes, my body firmly back under control.

James stood exactly as before with a pleased expression. "That was good, Claire. Are you ready to begin then?"

Too frightened to speak, I merely nodded and licked my suddenly dry lips.

Much like my earlier confession, I watched his hand moving toward my own except I felt like it was someone else's. Mine was some stranger's body and I was standing beside her, seeing this from the outside. When our palms were about an inch apart, I felt the hum begin, lower and quieter than I was used to. He *was* different than a human.

My eyes sought his. They quickly became my gyroscope, helping me balance here in this strangest of situations. He saw my surprised reaction to his feel.

"I will be easier to work with because I am not human. My emotions are much more fleeting and almost feel..." Here he became uncertain for the first time since I had met him. "I guess you would say that my body has been dead for so long that my human emotions have dulled. They are in my head, but do not affect my body as your kind's do."

95

Hmm, that was curious. I felt it building, the unstoppable urge to touch him. He'd said no harm would come and that he would help shield me, plus I had to put my hands on his. Again I felt that inexplicable pull toward him, but now it was total. The tug was in my head, in my stomach. I could feel it even in my very skin.

Dropping my resistance, I brought my hand down onto his, lightly then more firmly. I knew instantly that it was too much too soon. His feelings rushed up to me. They were so fast and fleeting that it was hard to focus on what I was getting as they flooded into me. With an incredible sense of relief I also found that with them shifting so quickly they were easy to block. It was like I had a box of his emotional "thoughts" and they were wrapped up with enough cotton that I could choose which one I wanted to grab and analyze once I got used to the pace.

I caught glimpses of faces and places from different times go flashing past me. Fascinating. Would I be able to do this when my training was complete?

Almost as rapidly as I had begun to read him, James pulled his hand back and put it in his pocket. He was breathing hard and his eyes were dark again.

"I don't understand. That was great! I was able to separate each emotive thought you had and if I had more time, I could have read them." It was hard to contain my exuberance. This was more than I had ever hoped I would be able to do. It was like mind reading, but more than words, I could feel flashes of what he felt about each person and place though too complex to understand in the glimpses I'd been exposed to. Realization struck me then and I felt the guilt over what I'd done.

"James, I am sorry, that was intrusive, wasn't it? I should have warned you. You said you'd shield and I figured I

96

would just go for it. Like ripping off a band-aid." I couldn't meet his eyes out of embarrassment.

Just then, the teakettle whistled making both of us jump to our feet. Carefully, so that we didn't touch again, James carefully stepped around me before turning to go to the kitchen. "Have a seat, I'll be right back with your tea."

"I'll help." I wanted something to do with myself to help dissipate the awkwardness.

"No," he said too harshly and too quickly, holding up his hand to me.

The rejection and humiliation burned hot. He offered to help me and when I wasn't offending him, I bowled him over like an overeager Labrador. I worried this time I'd pushed him too far and now he would take me home.

He seemed to understand how I was feeling. His voice was meant to soothe as he broke into my thoughts. "Claire, you have a stronger ability than I was ready for. It took me by surprise is all. I will be better able to help you if I eat before we continue."

Instantly, I felt the color drain from my face. My heart leapt into my throat. He was going to eat? Me? No, Stephen said he didn't do that.

"Relax," he assured with a small grin. "My supply is in my refrigerator. If you would have a seat and give me just a few moments, I will take care of my needs and return with your tea."
"Oh, okay. That's, um, thoughtful." Well, that was arguably the weirdest conversation I'd ever had. Feeling better about a lot of things, confused about others, I sat down on the couch and pulled my legs up underneath me to wait while James went about his business. Left to my own nosiness, I

took the time to look around. What had seemed so clean and streamlined about the house initially I now saw as sterile.

Most people have pictures around their house showing hints of who they are. Pictures of their hobbies, people they know and love, places they've been. I hadn't noticed it at first, but figured out in the lack of what I was seeking that I was hoping to learn more about my handsome tutor. He spoke formally at times, so I thought he was from at least the turn of the century when English got more mixed and slang became more acceptable. Or, maybe he wasn't American initially and had learned it later. The foreign exchange students I had met in high school had learned what we called "British English" which was way more formal than our own American version. Of course I was also looking for evidence of a girlfriend. She would have to be pretty amazing to get this guy and, I assumed, she would have to be a vampire too, or it wouldn't be fair because she would be too scared to break up with him.

I had put the cashmere throw on my lap while I was deep in thought about the hottie in the other room who was quickly becoming an incredibly fascinating person. Uh oh, double trouble. Great to look at, better to talk to.

Switching gears for my own safety, I looked around me. This was a comfortable house, I was tired and it was safe here. Relax, I thought as I closed my eyes for just a minute. I could return myself to a steadier place while I waited, thinking we could work that much better when he returned.

It couldn't have been more than a few minutes that I had been asleep when I awoke to his voice in my ear. "Claire, I should bring you home."

I sat up with a start, nearly smashing into his face in the process. He must have been right in my ear. Good thing he moved so fast or we'd both have serious goose eggs on our foreheads; well, I would anyway. "No, I'm alright. Please, I'll be fine after I have some caffeine."

He didn't look convinced, but I wanted a chance to prove myself after the earlier debacle. We couldn't end our session like this or it would be our last. "Are you certain? I warned you these practices can be draining. If you are already tired, I don't want you to pass out on me." He grinned teasingly and I felt my stomach flip. His color was closer to human, feeding must give him color as well as warmth, which explained the difference I saw in his pallor earlier as well.

"Let me have a cup of tea and I'll be among the living again." I froze and shot a look at him unable to read his reaction. Not sure if I had done damage or not, I concentrated on my tea.

After a few sips I put the cup down, pushed the blanket aside and stood up. "Okay, let's try this again. I'm ready."

He stood as well, so gracefully it was inconceivable, mesmerizing even. "Yes," he agreed cautiously. "But this time, you hold still and I will come to you."

We both put our palms out again but this time, obediently, I held perfectly still. When we touched, it was not like before. He was completely shielded and I had my first feeling of just someone's hand. This was just touch. I felt the solidness of his palm, the coolness of his skin. I felt *him*. I was unprepared for what it would do to me. Before I realized it, I was weeping; uncontrollably weeping.

James instantly pulled his hand back and I heard the confusion in his voice. "I was shielded, you shouldn't feel anything."

That just made me cry harder. I couldn't look at him. Through my sobs, I tried to speak. "I don't. That's it; I've never felt...nothing before."

99

He understood that and closed the last step between us. As I saw his arms coming up, I jerked my face up to his and he saw my panic.

"Trust me. You'll be safe." James put his arms around me, letting his shields block out everything and give me peace. I finally felt what it was like to be comforted by an embrace. I wept for everything I'd never had, for the fear that made me cringe from a hug instead of lean into one. I felt him lift me up with one arm, sweeping my legs up with his other and without the slightest indication of exertion, he sat on the couch pulling me up into his lap. I tried to tell myself he'd seen it all before working with people like me and then cast that aside, preferring to think this first embrace was special for more than just me.

It seemed like I cried forever. I finally stopped and sat quietly enjoying the repetition one of his hands provided as it gently smoothed my hair. My face lay against his chest affording me a nose full of his smell, which I gradually became aware of as I calmed down. It was a combination of vanilla and a musky spice that I couldn't quite place. It was so captivating that I couldn't get enough of it. His body had cooled, and now I was as well where we touched. That was okay with me because him holding me was different than any other contact that I had ever had and I wanted it to be just that, different. It made it even more special. I committed the feeling to memory since I didn't know if I would get this from him, or anyone, again. But I didn't want to overstay my welcome so I began to pull away.

"Where are you going?" he held on to me sounding displeased, his grip tightening slightly as if he too wanted to keep me with him. I stopped myself from groaning aloud as I thought of how I wished that were true.

"I think you've been more than kind. It's probably time for us to get back to work." Might as well offer him the out now

100

since he couldn't have planned on doing this all night. "Unless you would like to call it quits for the night."

He was bewildered. "Why would we give up?" He let me pull away enough so that he could look at my face. "You are a human and this must be overwhelming to you. We can work through this when you are ready."

"Have you always been so wonderful?" It sounded so reverent, I regretted saying it the second the words left my lips. Now it was out there. The dumb, overly emotional human thinks the vampire is wonderful. I should seriously consider cutting out my own tongue.

James regarded me with a quizzical smile, "Not everyone would agree that I am wonderful. It is flattering that you would think so, though. Thank you, it is nice to hear every few decades." He was thoughtful for a moment before going on. "Yes, I am different than others of my kind. It suits me, this kind of work."

Then he did allow me to pull away, but my legs remained on his lap. I tried my tea. It was cold. "I don't suppose you have a microwave, do you?"

"Yes, I do. Just a moment and I can heat that up for you, I can't have you falling down." He lifted my legs off of him and set them next to him on the couch before he rose up to take care of my tea. "Stay put," he added; I couldn't tell if he was kidding or not.

This time I didn't fall asleep while he nuked the tea. It helped that it was only about thirty seconds. "Thank you, I need this," I said, reaching for my cup. It felt good to just hold the warm teacup.

"Drink that and we will begin again." He resumed his original position, sitting in the chair across from me while he waited.

101

Always a good girl, I did as I was told and drank my tea. We were perfectly comfortable sitting in relative silence. I would have thought I'd feel awkward after my breakdown in front of him, only I didn't. It made me feel even more drawn to him, like he and I were supposed to be around each other. Maybe in some way we would be able to work that out, even if just as friends. I needed this man in my life, it was a compulsion beyond my control.

Setting my cup on the floor beside me, I placed my hands on my knees to push myself up. "Okay, let's do this thing."

"Are you certain?" He eyed me warily, possibly anticipating more tears.

"You've been more than patient and we have to have something to show for tonight's efforts before I leave here." It occurred to me I was being awfully presumptuous and again offered him the graceful exit. "That is, if you have the time? Do we have a limit as to how long this can take tonight?"

"I have set aside my evenings for you for the present, so until further notice, I am yours," he added with a one-handed flourish.

Whew, my head was spinning, heart racing. I saw him duck his head hiding a smile. Was that some sort of joke of his? With a momentary stroke of horror, I worried he could sense my physical reactions. I had better get myself under some form of control before I humiliated myself for the millionth time in front of him.

Standing, I tried to sound calm and sure of myself. "Okay, back to your way? You touch and I stand still?"
He recovered himself, all business again. "Yes. Be still, I'll block completely to start and let you in slowly."

We went back to our positions and he slowly laid his hand on top of mine. Again, I felt no emotional energy coming from him and although I choked up, I kept control. He looked at me, silently questioning. I couldn't speak but nodded that I was all right. He allowed the first taste of emotion leak through. It was again, like something wrapped in cotton and he'd slowed it way down. I had to really concentrate to "grab" it and examine it, feeling it with my mind. I reached out tentatively and got through the shield wrapped around it to find an emotional memory of James driving. He loved his car. I felt it coming off the memory quite strongly. I had to laugh. I saw him smile as well. He could tell what I was looking at, interesting. I admired his control, he obviously was able to choose what he shared with me. Fascinating.

We broke off our contact after he showed me how he felt about the feel of rain on his skin, reading his favorite books and building his house though that one had been a long time ago. He loved them all. They were all safe and uncomplicated memories. Though I was excited by the progress we had made tonight, I realized that he had not shown me anything that gave me any indication of who he really was.

I yawned then and James looked at the clock on the dining room wall. "You'll need to get back. Do you have class tomorrow?"

Noticing that it was getting late, I agreed that I should go even though I would rather stay here. I looked around for my coat, but he must have hung it up when I wasn't looking. "What day is tomorrow? Thursday? No, but I meet with my Psychology study group at ten so nothing too early."

He brought the tea tray back to the kitchen and returned by way of the wall behind the couch. It was where the stairway went up. I hadn't noticed the closet there, built into the wall. His hands disappeared into the closet and returned with my coat, which he held out expectantly. Again, I didn't mind when he did it, so I walked over and let him help me with my coat.

James' voice was warm and low. "Let's go then," and he surprised me by putting his arm around my shoulders.

I looked at him puzzled and he started to drop his arm. "Does this bother you? I thought I would help you to the car. You're unsteady and your color has faded." His gaze wavered uncertainly.

Smiling groggily up at him, I realized how close he was and my senses were filled with him. "That's nice of you." Not that I minded his arm there, even if I wasn't tired. "Thanks."

Sure again, he let his arm resume its position, only shifting slightly behind me as we walked through the front door. We drove very fast again after he put me in the car and helped me buckle in. I was looking at the library doors within minutes of leaving his house.

Stopped in front of the building, he seemed to change his mind. "Which dorm do you live in? That would be better given the time of night. It is easier to keep you safe if I'm with you." His tone had grown more comfortable and less formal around me through the course of the evening and I didn't mention it for fear he would change back if he realized it.

It felt good to have him worry, even if it was just his oath to Stephen and his family to keep me safe. That was one more person who would notice if I was gone. "I'm over on the other side of campus, overlooking the freeway. You know, the big one with the 'A' on the side." It was the tallest building on campus and the school used it to advertise.

He nodded, wove through the campus streets and had me to my front door in about a minute and a half. My exhaustion was getting harder to hide even from someone not as observant as a vampire, and I was glad to be close to bed. "Thank you, James. It was a good night." I paused, "For me, anyway, I hope you were pleased with the progress." It sounded like a question to me, though I hadn't meant it to be.

He looked away from the windshield, resting his calm blue gaze on me. "I had a better night than anticipated. It was very educational for me as well. Would you like me to pick you up here tomorrow at the same time?"

My heart fluttered at the promise of another night with him; I hadn't botched it. "That would be fine. I don't have anything in the evening. Thank Henry for me, would you? He is a great one to have in my corner."

He smiled warmly, showing me his brilliantly white teeth and bid me good night. "I'll see you tomorrow, James," I mumbled back sleepily, shaking off the hallucination my lack of sleep had granted, that James' smile held a glimpse of overly long canines.

I floated in to the building and up to my bed where I slept like the dead until after eight.

Ch. 13

That gave me enough time to go for a long walk, something that always helped to clear my head, before showering and heading off to Psych Group in the morning. I had known the group meetings would be among my hardest, but they weren't bad now that I was building my new skill set. It wasn't because of unholy mental torture that I couldn't wait for it to end; it was because I was in no mood to talk about Freud and Skinner's theories on behavior with anyone. There was only one thing I wanted to do and it was hours away; it would be a long wait until after dinner tonight when I would see him again.

I worked at the library this afternoon and was actually more eager to get there than normal. Of course I wanted to see Heidi who I was scheduled to work with today, but I was most eager to see Henry. I hadn't seen him at work since learning about his real identity and now that I knew what he was, I wanted to watch how he worked. It was the most interesting thing to me to see how these creatures performed ordinary tasks in the real world. I wanted to work out what was real and what was myth.

But first there was another surprise waiting for me as I walked out of my building after lunch. "Stephen!" I surprised myself with my eager greeting. I was changing so much, so quickly, it shocked even me.

His face lit up in a huge, boyish grin, equally pleased to see me. "I wasn't sure what I was going to get back this morning." As I got within arms reach, he held a palm out gesturing in front of him and raised his eyebrows. "Walk with me?"

"Sure, I'm heading to work." It dawned on me then, "Hey, how did you know where I was?" I pulled away to see his face.

He was still smirking like the cat that got the canary. "You didn't think we would let you out of our sight now that you are part of the family now did you?"

Strange how warm that made me feel, that my new family knew who I was and still wanted me. Granted, they were none too normal either, but I was still flattered nonetheless.

Noticing a sudden tension in his body, I caught a glimpse of his face and leaned back, scowling at him. "Are you sniffing me?"

Immediately he stopped what he was doing. It was so fast, I couldn't be sure of what I saw, but it sure seemed like he was sniffing around my head. I barely heard him mumble. "You must have changed your shampoo. You smell different." Then, before I could say anything, he changed gears on me, drawing me into the thing I really did want to talk about. "How was it last night?" His body thrummed with his excitement. Boy was I glad he was blocking. My shields weren't strong enough for this intensity of emotion yet and I bet he would positively overrun me with his enthusiasm right now.

My stomach somersaulted at the thought of James and I hoped Stephen didn't catch it. "I think we did okay. His," I felt silly but found myself looking around furtively for witnesses, "kind is *different*."

His face was close enough to feel his breath on my face. "How does *your* kind see them?"

"Well, they are less intense than ours. It makes it easier to pick apart; like slow motion. I'm thinking eventually I'll be able to take what I know and put it to use on my kind." Turning back to face front, I mumbled, "That's what I hope, anyway."

107

Stephen was quiet, his excitement dimmed by his thoughtfulness the rest of the way. He appeared to be mulling something over. Once in a while he would shoot me a vacant smile, just to remind me he was there, I guess.

We arrived at the front doors and, turning to him, I felt a surge of affection and stepped forward to hug him quickly, "Stephen, thanks for everything. I've never had a friend like you before." He colored and his shaggy hair fell into his eyes as he tipped his chin down for a minute. When I touched him, his shields were fully operational so there was not a repeat of the other night. Impulsively, I quipped, "I've never had a cat before."

Stephen's eyes widened until he saw my playful smile. He growled back and I gasped. "You'll pay for that one." He gave my upper arm a gentle squeeze and moved off toward the interior cluster of campus buildings.

Funny, I had never noticed how feline his movements were even as a human. He glided even now as he walked away, his shoulders moved in a sensual rhythm with his hips, reminiscent of the big cats on nature shows when they are stalking prey. My glance wandered to where he was headed and I saw why. There was a handsome young man walking toward Stephen. He must be on the prowl, indeed. I let myself wonder briefly if he had ever used his talents on his "prospects" in order to capture them in his snare, even though he had told me the other night he wouldn't do something unethical like that. I hoped not, I liked the uncomplicated Stephen who was fast becoming a big part of my life. Seeing him close in for the kill, I spun and dashed the last few steps into the glass entry so I wouldn't be late.

The jubilant bubble I was floating on today expanded yet again as I saw my coworkers. "Hey Heidi. Hey Ben." It made my shifts go so much faster when I worked with those two. Ben and I didn't talk much, but we got along well enough that I enjoyed working with him, although Heidi was my favorite and now it was going to be even better.

Heidi came out from behind the front desk as I walked up to drop my bag and coat in the cubby behind the counter. She dropped her voice so it wouldn't carry in the open room. "Henry is looking for you. What did you do? He never asks for anyone." Her eyebrows were pinched up with concern and her face awash with worry.

I tried to appear nonchalant despite my heart's sudden acceleration. "Well, I can't think of anything. Maybe he just has news about a specialty book I ordered."

Heidi was a book lover at heart, which was why we got along so well. "What book did you order? Would I be interested?" It worked. I had distracted her for the moment.

Uh oh, think of something obscure but mainstream enough not to draw attention. "It is a rare translation of the Aeneid I heard some students in Philosophy talking about. They said this one was a hard one to find but worth it."

Score, I thought with a sense of relief. She didn't care for either the Greek or Trojan side of the war. The whole thing bothered her since she thought Helen of Troy was an irresponsible, flighty trollop. Personally, I liked the story. Call me a romantic, but I thought it was a wonderful tragic love story with a hell of a lot of adventure, to boot.

"Do you mind if I go find him?" I asked now that her concern was put aside. My lying skills were terrible and I didn't want my story to fall apart with further questioning.

She turned to head back to the counter with Ben, now seeming unconcerned. "Go ahead, I think I saw him in the upper level stacks."

Up I went, unease replacing my previous desire to see Henry. I wanted to talk to him and ask questions, fill in some blanks that I had from last night. Hopefully he wasn't calling me in to say that it was not working, or that now James had a better idea of what I could do, he didn't want to teach me after all. It was worse than waiting for test results on an exam. I could never find school as much of a draw as my sessions with James.

No. I stopped myself. James had seemed genuinely enthused about my abilities last night and even I had felt the progress. Maybe I wouldn't be awesome by Thanksgiving, but I would be able to try to help them. Plus, I wanted to contribute something to my new family. I felt that I owed them. We certainly didn't want crazed, bloodthirsty vampires killing all over the city. If we could encourage them to pass us by, count me in.

Sure enough, Henry was standing at his rolling cart full of books, looking intently at the spine of some forgettable new bestseller.

Henry didn't look up until I entered the aisle he was working in, though I was sure he knew I was there. From my limited experience with James I knew vampires had heightened senses, I just wasn't sure how much more aware they were because he blocked quite a bit. I had felt that too.

"Hello Claire, how was your evening?" Even though his voice didn't call to me as did James', it was still captivating and he drew me in without having to try.

I had looked around on the way up for any sets of ears, but checked again just in case. There were none within our immediate vicinity. "It was probably the most bizarre evening of my life." Was it more so than the night before that with the Andrews? "Okay, at least in the top two."

Henry's eyes lit for a second, briefly amused. "Yes, I suppose you have had quite a week so far." He grew more serious, "Is it something you would be willing to continue at or if it is too much, do you wish to stop?"

"Continue? Of course I want to continue!" My voice sounded shrill. "I'm doing well, James thought so too." I hated how childish I sounded.

My breathing became difficult. My reactions seemed out of proportion when it came to James. It must have been the strangeness of my situation. But the thought of not seeing, or touching James made my heart nearly stop mid beat.

Hand up to stop me, Henry's voice slid over me. "I spoke to James about your progress this morning."

Henry paused before he went on, he seemed like he was sniffing too. Shaking it off as my paranoia, it seemed more likely there was a biological reason for his pause. I was betting that he could sense my physical response and he was letting me calm down before continuing. "James confirmed that you have made excellent progress and he feels you have tremendous potential. There is nothing to be concerned about. We merely wanted to make certain you had not changed your mind."

Sighing in relief, I relaxed. I hadn't realized how desperately I'd wanted Henry to remain oblivious to my freakout last night. "Actually, it's quite the opposite. Now that I've worked with James, I think I can be more than ready in the next few weeks and even help you out with your situation." Did that come off as cocky as it sounded? "If you'll have me."

"Don't be too eager. This is a dangerous situation that you will be walking into if you participate. James will be with you, as well as my clan, but this is a strong coven moving into our territory; they pose a danger even to us. That is not

111

something to be taken lightly. We are working on finding some more allies willing to help if it comes to a fight but it will be difficult given our solitary natures. However, we cannot let this group onto our lands, the consequences are too great."

Henry seemed so concerned for his coven that I made up my mind; I was helping them no matter what. They were a good group who believed in something and I could get behind that.

"I understand James will be picking you up again tonight?" Henry broke into my thoughts.

It was beyond my control to stop myself from grinning like a mindless boob when I thought of another night with James. "Yes, he's a great teacher."

"Interesting," was all Henry said. He was staring rather intently at my face when my focus came back to him. He appeared thoughtful but I couldn't understand why, unless it had something to do with my obvious preoccupation with James while I was supposed to be concentrating on how to help them with a life or death situation.

I stuttered and blushed my response, overall making it ten times worse as I tried in vain to explain away my eagerness. "I am just so happy to finally be working on my abilities. Maybe things will be better for me now." Wow, did that sound dumb. I was so not nearly smooth enough to hang out with these guys. I felt so inadequate it was painful.

Henry tipped his head, meeting my eyes, and looked right through my babbling; I was sure he was seeing directly into my thoughts. What he told me astonished me. "I have known James for some time, since he was very young. It has been a long time since he has had someone of interest in his life. Has he told you anything about his past?" I shook my head, afraid to interrupt. "It is not my place to share all of it.

However, I think that you should know something about him. James grew up in a different time and has different priorities than you might be able to understand. Through no fault of his own, he lost most everyone who was important to him. He tried to go on despite those setbacks, and was achieving some amount of success as a young man until he was changed," he dropped his voice, "into one of us. James did not choose to change and his was a horrific experience, but it solidified some things for him, such as his desire to help others. It has become a compulsion, that is why he does what he does. It helps him as much as it does you."

"Thank you Henry. I appreciate your candor. This is all so new to me, it's a lot to take in but the more I can learn, the better I can handle everything." My affection for Henry was growing rapidly. He exuded paternal kindness and compassion, but I pictured that cool customer the other night on Troy's doorstep and reminded myself there was another side to the man even if it was hard to fathom.

He looked abruptly at the ceiling over my shoulder, "I can hear Heidi coming. She's worried about you, you know. She is scared that you're going to be fired."

"Yes, she was on me the second I walked in today."

"Right then, back to work. And good luck tonight. We are pleased to have you on our side." Henry smiled at me and put his book down on the rolling rack.

Watching him, I knew what he was going to say and wanted to avoid it. Turning on my heel, I started to walk away, "I'll go see about Heidi."

"Why don't you stay here and take over the fiction section for me. When Heidi gets here in a moment, she can help you."

Damn, I knew it. Oh well. "Thanks Henry."

He was right, no shock there. Heidi was just seconds away from turning the corner and Henry waved a quick good-bye to us as he glided smoothly off to some other task. The two of us settled in to an afternoon muddling through murder, mayhem and smut. Good times.

Ch. 14

I was eagerly waiting at the front doors of my dorm ten minutes early. It was hard not to feel like a school kid waiting for the bus, except that I had never been this excited for the bus.

"Hot date?" Came the mildly interested comment from the tall blonde girl working at the front desk.

"Sort of," I mumbled back distractedly, not wanting to discuss my social life with the snide door monitor. My thoughts were elsewhere.

James and I had been working together for a week and each night I waited just as eagerly as I had the first. He'd been an encouraging teacher, although, at times he would withdraw and I would worry that I had said or done something to offend him. Inevitably, he would excuse himself to the kitchen to return renewed and ready to resume our lessons. He had promised something special tonight and I was beside myself with anticipation. The difficult part was keeping my overactive imagination in check.

A flash of black caught my eye and I turned back to look out the door. He was stepping out of the Audi and actually coming to the front door. I watched him approach while I felt around on the chair next to me for my coat and purse. I heard the blonde's breathing change as she noticed my "date." He was arresting in his faded blue jeans and dark blue shirt. To her credit, I was as breathless as the door monitor when James stepped inside.

"Ready?" His grin lit up his entire face. He looked sincerely happy to see me and my knees felt weak. I enjoyed his act for the blonde and easily played along

I smiled back. "Absolutely." This was going to be the best few weeks ever.

****

It was several hours later, we had been working diligently and I'd called for a break. James had put the kettle on and we were idling in the kitchen, waiting for the water to boil. It felt domestic and homey, my ease around him had become second nature since that first awkward night.

His smooth voice broke the silence, "Can I ask you something?"

"Sure, anything." I didn't have any secrets. I was pretty sure he even knew what I wished he didn't. He probably also knew that I was all sorts of nuts about him, he'd been pushing my boundaries on blocking hard tonight.

"Anything?" He raised an eyebrow archly at me. I wondered if he knew the effect that he had on me as my heart started hammering its staccato beat.

Awkwardly I nodded, "Yeah, I don't really have some secret life or anything."

He gave me a dubious look. "Don't you?"

"Yeah, I guess I do now. But you know all that," I admitted with a sigh.

"I would like to know if you feel comfortable enough to take a field trip with me."

"A field trip? Where?" I tried to imagine where we would go on a field trip and felt a quiver in my core. It didn't matter, as long as I had him with me I knew I'd enjoy it.

He turned the heat off the whistling teakettle and answered without turning around. "I would like to take you downtown. There is a nightclub frequented by my kind. It would give us a chance to test your distance, something we have been unable to do up until now." He turned to catch my eyes, "If you're willing."

My heart skipped a beat then started to pound. We were going to a vampire hangout with me smelling like a snack?

"Claire, I won't let anything happen to you." His smoky eyes were sincere; it was impossible not to believe him. I wondered for a fleeting moment if he was using any of his vampire tricks on me to get me to agree.

Feeling oddly assured and eager to prove myself, my mind moved to more practical concerns. "Am I dressed for it?" We were both wearing blue jeans and I was wearing a light green sweater that I hoped, for his benefit, would be flattering. He outshone me of course, but when wouldn't that be the case.

James stood up and, putting his hand on his chin, made a show of giving me a once over. I was not successful keeping the heat out of my face. Giving a grim nod, he replied, "It'll have to do."

I could feel my self-esteem take the hit. Of course someone so beautiful would see me as completely ordinary, I knew that already. But before I could berate myself any further, I heard him laugh warmly as he shook his head. "Why do you doubt your appearance? You look incredible." My disbelief must have leaked out. "No, really. You are a stunning woman. I find it hard to believe that you have no suitors." He hesitated and I thought I saw a flash of darkness flash across his features, jealousy? No, that had to be wishful thinking. "Do you, Claire?" The dark edge to his words tickled up my back.

117

I laughed dismissively at his question. "No, I have never had a boyfriend."

James feigned surprise like he hadn't had access to all of this in my head for the last week. "Never?"

Crossing my arms, I looked severely at him, done joking. Pushing this way to make me discuss a painful subject with someone whom I particularly did not want to discuss it with was cruel and I didn't appreciate it. "If I can't shake hands with someone without losing control, how could I have had a relationship? Think about it. You're the first person that has even had his hands on me for more than five seconds, aside from a few unfortunate incidents here and there." My strong stand had ended with a fizzle as I thought about what I was saying. It was kind of sad really but between Stephen messing with me about dating all the time now, his favorite pastime I was learning, and now James picking up the torch, I wanted to let him know it was an off limits subject.

"How lonely you must have been." He didn't say it condescendingly so it was not *as* horrible as it could have been, but it still hurt to have him look at me like that with something akin to pity in his eyes.

"It will soon be your choice whether you want to share your life with someone or not. I promise you that."

I tried, but failed, to hide my lack of enthusiasm, considering the one person I wanted to share my life with was not an option. "That's something to look forward to. How about we go meet some vampires?" In spite of his assurances that I would not be harmed while in his company, I had serious doubts about our destination. The best I could do was to try to swallow the fear building in the back of my throat while in my mind's eye I saw James at his most frightening, times twenty.

****

The car ride was unusually quiet. Vampires had no awkward need to fill silence with small talk, a detail that suited my inability to take part in it perfectly. I used the time to practice my shields and calm my mind currently racing faster than the Audi. It didn't take long to reach the nightclub. We pulled into the warehouse district and parked on the street near a coffee shop so dark inside it was hard to see the people through the windows. It must cater to the goth and artsy crowds so prevalent in this area.

Upon parking, James was around and to my door before I could unbuckle, as usual. I didn't mind that he kept in close proximity to me. We walked so close; we were almost touching. We walked just two storefronts down and reached a rough looking brick faced building with a hot pink neon sign that should have read, "Glamour", but part of the sign was burned out, making it say only "lamo." Smiling at the connotation, I looked questioningly at James.

"We use our Glamour for more than just changing how we look. We can also make a building seem unappealing to your kind. It helps to keep us separated. Sometimes, segregation is good."

I let that one roll around in my head for a moment before I felt something cool in my hand and glanced down. He had taken hold of me as he opened the door. When I looked at him again, he was unable to hide all of the tension in his jaw. "Claire it is better if they think that you are mine. Is that alright with you?"

Scared as I was, I still managed to have a keenly physical reaction to his request. Pretending I was unaware that he could certainly hear and feel it now that we were touching, I gave him a tight lipped smile. "I think I can manage that." As he turned away from me to walk in, I thought I saw some foreign emotion on his face. He was blocking so I couldn't

119

feel anything, but I noticed a vagueness to his gaze and wondered what could be distracting him. Sighing, I realized he was concentrating on work, which was what we were here for and I should be doing the same. Subdued, with my heart in my throat, I followed him into the doors.

Walking in, I was disoriented immediately. There was a loud punk band playing on the raised stage at the far end of the bar. The flashing strobes were seizure inducing and the bodies on the dance floor were not exactly packed sardine tight, though there were far more than I found comfortable. As much as I welcomed an excuse to put my hands on James, I didn't want to be on that dance floor with all of those vampires crowded so close.

James pulled me in tight to his body so that I could hear. "I'm sorry, it is crowded on Friday nights but my informant tells me it is a safe crowd."

"What do you mean 'safe'?" Surveying the sheer number of bodies around us I considered the possibility that the word had a different meaning for him than it did for me.

He lowered his head to speak into my ear. "I have had someone watching this place for the past few nights waiting for a time when the patrons were less than gifted. We want to keep your education under the radar for now."

It was hard to concentrate on what he was saying beyond the fact that he was once again keeping his oath, a fact I was eternally grateful to the Andrews clan for thinking of. I was currently completely molded to his left side and he smelled incredible. I hoped he would never move. He did though, he swung to the right side nearest the bar and started to maneuver gracefully between the heavily occupied bar and dance floor heading toward the tables in the back, I was guessing, as he pulled me along.

I was correct. We reached the first table in the row nearest the dancers. It was still loud, but we were able to hear each other due to the fact that we were sitting with our chairs nearly touching and his lips brushing my ear as he spoke. I was glad to be sitting since my knees would have failed me, no doubt as the reality of what we were doing sunk in. "Do you mind?" He asked as he put me to the inside, taking the aisle himself. He put his right arm around my waist. "I can help you block better if I am touching you. That way you can concentrate on what you need to do."

"I'm okay," I breathed at him. Good thing he had supernatural hearing as I was having trouble speaking. Not sure what I should be doing, I waited for direction as I studied the people around me. At first blush, the nightclub goers appeared much like humans, dancing, talking and drinking. However, upon closer inspection it became obvious that they were all better looking than the average human, most, but not all of them, were gorgeous. That was a myth I was secretly pleased to see debunked. And everyone drank what appeared to be red wine regardless of the shape of the glass. I couldn't be sure, but I didn't think there were more than a handful of humans here.

"Is this too much for you?" He leaned in close to my ear and the tips of his lips brushed my ear again, making me shudder. He had to feel that one since we were snuggled up so tight.

Closing my eyes, I had to focus on my breathing so that I didn't pass out. "Mm hmm." Overwhelming was an understatement.

James noticed I was having trouble, but I hoped he didn't guess what part he played in that. Again, I wished that I could feel him. I'd never wanted to know what anyone else was feeling, but I would have given anything to know how he felt at this moment about our safety, about his belief in my competence, about me. "What would you like me to start with?" I was finally able to ask. It was best to distract myself.

"Let's have you try that red haired woman dancing near the bar, the one with the tall black man in blue leather pants, he's hard to miss. I will take away my arm and see if you can get anything from her. Try to be specific and focus just on her. I'm right here if you need me."

I'd never tried to pinpoint someone before, but was getting stronger with my training. I was as curious as James to see if this would work.

I felt the chill of him fall away from my back and missed it. I quickly shifted my focus to the red haired woman dancing by the bar just about ten feet in front of me. She was sexy as only a vampire could be. She was grinding on the leg of the tall, elegant black man glued to her front. Then, when I tried to reach out to her, I felt something tingling in the back of my skull. It got stronger when I saw past the redhead to a brunette over her left shoulder and at twice the distance. Her eyes were focused on me, of that I was sure, and once I had seen her I could not stop staring at her. Following the slow, soulful beat of the new track were slight hips sheathed in purple leather and topped by a black studded belt. Her sheer white Ramones t-shirt stretched over her small chest. Though her body was enviable, it was her face that was hard to ignore. Her expression was one of pure unadulterated bliss as she danced with two young men, one white, one Asian. She tossed her head back and forth, swinging her long purple streaked black hair flashing blue when the strobes caught it, her arms up over her head. I didn't understand my draw to her, but there was no looking away. Fearing failure, I tried forcing myself to think of how the redhead felt, then *finding* her. Trying to disengage from the brunette, I found that I could not. I started to sweat.

"Do you need help Claire?" James' voice was an intrusion and I shook my head to make it stop.

Then, finally I felt my shields cave and I felt her. She was filled with lust and some new feeling that felt like hunger, but not quite. She meant to make the men fight for her. It turned her on. Suddenly, I felt a mental jolt hit me like a slap. Startled, I looked up and she was staring right at me still, only now her blissful expression was gone, leaving her angelic features twisted with loathing. I tried to pull back when she'd caught me, only she wouldn't let me and I felt her lust starting to cross over. I felt the beginnings of it creeping into my body. Seeing my discomfort at the intrusion, her mouth twisted into a cruel smirk and she flooded me. That is the best way to describe it. I was instantly awash in her desire, unable to think of anything else. There was no separation between our minds. She'd made her way through my carefully crafted defenses like paper and her sexual push into my head was a full immersion. I had enough time to curse myself for being a fool not to take James up on his offer to help bolster my defenses before I felt my mind fall far behind and watched as hers took over.

Mortified, I felt the desire to turn to the man next to me and satisfy the hunger now mixing with my own pent up feelings for him. I put my hands on my knees, fighting to control what was building within me. *It wasn't mine* I called from my tiny corner. Not entirely.

It was odd, I usually had to touch someone to get this strong of a reaction. And she wasn't like reading James, the feeling she'd shown me was much sharper, or it was due to the fact that her lust was so similarly mirrored in my own thoughts tonight, again I cursed myself for being naive. Or maybe she was sending it straight into me on purpose. I didn't have time to think about it. All I could do was to try to fight it before I did something foolish.

He hadn't seen the brunette, but James saw me struggling, put his arm around my waist again and I felt him project his shield, helping me block out the woman's desire. I dropped my head to the table then and he put his head next to mine.

"Are you alright?" His voice was heavy with concern. Neither the sound of his voice nor his words themselves could distract me from the brush of his lips on my ear or his hair tickling my cheek. I wanted to cry with the effort not to touch him and clenched my hands on my knees so hard my fingernails made small indents in my hands.

"Could you get me something to drink? A water, maybe." It came out raspy as I tried to get a hold of myself and to put some space between us. The flooding had stopped with James' touch and I chanced a glance at her. She was doing a great job of pretending none of this had transpired, back to dancing with her men, a little smirk on her face.

I could tell he didn't want to leave me and to my regret, he sat up and raised his hand to signal the waitress who came at once. They spoke quietly. Of course, they didn't need to yell over the noise with their super special hearing. Within a minute, he had a glass of something red that I didn't want to think about and I had a glass of water sitting in front of me. I took my time sipping at it, pretending I didn't see my hand shaking.

Finally I felt him lean in again, sliding his hand up my back while his face came tantalizingly close to my neck as he spoke. I vaguely heard him, concentrating on the cool breeze that was his breath raising goose bumps on my flesh. "Claire are you okay? Did it work?"

I nodded first, trying to pull away, then, taking another long pause to sip my water. I thought I could finally trust myself. "Yes, I'm okay now. I found one farther away. It wasn't the redhead, it was the brunette with the two guys over there to the left. She has to be twice the distance." Starting to feel more myself again, I gave in to the excitement of what had gone right. "I did it! I felt her."

He met my shining eyes with his own, dark with something unexpected and smiled slowly flashing a lot more tooth than I was used to seeing. His exuberant embrace was unexpected, and I felt something more than friendship in his hands as he rubbed them across the back of my shirt. His stroking brought back the barely beaten desire I had battled so arduously and did not have the strength to fight again. I felt the familiar tugging of my unexplained connection to him telling me to give in. It was more than I could bear and I threw my arms around his neck and pulled his face to mine needing him more than air.

Ch. 15

It was definitely morning when I opened my eyes. I could see the white glow of the sun coming around the edges of the curtains. They weren't my curtains. The crisply tailored, midnight blue silk drapes did not match the plain tan cotton curtains that ended halfway down the wall of my dorm room. This fluffy down pillow and matched blue comforter were also not mine. I stretched slowly, feeling sore in a very new way. Oh my gosh, it hadn't been a dream? Holy uh oh, I was in *his* bed!

Last night came rushing back as I lay there. After I had kissed him and he had kissed me back, we had left the club. We drove back here, unable to keep our hands off each other in the living room, shedding our clothes as we clung to each other. He kissed me as he carried me up the stairs and into his room where we had made love. The memory made me flush in embarrassment at my own boldness.

Not being experienced, I didn't know if it was always like that, but I didn't think so from what I'd overheard from my peers. And felt. It was not uncommon for the girls to be upset or feel disappointed in their experiences. Not me. Maybe there was something to immortality. He had probably been with hundreds of women and was far more knowledgeable than the young men the girls at school had lain with, or it was because of how I felt about him. I didn't want to think too hard about it; surely I was one of a number of women and one he would inevitably forget, but in this little moment I could cling to the notion that last night had been special for us both.

As I lay there, remembering the events of our night together and considering how I might feel about him in my head, I felt him stir behind me and I froze. What would morning be like now that our heads were clearer? Awkward? Would he regret it or tell me that our time together was at an end? I felt my whole body cringe as I thought of being cutoff from him.

"Are you awake, Claire?" His voice was cautious. Great, he was trying to figure out a nice way to get rid of me.

"Umm, let me find my clothes and I'll be out of here in a minute." I started to throw back the covers and paused in my escape discovering that I was stark naked and *all* of my clothes were either down the stairs or on them.

Lightning fast, his arm shot out and wrapped around my waist, pulling me up against the front of his body. Oh, he was also naked, I realized with a flutter in my stomach. I blushed and lay perfectly still.

"It's Saturday, do you have somewhere you need to be or could you stay a while?"
Was he just being nice? "I, uh, don't have anything until later this afternoon. I'm meeting my folks for a late lunch." I dared to let myself hope for something other than the worst. "Why?"

With our bodies touching, I could feel the rumble of his voice against my back and I closed my eyes, enjoying his closeness. "Would you like to join me for breakfast? I'm a pretty good cook."

"Sure, if you don't have anything, uh, more important." I tried not to sound too grateful.

He pushed up onto his elbow and gently guided my chin around. I twisted to follow. "Claire, do you think last night was a mistake?" No way, he actually looked worried.

I tried to make the words come out steady. "It wasn't for *me*. Was it for you?" I didn't think I could live through the humiliation if he said yes.

127

James' reply was halting. It was a side of him I had not expected. "No matter what you might think, I do not take lovers easily. It has been quite a while since I have brought anyone to my bed and no, I do not consider it a mistake."

I searched his eyes, dark with emotion and felt my uncertainty fizzling, the memory of Henry's speech in the library coming back to me. "So, it wasn't just physical for you?"

"No. I can't explain this draw I feel to you, but I will not deny it any longer. When I sensed the power of your wanting last night, I couldn't stop myself. I am not proud of myself for taking advantage of you when you were weak with *her* desire. But my own was too strong to deny." He nodded at my shocked intake of breath. "I smelled a stranger on you when she pulled you in, I knew it wasn't the one I'd asked you to try. Are you angry with me for making your first experience with a man a dishonest one?"

"You knew I picked the wrong one?"

"It doesn't bother you that I took advantage?" He refused to be deterred.

Raising my hand, I reached out to touch his smooth cheek and watched as my fingers traced the bottom curve of his jaw. "Nothing happened that I didn't want." Remembering what he had said about it being my first time, I offered him a timid smile and felt my cheeks warm. "I hope it was okay for you, we're kind of unevenly matched in experience."

He lowered his face to mine. I felt his cool body molded to every inch of mine and the fire banked last night was rekindled within my body. His husky voice brought me back. "Experience can't hold a candle to passion, a place where you excelled."

128

I felt the heat burning down my neck and watched his eyes track, following it. Remembering a key sticking point between our species, my hands flew to my neck and my fingers searched for the marks I feared were there.

"I didn't bite you." James' face clouded and he pulled away, offended. "I am old enough and strong enough to resist the call of your blood, tempting though it may be."

Once again I felt foolish. "I'm sorry. I only know what the stories say. I thought that was what happened when our kind were together, you know, physically."

The tension eased in his eyes. "It can make for a more intense experience to be bitten during sex. Being bitten can be a frightening or pleasant experience, depending on what the vampire does to your mind when he bites. It is the same with marking." He paused a moment, it almost seemed he wanted to take that last comment back.

"What does it mean to be marked? Is it different than just being bitten or changed?" I'd never heard of being marked; until now, I thought there were only two reasons for being bitten by a vampire: food or convert.

James' brows knitted in thought while his hand played with a clump of curls lying on the pillow beside me. "Being marked by a vampire is not something to be taken lightly. It binds a human to the vampire for the remainder of their existences." I watched his face, still wondering how he would feel about being bound to me, still confused by my disturbing need for him. "Have you ever marked anyone?"

"No, I have not." He took a deep breath and closed his eyes. "Let me start at the beginning to clarify a few things. I suppose you will need to know all of it soon anyway." He left the hair alone and his eyes returned to my face. "Intention is the key to what happens with the bites. If the vampire is hungry then a bite can be for feeding or draining and death." Seeing my face at that, he added quickly, "Few still do that, it draws too much attention. Most find it best to take small amounts from several sources and leave the donor alive with no memory of the incident. If the vampire goes too far and doesn't want the donor to die, he might choose to inject his venom and change the donor, but the donor must also drink from the vampire before expiration. It doesn't always have to be the same vampire. Another vampire can come in and save the donor with his own venom, like what happened with me." The guarded look on his face stopped me from asking any more than that, as did Stephen's warning that these stories were very personal. Having sex once didn't mean he was going to tell me everything about himself and I knew that.

"One can also be marked," he continued. "A mark is given when a vampire takes a small amount of blood and injects incremental amounts of venom on several different occasions. Again, the human must also take blood in return. Each mark changes the human a small amount and binds him or her to the vampire. After three such marks, the human is changed over completely to a vampire."

"I thought you just got bitten one time and that was it." Admittedly, I didn't know much about vampires. That would have to change, especially since it appeared I was involved with one. "What else do I need to know?" I looked at the sunlight and pointed at the window. "What about that?"

"The sunlight? That is a bit trickier. You probably remember from our training what my feelings are like?" I nodded. "They are fuzzy, less clear, than your own."

"Yes, I remember."

"When we are newly changed, our sensitivities are *more* intense than your own even. We still have the residual human physical feelings and the new vampire sensitivities

130

combining for an incredibly intense experience. During that period, it is best to avoid sunlight because it burns our skin. Not that we will combust as the legends say, but it hurts like a flame to the flesh. As we age, the physical sensitivity fades and we learn to ignore the tingling, and can walk around unharmed in the sunlight. I prefer to wear sunglasses, my eyes have remained sensitive all this time. Of course some choose to only move about at night. Since we do not sleep, we have the choice."

"James," his name felt even sweeter on my tongue now that we were intimate. "How old are you, do you mind my asking?"

He laughed. "Now you ask? After all the laws have been broken?"

"We are both over eighteen." I chuckled. "No laws were broken, except maybe decency laws. What if you were old enough to be my father or grandfather?"

"Oh, I could be that; several times over."

My jaw dropped. "Seriously?"

"I was born in Quebec around 1842. It is hard to be sure because I wasn't born in a hospital and the records were not kept as accurately as they are now. My parents were part of a large number of emigrants coming from London that year. They sought better fortunes in North America. It was very common then and I was born not long after they arrived."

"Oh my gosh!" I didn't know what to say.

"Yes, suffice it to say that I am old enough." His face was closed, guarded once again. "Does that bother you? My age?"

131

I thought seriously about it for a minute. "No, it doesn't. What matters is now. As long as you want me here, I'm good." Holding my breath, I realized I had put myself out there for more than just a physical dalliance without meaning to do so.

He pulled me on top of him as he rolled over and chuckled darkly, "Oh, I want you all right."

Ch. 16

James and I enjoyed the very late breakfast he was able to scare up in his kitchen. Apparently, he occasionally had human and weres for guests and carried a limited supply of food. After the long night and morning of activities, I was voracious. He was right; he *was* a surprisingly good cook and made me a huge breakfast of eggs, toast and bacon. I ate it all.

Stephen hadn't been wrong about how James and Henry fed. James sipped on a travel coffee mug while he sat with me at the table for breakfast. "What is that?" I asked without thinking.

He looked down his nose over the table. "You know what it is."

"Oh," I felt stupid. "I know *what* it is. I was thinking about *who* it is." From the look on his face, I was guessing I was starting to make him mad. Stumbling, I tried to clarify before it got worse, "What I mean is, does it bother you? Having to drink blood knowing it's from people?"

"At first it did, when I didn't have control, and sometimes, it didn't end well."

Gulping, I realized I had tried to avoid thinking about that part of James. Seeing him as a monster.

"After a while, I was able to streamline the process and occasionally I would take a partner who would willingly feed me." He saw me thinking about that one and moved on before I could think very hard about it. "That was never my preferred method. I don't like to mix sex and blood like some do. It was merely a necessity of the time. Now that we have the option of the blood bank, I choose to keep my pleasure separate from my feeding."

133

Funny, I hadn't realized how much of my knowledge of vampires was wrong. Knowing that sex didn't equal blood loss took away a ton of my reservations about dreaming of more with James.

James looked at the clock on the dining room wall and pushed his chair back. "I'd better get you back soon so you have time to change before you have to meet your parents."

"Yes, I would like to clean up a bit." It was strange how unselfconscious I was with him; I felt at home here with him. Whoa, too fast. Well, either way, it was good to be comfortable with him since we were still going to have to work together for the next few weeks at least. After that, I wasn't sure how things would end.

Ch. 17

My parents and I had agreed to meet at Grandma's Restaurant down at Seven Corners, a trendy part of town off campus. It was usually pretty slow on a Saturday in the late afternoon. Part of the reason that I picked such a public place was my parents' adversity to public displays of affection. I was ready to test my shielding, but I didn't want to hit it with a battering ram.

My parents were notoriously early, so I made certain that I was there a full fifteen minutes early. Sure enough, they beat me there.

Mom was first, squealing as she ran up with her arms held high coming in for the hug. I was unusually happy to see her as well. We hugged with limited shockwaves that gave me an extra surge of joy and I even hugged back. Mom rocked back, shock registering on her face. Shrugging it off, I joked, "Can't I be excited to see you?" Dad was next, predictably more subdued. We were seated quickly due to the lack of customers at this hour, so no more hugs before lunch. They were eager to hear how college was treating me.

It was easy to make conversation with them; it really had been too long since I had seen my folks. "My classes are great! I love them and the professors are really interesting. Most of them seem honestly happy to be teaching and are passionate about the subject matter." This of course led to a whole new round of talks about the courses and what major I might be choosing. "I don't know, we'll see what grabs me. I'm just not sure what I want to be when I grow up."

Dad wanted to know how work was at the library. He was the one who had taught me to love books. "My co-workers are fantastic and I'm getting kind of tight with Heidi." I felt myself gushing, a little drunk with the joy of a normal family and my night with James. "She's a junior and she's really nice." I skipped over James and Stephen for now. I wasn't sure how to explain either one without giving away too much. They would never have thought of asking about boyfriends, so I dodged a bullet there as well.

"Is your boss nice to you?" Mom wanted to know. She was positively beaming as she sat across the table from me. It felt so good to know I was being a good daughter for once.

Smiling, I replied honestly, "Henry seems to have my best interests at heart and has really put a lot into training me. I like him quite a bit."

"Good to hear. Are you still thinking you might want to be a librarian? You know they make good money and can work in any town. You certainly love books enough and have the right mind for the reference systems." Dad was the expert at relocation from years of military transfers and he knew I'd considered the career but couldn't guess why working in a research library away from the general population would appeal to me.

We talked for a few hours until we couldn't handle any more soda and we had eaten our fill. Agreeing to talk soon about Thanksgiving, I was able to hug Mom and Dad good-bye before parting ways.

"Honey, we can drop you at your dorm." Mom was upset that I didn't want to accept a ride in the minivan.

I was being honest when I told her, "Mom, after all of that food I think I *need* to walk. Next time you come, we can go up and you can see my room. It's just such a pig sty right now and I don't want you to see it." Waving, we parted in the parking lot. It was with very light feet that I started back. Realizing Mom hadn't had a drink all through lunch made me smile; thinking our family had a chance for normalcy.

Now I was off to get some studying in before meeting James in just a few hours.

In a happy fog, I floated for a few blocks, oblivious to my surroundings when I suddenly heard the screeching of tires in my immediate proximity.

The next thing I knew, I looked up to see a dark blue sedan stopped right next to me on the street and the dark haired dancer from the club and her Asian boy toy coming at me fast, both looking murderous.

I barely had enough time to register what was happening. By the time it occurred to me I was in trouble, I had taken one step in the opposite direction and felt two sets of iron strong hands grabbing my arms. "No, wait," was all I got out before something went over my head and my feet left the pavement. Once inside the car, we drove rapidly, into an area where the stoplights were spaced further apart. My ears were pricked for any clues as to where we were but there was nothing outside of the occasional sound of another car passing. I was guessing we had driven into a neighborhood just outside the city when they stopped, hauled me out and up a few steps into a house where I was tied to a chair with my hands behind my back and the bag was removed from my head.

Glancing around, I saw my captors again. They were angry and scary, but were uncertain what to do with me. The woman was on her cell phone arguing with someone too fast for me to understand. She snapped it shut and looked at me with a seething hatred.

"What the hell were you doing in our club? How did you like the taste of your own medicine?" She moved so fast, she closed the ten foot gap between us in a hurry and was in my face, fangs out, eyes black. She was less human in that moment than Stephen when he changed into a mountain lion.

Sniffing at my face, she spat, "I smell vampire on you. I know who you call Master."

Terror doesn't even start to describe how I felt at that moment. I was sure I was going to die. I just wasn't sure how much it was going to hurt. My friends could help me, except they had no idea where I was. I was going to die here scared and alone. The fact that I was concentrating on my shielding was keeping me from completely coming undone; it gave me something else to focus on other than my imminent demise.

From this close, I saw that she was probably just over my age. It was clear that she was in charge and not the young man with her. Like Stephen he was very short, maybe five foot four and of slight build, making it hard to guess his age. His eyes continued to flick to her for direction, giving a clear indication that he would do whatever she said. He spoke timidly and cringed from her out of fear of reprisal.

"Gina, you heard him. He said we have to wait for him. I don't know what he wants from her but he wants her able to speak."

Her black eyes were flat, that same cruel smile I'd seen last night curled her lips. "He didn't say I couldn't touch her though, now did he?"

My stomach twisted and I thought I was going to throw up right there. "Please, I don't understand. I just went there to meet a friend." They had *me*, but I didn't know if they knew about anyone else's identities and I certainly wasn't going to give them anything new.

Gina turned back to me showing me some tooth from under her twisted lip. "Oh yes, your friend James. I am very familiar with James' ideals. His sympathy for humans is revolting."

138

Okay, she knew James, that didn't mean anything. Maybe they all knew each other. There couldn't be that large of an underground supernatural community here in Minneapolis, could there? My mouth was staying shut. I'd heard that if tortured, the best way to handle it was to stay quiet as long as possible, then when it got really bad, give false information. I could tell her a story or something. I didn't think she would care what she heard from me. She had decided to kill me already. I could see it in her eyes. To take my mind off of it I tried to think of a story I could change the names in and get the most play out of, maybe a TV show since no one seemed to own one of those.

Distracted as I was, her slap took me by surprise. I've never been hit before, and definitely not by a crazy strong vampire who liked to inflict pain. The fact that my lip split open wasn't a surprise. The way her eyes darkened and she licked her lips though, that sent ice running down my spine. The shock of the impact had brought with it some twinkling and hazy clouds on the edge of my vision. The few remaining barriers separating our minds fell and I *felt* her thirst for my blood.

My stomach turned and I retched, vomiting on the floor at my feet. My lunch hit her shiny black boot and she stared at it, blinking slowly. Looking up at me, she shook her head and growled. She hit me again with the back of her hand and I saw an explosion of light. Gagging, I choked on the blood running freely inside my mouth.

The little man stepped in front of Gina. "He said she had to be able to talk. She can't talk if you break her jaw. Enough for now."

Though it clearly took every ounce of her self-control, she stepped back and they left the room together, with her growling under her breath. He shut the door behind them.

139

When the door closed, I began to cry. My face hurt. I could feel the swelling and my tongue found where a back tooth was now lifting out of its spot. Blood was all over my shirt and inside my mouth and it was mixing with the acidic aftertaste of sick. The taste made me gag, so I spit and out came the tooth. Dammit! I wished I could say good-bye to my family, and James. My parents were going to be so upset. We'd only just turned a corner. I hoped my parents wouldn't blame themselves for not making me ride with them.

I lost track of time as I sat there. I'd had enough time to get past the first taste of fear and had moved on to wondering when, or if, someone would notice I was missing. Maybe James would miss me when I didn't show up tonight but I didn't believe he would be able to find me before it was too late; how could he? Or if Stephen could follow my scent all the way here, I was guessing it still wouldn't be in time.

Maybe I drifted off to sleep or I blacked out, I couldn't tell. The blinds were drawn in the room, though I thought I saw streetlights come on at one point. The house was deathly quiet with only the occasional clicking on of the furnace now and again to mark any sort of passing of time. I jerked when I heard the knob on the door creak, holding my breath as I watched it slowly twist and push open. My tongue felt like it was taking up my entire mouth and my lip was swollen, but thankfully, had stopped bleeding.

The door swung out of the way and through it walked a tall, thin man dressed so impeccably I heard the accent before he could open his mouth; British. "Hello Miss, my name is Bradley. I am so sorry to see you in such a state. Are you well enough to answer some questions?"

I tried to speak, to tell him what to do with his questions, but my mouth was dry and my jaw ached. My whispered response was hoarse and didn't sound at all tough. "I don't know anything."

140

He looked pleased, regardless. "No matter. You aren't here for what you know, but rather for who you know." Bradley spoke quietly over his shoulder to someone outside the room, "Please get our guest some water." It was a brief moment and the small man returned to hand a glass of water to Bradley. He, in turn, held it to my mouth and tipped it for me to drink. I could barely swallow but was able to sip enough to wash down the blood and wet my mouth to speak.

"Thank you." It couldn't hurt to try to be polite. My eyes remained on Bradley as he handed the glass back to Gina's boy. It was hard to tell what this one's plan of attack was but I wanted to be ready.

"You're most welcome. Tell me, why did you enter my nightclub last night and go digging through the minds of my children? What were you hoping to find?" His deadly tone belied his innocently open features.

My stomach dropped. Children? Was he responsible for these two degenerates? I stuck with the story I'd given Gina. "I met a friend there for a drink, that's all."

"Interesting friends you have. I knew James long ago when he was new, and his Master as well. Birds of a feather those two, I did not like them then and I do not like them now. Did you know that they are working very hard to close this city to anyone who does not share their views on humans? There are many of our kind that do not find their position agreeable." He moved closer to me and bent at the waist so he could look into my eyes from less than a foot away. His were black and cold; unfeeling. "What a wonderful way to start a war."

When he leaned away I saw that he wouldn't let me out of here. I felt it in my bones and started to tremble; I wanted to gag and was glad my stomach was empty.

"Tell me, what do you think your friends would do if I sent them your head, just to show them what I think of them telling me how everyone else needs to hunt?"

Past my breaking point, there was no stopping my choking sob. I had decided not to tell them anything. That didn't mean I couldn't be frightened.

Frowning thoughtfully at me, Bradley put a finger under my chin and turned my head one way then the next, sniffing. Deciding something, he stood abruptly. "They don't use her for food; maybe she has some value to them alive. Let's see if they are willing to trade." He pulled a small silver phone from his pocket and dialed. The volume was down so I didn't hear the other side, but I watched Bradley's face intently as he spoke.

"Henry, I am so pleased to hear your voice. Have you thought any further about my request for my friends' entrance to the city? It seems your watchdogs are unwilling to let them pass and they are growing restless." He listened for a moment before politely responding. "Mmm, that is too bad. You see, my friends are ready to come to me now. Their business with William in Milwaukee has resolved rather quickly." He paused and I thought I saw a flash of a smug smile, "Yes, they were less of a challenge than anticipated." Not hard to guess which side his friends came out on in that one. "I wonder if you would be willing to trade? Maybe something that has recently come up missing?" After a short pause I saw him smile as he gloated at me. "I have recently found myself in possession of a human female. Pretty little thing. She was in my club last night without an invitation. Though I must say, she is not quite so pretty now." His dead eyes rested on me and I couldn't break away. I watched them for a sign of my fate.

After a long pause, I saw Bradley's mouth curve into a smile that failed to reach his eyes. He had won. "Well, I appreciate your reason Henry. It has been a pleasure once again. Do tell James he needs to keep his pet closer to home next time, preferably on a leash. Where would you like us to deliver her?" He rolled his eyes. "Yes, we will deliver her alive."

After agreeing to deposit me by the falls in Minnehaha Park, the phone snapped shut and Bradley turned on his heel to leave. I heard him in the other room speaking to the two waiting there.

"Don't do anything too damaging. We are required to hold up our end of the bargain and I promised she would be alive. It sounds like James is partial to this one. Wrap her up, drop her off and meet me at the club later. We have much to do to prepare for our visitors. They will be here within a few days."

I was stuck on his wording. *"Too damaging"*? What did that mean? In answer, Gina came in looking pissed. She tore off the duct tape I'd been bound with and jerked my arms up severely behind me. The pain brought tears to my eyes.
"Why?" I wanted to know what her personal vendetta was with me, but couldn't articulate any more than one word phrases at that point.

She sneered at me, her fangs glinting in the dim light of the room. "I hate humans. Especially those who don't know their place." She pushed me out the door and the Asian boy toy was waiting to drop the bag over my head again as she used my sore arms to maneuver me back into the car. We weren't in the car for more than a few minutes, so I figured we must be pretty close to the falls. I didn't believe it. They were really going to let me go. Guilt weighed heavily on my heart. I had been used to let in the very group I was hoping to help keep out.

After the car stopped, Gina jerked me out and pushed me hard enough to knock me to my knees. She pulled the bag off my head and I saw the telltale streak of orange sunset

143

bouncing off the clouds at the edge of the horizon, before she hit me again and I blacked out.

Ch. 18

When I came to, I heard voices but they were so far away I could make out no more than rumbles. My head was foggy so I lay still while I pieced together what I knew. I knew I was in a house because I was in a bed. Blinking in the faint light, I recognized the bedding. I was in James' bed. Safe. As the thought registered in my pain riddled brain, I felt the tears start to well. When I didn't think I was going to come home, *this* was the home I'd feared I would not see again. Not my dorm room, not my parents' home but this one. Now that I was here, relief surged through me. I wanted to see James right now, to know that this was real, that this wasn't a dream.

Swinging my legs over the edge of the bed, I sat up. It was too fast. The room spun and I felt faint; I held on tight waiting for my head to clear. I had to see him, I was desperate to make sure this was not a hallucination. My feet hit the floor and I took two hurried steps to reach the doorway. The door had been partially closed and I fell against it. By the time I had the door open, he was there, really there, standing in front of me. Letting go of the breath I'd been holding and the door holding me up, I collapsed.

His hands caught me and swept me up faster than I could fall. Forgetting my shoulders, I tried to bring my arms up around his neck and stifled my cry. I heard his quick intake of breath. "Claire are you all right?"

My head was killing me, my vision was blurry, my lip had re-opened and was bleeding, my jaw ached, I couldn't lift my left arm, and I was here. I was fine. There was a bigger issue now and I knew who was responsible for it. Taking a quick look up at his tight face, I knew I'd failed and had to look away.

"I'm sorry, I didn't tell them anything but they knew about the club. She recognized me. It was dumb of me to get snatched. I should have let my parents drive me home." I knew I was rambling, but I couldn't stop. Because of me James and Henry and others like them were in danger of being exposed. If violent vampires moved in and drew unwanted attention, it would get too risky for them to stay. James would have to leave. I couldn't begin to wrap my mind around the potential human cost of the new regime.

I chanced a look up at James and saw that his jaw was locked and he looked ready to explode. My despair reached a new low. I felt the tears at the back of my eyes and fought them. I had to get out of here, away from him and his disappointment, and mine. Wiggling in his arms, I tried to get loose. "Let me go."

He was trying to be gentle, but wasn't going to let me go. He held me firmly around the waist. "Claire I am not letting you go anywhere without me again." Shocked, I paused in my struggles and waited. When he spoke again his voice was rough, his expression troubled. "I almost lost you today. No one is angry with you for what has happened. How could anyone have seen it coming? We had no idea they sensed what you were doing in the club the other night. That was entirely my fault, I should have checked the place out myself before bringing you in there. I am the only one to blame in this scenario." When he reminded me of the club, I thought of Gina and shuddered.

James gathered me closer to him and I heard the concern in his voice, "We should get you to a doctor, Claire. You have a concussion, possibly a cracked skull, a dislocated shoulder, which has been fixed but will hurt for a while and you lost a tooth. That is a lot of damage for a human body to take."

"No!" I shouted, grabbing on to him with my good arm. "I don't want to go to the doctor. I want to stay here." There was no releasing the death grip I had on his shirt. "What if they find me there?"

He didn't speak to my objections, only called quietly for Henry. He was up the stairs in seconds, his paternal features mild. "Bradley is not a forgiving man, Claire. He would not have easily let you go had he not wanted something from us. I agree it is best that you not leave just yet, we will care for you here as best we can."

I nodded, placated for the moment. "It was the brunette woman I felt instead of the redhead you had suggested. Gina was her name. One of the men that was with her that night at the club, the young Asian one, was at the house where they brought me." I came back to the point I had brought up when I was rambling before, "She said she knew what I was doing at the club, James. How did she know? She just hijacked me and I was powerless to stop her. I was so stupid I didn't realize it meant anything or I would have told you." I wiped at my eye threatening to leak. "I didn't accidentally channel her, she flooded me."

He and Henry exchanged glances. James spoke first. "I didn't know they had one in their midst. She must have been well guarded at the club; I didn't sense her. I should have done my own sweep. I will speak to my source." He growled the last.

"What are you guys talking about? What is she? Who *is* Bradley and why do they hate humans so much?"

Henry filled me in. "Bradley is a very old vampire and has always preached about a return to the dark days. He does not agree that humans should live free in our world and has been in the wings many times when humans and vampires clash, fanning the flames of genocide and war as a cover for massive hunts. But, his club is friendly to all vampires and our ruling Court has made public places neutral ground so that our kind can come together if we so choose.

147

The woman is one of Bradley's children. He changed her not long ago and they refused the assistance of the Court in her transition. She is still finding her strengths with only his guidance; she must be a Sensitive, like James. They are sensitive to others' gifts. That is why he is able to help in training others. He feels it when you are using your ability and can help you to shape and control it, much like when you channel. When someone like this child comes along and she doesn't have someone help her to shape her ability, it can drive her mad."

"Mad how?"

James spoke up his voice was back under control. "You know how your gift felt to you before you met us and began to control it?" I nodded. "You thought that you were crazy and couldn't control your emotions, constantly being invaded by those of others around you, right?"

He waited for me to remember. No need, it was all too fresh. "Combine the sensitivity of being newly changed with the constant barrage of stimulation already bombarding her from all sides. This woman is quite literally being driven mad by the nonstop 'noise'."

I put myself in her shoes and felt pity for her. "She blames humans for the noise, that's why she was mad I was in the club. That's her quiet place because she can block out a vampire's 'stuff' so much easier. She wants to kills us because she thinks if we're dead it will stop the chaos in her head." The thought made me cold all the way through and as wrong and terrible as her ideas were, I understood. I empathized with her.

James did not loosen his grip on me. "I will never let her hurt you again. I've sworn it. You're safe here with us."

Ch. 19

A few hours later the doorbell rang while James and I were sitting on the couch. I was wrapped in my favorite blanket and drinking a cup of tea. Fortunately, I wasn't holding the teacup when the bell rang, I startled so badly I would have been wearing it.

Henry came out of an upstairs room and announced. "It's Stephen. He's here to get your key, Claire."

Alarmed, I swiveled my head from one to the other. Stephen walked in as I asked him. "Why do you need my key?" Only my eyes were visible over the back of the couch but he could hear the warning in my voice.
It was James who answered for him. "You're staying here for a while. I cannot protect you while you stay in the dorms. Stephen will need your key so that he can get your things."

Indignant, I tried to stand up and ended up flailing to escape the blanket tangled impossibly around my arms and under his leg. Giving up, I settled for a stern frown from my spot on the couch. "There is no way Stephen is digging through my underwear drawer to pack my bag. No offense Stephen but you don't know what I need of my books and toiletries. This has been bad enough without people going through my things."

Stephen had come around the couch and got a look at my face. It must have been bad. I could feel the swelling and had been avoiding mirrors so far. His features steeled before he could recover his easygoing mask. I had my first inkling that there was something more behind Stephen's nonchalant attitude, something I'd been hoping would eventually have peeked out in time. "I am so sorry, Claire. Would you like me to beat her up?"

149

"As a matter of fact, I would like that very much, Stephen."
My laugh was cut short by a grimace. It hurt to smile.

James put his arm around my back again and lowered his
voice. "I can't let you leave here. You're lucky to be alive
and we don't know where these people are, nor do we know
when in the next few days the newcomers are crossing into
our territory. We have only days now instead of weeks and
you aren't safe from any of them now that they know you are
special to me."

I wanted to stop at his mention of my being special but there
were more pressing matters if I hoped to retain some small
portion of my dignity and independence. "Henry, Bradley
said you have watchdogs keeping an eye out for the new
group so we know they haven't come across the borders yet.
Don't I have another hour before I have to go under lock and
key? Stephen, you could go with me just long enough to
pack my own things and come back, couldn't you?" I tried
to reason with James. "I promise I have no problem staying
here but I need to go and explain to the staff that I will be
staying with a friend for a while. It wouldn't be hard to
believe I was mugged and am scared to be alone." I pointed
to my face. "After I pack I'll come right back."

James considered my request for a moment and looked to
Henry and Stephen. "Why don't you two talk to the sentries
at the southern border and find out if there's been any
movement? It would take them at least a few hours to make
it from there. I can check with some of my contacts in
Milwaukee to see if we can get a handle on what time they
left while I go with Claire to get her things. We will meet
back here later tonight." He turned to me. "If you're leaving
here, it's going to be with me."

Under the circumstances, I didn't let my independent female
spirit be wounded. No one made me feel safer than James.
It would be fantastic if he would never leave me alone again.

Stephen and Henry both agreed to the plan and James helped untangle me so I could get up. Henry, holding up a finger to wait, disappeared from the room and returned in a few seconds holding a glass of water and something in his hand.

I looked at him questioningly and he opened his hand revealing some large white pills. "Now that we have all thought this through, I think it is safe for you to take these. They'll kick in about forty minutes from now when James has you safely back here and tucked in to bed. By then, you will be grateful for the relief." Normally, I didn't like taking medications, though I saw a huge benefit to dulling the pain in my jaw and head. Downing the pills, I watched James put on his sunglasses, making ready to drive me back to campus.

His features were tight around his shades as he silently helped me into my coat and out the door. He never took his arm off of me except to walk around the car and get in, scanning our surroundings the whole time. During the drive to school, the air in the car between us was uncomfortable like that first night again. Things were going so fast now. It had been just two nights ago, James and I had gone beyond teacher and student and now, for all intents and purposes, I was moving in with him under the guise of protection.

"You know this isn't your fault James. I could stay with the Andrews, too." Staring straight ahead was easier for me than eye contact. I felt him grow still. "You don't have to take me on while this is all getting sorted out. If this is... whatever it is, then I can't go and move in with you. I don't want either of us to feel pressured or anything because things have gotten, um, complicated." I would never forgive myself if I lost a chance to have something with him because he felt rushed or crowded or whatever and took me in out of a sense of obligation.

Without warning the car whipped across two lanes of traffic, onto the shoulder and skidded to a stop on the side of the freeway. Scared to death I'd committed some awful offense

151

I stared over at James' profile. Cars went screaming by us at 70 miles per hour while he stared straight ahead through the windshield. His face was frightening in his anger, his total stillness promised violence.

"Claire I want you to be perfectly clear about something. I am very old, though I am not too old-fashioned to be practical. You will stay with me where I can protect you because I love you. I will not lose you again." He tilted his head curiously. "Are you unwilling to stay with me?" Even with the anonymity of sunglasses, I could feel his eyes burning into mine. "If it makes you uncomfortable, we can have Stephen come to the house as well to make you feel more at ease."

My brain was swimming. Maybe the pain meds were kicking in or it was my concussion. "What did you say?"

He aimed his gaze forward again, grinding his jaw in frustration. He growled low. "I said you could have your cat come over if you don't want to be alone with me."

Shaking my head, I stuttered. "No, before that. You...you love me?"

Lowering his sunglasses, he turned his dark eyes back to me. "I said that I love you and I will do everything in my power to keep you safe."

Slowly, his words sunk into my concussed brain, I felt dizzy. "James, I love you too." I was breathless as I reached over, wrapping my good arm around his neck. I kissed him gingerly feeling better than I had in a long time, injured or not. That tugging sensation inside me gave me a funny little tweak. I took it as a good sign.

Ch. 20

We walked into my building, James' arm around my waist, protectively drawing me into the shelter of his body. Now that I knew he loved me, I couldn't get close enough to him. I only wished I could have moved my mouth enough to kiss him harder, but I had to admit that last one had hurt. When we got to the desk I took my ID from him and showed it to the girl, leaning out of his shadow so that she could see it was me.

"Oh my God, what happened to you?" It was the blonde who had gawked at James the other night. Was that all it was, just a few days that had passed? Things were so different now, for better and worse.

"I got mugged. I'm here to get a few things and then I'm going to stay with a friend for a while. Until I feel better." I tried to speak as clearly as possible. It was difficult, I had to open my mouth to speak so much louder for humans. It was convenient to have a vampire with super hearing for a boyfriend when your jaw hurt and your lip was tight enough to burst.

The blonde looked at James and probably thought she would give up a tooth or two of her own to spend some time alone with him. I felt a twinge of jealousy. James tightened his arm around me. "If you don't mind, Claire has had a long day and I'd like to get her home and resting as soon as possible. If anyone comes looking for her you can tell them she's gone for the time being and you have no idea when she will return."

The blonde's eyes went glassy and she nodded mutely. He wheeled me to the elevators, passing the curious looks of other students on the way. We were positioned with my bruised right side toward his body hiding my face. We probably just looked like we were snuggling close to anyone passing by, although the only glances we drew were from girls and those were most likely due to James' good looks. I could have been a rhinoceros and no one would have paid me any notice.

He took my key when we reached my room and opened the door. Once inside, I found my suitcase in my closet and set it down on the bed. I sat down next to it and put my head in my hands. I felt the bed move as he sat down beside me. His hand stroked the back of my head. "It's going to be okay. We will all fight when the time comes."

The guilt I had been feeling for the past hour erupted in a tired and pathetic whine. "I know, but why do you have to fight for me? I don't want anyone to be hurt on my account. Can't we just leave the country or something until this all blows over?"

"Claire, we would still fight even if you were the only reason, but you aren't." I met his eyes, trying to read him. "There is much more at stake than you or me. This is a fight for territory and also a skirmish in a much bigger battle. Our kind is approaching a war between those who want to live side by side with humans, and those who want to hunt them to extinction with the exception of food stock."

"Why?" Now I understood why Henry was taking this encroachment so seriously.

He sighed, resigned, "Why does any group hate another? From the time that Lillith was cast out of the Garden, our kind has fought your kind and now is no different. Humans have stronger weapons and greater numbers and we have greater physical strength and abilities, and that's without factoring in which side has the most launch codes. Henry is just one of many across the country and across the world who are working to keep things as they are. Us in the shadows, humans thinking they are the only intelligent species on the planet. Sometimes, some vampires kill humans to feed, but that is the natural balance. Our side can't be the dominant side because we are too hard to kill and our potential for damage is too great. If one of us gets out of hand, we handle it internally with the greater population none the wiser."

"Don't look so surprised," he teased, "we've been around as long as you have. We've developed our own rules that we live by." He stood and changed the subject. "Let's get you packed up and back home."

"Home," I repeated after him considering what that meant for me now. Staying at James' house until this passed. What then?

He put a hand on my elbow as we stood. "My home is yours for as long as you want it. But you have to explain it to your parents when they come for a visit," he teased. It was enough that he loved me and I loved him and I didn't dare think beyond that for now. I gave his arm a squeeze in response.

It didn't take long to pack up some clothes, my books and laptop. Really, everything else was superfluous. Once we returned home, Stephen, Henry, James and I all sat down to figure out who would drive me to school, walk me to my classes, pick me up and take me to and from work. I was never to be left alone and though I knew it might save my life, I also couldn't help but wonder if it was all really necessary.

"Don't you guys think you're going a bit overboard on the protection? I'm just some human to them. Yeah, they roughed me up, but I am still just a human. They don't need to concern themselves with me anymore; they got what they wanted." The painkillers were acting like anti-anxiety medications now and I was the calmest of us all.

155

James growled ominously when I mentioned the violence, but explained the situation in a way I hadn't considered. "Claire, they have found someone more vulnerable than us that has proven to be a weakness for me. That might be a bargaining chip they look for again. Besides, Gina might seek you out just because she is crazy enough to do it and now she has focused her anger on you. Either way, we will not risk you, nor will we lose the opportunity to capture any of those bold enough to come for you again."

James and I had been sitting together. I was leaned against him, legs across his, Henry was on the opposite side of the couch and Stephen was in the chair. Stephen had seen us sitting together earlier but having James point out my special status with him caught his ear and he perked up.

"Hey, did you two hook up and not tell me?" He wagged a finger from one to the other, shaggy hair hanging in his eyes. He had never felt more like a little brother to me.
James glared at Stephen. "Watch it."

"Geez, James, he's just being Stephen. Don't get your nose out of joint." I rubbed his chest playfully. The feel of his body was fascinating. His chest was firm, more so than muscle; it was like touching surgical rubber stretched over steel cables. Despite my physical ailments and the constant dose of painkillers Henry had me on, I was quickly becoming distracted as I started to think hard about James' body and what it felt like under my hands and against my skin. His hand caught mine when it lingered too long on his chest. Flicking my eyes up, I saw he was amused at my attentions and trying to be serious with the others in the room. Slightly out of wack from the meds, I leaned into him, content to just feel his voice vibrate my head as it lay against his chest.

"Sorry, Stephen, I was raised to never speak so casually about affairs of the heart."

Stephen joked back. "I didn't know we were talking about an 'affair of the heart'. I thought we were just talking about a little action."

James growled again and I lifted my head up enough to shoot Stephen a look. "Don't you know to leave well enough alone?" Meanwhile, my half-baked mind was trying to wrap around James' sudden need to publicly claim me as his, I was warm all over.

Stephen laughed, undaunted, rising to go to the door. "Yeah, I have my own affair to get back to but I'm not looking for a heart."

"You will be back here this evening with your family for us to discuss how to go forward," Henry spoke calmly, though I heard the hint of a command in his tone.

"No problem, we'll be here. I would assume you need some stealthy cats to back you up as usual?" Stephen seemed awfully cocky about his prowess.
"Watch yourself, Stephen. I have no desire to lose you to carelessness. Things are heating up and we all need to use extra caution now." Henry was ever the voice of reason.

Not Stephen. "Don't worry about me. I'll be back after dinner, ready to serve and protect."

Ch. 21

We met with the Andrews clan to draw up patrol zones. We had the dual tasks of monitoring the movements of Bradley's vampires and splitting my escorts' duties between James and Stephen. The werecats and vampires spoke further about the mysterious happenings in Milwaukee between an ally of Henry's and the violent vampires now coming here to work with Bradley.

The Andrews and vampires discussed names of contacts all over Minneapolis and into Wisconsin. They were trying to figure out why no one knew what had happened in Milwaukee. All were assuming the worst but hoped a witness or survivor would have surfaced by now. It was a puzzle given their considerable grapevine for information gathering. James was spooked that it had suddenly dried up. I could tell he wanted to investigate for himself but didn't want to leave me. I had tried to object and send him out; he'd given me a look that closed the subject.

He was stubborn, that much I'd learned by now and I knew not to push. Henry decided he would try to call Dan, a vampire he knew with a club in Milwaukee. He was trustworthy and in the know; most vampires hit his place when they first came to town to find out who might be in the area. Henry and James hoped he would be able to shed some light on what had happened so that they could better establish what kind of force, beyond the little James had gleaned, was coming our way when the coven arrived this week. But when Henry called, Dan's line was out of service.

During the meeting, the clan was oddly disjointed. Stephen was distracted and elusive on what he would be doing, which Tara played off as Stephen being involved with someone new, yet it didn't seem right. He wouldn't answer any questions about where he was going to be and refused to commit to any specific times when he would be available to run area patrols interchangeably with his family. Stephen was definitely the most cavalier of the clan, but he was being downright irresponsible, a detail I found particularly hurtful since he had been the one concerned enough to bring me into the fold in the first place.

Maybe it was the painkillers, but I couldn't quite identify what felt wrong about Stephen's protests as to why he couldn't be more help in the grand scheme. James, disgusted with him entirely, threw up his hands, demanding the rest of the clan make up for Stephen's unreliability. Henry made a final ruling that he backed James and that was where it ended.

****

Later that night, lying in bed with my bruised face resting on James' cool chest, using it as an ice pack, and my head somewhat cleared of drugs, I could finally ask something that didn't make sense to me.

"James, it seems like the war and Bradley are a vampire problem, yet the Andrews are putting in a lot of effort to help. Why is that?" I strained to see his face, barely able to make out the pale outline of his face against the dark of the sheets. He had blocked his emotions from me so I couldn't readily guess.

"Have you heard of witches' familiars?"   He replied hesitantly.
"You mean like the black cat thing?"

"Right, well some vampires have something like that. It is referred to as having an animal to call."

"The mountain lions are Henry's animal?"

"Yes, specifically, the head of the Andrews clan.   He imprinted on Henry a long time ago. I am not sure of all of

159

the details, but I know Troy was at one point bound to another vampire. He was a cruel master and demanded the cats hunt for him. Henry helped to free them from their bond and it transferred to him. Now they are bound to each other in a sort of symbiotic relationship. The Andrews clan now has free will and can live autonomously with one exception. Just as they cannot refuse Henry's request for help now, he could not refuse them if they asked."

"What is your involvement in all of this? Are you helping because you *want* to or do you *have* to?" The compulsion Henry had mentioned that James had to help people would explain his cooperation easily enough, though hearing about all of these bonds, I couldn't help myself from worrying that James was bound to his mentor by more than mere friendship.

James frowned at me. "Henry was a good friend to me when I had no one. He helped me when I was having difficulty with some complications after being turned. I agree with Henry's efforts on behalf of humans and choose to help him." His features softened as he gently kissed my nose. "It is an alliance that works for us and it has been good to have a friend these many years."

"What were the complications?"

"Always the curious one," he teased. "Sleep now, we will have plenty of time for that. Besides, you have school tomorrow, young lady."

Too tired to disagree, I closed my eyes and drifted off while he kept watch for the boogeymen.

Ch. 22

Monday morning. I had an escort to my Psychology class and, though I believed the guard was unnecessary, I have to say, I didn't mind the extra attention from my super sexy escort, looking very mysterious in his ever present shades and dark coat. James drove me to campus, parked the car and walked hand in hand with me to the door of my classroom. To all appearances we were just like any other dating couple, except we had the responsibility of trying to prevent a brewing vampire war from erupting so that free human beings wouldn't be wiped out. Still, today, life was perfect.

After class, Stephen picked me up and we walked to work. He had some studying to do in the library anyway he said, and once I was there, I would be Henry's charge. Heidi and Ben had become suspicious of all of Henry's extra attention. To placate them, I told them both that I had confessed to Henry my wish to be a librarian so he was putting some extra time into me. Fortunately, they were very sweet about it. Ben was going to be a finance guy so he thought my wish to work with books was a waste. Heidi didn't know what she wanted, even though she was halfway through her junior year. She said she was just jealous of my decision-making ability. I figured it wasn't a lie on my part since I hadn't ruled it out as a possibility, although it no longer felt like my only option.

On our way to the library, we had a long walk across campus, which led us through the park. Augsburg's campus housed Minneapolis' oldest park across the street and down a flight of stairs from the main part of the school. We were halfway through the park when Stephen hopped sideways closing the small gap between us fast until our arms nearly touched. I barely kept my feet as I looked up expecting him to make a joke.

161

But the look on his face was severe. I had never seen him look dangerous. He did now. His changed demeanor had me searching around us for the threat that had to be nearby. It didn't take long to find her. Gina stepped around a large oak tree just to our left and blocked our path on the walkway. We could easily have stepped around her, which would have left our backs open to her. We stopped.

"Stephen," she crooned not taking her hate filled eyes from mine. "I see you are still doing as you are told like a good kitty. Does your Master pay you well to babysit?"

A familiar tingle raced up my arm making my hair stand on end. I recognized the sensation of him changing forms. "Stephen, no." I warned hoping to distract him and unwilling to risk putting a hand on him in such a volatile state. It wouldn't help matters if I lost it and just ended up making him twice as mad. I wasn't sure of the rules, but I figured it probably wasn't okay to turn into a mountain lion on a college campus in front of dozens of witnesses in broad daylight.

Stephen snarled at her. "*I* have no Master. Can *you* say the same?"

Her eyes narrowed yet she ignored his question. "Yes, Stephen, do as you're told. You know what happens to bad kitties." She stood just feet from us, and closed the space in one gliding step. Gina put her clawlike hand on Stephen's cheek and stroked it, putting her face to his. I half expected her to kiss him. "I heard what happened the last time you misbehaved for your *old* Master. Maybe we can arrange something like that for you again to serve as a reminder of who is the stronger species." Turning on her heel, she sauntered off, calling over her shoulder as she did. "See you soon, dears."

From my nearness I could feel him shaking, I wasn't sure if it was anger or his effort to remain human. "Damn it, I hate that woman already." He was angry, not afraid.

Curious, I asked him. "Stephen, how did your old master punish you? You're so strong."

His jaw was so tight I was sure I would hear a tooth break soon, but he breathed a few deep breaths and pulled me along. Resuming our walk to work, Stephen was silent for a while. Eventually, he answered me. "Silver." I didn't understand, so I waited patiently for him to continue. "Silver hurts and temporarily paralyzes supernatural creatures. The entire time it touches our skin, it burns and will give us scars. Given enough time it will burn through until it touches blood. Then it kills."

"I've never seen scars on you. Where did he touch you with silver?" We stopped walking and I turned to face him so that I could see his expression. His eyes were full of remembered pain.

Without speaking, Stephen grabbed his pants at the knees and lifted his jeans. He was wearing low socks and I could clearly see the skin at his ankles. I gasped in horror. The flesh just above his socks was forever marked by wide bands of melted white skin, so thin in parts they were nearly transparent.

"Oh Stephen, I'm so sorry." I shored myself up enough for a short hug. He squeezed me back.

His voice was choked as he pulled away roughly and spoke. "Come on, we'll be late and I need to let Henry know they're following us. At least they can't do anything to us in public like this. Even Bradley isn't that bold. Yet."

Ch. 23

When work was over my personal hero picked me up from Henry's watch and we went home for an early dinner before heading back to campus for my evening Eastern Philosophy class. Having heard about her visit, James was on high alert, scanning for Gina the entire time we were outside of his house, but she didn't appear again.

When my day at school was done, I sat studying at the dining room table while James was researching an upcoming trip to Scotland on his laptop. I was so deep in thought about the psychosocial aspects of human sexuality that I didn't hear James the first time he said my name.

"Claire," he teased. "Oh, Claire."

"Hmm? Sorry, interesting topic." Folding a piece of notebook paper into a bookmark, I closed my textbook. "What did you ask me?"

"I asked if you have ever been to Scotland. My next trip to Edinburgh is scheduled for next week. I was supposed to leave Sunday. However, in light of recent events I don't feel comfortable leaving you here." He was rocked back in his chair watching something on his monitor.

"So you're telling me you would get in trouble with your editor and blow a piece just because of your girlfriend's dumb luck? Not bloody likely. I think you want to whisk me away to faraway lands and do unspeakable things to me with no one to stop you," I teased playfully.

His eyebrows rose archly as he took the bait. "Do you have any objections to that?"

"None in the slightest. How long were you going to be gone?"

"We would leave Sunday and return Wednesday. That gives me time to do some travel pictures, write the story up quickly and attend some meetings."

The dismissive way he mentioned them caught my ear. "What meetings, James?"

His chair came down. "Henry has asked me to speak to some of my contacts in Edinburgh about what is happening here with Bradley and his incoming coven."

"Is it smart for me to go with you if you are doing vampire things?" In spending more time with my new friends, I had become privy to lots of information previously unknown to me about our world and theirs. For example, yes, some vampires hated humans and saw us merely as food. Others, though opposed to our extinction, were not enthralled with the idea of us in their business or knowing about them. James and Henry were crossing a line by bringing me into the fold. Granted, it was due to Henry's animal connection that I had even been introduced. Still, it was not something the larger vampire population would be taking lightly when they found out.

I was fairly certain Bradley and his lot were spreading all sorts of propaganda about our family right about now. It wouldn't surprise me at all to hear his crowd arguing that I would blab the whole thing and they would all have to go into hiding in the woods somewhere. If there was one thing I had learned about vampires and weres, it was that they loved the modern conveniences of city living. There were not many farming vampires or werewolves, so needless to say, they would be pissed off if they had to go into hiding somewhere off the grid.

James didn't want to answer my question but when he did, he met my gaze unflinchingly. "If we are to have a future together, we must eventually make our appearance before the

165

members of the Court for approval. We might as well do so now, it might even afford you some extra protection."

"What are you talking about?" Never in any of our conversations about how his society was run had he mentioned such a technicality. "There's an approval process?"

He nodded once, slowly. "Yes, vampires wishing to consort with humans are left to clean up their own messes when they're finished." I gasped. He went on calmly, "The few who seek a longer term arrangement must gain approval through the ruling body. If we are to maintain the necessary secrecy to survive, we can't be running around telling everyone how vampires make for great lovers." His attempt at levity did nothing for the fear in the pit of my stomach.

"So we have to go meet with the mightiest of mighties on their turf, and ask if it's okay that I'm your girlfriend, while you are *also* there asking for help reining in one of theirs? Doesn't that just prove Bradley's point that your loyalties are confused?" This didn't sound like a vacation I wanted to go on at all now. Screw Scotland. I'd go sometime when I was old and I would take a bus tour of old castles or something.

His brows knitted in consternation. "You sure have a way of putting a damper on my vacation plans."

"This was supposed to be work, not a vacation. Now, it sounds like I'll be asking a bunch of vampire politicians if they'll let me, a lowly human, keep on breathing." How could he not understand how I could be upset? I was a human. These were vampires. Some of who wanted to wipe out my kind.

"Claire," he laid both hands on the table. "Do you think I would put you in a situation where you are in any significant danger at all?"

"Significant?" I squeaked.

"Asking for an audience with the Court is a formal occasion, yes. It does carry some amount of risk, but it is both manageable and necessary." He held up a hand to postpone my arguments. "However, they will not disagree with our relationship. Henry and I are held in high regard due to our history with the Court. And then there's the biggest piece of evidence on our side, you haven't said anything."

"What do you mean, 'I haven't said anything'?"

"Exactly how it sounds. If you are deemed to be trustworthy and will swear to uphold our secret, you have nothing to fear." He reached for my hands across the table.

After a long moment of consideration, I realized that the details under which I met his "people" didn't matter. I would follow him into the jaws of hell if he asked. I took his hands, "If you are comfortable with this, then I am too. I have to trust you on this one since I have less than no experience with meeting in-laws." He threw back his head and laughed and I couldn't stop myself from smiling at the sound. A couple of happy fools; that was us.

Ch. 24

What a week. Saturday night I had almost died, Monday night I learned that I was only a week away from meeting the vampire Court to not only ask for help in dealing with some angry rogue vampires wanting to destroy the human race, but also to present myself as James' human consort. It was only Tuesday and, as if I didn't have enough on my plate, my cell phone rang. It was my mother with another bombshell.

"Hi, Mom."

She sounded hesitant, my ears pricked suspiciously. "Honey, I think I owe you an apology."

Uh oh. I sat down on the couch. "What is it Mom?"

"I don't think I told you about your cousin Vanessa's wedding, did I? It's this Friday night in Duluth." She knew she hadn't told me or she wouldn't be tiptoeing.

"Um, no Mom. You didn't." I rolled my eyes at James who had just walked in to find out if Stephen was calling in. Nobody had heard from him since last night. "I didn't know anything about a wedding. That is awfully last minute, and I have something I have to do next week so an overnight in Duluth on Friday night isn't exactly convenient." I made my eyes huge and James figured out it was Mom. Moms and daughters, that one was timeless. He leaned against the doorframe and crossed his arms making no bones about the fact that he was eavesdropping.

"Claire, I am so sorry, this one is all my fault. I put the invitation on the fridge." That was always our warning system in the house while I had lived there. "It just never clicked that I had to call you. I'm not used to you being gone yet." I heard the cry coming on, reflexively moving to

168

avoid it. I knew I was going to cave. I also felt bad for her, she really had forgotten or she wouldn't be groveling.

Glancing over at James, I spoke to him as well. "All right, Mom. I'll tell you what. I'll come to the wedding if you can email me the specifics. But I'll have to drive home afterward so I can't stay too late."

She squealed jubilantly. "Oh Claire, Vanessa will be so happy. You two used to be so close when you were kids. This will mean a lot to her and her mother. Don't worry about a gift, we'll put your name on ours." She prattled on for another few minutes and I raised my eyebrows and shoulders to James, asking if that was okay. He nodded that it was okay with him. She caught my attention again when she asked if I would be bringing a "plus one," she sounded hopeful. "You know, a friend to share the drive? What about Heidi?" She suggested helpfully.

"Yes mom, there *is* someone I would like to bring. Is that okay if I have a date?" Even if she had to agree to be the narcissistic Vanessa's personal attendant, she'd make sure there was room for me to bring my first date. She would be dying to meet him, I was sure. "Mom, I have to get going. I have some more homework to do before I head to work." Snapping my phone shut, I sighed and sank back into the couch cushions, closing my eyes. They popped back open when I heard the soft voice chuckling under his breath.

"Looks like I'm going to meet your family, hmm?"

***

"*Who* is watching the house?" James barked grumpily at Tonya just coming in after a night's patrol in the neighborhood. Bradley's crew was still missing and, as if the patrols weren't enough and the Andrews weren't already exhausted from ranging all over the city, they had added checking in with the were network, both local and distant to

169

their duties. They were all trying their best to find out what they could about what was happening with the incoming vamps and Bradley's coven. It was as if they had up and disappeared. It was pushing everybody to the breaking point.

Tonya snapped back, the strain showing in the lines around her eyes. "Who the hell cares? I just pulled a double and I need some sleep. At least if they hit the house we'll know where they are." She threw up her hands and stalked away to take a nap in one of the two spare rooms upstairs. Who could blame her, her house was a good half hour from here and she'd been on her feet for a full day already.

There was some unspoken tension in the house due to Stephen's current preoccupation. He was being intentionally vague whenever anyone asked him to help out and he wasn't answering his phone when Henry or James called. His family of werecats and vampires plus one human were all trying to work together to thwart any incoming attacks, strategize for next week's meeting with the Court and train me up fast to help, should the need arise. We were still hopeful my abilities would come in handy when and where we met up with the other coven.

"This is ridiculous," I said flipping open my phone. There was nothing I could do to help while I watched my family run themselves ragged trying to save the world; the least I could do was try to see if I still held any sway with one of them.

James watched me dial. "What are you doing?"

"I'm going to call Stephen and find out what's going on with him. Everybody's fighting and tired and I'm worried someone's going to get hurt because they make a mistake out of exhaustion. And for what, why won't he talk to anyone?" I was personally upset with him because I was supposed to be his friend and if he was having trouble with something, I wanted him to feel like he could come to me.

"Claire, I'm surprised. Usually you are his first defender."

Sighing, I lightened up. "I'm going to try to talk to him and see what is going on. This is just so unlike him. I don't get it." Being this tired constantly surrounded by so much tension was making me weepy. I felt the tears gathering behind my eyes. James saw them too and pulled me in for a hug, still careful of my bruises, which were almost gone by now. He and I were amazed at how quickly my body was healing. I was still missing that tooth though. When this was all done, I'd have to get in to see my dentist.

After all that, reaching Stephen was kind of anti-climactic. He answered his phone on the first ring and, giving James a hopeful smile, I wandered away. He said he had been at Troy's, currently standing vacant with everyone at James's house. He even seemed eager when I told him we had to meet tonight. As a matter of fact, he offered to pick me up from work after I closed up. Other than sounding tired, Stephen hadn't seemed any different than normal during our conversation.

Hanging up, I was standing in the kitchen puzzling over my odd exchange when Troy came in to get a drink.

"Troy, is Stephen up to something?"

Closed lipped, he filled a glass with water. "That is a good question. I heard you're coming back here later, so I guess we'll all find out then." He frowned into his water as he took a drink.

I had a feeling Troy was keeping something and his easy attitude about his brother turning up, all of a sudden willing to talk, made me sure of it. If not for the fact that we were all due to talk tonight, I would have pushed. But, in light of

Stephen's offer, I didn't burn the goodwill between Troy and I that it would have cost me.

His expression lightened as he turned the tables on me. "How about you? I heard your family is to meet your new beau." I thought I saw a twitch at the corner of his mouth.

"New beau?" I guffawed, "Try *only* beau. I just don't know how I feel about him meeting my whole entire family so soon. Especially with cousins, grandparents, the whole shooting match. He'll take one look at them and run for the hills. Or I'll crawl under a rock and die of embarrassment if they trot out some awful 'when Claire was young' story. It isn't fair. It's not like I will ever meet his family and see where he comes from. He has no way to compare."

"You know, that is hard for creatures like us." Setting the glass down on the counter, Troy looked at his hands braced on either side of his drink. "I know that you *know* we are older than we appear. What you don't *appreciate* is the cost of that longevity. When we first changed, our ages froze or in the rare case of a younger animal, they become pubescent during their first change and it becomes permanent thereafter.

At first, we enjoy it when we feel the strength, power and speed. Our kind's amazing ability to heal; we are nearly indestructible and it is intoxicating. It can be very difficult for those who are young souls; it is as though they cannot fully grow and mature mentally. But, over time, we watch those we love age, weaken and die. Some of our kind cannot handle it and their minds twist in sickness. When that happens, our Council steps in to control the situation."

"You mean Stephen. He can be older than his years one minute, the next he's off being an infuriatingly immature kid." It made a lot of sense when put in perspective. What would I do if I froze today but lived on beyond the lifetimes of everyone I knew? "But look at the rest of your family, and Henry and James. You are all such old souls. Why is it so different for you?"

"Claire, enough sorrow will age mortal as well as immortal souls. When you see enough tragedy, part of your soul dies. Have you ever met a human who has seen true horror?"

I had. On base at Miramar in San Diego, Dad had introduced me to one of his heroes, Pat Murphy. Pat had been a boy, serving as an Airman on a carrier during World War II in the Pacific. When he spoke of watching kamikazes fly their planes right into the guns and ship decks, killing themselves senselessly, trying to take as many lives as possible before dying themselves. He had been so sad; it had been physically painful for me to be near him feeling the intensity of the emotion rolling off of him all these years later. I nodded, understanding.

"I have things I must do." Touching my shoulder as he walked past me, Troy smiled comfortingly. "Don't worry Claire. You know who he is, that tells you enough." I wasn't sure if he was talking about James or Stephen.

Ch. 25

The day passed relatively quickly with my upcoming papers for Philosophy and History and work in the evening. Heidi and I talked about her latest dating fiasco with an upper classman, Matt something or another.

Heidi and I still only hung out at work, but we both came in early and stayed late to talk to one another a lot. I hoped that when things calmed down with the scary part of my life I would be able to invite her to coffee. Right now, it probably wasn't safe for her to be around me as much as she was.

Heidi's fun personality and animated way of speaking made every recounting of her awful dating adventures hilarious even if they were all kind of sad in a way. Still, it didn't seem to bother her *too* much. She seemed determined to repeat the same formula over and again. It didn't make sense to me, but then again, never having been on the dating scene before, I couldn't pretend to understand the nuances.

"I don't get it." She was still going on about Matt. "I told him I wouldn't go to his house with him, so what does he do? Drives me there and refuses to take me home. I had to walk. What did he think was going to happen? That I would do whatever he wanted so that he would take me home? I can't believe I thought he was different."

I could have told her she had terrible taste. Choosing only the least reputable from, I think, every athletic team Augsburg had. Heidi had run the course with them all. Some lasted for a little while, others were less than twenty-four hour relationships, but all of them inevitably flamed out in fiery train wrecks. And Heidi dealt with them all in the same way; she would change her hair color, sulk for a few days and refuse to unplug from her ipod. Then, poof it was back to the chipper girl we all knew.

"Heidi have you ever thought about being *friends* with a guy first?" I wondered aloud slipping a book into its designated spot. I stopped myself right there, now I was giving dating advice? Me, of one boyfriend total in a lifetime, what did I know? Sure, James was a nice guy but his enemies could kill me.

She shot me a look like I had grown a second head. "Why? If I am going to date him, why try to be friends first? Otherwise, when it all goes down, I lose a friend *and* a boyfriend. I'd just as soon get in and get out. Minimum damage."

I decided on a safer topic. "So, have you chosen a major yet? Registration opens in a few weeks for second semester. Tick, tock."

She groaned, rolling her large brown eyes, sharply accented with thick black eyeliner. "Don't remind me. My folks are all over me. I just don't know. Can't I keep it general forever?"

"You can, it just isn't going to play as well when you are interviewing for a job after graduation." Down the road of majors and school we went. It made it easier for me to pay half a mind to her and the other half to the upcoming events in Scotland. James didn't want to worry me, but I could tell it was more serious than he let on.

My time with Gina and watching everyone run themselves ragged in the aftermath had given me inspiration on how I could help. I got the idea from Stephen. When he'd first told me about his ability, he had shown me how he could project a directive into someone's thoughts. I wondered if, with practice, *I* could do something like that. Could I take the emotions around me and channel them into someone else, or could I take some of my own or those in my memory and project them outward? Even if it only bought us an

175

extra few seconds or provided a distraction it might be worth it.

Several hours later, we had the library put back together despite the students' best efforts otherwise. The last one in the building, I was in the basement among the religious texts when I felt someone else and reached out to check if it was Stephen. He was supposed to have been here by now, it was almost ten.

My shielding had grown stronger, but sometimes when I was alone I brought it down to give myself a break. It was also an experiment I was trying, to drop it and "sweep" for people and non-people at regular intervals. Like my own built-in security system. My distance testing at home and here during my shifts had proven I could feel someone roughly one floor away from me without much effort. I was hoping to push for more before we left for Europe. I knew everything would be different after that and I wanted to prove myself useful to my "family" come what may.

My skin prickled and I felt a surge of rage from the other party. He was nearer than I first thought, or he was moving. Reaching out again, I felt the rage growing, and then disappear in a flash. I felt the emptiness as strongly as I had felt the anger just a moment before. Uh oh, that was shielding. Whatever he was, he was hiding.

Panicking because I didn't know how many there were or how long I had, I instantly felt sweat bead up on my upper lip as I flashed back to my time with Gina. My hand was shaking and I dropped the phone back into my pocket twice in a row. The denim finally relinquished it and I was able to get it out and dial.

James answered on the second ring. "Claire?" He sounded worried right away.

Crouching next to the tall shelving that normally brought me such comfort, I whispered. "Someone's here. I felt him. He's not human." Trying again for another sweep, I was disappointed. I wished he would lower his blocks so I could gauge the distance again.

"I'm in the car." I heard the door shut and the engine turn over. "Stay with me."

I had never been much for panicking, but that was before I found out monsters were real. Oddly enough, I found some tiny speck of peace in knowing that the vampire chasing me was not Gina. Funny, I'd never thought of myself as an optimist.

I checked the time on my phone and by my count James was at least seven minutes away even if he broke every traffic law known to man. Seven minutes was a really long time to hide from a vampire. A little voice in my head told me the vampire had gotten Stephen and that was why he wasn't here. Stubbornly I refused to listen. The phone banged my head and I realized how badly I was shaking. I was petrified.

My brain slowly started to churn again and I tried to use my knowledge of the building to my advantage. "James, am I better off in the elevator?"

"No, if it is a vampire, he can get in anyway and you limit your means of escape. You're better off leaving yourself options."

I extended myself out again, feeling for my hunter. I was extra sensitive in my approach to remain undetected. I felt a tingling on the edges of my periphery. Was that his shield I was feeling? It would be cool seeing how far I had developed my talent if I didn't think I was moments from a painful death. He felt like he was upstairs, but I wasn't sure if he was on the first or top floor. The only thing I could

177

think of was to get to the front doors and make a break for the outside. It sounded nuts, but maybe I could find some other people. There was a chance the hunter would not want witnesses. I hated to think I might get someone harmed, but I couldn't just sit here and wait for him to find me and kill me. Or take me to *her*, to Gina. That decided it.

Thank goodness for my practical fashion sense. I was wearing jeans, a black sweater and black Converse. Sneaking quickly, but quietly, I whispered to James on the phone.

"I'm going to try to get outside and aim for people. I need to be able to run, I'm hanging up. I know you can find me." Our connection was stronger than either of us understood and I knew I could trust it right now.

"Claire, please." I could tell he was desperate, but what could he tell me to do? There was nothing a human could do against a determined vampire, except to buy time while she waited for someone who could.

"I love you." I closed the phone before he could even answer and put it in my pocket as I started for the back stairs. Maybe the hunter wouldn't think of this route. Thank goodness I was on carpet and could scoot between racks, keeping to the darkest ones along the right side until the open entryway. Up to a few minutes ago I had never considered the sunny open part of the library as anything other than warm; now it was exposed and I dreaded crossing it. My shields were still down, searching, but I had lost the tingling. Maybe my own nerves were getting in my way. I'd have to look into that, but not now. Now, I had to run.

Edging along the front windows in a low crouch, I had finally reached the front doors. My hand was on the glass, ready to push when I felt him. He was close. I looked around but saw nothing, the hair on the back of my neck went up anticipating a hand or set of teeth. The thought of teeth did it. I got the nerve to push the glass door open and launch myself out into the night. Out into nothing but a quiet night with no one else in sight.

My feet went as fast as they could travel, slapping the concrete as I ran full out toward the quad. My mind was sifting through my best possibilities for ten o'clock on a school night. The air had turned cold in the evening hours and burned in my lungs as I sucked it in by giant mouthfuls. My best bet was to cut across the quad and over to Riverside Avenue just on the other side of campus. It was about a quarter mile, but it was a busy street and I would be guaranteed to find plenty of traffic, pedestrian and automobile.

Still I ran, putting everything into it that I had. Years of hiking and keeping in decent shape helped, but fear was my strongest motivator. I had just passed the last of the school buildings and was within sight of the bright lights on the hospital on Riverside. That was the direction James would be driving when he came off the freeway. He would see me if he could get there in time. It was so close. I tried to put more speed, doubting it really made a difference. I was pushing my physical stamina past its limits already.

My path brightened as I jumped down the short set of stairs from the quad, skirting the edge of the darker park, and ran across the walking path under the streetlights marking the edge of the open lot bordering the street. It was abandoned, but I saw headlights going back and forth on the street beyond. When I was about halfway across the parking lot I felt a gust of wind from behind and felt someone just about on top of me. The terror rose up my back and I imagined I felt someone touching me from behind, grabbing me, when I saw one of the cars on the street turn.

It turned left toward me, cutting off an oncoming van left swerving and honking angrily behind it. The headlights bounced through the darkness as the car jumped the curb and raced my way. It slid to a stop about five yards in front of me. The door flew open and out jumped a very fast moving vampire hurling himself over the car. He virtually flew toward me and I felt the presence behind me evaporate. And then we collided. When we met, he grabbed me and cradled me against his side, spinning to dissipate the impact as he stared over my shoulder, struggling for a glimpse of the one who was getting away. I could tell that he was torn. He wanted to pursue yet he refused to leave me alone. He remained vigilant for a few blinks more before turning his attention completely to me.

"Are you hurt? Did he touch you?" He pulled back only far enough for his eyes to search my face and body for any signs of trespass.

It was too soon to speak. My body was spent and I was sweating heavily despite the chilly fall air. My lungs burned as I struggled to get enough air into them. All I could manage was a shake of my head. I wasn't physically harmed, although my nerves were shot. My arms went around him and I pulled myself in as close I could get. It still wasn't enough to make me feel safe.

James walked back to the car, mostly carrying me since my legs were failing. He put me in the passenger side, buckled my seat belt after my shaking hands dropped it and walked around to his side. Throwing the car in gear and squealing the tires coming out of the lot, he didn't speak again until we got home.

My eyes tracked James, following his swiveling scans, as he came around to my side and helped me out. Sweeping me up, he had the front door open, us inside and the door locked behind us before I could have even closed the car door by myself. Once inside, I heard and felt the warm bodies of the Andrews's clan and Henry. They were all speaking at once. James and Henry spoke too quickly for me to hear most of it but I caught a few words. "Gina's friend" was all I needed

180

to hear to feel sick. I struggled to get down, but James didn't want to let go. I finally had to say, "I'm going to be sick." He half carried me to the bathroom off the kitchen and set me down barely in time for me to empty my stomach into the toilet. I threw up over and again until I had nothing left.

Sitting down on the tile floor I put my head in my hands, the shaking became uncontrollable. My teeth started to chatter and I hugged my knees to my chest. I felt a cold washcloth against my forehead and looked up. His blue eyes were black with heat. "I will kill him for this." With everything in me I knew he meant it, but it didn't make me feel any better.

The front door jiggled and I screamed. James spun so that he was in front of me, crouching defensively. Troy and Henry flanked the door and Tonya stood at the ready beside her brother. The doorknob turned and we heard the lock pop. The clan members relaxed just as the door opened and in walked Stephen. He looked around at everyone in surprise. At least he had the good sense not to make any jokes. I could see his eyes searching the room, not seeing who he was looking for. His appearance was disheveled and his skin flushed. Stephen's huge eyes landed on me and the panicked edge slid from his face as he heaved a huge sigh of relief. It was not to last.

In the half of a second it took for Stephen to enter the house and find me, I had only enough time to hear the growl next to me explode and I felt James launch himself at Stephen. It happened too fast to register in my head until I saw the couch jump sideways as the two bodies crashed into the backside of it.

It was hard to tell if Stephen was as surprised by James's attack as I was. By the time I had scrambled my way to them Troy and Henry had pulled James off and were trying to restrain him while Stephen held his face in his hands.

"Where the hell were you? He almost had her." James spat at Stephen. I could see the wild violence in his black eyes and his lips were pushed out unnaturally from his gums. I gasped as I saw his fangs fully extended. I had never seen this side of James before, the vampire in him. He wasn't himself, he was unrecognizable as the man I loved. Shocked, I gasped and my hands flew to cover my mouth in horror. His head whipped around at my noise and grasped what I was seeing. James went still under their hands and closed his mouth and eyes. The mouth regained its normal shape and when he opened his eyes again they were blue, dark but blue. Gone was the monster as suddenly as it had appeared. I would have doubted what I'd seen if it wasn't for the evidence I could see leaking through Stephen's fingers.

With James subdued, Troy and Henry relinquished their holds and Stephen took a seat next to the back of the newly relocated couch. His hands were covered in blood. When Troy moved his hand aside to assess the damage, I saw with a shock that pieces of his cheek hung in ribbons under his eye. His perpetually twinkling eyes were flat with pain.

Stephen spoke, his voice tortured. "I got there at ten till, like we agreed. As soon as I walked in I smelled him. I ran as fast as I could, following their scents. I caught up to where they crossed in the parking lot." He broke off, putting his head back into his hands. "God, I thought he got her and I couldn't track him. He just disappeared and I thought you were gone. I didn't pick up James' scent until my second pass and I came straight away; I wasn't sure what I'd find."

Stephen looked over at me and I wanted to cry from the pained expression I saw there on his mangled face. He was bleeding and there he was, worrying about me. "Claire, I was there. I swear it."

I got up from my seat on the floor and walked over to him. Sitting down next to him, I put my arm around him and he laid his unmarred cheek on my forehead. "I'm so glad he got to you in time." Rubbing his shoulder, I sniffed, letting several fat tears roll down my face.

Seeing James as not yet ready to listen to reason, I peeked over at Henry. "Please, it isn't his fault. They knew our schedule and how to get around it. I think we should figure out how to best defend ourselves from here. For now."

Henry grunted. "Claire, I agree that for the time being you will stay here. There is a reason Bradley wants you so badly and I don't think that we want him to succeed. I would have to assume he's gotten wind of your upcoming trip and does not want you to go, which means it is imperative that you do. With him acting so recklessly, we have a good chance to bring the justice of our Court down on him. They cannot possibly ignore our request this time."

"Stephen, I must apologize. The strain of this constant threat to Claire and to all of us is maddening. I have acted poorly." James had regained some amount of control.

After a tense moment, Stephen nodded at him. Tonya went to Stephen then saying, "If I don't get that stitched up soon it's going to heal crooked and your boyfriends won't think you're so pretty anymore."

Henry saw my confusion. "Weres heal quickly and timely wound care is essential to prevent any long term deformity."

Quick healing. My hand traced the line of my jaw now almost completely healed; only a few days what should have taken weeks. My eyes traveled from Stephen to James. Could I be like them from being around them or did it have to be something more physical. James caught me staring at him and gave me an odd shrug. I gave him a tired smile and shook off my concerns. There were other things to worry about for now.

183

****

It was much later, after hours of brainstorming over what Bradley and his gang of malcontents were up to that I finally admitted I could no longer stay awake and I said my goodnights. James wouldn't even let me out of his sight to go to sleep. He walked up with me and as we lay down together, I remembered that I had something I needed to leave the house for this week after all. Something almost as scary as facing the Court.

"James, we still have my cousin's wedding. If I cancel my parents will never forgive me."

"I'll be with you. You'll be fine."

"I know, but will you? You've never met my family." I wasn't entirely joking.

He chuckled softly.

"No seriously. I have never brought anyone home to my family. They would be all over you even if you *didn't* look like you do."

We lay facing each other and I adjusted my pillow so that I could see him unobstructed. "Love, I assure you that I have faced worse humans and supernatural enemies. I can handle this." His tone changed. "Are you worried about *me* or are you worried about *you*? We're going to be alone together." The incident with Stephen earlier had shaken us both.

Putting my hand on the side of his face, I looked at him. He was the James I knew and loved. The flash that I saw of vampire James had been terrifying, but I felt safe because I knew his strength and violence would never be turned against me. "James, I can't deny it was frightening to see you like that. Stephen's my friend and I love you both. But I trust you with my life." I shrugged my shoulders and gave

184

him a playful smile. "I sleep in your bed. There's no better proof of my trust than that.

I could see the relief in his jaw and the set of his shoulders. "I swore an oath, do you remember? I failed you once, but it will not happen again and you will *never* come to harm at my hands."

We had not made love since that first night. Now that I lay close to him, I felt a need to be closer and leaned in to kiss him. He felt it and I saw the same need in him. It was quite some time before I drifted off to sleep.

Ch. 26

Wednesday morning broke cold and damp. It was a perfect day to stay in bed all day. As much as I tried, James eventually insisted that he had to make some calls to finish making our travel plans and to call the office to talk to his editor.

I stumbled downstairs to find breakfast and was foraging in the cupboards looking for the English muffins. They were in the pantry with the canned goods. James could follow a recipe, but had a vampire's inability to categorize foods like a person does. Probably because it had been so long since they had tasted it, the memory of each food had faded. And packaged foods, forget it. That was after his time. Smiling, I was picturing my poor James trying to grocery shop when I heard the doorbell.

Listening for the sounds of people in the house I'd grown used to, I realized I didn't hear anyone going for the door, so I shuffled through the living room to answer. Opening the door halfway I saw a young woman, maybe in her mid twenties, standing on the stoop. She was shocked to see me, her mouth hung open and her large brown eyes, surrounded by too much green eye shadow, were saucers as she stared. While she gave me a bold once over, I pictured what she was seeing and felt my cheeks warm. When I had finally gotten out of bed this morning, I had put on one of James' white dress shirts, I liked to smell him when I rattled around the house. It hung down to my mid thighs so nothing was showing but there was also no way to convince her I was the housekeeper. "Uh, hi. Can I help you?"

Thankfully her mouth snapped closed and her eyes went back to normal. "Now I know why James doesn't want to come to the office anymore. And, that explains the second ticket."

Oh, the ticket! How could I have overlooked that? That had to be costly and there was no way I could let him cover it. It would hurt but I could scare up enough to repay him. "I take it you work with James?" I asked curiously.

She smiled. "Yeah, I'm his assistant, Beth. I've worked with him for about a year now. I make his arrangements when he asks and research any details of his trip he needs help with." She extended her hand and I shook it.

"Would you like to come in?" As I spoke, I felt a breeze and an arm went around my waist, pulling me close. I leaned in without thinking as I recognized James' musky sweet scent. He had snuck up using the partially opened door as a blind for his speed.

"Beth, thank you for bringing that by today. I've been a bit," he stumbled uncertainly, "busy around here. I've only just hung up with Josh." He reached out a hand and Beth put a large envelope in it.

"Josh is my editor," he clarified for my benefit. He looked down at me, a mischievous light in his eyes. "I see you've met Claire?" His smile put a proud bubble in my chest. I could just imagine what Beth was going to share at the office when she got back.

"I just invited Beth inside." Glancing back at her, I added, "for some tea? Or coffee?"

Beth looked from James' possessive posturing to my casual dress and smiled politely. "No, you two have a lot to do before you leave on Sunday. James, I'm sure I'll talk to you when you get back. Claire, it was a pleasure to meet you." She grinned again and waved as she turned to leave.

Pulling me back in order to close the door, James looked down at me and I saw all the playfulness was gone. Misunderstanding, I began, "James, I am sorry if I just

187

started something for you at the office. I should have considered how it would look with me in this," I put a hand over the open collar in a nod to decency.

He rolled his eyes. "I don't care if she puts a picture of us on her Facebook page." He frowned. "I don't want you answering the door right now." Before I could object that he was being overprotective, he went on. "That could have been a vampire and you would be gone right now."

The nausea I felt and the sweat that sprang up under my arms and on my lip were instant. It felt like I was three years old again and I had done something naughty. "I'm sorry," I said in a small voice, looking shamefacedly at my bare feet.

His fingers stroked my cheek. "You have nothing to be sorry about. Let's just try to keep you safe until all this is over."

It sounded so ominous in my ears, 'when this is over'. I hoped I wasn't the only one concerned about the possibilities for that upcoming end.

Falsely bright, James stepped back and grabbed my hands. "Don't you need to do some shopping?"

"What?" Shopping was the last thing on my mind right now.

"We have a wedding to attend in two days where you will unveil me." He waved his hands up and down in front of his body like a game show hostess. "Then, maybe something a bit more formal for my unveiling of you in Scotland."

"Uh oh. What does a human wear when she is being presented as a girlfriend or snack to ancient vampires?" I didn't feel the lightheartedness I tried to portray.

"Why don't I send you with the girls to the store and you can figure that out. They are pretty familiar with our vampiric flair for drama." I could figure out what girls he was talking about and I wasn't so sure they would care for their assignment. He misinterpreted my reticence. "It is too risky for Bradley to mount an attack in a large department store in broad daylight and this might be your last chance to get out before we go."

Ignoring his misguided reassurance, I latched on to his other comment. "So is that part true? Vampires *do* like to dress fancy?" I had seen the movies and the vampires were always dressed to the nines.

"Some do like to dress dramatically all the time, but most of us live amongst humans and try to tone it down a bit. Look at me, I am always understated." He looked so innocent, like he actually believed what he was saying.

"Are you kidding? You could be wearing a potato sack and you still wouldn't be understated." With his looks, it was hard to imagine him blending in to the crowd anywhere. Could Patrick Dempsey fit in at the local grocery store on a Saturday morning? Not even in sweat pants.

Ch. 27

In a shopping threesome I never thought I would live to see, Tara, Tonya and I wandered through the Macy's downtown store. James and Troy had agreed to let me out of the house with the two cats accompanying me, daylight or no. As much as he tried to tell me he wasn't worried about a daytime attack downtown I could still see how hard it was for him to let me out of his sight. I had the feeling Henry had more to do with it than James, something that had me very scared. If Henry wanted me to pass inspection there was no way it was as inevitable as James would have me believe. That was just one more thing that made this shopping trip with two women who disliked me even more enjoyable.

We went through Macy's on a mission. Something fitting for a fall wedding for a cousin I hadn't seen in years. Normally I wouldn't stress out about it, but knowing that my family would be paying a lot of attention to me due to my sudden appearance with a date, I was very self-conscious. And what a date he was. Without realizing it, I had stopped in the dress department, thinking of James' hands on me, the way that he kissed my neck, just to the inside of my collarbone. I became aware of a frustrated sigh close beside me. Oops.

Turning to make an apology, I saw some dress possibilities on the racks behind them. Grateful for the distraction, I went between the two of them and into the nearest rack. The girls were surprisingly helpful. Tara showed herself to be incredibly skilled at matching my coloring and style. We settled on a gold satin sheath dress with a wide, light green upper bodice and straps that brought out the tiny flecks of green in my eyes. It was perfect and we even found a matching gold shawl to throw over my shoulders.

Tonya's shoe instincts proved exemplary. She found a heeled sandal matching the green in the dress perfectly. It was upscale enough for the wedding, but low enough to let me dance if the opportunity presented itself. Dancing. That thought stopped me in my tracks.

Dancing, on the rare occasion I had tried it, had never been enjoyable. However, despite my best efforts to avoid it, I had learned how to function on a dance floor with a reasonable amount of aptitude. Now, I relished the thought of dancing with James. It struck me, not for the first time how strange it was that I felt so closely bonded with James so quickly. Again, I assumed it was because we were meant to be together and this must be true love. Not that I would say that aloud; it sounded hokey even to me. But, how else could I explain the depth of my feelings for a man I had met less than two weeks ago. We had been spending a lot of time together and had been in some pretty emotional situations. And besides, people had fallen in love and gotten married in two weeks before. I felt the tentative peace settle in as I justified my devotion.

Finding the perfect dress for the wedding had only taken us an hour. It was lunchtime, my stomach announced noisily. Tonya smiled. "I agree. Anyone for sushi?" Of course the cats wanted fish; at least we had found something we had in common.

The three of us wandered down Nicollet and cut down Eighth to Hennepin and over to Seven. Seven was a bar I had read about in the Star Tribune. I never used to read the paper, but now that I knew the travel writer, I had to admit I had started reading some of the sections when I found them laying around the house.

The story I'd read didn't do the place justice. I knew they had all of the floors and the rooftop bar in the summer but I hadn't realized how many floors that was. They had the whole building. Following Tonya's lead, I let her heels on

191

the polished concrete guide me while I studied the sparsely modern décor in the dim light. Even midday the place could convince you it was after hours in Manhattan.

Once we were seated and looking at the menus, I saw Tara examining the cocktail menu. "Tara, how old are you?" She looked at me like I had a screw loose and Tonya bristled as well. I wasn't sure why they were so upset, then I realized there were two answers to that question. Feeling the red come up my neck, I stuttered, "I mean, how old does your drivers license say you are?"

Less annoyed, though still tight around her mouth she replied. "I'm nineteen. I think it's a good age for me."

Turning to our third member, I wanted to satisfy my curiosity there as well. "Tonya, how about you?"

Tonya was still scanning her menu and over the top of it I heard her answer. "Twenty-two, just like Troy."

Our server, a young black man named Thomas swaggered over, his eyes locked on Tonya. "Can I get you anything?" He gave her a wink.

Tonya, however, did not reciprocate. "We will have the Seven, Dynamite and Spicy Tuna rolls." Looking him right in the eye with a cold stare that would have sent most men packing, she answered him crisply. "And that's it." Getting the message, he cleared his throat and his professionalism returned. "I'll put those in and I'll be right back with three waters."

The bar wasn't very busy. It was lunchtime on a weekday and the nearest occupied table was on the opposite side of the restaurant. I thought it was safe to try to get some questions answered. This whole "thing" was all so new and I'd been so wrapped up in James that I hadn't learned much about my honorary clan.

192

"What do you do as time passes?" I was looking down at my menu. "When you don't get noticeably older?" There was no response for a minute, so I chanced a look at Tonya. She was glaring at me. A sideways glance confirmed that Tara was doing the same. They looked so much alike and I wasn't going to back down, I had to ask. "Are you really sisters?" Maybe that one would be less offensive.

Tara let out a big sigh. "We didn't start out as sisters, but we've been through a lot together." I sat perfectly still so as not to upset her or make her stop. "See, to become a part of our family, you have to have a certain something happen to you. Sometimes it is on purpose, sometimes it is accidental." She seemed to be open to sharing as long as it was ambiguous to those around us. I didn't think it would help if I pointed out to her that humans don't have as good of hearing as *they* did or the vampires. I just let her go on, hoping to learn as much as I could by being a silent audience.

"Tonya *is* older than me in some ways, but technically, I have lived more." Raising one eyebrow, she hinted that there was more to that story.

"Tonya was older when she joined the family but you've been in longer?"

Tara was pleasantly surprised that I was not as thick as she had presumed. "Yes. She *chose* to join us a bit later."

"Chose?" I interrupted, staring at Tonya.

"What did you think Tara meant by "something had to happen" to bring us together?"

"Well, I thought something happened that triggered it, that it was already inherent within you." What was a human equivalent? "Like growing boobs or something."

193

Tara erupted in laughter. She laughed so hard her eyes watered. Tonya was stifling her own amusement as well. They both loosened up after that and saw they were not going to be overheard by the other table.

As Tara was pulling herself back together, she took a sip of her water and I couldn't help but feel hopeful. I was starting to have some fun with these two and could see a big upside to gaining their respect. I had never had girlfriends I could talk to about *anything*. And considering my world just got a lot more complicated, it would be even better to have them.

Tonya took up the story, and still cautious, continued in a low voice. "The common shared experience my sister is referring to is the infecting bite we must suffer to make the change." She smiled when I paled.

Nodding, she continued. "Yes, those stories are true. One must be infected by the bite of an animal. It doesn't work if they are in their human form. Tara was bitten by a cat ranging in her area. She accidentally got between him and his kill."

My words came out before I could think to self-edit. "Kill? Was it animal, or…"

Tara responded flatly. "Human. I was trying to help but it was too late." Life flashed back into her eyes as she shook off the dark memory. "Depending on the were's control over their beast, human kills can be chosen. Sometimes they are even preferred."

That was a twist I had never considered. Somehow I couldn't see Stephen, Troy, or even one of these girls hunting down a human being to eat them. I *hoped* I would never see that anyway. "Really? What do you mean 'depending on the control over their beasts'?"

194

"You have seen that some like James and Henry are more human friendly than others like them, correct?" I nodded assent. "Well, weres are also divided on their affection for humans. I have known some that were discovered and pursued over the years by humans and, in frustration, now see hunting the humans for meat as justified revenge." At my gasp she smiled and pointed out, "Obviously we do not encourage such behavior. But be careful because not all of our kind share our clan's perspective on humans."

Clearing her throat, Tonya picked up the thread. "I, on the other hand, had heard of animals such as this and envied their strength, I saw it as an escape. I'd heard stories of a night creature near my home and during a full moon I took a sheep off of our farm and brought it far into the woods where I had heard hunters talking about the creature. They had come across large kills, like moose with a lot of meat taken off of them. The sheep was a big one and I knew that to bring something large in for the kill, I would have to maximize the blood scent. I slit its throat and with the legs tied, I dragged it all through the area. Then, I sat down to wait. It wasn't long before one of them was drawn in by the smell. I asked to be bitten, thinking he would understand except he was frenzied by the blood." She closed her eyes and paled from the memory.

I felt sick when I thought of her being ravaged by a cat as large as Stephen. My throat closed to choke down the bile. Sipping my water, I thought how absolutely terrifying that would have been for her. I couldn't imagine what could have been so horrible in her life she needed to escape to welcome such a thing.

Our food came and our reformed waiter looked only briefly at us to ask if there was anything else we needed for now. We all shook our heads and plated our sushi. The rolls looked great and we were hungry. We talked a little about some other stores where we could search for my more

195

formal dress that I would need to meet the court in Edinburgh.

Tara thought I should wear something more like a ball gown, which I could get back at Macy's. Tonya thought I should go more exotic. Maybe something Asian. Motioning toward me, Tonya embarrassed me by asking me to stand up. I wasn't sure why but didn't want to upset our newly forming friendship by being disagreeable so I did as I was asked. Tonya indicated with her hands toward me. "Look at that body. A ball gown hides too much. She needs to strut her stuff and impress the hell out of them if they are to decide favorably."

"What do you mean *if* they decide favorably?" The look they exchanged was all I needed. "I *knew* it was more serious than he let on." I was furious and underneath that I was terrified. "How can he lie to me like that? Aren't there enough monsters *here* who want to kill me without having to fly me half way around the world to be killed by *special* monsters?"

Tara was looking at me steadily. "Do you think so little of James that you do not trust his judgment?"

"Of course I trust him, but when you say they might not 'choose favorably,' how am I supposed to feel? I'm nervous. No, I'm scared stiff that I'm not coming home."

They both sat quietly for a moment. Tara popped a piece of spicy tuna into her mouth and Tonya ran her finger over the sides of her water glass. Tonya spoke first. "You love James." It wasn't a question. I nodded. "He loves you." I started to open my mouth, to mention some of my doubts on the equality of that emotion, but the look she gave me said that this was also not a question. Again, I nodded. "Trust me when I tell you that James has not had a human consort in a *very, very* long time. Henry tells me he has never brought *anyone* to the Court for approval so this is a huge

196

deal for him too. Please trust that he will be certain to keep you as safe as possible." She saw my eyebrows shoot up and maybe she had seen the sheen of sweat start on my forehead. Their kind could sense that stuff incredibly fast. "Yes, there will be some risk involved, there always is in these matters. However, they will not demand an action right then. They never do from what I understand. They like to consider things for a while and if they decide against you, they tell him to end it or send someone to 'clean up' as they put it if he is unwilling. Quite honestly, the only time I have heard of that happening is when someone picks their human unwisely and James has not done that." She shrugged seemingly unaware of the effect of her compliment on me. "I think they just like to relive the glory days of holding Court and find reasons to have people attend them."

Raising her hand to flag our waiter, Tara took a last swallow of her water. "Well, let's go get you sexy then."

Sexy was not something I had ever considered myself so I couldn't help but giggle. "We can try."

Ch. 28

It was nearly dinnertime when they dropped me off at James' house. He was waiting for us and opened the door as I came up the walk.

"Well, aren't we the eager beaver." Tara muttered under her breath.

James heard her when he opened my door. "I miss her when she's gone." His eyes never left mine as he called back to them. I could feel the heat come right up the back of my neck, ducking my head to hide my reaction. I felt him put his arm around me as we crossed the thresh hold. His lips tickled my ear as he whispered. "You know I get a private showing." His fingers tapped the bag with a rustle. My ears burned hot, despite the eager shiver that went up my spine at the promise behind his words. I barely heard the engine fading as the girls drove down the street.

His hand slid down my shoulders lightly trailing its path down my back, ending low on my waist. "Shall we then?"

Yes we shall, I nodded, not trusting my voice.

We went upstairs to "our room." I was able to get myself out of my jeans and long sleeved tee and slapping James' hands away when he tried to help pull my shirt over my head. "You behave and go sit down over there," I pointed to the chair in the corner opposite the bed. Dutifully he sat resting his hands in his lap. It was awkward at first with him watching, but I began to enjoy it and took my time when I heard his breathing stop. First, I tried on the dress for the wedding. I had to go to him to be zipped up. James' fingers lingered at the top of the zipper, tracing my shoulder blades. I had to close my eyes and take a few deep breaths to keep control of myself.

"You sir, are not helping." I felt his warm breath on my back as he chuckled softly. He had just fed if the warmth of the reheated blood had not yet faded from his lungs. "Did you want to see my dresses or not?" Uncertainty crept into my voice. "I *would* like to know what you think of them. I don't usually have people paying that close of attention to me so I'm pretty nervous about all of this."

His hands rested on my bare shoulders and he turned me around to face him. Blue eyes penetrating my own from just inches away. "You are a beautiful woman and you will make the bride weep for jealousy." My heart skipped, James smiled when he heard his effect on me.

"Were you this smooth as a human or have you just gotten good with years of practice?" I teased.

He didn't answer instead he held me out at an arms length and let go. Crossing his arms, he made a show of giving me a once over. He walked all the way around me, his scrutiny only serving to heighten my paranoia that I had chosen poorly.

"What do you think, do you think I look good enough to impress the family?"

A hint of a grin lifted one side of his mouth. "Love, you are breath taking."

"You are so good for my ego, James. I don't know that I believe you all the time, but I like to hear you say it." I leaned in for a kiss.

Sighing he pulled away. "We'd better stop or we'll ruin that dress before you have the chance to show it off. That would be a shame, it looks good."

I smiled and turned around. "Unzip me, please."

"With pleasure," came his rough reply. He unzipped me then continued to help to slide the dress off of my shoulders and down my body. It landed on the chair he'd vacated with a soft rustle.

Ch. 29

I rolled over next to him in bed and smiled lazily. "Care to try the second dress? The one for *them*." It was hard to hide my trepidation over the whole thing.

Propped up on an elbow, my hero didn't fail me. "If the Court doesn't approve then we will simply run away together. They cannot destroy what they cannot find." He said it without the faintest hint of jest and I wondered if he was serious, if we could do that.

"James, can I try something?"

He lay perfectly still and looked into my face, studying it with a mild expression. "Feel free."

Putting my hand out, I laid it very gently on his bicep. It was hard to concentrate when all I wanted to do was to run my hands over his body. My addiction to him was powerful and it took all of my focus to bring my thoughts back to my experiment. Re-focusing myself, I stilled my hand and lowered my shields carefully. I could feel that he had lowered his enough for me to try this. Despite his apparent lack of curiosity I knew that he was very aware of everything I was doing and was following my lead.

Like we'd done in our first sessions together my mind reached down only this time I was more specific in what I was looking for. I knew it as soon as he figured out what I was doing and I felt my access closing off. Flicking my eyes up to his I pleaded gently, "please."

Outwardly he said nothing. Inside I felt the barriers evaporate. I gasped and jerked my hand off of his arm. Seeing James' normally confident face vulnerable moved me almost as much as what I had felt. He had let me feel his love for me. It was overwhelming. Not like it used to be when I touched people without shielding. It was astonishing in its strength and certainty. It wasn't fleeting like all of his other emotions; this one had been stronger and more established. His love for me did not feel vampire, it felt human.

"You love me."

The uncertainty still wavered in his gaze. "I told you that I did."

"But, you *really* love me. Like I love you."

He wrapped me in his arms then and let me *see* it again. Lying there with him, I was overcome and felt the tears roll down my face and splash his cooling chest. His fingers lifted my chin up to look at him and I was ashamed of myself. "Look what you've done to me James. I don't cry and here you are making me cry all the time. I've lost track of how often I've gone gooey this week."

Kissing my tears he answered tenderly. "I won't tell."

"James," not trusting my voice enough to answer louder than a whisper, "I've lived my whole life pretending it was okay that I was never going to have anyone. Even when Stephen got me started the best I hoped for was a little more peace and quiet. My life was going to be so simple. Now you've ruined all of that for me. I feel as though if you went away it would tear me apart." Hating the raw need I could hear in my voice, I continued, my words spilling forth unchecked. "Promise me you will stay with me."

"Forever, Love." His eyes were nearly midnight.

"But what if things change for you? What if I'm not approved? You can't really leave your life behind, even for an oath." I didn't want to think of him ruining his life for me

202

if things changed. Even I knew love couldn't last forever for a human and a vampire. Not *his* forever.

He cut me off abruptly. "You are a stubborn woman Claire. I love you for you. Not because of my oath. However, that does require me to stay *very* close by at all times." He nuzzled my neck giving me goose bumps. "I hope you don't mind?" My doubts could not outweigh my need to be close and I let him change the subject.

"Didn't you have another dress to show me? Something that will impress the hell out of the Court?"

Sighing, I sat up. "Are you making me leave this bed?"

He pulled me back down with an impish grin. "I will *never make* you leave this bed. We can have someone send food up a few times a day and stay here forever. But I do like the fashion show. It is very flattering knowing this is all for me."

Confidence inspired by his declaration made me reckless. "James, this," I waved my arm over my nude body and his eyes followed, "is all for you. The dresses are for our respective families. But it does help that you like them."

"The Court is not my family." He grew somber. "However it is necessary to gain their approval for our long term courtship or they will not leave us in peace."

"Then don't let it be said I was rejected for poor fashion." I declared with false bravado. Rising from bed I did my best to saunter over to the dress bag hanging over the back of the closet door. The show was back on for my audience of one and this time I put a little more swing in my hips.

I heard him growl and smiled as I grabbed a bra to put on. The dress wouldn't look right without it. This one I could get on by myself and I did so with my back to him, a gutsy move by me. It felt good that I heard his breath stop as I turned around to face him.

Tonya had won. We went exotic. She said that it set off my dark features and prominent bone structure. My cheekbones had always bothered me. I thought they stuck out but Tara and Tonya had decided that they were elegant and should be shown off. The dress itself was a black classic Chinese style that ended mid thigh. The neck had a higher collar with gold knotted buttons in a diagonal line down to the bust. From there the buttons were internal and not visible leading to an uninterrupted line in the design, allowing it to hug my body in ways that left little to the imagination.

"I'll have my hair up, maybe in chopsticks. You know, keeping the theme," I said holding my hair up for effect. He was staring at me, body propped on an elbow. It was bugging me that he still hadn't said what he thought of it. I was beginning to feel my nerve waver. "Well, do you like it? Do you think *they'll* like it?" Holding up a finger I made a short dash for the pile of bags. "Oh yeah, the shoes." Digging them out, I put on the high satin heels and did a small spin with my arms out. "Well?" It was killing me he wasn't talking. This was nerve wracking. What I was wearing, where we were going. I needed some reassurances that we were going to be okay. That I was going to live to see Christmas. "Come on James, I'm dying here. Opinions?"

Standing up completely nude, he walked over. It was my turn to sigh. I was sure he could hear my heart thumping with both fear and excitement. He was always in tune to my reactions. It made me self-conscious that everyone in this house had super senses and knew when I was feeling anything of any importance.

"This has me worried." His eyes were dark, hooded beneath his lowered lids.

My stomach knotted. "What? Do you think I should return it?"

He grabbed me and folded me into his arms. "No, I am worried someone will want you for his own and I will have to defend my claim. It could get ugly."

It didn't matter whether he was just saying that to make me feel better, I liked hearing him say it.

Ch. 30

We all spent the next day around the house. Tomorrow was the wedding and we had a lot to do before James and I would be indisposed for the evening. The Andrews were in and out all day, still ranging far and wide to learn what they could.

So far neither James nor Henry had been able to get any information from Milwaukee. It was as if William, the leader of the coven out there, had just vanished. There had been a suspicious fire at his office, but no other information could be found. No witnesses, no nothing. Henry said that there had been times in the past when William had taken his coven and "gone underground" for safety.

Another one we had not been able to find was Stephen. No one had seen him since the night of the attack at the library and we all felt his absence. His clan tried to cover for him. It seemed to me they knew something we didn't, since they didn't complain about it. Tara wasn't the type to let him slack in his duties unless something was up. They just agreed that he was uncharacteristically absent of late. I needed to see him before I went to Europe.

I called his cell phone and he answered on the third ring. There was a tremendous amount of noise in the background. I had to concentrate on his voice, but still had a hard time differentiating the sounds around him. It sounded like he was near a train yard or train tracks.

"Claire," he panted out of breath. "I was going to call. Can you get everyone together at the house later?"

"Sure, Stephen," I thought it was awfully easy to get him to agree to meetings, hopefully this one worked out better than the last. "We're all around today so it shouldn't be a problem. What time are you thinking?"

"I should be back around five. Can you get them together then?"

"No problem, Stephen." His wording struck me strangely, "Back from where, Stephen?"

"I'll explain when I get there. See you at five." The line went dead.

Perplexed, I was lost in my own head when Troy came into the living room where I was lounging on the couch. Even though he spoke softly I started, nearly dropping the phone still in my hands. "Who was that, Claire?"

"Stephen. He said he wants a meeting with everyone at five tonight when he gets back. Gets back from where?" I hoped for a hint.

"I'm sure he'll explain when he gets here."

"Troy, what's going on here?" I worried he was in trouble and needed help or maybe he had been sent away. My instincts said his family knew what was going on although I didn't think Henry or James knew any more than I did.

Troy couldn't be motivated to give up anything. "I'll let Stephen explain himself."

"You know this whole 'I'll live for a super long time so I have all the patience in the world' thing gets really old. My time is limited and I hate to wait."

Troy chuckled and left the room. I failed to see the humor.

Ch. 31

I had tons of homework since I was gone the better part of the week on a "medical leave," while I healed. Most of it remained unfinished, staring up at me from where I spread it out around me on the couch. My mind was a mess and it made the day creep slowly by. My previous suspicions were confirmed when, with my shopping errand complete, James was no longer willing to concede daytime as safe. He had declared me housebound and was himself unwilling to leave me for any reason. As a result, he was spending a lot of time on the phone and confined to his upstairs office. He was checking with people from all over the midwest trying to find out anything he could on the incoming coven and how they fit with Bradley.

Eventually, I could stare at my books no more and tucked them all away in a pile next to the couch and followed the hum of James' voice up to his office. His office was in the first upstairs bedroom on the right. The wooden furnishings were minimal and masculine, in keeping with the rest of the house. In my mind's eye I could see him sitting at his desk staring at his laptop with his back to the bed and night table. The small bookshelf filled with travel books he occasionally referenced acted as a table at the foot of the bed. Since no one had been sleeping in there this afternoon, he had virtually locked himself in since breakfast.

Before I was halfway up the stairs I knew he was speaking to a human, most likely someone at the paper because I could hear parts of actual words. It was always lower and deeper, harder to distinguish when he spoke to other vampires or the cats. I would assume it's because they'd grown accustomed to hiding their voices that they always talked to each other like that. Though I was sure he could hear my approach, I tried to sneak anyway. He seemed to be losing patience with whomever he was talking to; at least, it sounded that way from the one side of the conversation I could hear.

"It doesn't matter to me what they think. Yes, I want to stay there. Because last time I went I was barely in my room, if you must know, and I doubt that will be the case this time. No, you're right, I don't have to share any more than that and I don't intend to. I don't care what he has budgeted, he isn't the one paying for her." He paused while the other party responded at length. Sighing, he reached the end of his tether. "I don't care what they're gossiping about in the office. The point is that I am required, by contract, to write an article and I will write one. The fact that I choose to bring a companion and," his voice raised as he spoke over some objection from the other party, "and my companion is a woman whom I happen to be involved with is not the office staff's concern." My pulse went up when he flicked an eye my way. He had noticed me, of course, though I wasn't sure if what he was saying now on the phone was for my benefit or the other party's. "We have our travel plans made. Whether I pay or you do is not my concern." Hanging up, James closed his eyes and rolled his chair back from his desk, waving me over to join him.

Settling onto his lap, I snuggled in as he brought his arms up to wrap around me. I put my head on his chest and listened to his silent heart. It wasn't as creepy as I would have anticipated. His stillness was something that I found comforting now that I was used to it. Maybe it was because I had never lain with anyone before and had nothing to compare to. Either way, I didn't find it odd that his heart didn't beat or that his breathing was merely habit. That and the act of bringing air into his system allowed him to appear human to others and to smell scents around him.

Sitting here with him, it didn't bother me anymore that Stephen was coming in a few hours for a meeting about something that I could only wonder at, or that we were going to the wedding for a cousin I could barely stand where James would meet my whole family tomorrow, or that in just a few days I would be neck deep in vampires who might not like me. Being with James made everything bearable because I was here with him. It struck me again as odd that we were so in love so quickly. That was on my mind a lot lately. And again, I tried to justify the strangeness of it on the "quality" of time and how many hours in each day we had spent together. With him not needing sleep and always being around, we pretty much talked around the clock. I never *had* slept well, so I was up in the night often enough to talk to him then, and of course during the daytime when we worked together and just went about the business of being.

"James, I should never have opened the door in just your shirt. I didn't mean to cause you any trouble at work. Gossip is never fun." I did feel bad, yet at the same time I was happy that they all knew now that he was mine. He wasn't the only one who was possessive.

"Claire, I told you I don't care that they know I have you in my life. Did I tell you Beth is a pot stirrer?"

I noticed he was trying to look more upset than he really was. One corner of his mouth twitched and I knew he was secretly amused.

"Sure, she likes to get everyone up in arms so she did a very thorough job of describing you and what you were wearing and how well you distracted me."

I flushed. "How do you know, did she tell you?"

"No, my editor and I have worked together for a few years, and he wanted to know who the hot little number answering the door in my clothes might be." His eyes twinkled merrily, he was definitely finding it entertaining to be causing a fuss at the office.

"Oh no!" I groaned. "You mean she told them I was virtually naked answering your door?"

"Oh yes, you would be happy though. I guess Beth was honest in her description of you. She explained how attractive you were and how I couldn't keep my hands or eyes off of you. Apparently we barely managed to keep our hands off each other while she was here; we practically ran her off."

Mortification turned to giggles. "I can only imagine how the girls in the office feel about that one. You being off the market has to be causing some tears over there."

He shrugged offhandedly. "There can't be that many. I was always polite when I declined any offers."

"Offers? How frequently do you get propositioned at work?"

He pulled me in close, probably so that I couldn't see him grinning in the wake of my jealousy. "They didn't ask as often as you are imagining. And don't worry, I have never been anything but a perfect gentleman with the staff."

Keeping my eyes to where I was fingering his collar, I asked him under my breath the question I couldn't manage to get out of my mind, even though I knew I should, "James, everyone keeps telling me how long it has been since you have had a," what word to use here, "lover. How long has it been?"

He went still under me and I started to think he wouldn't answer at all. "Claire, I told you that I do not take lovers lightly and you were the first in a long time. I am willing to talk to you about my past, but first you should ask yourself if you really want to know all of what a man has done in a century and a half or if that has any bearing on what you think of him."

I didn't answer him right away, stroking his collar smooth unnecessarily as I contemplated his counterargument. When

I answered I managed to meet his eyes with some degree of certainty. "I want to know everything about what makes you you, but I guess I don't know if I want to know *that*. Let's hold off on the long list of lovers for now. Especially since I only have one on my list. It's kind of humbling."

He looked down at me, expression troubled. "Does it bother you that we are not equally experienced?"

Thinking about it for a moment, I was able to reply honestly, "No, I got lucky and found the right one on my first try."

He squeezed me against him and kissed my head. It was hard to hear him as he mumbled into my hair, "My list is not so long as you might think, my love." When I tried to look up to see his eyes, he held me tightly to him so that I could not.

Ch. 32

Five-thirty and still no Stephen. We were all together in the house, it was fully dark outside and none of the many sets of eyes watching for him had yet to announce his arrival. Henry had arrived about forty-five minutes ago in anticipation of Stephen's news. I was pretty sure the Andrews knew what we would hear tonight, while the vampires and I were very eager to learn what our friend had been up to this past week.

James and I were at the table having a snack. I was munching absently on an apple and James was drinking from his travel cup while working on his laptop. Troy was on the couch reading a National Geographic, Tonya and Tara were upstairs and Henry was on the chair in the living room reading a book that looked very old and brittle. I had been watching everyone and noted how perfectly human we all looked. No one would know that we were unusual in any way if they were to happen by at this moment.

With silent, catlike grace, Tonya and Tara appeared out of nowhere at the bottom of the stairs behind the couch. Tara spoke up first, "Stephen's here." I couldn't help jumping and almost dropped my apple, catching it just before it hit the floor. My reflexes were improving I noticed. Interesting. James lifted an eyebrow at me, he had noticed as well.

Troy eyed Tara expectantly. She shook her head the tiniest bit and sounded disappointed. "He's alone."

Now I was sure they knew what he had been doing. Who was the other person he was supposed to have with him? I hopped up from the table so fast I banged my knee on the underside of the table. *Yes, still human*, I growled at myself. Tonya glanced over at the sound and snorted. I thought I heard a derisive comment about humans from one of the cats.

The doorknob turned and he was there. My heart leapt into my throat as I watched my friend walk into the living room. Tonya shut the door behind him. Stephen looked like a soldier returning from war. He had bags under his eyes, his shaggy hair was dirty and greasy, dried blood crusted over one ear and what I could readily see of his face and arms was covered in partially healed scratches and gouges. Most alarming was the fact that he was almost as pale as Henry and James when they were hungry. Because he was wearing a t-shirt and jeans, I couldn't see any more physical evidence of the price of his week away, but I ventured to guess that he was probably damaged under his clothing as well. The left cheek James had almost torn off a few days ago was still swollen and yellowed, even though it should have been healed by now. It was almost hidden under a large, fresh, purple bruise distorting the side of his nose.

"Stephen!" I rushed to him.

He saw me coming and put an exhausted smile on his face making him look more like my reckless young friend. When I threw my arms around his neck, he rocked back and winced, groaning with the impact. Cursing myself for my thoughtlessness, I pulled back and looked into his hazel eyes seeing fatigue and torment. "I'm sorry. You're hurt, what was I thinking? Come sit, can I get you something?" I asked as I led him by the hand to the couch. Troy had moved over to make room on the end closest to the door.

Stephen followed and sat with me taking a spot next to him. Henry remained in his chair, James stood behind him and the Andrews sisters took up seats on the floor in front of the couch, graceful as always.

Troy locked the door and prodded him to speak. "Stephen, I'm happy to see you back with us. I think it might be best

214

to catch everyone up before you tell us what you have learned."

Stephen sat up straighter with visible effort. "Our local search for information on the incoming force was not fruitful, as you know, so we decided I should sneak out to do some investigating in Milwaukee."

It occurred to me that because of his youthful countenance, I underestimated him. He was clearly much more capable than I gave him credit for. Maybe that was a common phenomenon and was why he was chosen as the spy.

He went on. "We weren't sure what their business had been in Milwaukee, but knowing they were friendly to Bradley and he isn't friendly to us, we thought it best to act the part of a defector."

"We?" I aimed my suspicious glare at Troy.

Troy explained the reasoning, undaunted, "Vampires are infamous liars and we couldn't begin to know which ones to trust other than those here in this room. To avoid detection through any means known or unknown we thought it best that only our clan know the details of Stephen's mission."

The thought that there were more unfriendly vampires beyond Bradley's private army, possibly even within Henry's own coven, gave me pause. I sought James' eyes and saw that he was not surprised by Troy's words. A brief survey of the faces seated around me revealed that *only* I had been oblivious to the dangers lurking beyond the one known threat.

Henry regarded Stephen with clear respect. "Please Stephen, go on."

215

"When I got to Milwaukee it was a mess. The leadership there has been massacred. I'm sorry Henry, I know you and William were allies."

Henry and James stared at Stephen in shock while the Andrews' took the news in stride. They had heard this before.

Weary, Stephen lay back on the cushions behind him. He was whipped. "No information was getting out because the coven we've been waiting for and their leader, Gaston, were very thorough. There were no surviving witnesses. The most I could gather was that Gaston and his coven came through Chicago from out of nowhere a few weeks ago. He runs his coven like a military outfit. He has four others with him, three men and one woman and they all have experience with 'wet work. I'm sure you're familiar with the term. They came up, and in typical vampire formality, requested an audience with William. I got there too late to help," he told the vampires apologetically.

Henry's face was impassive, anything he was feeling was well hidden away. He gave a simple nod; they must have been close. Henry was having a lot of trouble with Stephen's news if he was locking himself down like this; I could see the stillness in him as he tried to carefully maintain his composure. James stared at Stephen, eyes and lips very tight waiting for him to go on.

"William and his coven weren't a big one, but I would assume strong enough to hold their own. I couldn't get a solid number from anyone there, though. Do you two know how many were loyal to him?"

James replied coldly. "There were thirteen in his coven."

"Well, William's coven accepted the request to pay their respects last weekend. The little I could get was that Gaston told William they wanted to join his coven, and since that

216

would upset his patron Bradley, they needed to keep it just between the two of them. Because William honored his request for secrecy, no one but the members of the coven were present when Gaston and his crew showed for their requested 'private' meeting. The last anyone saw of William's coven was when Gaston walked into the downtown office and they locked up Sunday night. Whatever happened is gone with the evidence. The building was burned to the ground along with the adjoining two buildings. There are no signs of what might have gone on."

Five vampires had taken down thirteen. I marveled at the power they must have, while at the same time feeling the loss of at least thirteen more we could have counted on as friends, should we find ourselves at war.

Stephen's eyes were closed, his breathing shallow. This trip had cost him much both emotionally and physically. "Stephen, if the battle was over when you arrived, then what happened to you and why have you been gone so long?"

Turning his head, he opened his haunted eyes to me suddenly lifetimes older. "When you thought I was chasing guys last week, you were right; it just wasn't the fun kind. I ran to Milwaukee and was trying to get into the city. With the leadership of a coven gone, there are a lot of other not as friendly groups trying to fill the void. Everybody is seen as a threat and there were a few skirmishes when I tried to get through."

"But when I saw you a few days ago, you weren't hurt." Well, that wasn't entirely true. He was unharmed until James tried to kill him on my account. As if he'd heard me, James glanced over, although he didn't look very apologetic. Actually, he looked like he was on the verge of getting very scary, very fast. His eyes had changed to black and I saw the beginnings of fangs starting to grow from behind his tight lips. Henry's control was better. His face and body were

217

still with no feigned breathing giving him the air of a dead man. I wasn't sure which reaction was more frightening.

Stephen's voice cut in on my musings. "It wasn't my body that took the beating the first time." I whipped my head around, confused. "*Someone*, I'm assuming Bradley, has brought up another coven, hoping to set them up to take charge of the city in William's absence. There are only three of them but they're strong and at least one of them has abilities I've never seen." Rubbing his eyes, Stephen was growing visibly weaker. He had to get some sleep soon. "The leader is Sasha, a Cajun woman with an amazing ability to stun. She was able to knock me down from a full run in my animal form."

Tonya gasped in shock.

"Is that harder than when you're in your human form?" I asked, ever the naive human.

Tara was subdued without a hint of sarcasm. She must have been pretty upset too. "When we are in our animal form, we are at our strongest. Almost as strong as a vampire and our animal form usually keeps us immune to any of their mind tricks."

"So this woman was able to knock you down when you were a cat? What else happened?" I reached out and took Stephen's hand. He squeezed it tight enough to hurt. My shields were taking a beating from the waves of anger and fear I felt emanating from him. His exhaustion was apparent in his inability to keep his own up with any consistency. I could feel them come and go as he fought to focus, stay awake, and keep himself together. My poor Stephen, I had never felt as protective as I did right at that moment.

His eyes closed, Stephen whispered his response so quietly I had to strain to hear him. "She has two other women with her, also Cajun. Bradley just brought them up from

Louisiana but nobody knows why them specifically, only that they are close to taking the city because no one will dare take them on. I caught up with them in a park off the lake, where I'd heard they were hunting at night. Sasha took me by surprise. She held me still while they cut me up." He broke off as his voice caught. "No silver, no chains, just her mind."

"Stephen, what did she want? Why would they do that to you?" My instinct was to comfort him yet I knew his duty was to report. My stomach turned at the thought of someone causing him that level of pain.

"She wanted to find out what clan I was with and if I was affiliated with any covens. They were waiting for us."

Henry came back to life. His ghoulish mien mirrored James' and his voice was cold and dark. "Stephen, did she get anything from you? Can you recall?"

Stephen shook his head no. "She tried for two days before her hold broke. They got nothing."
"What does that mean, to break her hold?"

Henry answered me, voice tight and clipped. "Thirst. That kind of power is draining and requires a lot of blood to maintain. She had to feed."

Stephen nodded an affirmative. "When she broke her hold, I changed and ran back here as fast as I could. My equilibrium was off. They messed up something in my head. I fell a few times and got scuffed up, but changing helped me to heal most of it."

James slowly reanimated and walked toward Stephen with a curious look on his face. "Stephen, what else is 'messed up' in your head?"

219

Stephen's eyes popped wide open, he shot up in his seat. "What do you think she did?" His panic was hard to handle. He had been through so much.

I was having a hard time following what was going on, handicapped by my huge knowledge gaps. Regardless of my comprehension, the need to comfort my friend was reaching critical and I wasn't sure how much more pain I could watch him endure.

James crouched down in front of Stephen, hands inches from the poor man's knees when I broke in. "James, leave him alone. He's exhausted."

The sharpness in my tone brought James up short. His black gaze turned toward me and for a fraction of a moment I felt the stirrings of fear. Feeling my reaction to him, he turned back to Stephen addressing me over his shoulder. "Claire, there are things about us you do not yet understand. Vampires can do things no other creature can do, find things in your mind without your knowledge and then erase the memory of it. It leaves the trace of a scent and by using my sensitivity to her ability, I can track what she found. No one is accusing him of weakness. What Stephen did took great courage." He looked back at me some color back in his eyes, yet I saw a flash of his fangs when he spoke. "I won't hurt Stephen. I promise you that."

James' hands rested lightly upon the tops of Stephen's where they clutched his own knees anxiously. He sat rigidly on the couch. The pall in the room was suffocating as James tied into Stephen's ravaged mind.

James did something and Stephen's eyes glazed over and his face went slack. I saw the ghost of the girl in my dorm that night when James had told her what to say if anyone came asking for me. James' spine went rigid, his head jerked up and the low rumble emanating from his body again made me fear for what had been done to Stephen, and also what it must mean for us now. The rumble spiked to a roar and he broke off from Stephen jumping to his feet. "God damn her!"

His passion brought forth everyone's fears in a heartbeat. Henry took command. "James, what did she get? What did you sense?"

James was all vampire now, so preoccupied that he did nothing to hide it from me this time. When he turned around to answer Henry, the perfect skin had paled and hardened with the muscle cording taut below the surface. His jaw held clenched so firmly, he spoke only through his lips stretched thin over his fully extended fangs, which were visible through his snarl. I stared in fascination. His fangs were not long like a wolf, they were thick like human canine teeth usually are, only a half inch longer to make them more effective. This was how my James looked when he hunted and killed. The two sides of my lover were having a hard time meshing in my head. They were two different people and I couldn't marry the two together no matter how I tried. This James was a stranger, and he scared the hell out of me.

Jumping to his feet, James spoke furiously. "She rolled him."

Stephen cursed.

"She must have old magic from her human life. I would guess she was strong before she was turned, she hasn't been a vampire long enough to have such tremendous power. She knows the clan is allied with a vampire, the mark of the bond is too deep to hide." He rolled his shoulders. "She also saw enough of the school to know where we are. It is only a matter of time before she learns of the bond between Henry and the clan from Bradley's people and figures out exactly where to find us. Everyone Stephen knows through us is in danger." I could feel a sense of dread as he spoke my name and turned to me with cold, black eyes. "Claire, she saw you." I felt faint. "She knows you are also tied to a vampire. She believes it is the same vampire as Stephen. She is looking for a very strong vampire, one capable of holding you both. She spent a lot of time digging into that. She is most interested in Henry's identity, but that was protected by Stephen's bond. She will go to the cats' dens first. I didn't see my house or yours Henry so I believe we have a day, maybe more before she is able to sniff us out."

The room was quiet. As opposed to the chaos I was expecting, when they spoke it was rational. Troy spoke for his clan. "Henry, this is your fight and it is your play we follow on Bradley and this Gaston. But this woman Sasha has struck against my family, we must respond. I would ask you to grant my family leave to seek our own justice."

Without pause, Henry granted his request hinting he'd known it was coming. "I would think we have a day or more before our enemies converge here in Minneapolis. I leave to your discretion what you do with those days. I wish you luck in your pursuit. Let me know if I can be of any help. James and Claire, you leave tomorrow as planned and go straight from there to Edinburgh. They are least likely to look for you there." I caught James' look of surprise at the order. "James, you are responsible for keeping her safe until you can meet with the Court. If they get their hands on Claire it will hamper your willingness to fight and we cannot have that now. I am sorry but we can spare no one. If you want her you must protect her."

Stephen was barely keeping his eyes open. Henry continued to act as commander. "Tara, please take your brother to get him washed up and resting." Seeing Stephen start to object, Henry raised a hand. "Stephen, you have done more than any of us could have asked. Take this chance to rest. You will have your chance at revenge." That either placated Stephen or he lacked the energy to argue and he went with Tara up the stairs.

222

Making use of the opening, I looked to James to explain something he had said at the beginning, something I'd never heard before. "What do you mean she rolled him?"

When he turned to me his eyes remained dark, though the vampire was receding. I saw him fighting it down. "Vampires can see into people's heads; the older the vampire the better he is at it. She had to be strong to see into his thoughts even through his defenses. We were just lucky Stephen was strong enough to blur most of it for her in spite of all she did to him." Horrified, I listened without interrupting. I wished, not for the first time, that I wasn't being counted among our liabilities or that we had to leave them here to face who knew what. I was frightened what we would come back to.

Letting the others who actually *could* do something useful to help have a chance to talk, I wandered into the kitchen to get a glass of water. As I stood with my hand on the glass and faucet, a pair of familiar hands covered the tops of my arms. The coolness felt good in my anxious, heated state. Without a word I leaned back into him. My future was with him, I knew that. I only wished I knew how long that future would be. And how violently it would end.

The house was large, yet felt too crowded as the evening wore on and plans were made. I went upstairs to take a long bath in James' huge claw foot tub, closing my eyes so I could meditate and calm my nerves. Shielding was hard when the emotions around me were so strong and I was not nearly talented enough to withstand such a constant barrage. *Their* defenses were not enough to keep back all of the heat they were throwing out.

My meditation had succeeded and I was beginning to drift off into an exhausted sleep when I felt the water around me move. I slid over to let him slip into the tub beside me, pulling me onto his chest. I lay against him, enjoying his stillness.

223

The water eventually cooled aided by James' low body temperature. He pulled the plug and pulled me out of the water without letting go. I let him towel me off as if I was a child and lead me into the bedroom. He dropped one of his undershirts over my head and I put my arms through, enjoying the soft feel of the cotton on my chilled skin. Being taken care of was a luxury I had not enjoyed since my earliest childhood when I first became aware I was different from other people. Preferring distance to touch had its costs. His possessive touch comforted me as I drifted off to sleep. I didn't move until the dawn broke the next morning.

Ch. 33

When I woke, James was already downstairs. I could hear his low timbre mixing with Henry's softer tone and Troy's clipped manner of speech. I followed the medley of wordless tones downstairs, looking for breakfast. The stress of last night had left me ravenous. Curious. Stress usually made me nauseous. The change gave me hardly a second's pause. One more weird thing in my life wasn't going to freak me out at this point.

They were in the dining room, sitting at the table with a map out. James and Henry had their covered mugs; that was James' doing. I was grateful for the lids hiding the sight of blood so early in the morning. Troy's empty breakfast plate had been pushed off to the side. I knew he usually liked to eat a big meal and I was bummed I'd overslept that feast, my usual English muffin didn't sound like enough this morning. James' smoky blue eyes caught me as I entered the room and warmed when I smiled at him. He smiled back, perfectly relaxed, and I felt that tug inside my center.

"Good morning Claire." It never failed to amaze me how he could invoke such a physical reaction from me with the most casual of gestures.

Still a bit groggy, I pushed my hair back with my hand. I wished for the millionth time that I had gotten my dad's straight hair.

The English muffins were next to the toaster, I honed in on them the minute I entered the kitchen. Perfect. I put one in and set the kettle on the stove while I waited for the toaster to pop. The men were still talking in the other room and I was leaning on the counter, dozing, thinking how much it felt like a home with the sound of their voices trailing into the kitchen.

Feeling mellow, I walked into the dining room a few minutes later with my plate in my hand. James got up and motioned for me to sit in his chair since the fourth place at the table was taken up with atlases and books. He hovered between the others while I ate my breakfast and was almost done when the kettle whistled. Tea in hand, I returned a few minutes later to retake my seat.

I must have been more tired or distracted than I thought because I noticed that, although I could make out what they were saying, I wasn't absorbing the details. Instead of grasping what should have been straightforward plans, my lack of focus was blurring every few words so that I could no longer make sense of things. It didn't matter, their voices were all I wanted to hear, not the words. Knowing we were all here gave me some minor comfort. Rubbing my temple I worried a headache was coming on.

"Claire." James left them to approach me while I was finishing my second cup of tea. "Are you feeling alright?" He sounded concerned.

My voice surprised me. It was flat, my tongue sluggish and hard to maneuver in my mouth. "I'm fine. Did you get everything sorted out?"

He eyed me strangely. "Yes, we have everything pretty well ironed out, down to some much needed outside help. We were able to find some more locals willing to step in; William was respected."

Waving a hand limply in the air I cut him off. "You don't need to tell me, I heard you. I'm sure it will all work out. When are we leaving?"

Brow furrowed, he put his hand to my head, tipping my face back so that he could look into my eyes. "If it makes you feel better, we work very well together as a family, our clan and us. This will be over before you know it."

I smiled lazily, perfectly accepting. "Okay."

His features stiffened as he tipped his face and called out low and urgent over his shoulder. "Henry, come in here." Those vampires sure were fast, I thought to myself when Henry appeared out of nowhere.

James spoke too low for me to hear. This time I could barely hear even the hum of his voice. I usually loved to hear him talk about anything at all. Again, he turned my face to his and I saw his lips moving but didn't register anything he was saying. He looked in my eyes, lifting the lids and turning my head into the light. Henry checked my pulse and poked at me too before mumbling something else to James. He looked a little panicky as he followed Henry to the kitchen. Out of nowhere, I felt incredibly tired. Rising, I started to walk toward the couch. My heart started to pound in my ears and my vision blurred as the floor rose up to meet me.

Ch. 34

Eventually, I became aware of something cool and wet on my forehead and that I had somehow made it to the couch; then it registered what had happened. James had carried me here after I fainted. I'd never fainted in my life. Stephen gets tortured for two days and runs through two states to get home and *I* faint? I was mortified.

"Claire," his voice was thick with concern. "Claire, are you okay?"

My eyes fluttered open, and blinking, I took in my surroundings. I saw that there would be no hiding this embarrassment. The entire household was standing around the couch. The sound I heard was my own groan. Raising my hand to cover my face, I found my voice. "Can we pretend this never happened?"

Someone giggled nearby. I wasn't sure if it was Tonya or Tara. Either way, I wished they would find something to do away from here.

I rolled toward the back of the couch and willed them all to go away. There was a quiet shuffling as they left the room and then I felt the couch cushion shift. His hand was on my shoulder as he tried to roll me over to face him. Feeling exceptionally childish, I held my body tight and whined, "no" until he pushed a little harder and made me roll over in spite of myself.

I looked up at his eyes, dark with worry. "Claire, what happened?"

"Didn't you hear the thud when I fell?"

"No," he said sounding exasperated. "What I am asking is if you remember what happened *before* you fainted?"

"Yes, I felt really tired." I dropped my attitude; it wasn't helping.

He was nodding his head. "You looked pale. Your eyes were glassy as well. Maybe you are in shock."

Considering that, I canted my head to the side. "Yeah, but now would be a funny time. I mean, nothing's happened to me for a while."

His expression remained clouded as he was thinking and he spoke slowly. "I want you to take it slow the next few days while we figure out what is going on." Seeing my eyes beginning to roll, he spoke quickly before I could disagree. "It's probably nothing, but let's just keep track of your symptoms and see if anything else happens."

Reluctantly, I agreed. It felt selfish to take up anyone's time with my weaknesses while they all had so much to do.

"Are you still feeling up to the wedding? We can bow out if you want to. We could find a hotel in another town to wait until our flight Sunday."

"No," I surprised myself with my resolve. "I want to go. I have a chance to have a *normal* family function. I want that. Plus, I get to have the hottest date there."

"I was hoping you would want to go. I want to speak to your father." He was watching his fingers tracing the outline of my healed jaw.

I felt my eyes go wide. He chuckled. "Not about any of this. You must remember that I was raised in another time. In my youth, when a man wanted to court a woman he asked her father for permission. I would like to have the opportunity to do things right. It bothers me I haven't been able to speak to him yet."

229

I couldn't fight the laugh that bubbled up. "You *want* to meet my parents?"

He nodded, very serious. "I want to let them know my intentions. It would be nice to have *one thing* that we don't have to hide from them."

"We aren't hiding. People know I am here."

"Work doesn't count. Henry is your boss, and I believe your professors know you are staying with a 'friend'. Besides, I am trying to do the honorable thing here." He was starting to get agitated.

"James, have I done something that has upset you?" My nerves were starting my stomach churning and I felt dizzy again.
Reaching out to touch my cheek, James spoke uncertainly. "Claire, do you think your father will approve of you being with someone so much older?"

Taking a moment, I swallowed the disbelief at the comprehension that he could stare down death but had a perfectly human fear of a father's approval. "James, what parent wouldn't adore you? You have an exciting job, a lovely home and their daughter is crazy about you. Who cares that you're a few years older? They're a few years apart too. By the way, how do you explain your lack of a family? I should probably know so I don't say the wrong thing."

Winking, he grinned crookedly. "Haven't I told you about my trust fund? It explains the money, the lack of family and I have a legitimate excuse for being a prick once in a while."

"So, you're wealthy as well? Again I ask you, how could my parents not love you?" I sniggered. "I do." His skin right in front of me was a temptation. Stretching my neck I reached my lips to the base of his throat exposed by the open neck of his white shirt. My kiss turned into two and as I grabbed his arm to pull him close, I felt his body go still and he pushed me down out of reach. My hurt must have shown on my face. "What did I do?"

"Nothing." James' objection was harsh. He hurried to soften the blow. "Claire, you fainted about fifteen minutes ago and you are a few shades paler than normal. Although you are testing my self-control, I must ask you to wait until you are better. We should get a good meal in you first. Besides, I thought we would get on the road soon. I've always enjoyed Duluth and I thought we could get up there a few hours early and spend some time on the town." His brow furrowed. "You know, we've never had a real date."

"Yes, we have, remember the night we went to the club?"

James' face darkened. "How could I forget the night I introduced you to a psychopath? And for the record, it was not a date. It was homework."

I sighed, "Look at the up side." The look he gave me told me he didn't see one. "We've spent every moment together since that night. I can't see it as *all* bad. Can you?" Even with his recent declaration of love for me, I still worried it would fade in time when the newness of me wore off. What if I aged badly, what if he met some super hot vampire chick that could keep up with him better and wasn't going to die in seventy years? He'd said it himself, "a vampire's feelings are fleeting." How could I expect anything but what his nature promised?

Ch. 35

Bags packed and in the trunk, James and I were speeding up 35W by eleven. Normally Duluth was a two hour drive, but my chauffeur exceeded the speed limit routinely. I was fairly confident we would be there before noon.

On the way, we talked about nothing important at all. No covens, no psychopaths, not even our pending trip to Scotland tomorrow. Instead we talked about music. I confessed my guilty pleasure of 80's music, and he introduced me to blue grass. We agreed on some of the newer music getting radio play like Snow Patrol. We took turns listening to one another's choices made possible by satellite radio and iPod. Before long, we were debating electric versus acoustic guitars and how music has changed in the last century. He obviously had more experience with the earlier half of the century than I did, but he proved himself a patient teacher and willing listener.

Sure enough, it was just after noon when we pulled into Duluth. That was a record for me and I told him so. He was getting used to my teasing him about his driving and gave his now typical response, "my kind enjoys speed" and I was no more impressed with it this time than each time before. There was no point in commenting further. He could no sooner change the color of his freckles.

The music faded for no reason and I turned up the volume twice, unable to get the sound back as we pulled into the lot at a nicer hotel in Canal Park overlooking Lake Superior. After putting the car in park and turning it off, I felt his stare. "Isn't that a little loud?" He whispered.

"My hearing isn't as good as yours, you can't keep turning it down on me." I assumed he'd adjusted it when I wasn't looking.

"Claire I never touched it." He eyed me warily, guessing accurately that the change was with me and not the controls.

"Maybe I should get my ears checked." I snapped, frustrated with my weakness more than with him. My door slamming was mostly accidental but I was too close to tears to turn around and explain that.

He couldn't be vampire fast out here in public, so I used the time it took for him to grab the bags to pull myself together. He caught up to me as I was ogling the Victorian lobby décor. It was so beautiful and elegant. It struck me as very him, and I wondered briefly if all vampires got stuck in their time or if it was just this one. As "with the times" as James could be, he was certainly set in his ways from his formative human years. And as quickly as I had gotten pissy with him, I was on the other side of it. He walked up beside me and I turned my face up to him. Features guarded, he looked down at me, a bag in each hand and leaned down to kiss me chastely on the lips. Afterward, he nodded his head to the side and indicated that we should go to the front desk.

Riding the elevator to the top floor, I made a game of catching his eye and coyly glancing away; my goal was to make him smile and between floors two and three it worked. Leading the way, he carried the bags down the long hallway until we reached our room. James must have gotten the best room in the place. Ours was off the main hall, on a quiet wing overlooking the lake and our view was spectacular. We walked in, he tossed the bags down on the chair in the corner and I continued through to the balcony. Opening the door, I walked out into the shock of only mildly brisk air and took in the scenery. It was an unusually bright, sunny day in Duluth and the lake reflected the clear blue of the sky next to the fall colors lining the visible shoreline.

My hands were on the balcony railing, the light breeze ruffling my hair and just like that, my legs were swept up from underneath me as a low chuckle rang in my ear. James whisked me back inside and tossed me, giggling on the bed. I couldn't help but get caught up in the moment, his joy was infectious. Here we were, none of the bad guys following us for now, no constant checking in with anybody about safety or patrols. We were just two normal people in love. Sappy, but true.

"Well," his demeanor changed, making me catch my breath as he made his way up the bed, hovering over me. "We have almost five hours before anyone will be expecting us. Is there anything you *need* to do?"

Reaching up, I slid a hand into his hair and coaxed him closer so that I could wrap a leg around his thigh and pull him down to show him my first idea. It met with his approval, my health no longer a concern for him. Sometime later, we threw on our clothes and grabbed our jackets, heading out into the afternoon sunshine.

Ch. 36

James and I wandered in and out of some shops as the urge struck. Duluth was great for its boutique shops. I hadn't had anything since breakfast and even though I argued I wasn't hungry, James worried about another fainting spell so we stopped off at a coffee shop and I grabbed a vanilla latte.

We wandered into one of the shops advertising specialty woodwork and found, scattered throughout, beautiful sections of carved animals, doors and children's toys, antique wood inlaid boxes. One box in particular grabbed my attention, reeling me in while James made a loop around the far side of the shop to get a better look at an old door.

It was about the size of a cigar box and had intricate patterns inlaid on all sides with a stretched out map of the world on the top. Each continent and the larger islands was a different shade and type of wood. I recognized mahogany, pine, cedar, and cypress; there were a few others not so easily distinguished. I thought it perfect for James' office at home.

Patiently, I waited until he was heading for the door. "I'm going to use the restroom. Would you mind waiting at the tables out front with my coffee?" He gave me a curious look. Wrinkling my nose I raised my cup. "I can't take it in with me." He kissed my head, taking my cup before turning to walk out. When I was sure he was outside, I turned back and grabbed the box whisking it to the middle of the store and the counter.

The shopkeeper was a fifty something woman dressed in an artsy, burlap-like dress with some funky paint splattered glasses on a faux pearl chain. Dramatically made up eyes crinkled kindly at me over her glasses. "Quite a find, dear." I didn't know if she meant the box or James.

"Thank you," I mumbled, blushing like a fool as she wrapped up my package. She smiled again as she handed me the bag and I walked quickly out of the store.

Stepping onto the street, my gaze easily rested on James' back. He was sitting casually, to all appearances watching the people with little interest, unless you knew like I did, that he was studying each face for signs of danger. I couldn't help but feel a little sad seeing him looking so out of place here, waiting for me at a mismatched bistro set on a narrow sidewalk between bike racks and trees. He should be at a real bistro in Paris or somewhere much more cosmopolitan than this.

I was standing outside the door of the shop, staring at him with my gift in hand, feeling woefully outclassed, when he sensed me and shifted in his seat. Seeing the smile twist his lips when he saw me, I tucked away my doubts for the future in favor of the pleasures of now. That skill was not exclusively his.

As I approached, his eyes followed my arm down to settle on the bag in my hand. I wished briefly he didn't have to cover his eyes outside in the sun. I'd come to rely on them to read his moods. His eyes were the one thing he couldn't control and without them I was blind. Motioning for me to come over and sit with him, a crease settled on his forehead when I set his gift down on the table in front of him.

"What is that?"

"Go on, open it." I pushed it toward him, again fully aware he could hear my pulse accelerating.

Wordlessly, he took the bag and lifted the gift out very gently. Long pale fingers unwrapped the tissue paper from the box taking care not to let it slide on the metal table. When the last of the paper was pulled away, my eyes were focused on James' face. I had a second of trepidation that

I'd chosen poorly when he sat, paper held aloft in his frozen hand staring at it. It felt like an eternity before he reanimated and spoke carefully, "Claire, this is very thoughtful of you."

"Do you like it? I saw it and could picture it on your desk. You have all of those business cards and scraps of paper with restaurants and stuff from your trips floating around in a pile. I thought it might give you a place for them."

He leaned forward putting a hand on the back of my neck and his lips were brief but urgent. "I love it."

After he rewrapped it for safe transport, we continued our meandering way down the street. Holding hands and looking in shop windows wordlessly for the next while. When he tried to get my attention he had to squeeze my hand.

"I'm sorry, I was in my own world."

James gave me a quick grin and rubbed the back of my hand with his thumb. "I recognize that I don't offer up much from my past, it's just that when you have so many lifetimes they can blur. What makes sense in one may not make sense in another because it is a different life entirely." His expression was guarded.

I had thought about that before, how could I not? Yet Troy's words about family had been cathartic. I knew the man James was now, regardless of his people or what he might have done a century ago. "I don't mind. As long as you're here now that's all that matters."

Cocking his head at my ready acceptance yet again of his complicated life, James got a weird set to his lips right before he moved. It was so fast I wasn't ready and for a second; I was scared he'd seen someone when he plucked me out of the middle of the sidewalk and up against the building. I was taken aback never having approved of public displays of affection, but as usual, when he touched me I felt that visceral pull at the center of my insides and the world fell away leaving only him and his kiss. It was a moment before I recognized the sound of my name being called from somewhere nearby and my eyes rounded in fear.

James pulled me harder against his body and turned us so that he was between the voice and me. To an onlooker, it might have looked like he was maneuvering me to make out against the building. I knew he was putting himself in a position to protect me.

Peering over his shoulder, I followed the direction of the voice and caught a glimpse of my cousin Angie and her husband Brad walking toward us from two shops up. Angie's eyes were popping out of her head, one arm waving wildly while the other held on to her poor husband being dragged along behind her, looking like he'd eaten a bug.
Before he unwittingly killed a relative, I whispered over his shoulder. "It's family, false alarm."

Immediately he relaxed his arm and turned himself into me for another kiss, being very thorough trying to sell this one as a moment of passion on the street. I didn't mind although now I was *really* going to have them talking tonight.

"Angie, hi." There was no need to fake the breathlessness or flush in my face. I stepped around him and didn't argue with the hand he slid down my arm and into my palm. James took his protector status very seriously. I for one appreciated the support; family made me almost as nervous as bad guys. "Long time, no see. Hey Brad, how've you been?"

Angie was only a few years older than me and had married her high school sweetheart a year ago. They were a great couple, one of those that makes perfect sense to anyone who meets them for more than five minutes. She was a talker while he was the quiet type. Both were attractive, blond and tall. I had heard there was already pressure on them for

238

children, however, they enjoyed running competitively and camping too much to give in yet.

Angie was of course the one to speak for them. "Claire, how have you been? I missed you at *our* wedding. *You've* changed. The last time I saw you I think it was my mother's birthday. Weren't you sick or something? You stayed in the guest bedroom the *whole time*. Guess you got better." She eyed up my companion, her fascination readily apparent and it didn't take Brad long to figure it out. He was tense, not at all pleased with James as he stared at him icily.

My manners kicked in. "Angie, Brad, this is my friend James Thomas. James, meet my cousin and her husband Brad and Angie Carlson. I'm assuming you two are in town for the wedding as well?"

"Yeah, we have to grab some things they forgot to bring over to the hotel. We'll head over to the hall in a little while. So, James, you're *the* date, huh? Jeanette, that's Claire's mom, has been speculating about you *all* week." She stage whispered behind her hand, giving him a coy wink.

Brad cleared his throat attempting to be polite. I had always liked Brad. He was nice to everyone because that was just his way. It was never to impress or get something. I appreciated that he'd never pushed me to participate or insisted on hugging at functions when I clearly looked uncomfortable, and for that I loved him.

"Hey, Ang," he took her hand. "Don't we need to finish getting that stuff? They're waiting for us." He shot a glare at James who pretended not to notice the jealous attitude shift. Brad must have squeezed her hand because she yelped and glanced up, turning a deeper shade of pink at what she saw.

Angie, back on her good behavior, waved as her husband pulled her back to the other side of the sidewalk. "See you two tonight."

After they had gone, James and I both breathed a sigh of relief and I leaned my head against his shoulder. James kept his eyes constantly moving between the sidewalk and the street. So adept was he at his job, I knew if I looked at his face I would see only mild interest in his surroundings yet I could feel his muscles coiled tightly beneath the surface of his skin ready to spring if necessary. While I walked beside him, I thought about what Angie was going to tell my parents.

Groaning, I mentioned it to James, "You heard me tell my mom we were just friends and you were going to ask my dad permission to date me. Now Angie is going to tell them we were borderline indecent in the street."

"I don't mind if they know that you've let me kiss you. What about the situation makes you uncomfortable? Are you worried they will question your judgment?" One brown eyebrow flicked up accentuating his crooked grin.

"I don't really care about the rest of them, but yes, I do worry what my parents will think." I wanted to explain. "Just put yourself in their shoes for a second. Their only child, a daughter, who has never been away from home, is now off living in a dorm room alone with virtually no adult supervision. She has never dated and is innocent in the ways of men." The corner of his mouth twitched. "Hey, I *was* a complete innocent before you came along, I'd never even kissed anybody before."

"You didn't seem to mind." He was only half playful though, I could tell his feelings were mildly bruised.

What I had to say was important to me so I soldiered on. "Just listen please. Their daughter has been at school less than a month and this 'friend' she brought out of nowhere to go to a wedding with her has now been spotted making out with her on a public street corner. That just isn't how I was raised. I don't want them to think less of either of us for this."

He was watching the crowd while he digested what I'd said. Shrugging, he agreed. "Yes, that would be a hard report to receive as a parent. I will be on my best behavior tonight and will do my utmost to wow them. They won't even remember hearing anything from Angie by the time I am done with them."

Tightening my grip on his hand, I gasped, "You aren't going to mess with their heads are you?"

"Do you want me to?" He asked without flinching.

I'd never thought of *him* doing those kinds of things to people, definitely no more than a little convincing like he'd done to the desk attendant and that was for a good reason. Gasping, I heard myself justifying, "Can *you* do that? Do you know how to do what that *woman* did to Stephen?"

Sensing my discomfort, he tightened his arm around my waist, bringing my head into his chest. My heart automatically started to slow as I melted into his body and he lowered his face to my ear. "No, Claire, I would never do that."

There went my heart again and I pulled away. "You didn't say you *couldn't*, just that you *wouldn't*."

"Yes, I could."

"*Have* you ever? Done that to someone, I mean, against their will?" I whispered, knowing it was loud enough for him.

"Let's head back to the room and discuss this there." His features had hardened, I could see that around his shades.

Mutely nodding, I turned with him and let him lead. Our bodies drifted apart slowly on our way to the hotel, I had forced him to accept the loss of my hand for the time being. I didn't think I was necessarily angry, but I worried I could feel him distancing himself emotionally from me, getting ready to wall himself off and set up borders between us; what I could know and what I couldn't.

When our wandering had been random, we had gone up and down the streets and walked slowly. Now that we walked directly and with purpose, it only took ten minutes to arrive back in our hotel. A brief march through the hotel's lobby, and we were back in our room, locking the door behind us. Our balcony doors had been closed and I reopened them. I wanted the brisk breeze on my face to clear my head.

For the second time that afternoon, James came onto the deck with me; except this time was not as jubilant and the loss caused an ache in my middle. He held out his hand and, of course, I took it as he led me back into the room. Sitting down on the far side of the bed, he drew one leg up and toyed with his pant leg. I sat on the far side from him with my feet pulled up Indian style and picked at a loose feather sticking out from the down comforter while I waited for him to start.

"There are things about what I am that are frightening to humans. In the stories, humans tend to concentrate on the physical aspects, they choose to forget the mental side. It's too frightening."

I watched him, trying to keep my face open, not to pass judgment. At the same time, I know that I didn't want to hear anything that would burst my naïve bubble about him.

"We have the ability to enter people's minds, alter their perception of reality, mess with their memory; it all comes with the territory. When our bodies cross over so do our minds. We are no longer held in check by what is and what isn't. Our brains work differently. I can't explain it but I can see into places in someone's mind that just weren't there before. It's as easy as you can see if someone is happy. And all of that changes with age; the older the vampire, the greater the capability. I know you spoke to Henry briefly about me." I opened my mouth to explain and he interrupted, "It's fine, I'm not offended. Henry and I are very close and I trust his judgment. If he shares something with you about me, I'm sure there's a reason. But I must tell you it has been difficult. This time with you has challenged me to confront some things head on."

"Are you not comfortable with me? With my being a human?"

"No, your mortality is not the issue. What I am trying to explain is that I have my own doubts about myself, about *what I am*. And yes, I am tempted at times to use my advantages to achieve my goals faster and easier than the more traditional routes. However, as I believe Henry explained to you, there is something inside me that drives me, a desire to help both mortal and immortal beings. It prohibits me from using my abilities to harm an innocent, even if it seems necessary at the time." His brow creased again. "That doesn't mean I wouldn't fight to protect someone I love."

"It doesn't bother me that you don't talk about your past or what you've done in other lifetimes." I laid a hand lightly on his arm needing to touch him. "I thought about it the other day after we talked about your… your sexual history and I am okay with not knowing a lot of the details. I know who you are and the details surrounding that are unimportant." I met his eyes. "The one thing that I have to have is your honesty in this one."

James studied me before he dipped his chin and held out his hand. "I think that's fair."

We shook on our agreement and as soon as our hands touched, I felt dizzy. My insides twitched and tugged and I put my hand over my stomach, part of me expecting to be able to feel the flesh moving beneath it. The pull I felt toward him had grown to the point that I was afraid if ever he and I didn't see eye to eye, I would have no power to argue or to leave.

Lighthearted from our clearing of the air, James leaned forward and kissed my nose, keeping me from exploring the ramifications of my realization. I let his mood infect me and take my mind to a better place, not allowing it to be troubled at the potential loss of identity I was facing.

Ch. 37

At 4:45 promptly, James and I drove up to the gates of the Fairlawn Mansion overlooking the bay. An historic Victorian home built in 1891 and beautifully restored years ago to its original glory, it was a showpiece. The fall sun was setting over the bay, backlighting the scene with a dramatic orange glow. I wasn't sure if the small blue lights lining the walkway were for the wedding or if they were always there; the mood they created was absolutely magical. Lights shined from every window in the house, illuminating an awful lot of heads. Closing my eyes, I sank back into my seat giving a brief thought to driving away right now. A cool breeze tickled my bare shoulder when James opened my door. His silky voice added to my goose bumps and I absently wondered if that would ever pass.

"Claire, are you ready?" His voice glided smoothly into my consciousness.

Opening my eyes, I turned my head toward the sound and sighed, laying my head back into the headrest. "You know, it's hard enough to walk in there with most of my family having heard who knows what about us. Now you have to look like that." Lifting my hand I waved it at his body now dressed in a beautifully tailored dark blue suit over a crisp white shirt and light blue tie. The effect, when combined with his eyes and pale complexion was hypnotic. "They're going to be in a frenzy."

He stared boldly at me as he held out his hand and smiled. "I won't notice who's looking at me." Struggling to breathe, I took his hand and rose from the car.

We walked arm in arm up the illuminated path. I was glad to have the wrap over my shoulders, chasing away the chill of the unseasonably warm fall evening. His face nearly glowed white in the fading light. "James, when did you eat last?" I

245

knew he was usually very conscientious about feeding before going out with me but I hadn't thought about what he did "on the road."

"I was going to pick more up from my donor contact, but after what happened this morning," he shrugged self-consciously. "When you had your, ah, episode, I didn't get a chance."

How could I forget? I still felt like an idiot for fainting.

Putting his fingers under my chin, he forced me to look at him. "Don't worry, I've been doing this for a long time. I can control myself tonight." I let myself be reassured, despite the doubt pressing strong against the periphery of my thoughts as we strolled down the pathway.

When we walked through the front door, my suspicions were confirmed that Angie had been busy wagging her tongue. All eyes were on us and, to my ears, it got a lot quieter in the crowded entry. James put his free hand over where mine lay on his arm and I took confidence from him. Standing straighter and putting on a smile, I strode over toward a group of my cousins hovering near the front room where the ceremony was to take place. We had time for only the briefest of introductions before we were ushered to our seats. I had hoped to sit in the back, but we ended up in the middle. Either way, in a room of only about forty people, it wasn't as though we could easily lose ourselves in the crowd.

I had just enough time to turn to my date before the music started and mention something I had been thinking about since we had arrived here in town. "Thank you for coming. I'm having a great time on our first official date." He squeezed my hand and leaned in to kiss my cheek. Neither of us turned when the bride walked in.

My family was rather substantial, thanks to my father's four siblings and their own large broods. Mom was an only child like me, so we were often lost in the chaos when we all got together. Due to the sizeable flock, I had attended many a wedding in my time. However, up to now I had never really paid much attention to the ceremony itself, being too tied up with my "noise" to concentrate.

This one was non-denominational with a judge officiating in a way that I found suited my spiritual tastes. It was with a jolt of pleasure that I realized halfway through the ceremony that I could see James and myself up there exchanging vows. I snuck a look at him and saw him watching me out of the corner of his eye.

With a guilty smile, I brought my eyes back to the front yet couldn't help my mind from wandering a few more times wondering what it would be like if I had forever with James, not just human forever but the real thing. Would I change for him? I didn't have an answer ready for that question; it would have to be answered in time. There was one thing I knew for sure if I did change, I wouldn't want to be stuck at nineteen forever.

James met more family and friends in the receiving line. He was something to watch. In our time together, I had never seen him interact with humans beyond his assistant, and I had never seen him in a social setting. My female relatives were eating out of his palm and he had the men laughing several times. With enviable grace and charisma James put people at ease and drew them into conversations with each other, overcoming differences as well as any diplomat. I would have to tell him later, he should be a peacemaker in his next lifetime. He truly had a talent for bringing people together.

At long last we reached the bride. Vanessa had always been the beautiful one in the family and she never let anyone forget it; nor did her mother, putting her on the pageant circuit from three through college. She was a good person whose Achilles heel was her vanity. I saw her jaw drop when she saw James and I, and felt nineteen years of inadequacy fall away. I couldn't help but gloat for a fantastic couple of seconds. Then it was gone and I could be happy for her again, smiling and laughing like I'd never had a chance to with my family before tonight. When we got back into the car to head over to the reception at the hotel, The Suites in Canal Park, I couldn't help a few happy tears from leaking out.

James noticed them. "Was it that difficult? You seemed to be happy."

I dabbed at my tears with the corner of my wrap. "That's the thing. It was the easiest time I have ever had with them. I wish I had met you and the cats a long time ago." He reached over to take my hand.

"Me too. We'd better go." He winked playfully. "Word might get out that we were having a go here in the car."

I was still laughing as we headed onto the main street for the short drive to the reception.

Anyone who has been to a wedding knows that the ceremony is where all of the oohs and aahs happen, and the fun is at the reception. This was the first one where I got to really have some fun as well and I was looking forward to it by the time we pulled into the lot.

The hotel, not far from ours, was perched on the shore, its shape angling with the curve of the lake maximizing the natural views. The reception was in a large event room on the top floor; the water side was covered almost entirely in glass with the lights dimmed enough to allow the view of Duluth at night to decorate the room.

Lake Superior has its own personality and provides a lot of the character for the town. The guests were all seated at eight person round tables with white tablecloths. The head

248

table was round as well, something I thought was a lot more workable than a long table where everyone stared at the wedding party all night, demanding that they perform. It struck me that I was taking notes, making decisions about my own wedding should the occasion ever present itself. Glancing up I wondered if he had ever been married before. That was a first I wished I could be for him, knowing that my chances at being a first *anything* for him were slim.

Our table's occupants were milling about, everyone standing and visiting with champagne in hand before being seated for dinner. James and I were sharing a table with Angie and Brad, her parents, another couple who were friends with the groom Travis, and my parents, Jeanette and Doug. When I saw the name cards, I wasn't nervous like I had assumed I would be. It must be the high I was still riding from enjoying my family so much at the wedding. I was optimistic this was going to go well too.

"Mom, Dad." I hugged them both simultaneously, letting go of James' hand only long enough to embrace them and step back, feeling his hand automatically find mine. I hadn't been aware I'd done it until I saw my Dad's eyes follow it. Fortunately, he flashed me a smile and I felt the tension in my shoulders ease. With the duties my mother had at the ceremony, we hadn't spoken beyond my waving as we were leaving and Dad mouthing, "See you there." Mom had looked disappointed, but I saw she was more interested in my date than me. I'm sure she'd eaten up everything Angie had fed her.

Angie did hair for a living and was used to making small talk about other people's business. It wasn't something anyone held against her, one merely had to be careful what was said to our dear cousin, lest the whole world learn about it within twenty-four hours.

"Mom and Dad, I'd like you to meet James." I patted his forearm with my free hand, the other still locked firmly in his. Somewhere on the way here my happiness had crossed to euphoria and I was getting that dizzy feeling again, making me downright giddy; not a normal thing for me. James was eyeing me questioningly. My grin broadened stupidly as I introduced my parents to the most important person in my life. "James Thomas, meet my parents, Jeanette and Doug Martin."

James flashed them a radiant smile. "Mr. and Mrs. Martin, it is a pleasure to finally meet you. Would anyone like another champagne? Claire would you like one since it is a special occasion?" He looked at my dad adding. "If that is alright with you, sir? I am driving her and not to worry, I don't drink." I failed to stifle my giggle and he shot me a weird look.

Dad shook his head. "No, I'm taking it slow tonight but if Claire would like one, that's fine with me." He looked at my mother who was swiveling her head back and forth between James and I; she had a curious expression on her face. "Jeanette?" She looked over expectantly, clearly she hadn't heard the question. "James is getting drinks, would you like one?" She nodded and tossed back the small swallow she had in her first glass. "That would be fabulous. Thank you, James."

"James, let me help you. I want to see what else they have other than champagne." Swallowing, I rubbed my throat. "I'm thirsty but I'm not sure for what. Excuse us." Grabbing for his hand, I took too quick a step into him bobbling. Righting me adeptly, he turned to guide us to the drink table.

"Claire, what is going on with you? I've never seen you like this before," he whispered forcefully. Glancing up, I again saw the nerves he must be feeling reflected on his ashen face; his eyes were going dark. My insides lurched.

As soon as we were out of sight of my parents, we stepped off to stand by a pillar out of the way. My hand went to my throat again and I shook my head, "I don't know. I thought I was keeping everyone out but I have this weird lightheaded thing going on. It doesn't feel like me. Wait a minute." Closing my eyes and stopping with him, I stilled and felt around in my head like he'd taught me to check my shielding. It was there and strong. I tried to let go of James' hand but he held on. Opening my eyes, I looked up at him. "Let go, I need to check something." And I closed my eyes again. Reluctantly, he released his grip and my skin warmed where his cool hand fell away. As soon as his hand was gone, my head started to swim and I wavered. Wiggling my fingers, eyes still closed, I felt his hand close around mine again and my head cleared. I opened my eyes and looked up at him unable to cover the alarm growing inside me. "James, I don't know what is going on but unless I'm touching you, it feels like I did at your house when I was going to faint. My head's all muddy. No, not muddy. Garbled. At your house, I couldn't concentrate and now here it's like I'm hypersensitive, everything is happening so fast I can't catch it all."

He gave up any pretenses of appearing calm, his anxiety showing clear as he grabbed for my other hand and held it tightly. "Claire, I'm not sure what is happening, but something is definitely changing in you. Your heartbeat even sounds different, slow like when you're sleeping. It should be faster, especially with your anxiety. You are right though it is better when we touch. For tonight then, until we figure this out, we should keep in contact." The back of my hand went cold in waves with the stroking of his thumb. His gesture of comfort would have been more effective had I not seen the tension behind his eyes as he raised up my left hand to brush the back of my knuckles with his lips. Closing my eyes, I shivered.

"We are going to have to forego the whole budding romance act in favor of desperately in love for my whole family. We certainly can't try to explain some supernatural medical malady to this crowd," I sighed.

James' more heartfelt deep chuckle was a relief. We exchanged a glance. "I believe I can manage that one."

We headed over to the drink table covered in champagne flutes filled with the golden bubbling liquid. We grabbed one for my mom and, feeling suddenly very dry, I changed my mind and grabbed a flute for myself. Before James could object, I had tossed down half a glass with a choke. He was staring at me with his eyes wide, "Claire, what are you doing? If you are having trouble controlling yourself, you shouldn't have alcohol. I didn't even know you drank."

"I don't," was my honest response. "But my throat is really dry. It must be nerves. I would swear it burns. I hope I'm not getting sick." It was an unfamiliar feeling, different than a sore throat.

James' entire body suddenly hummed with tension and in one swift motion he set down my mother's glass, wrapped his arm behind my back swinging us around and virtually carried me out the main doors into the hall and ducked into an empty alcove. His arms went up against the wall on either side of my head and his eyes bored into mine from inches away. Without prompting, my body began to respond and I felt myself being pulled away from the wall, my hand rubbed down the front of his shirt.

"Claire," his voice was urgent as he broke into my scattered thoughts. "Claire." I felt his hands come down onto my shoulders and the cool contact helped to focus my thoughts. My eyes found his and saw the worry there within the dark eyes staring at me. "What did you say about your throat?" He demanded.

"It could just be a sore throat. Maybe that's why I've been feeling off lately."

"No," he pressed, "the throat. Sore how? Describe it"

"Like I said, it's sore but not. I can't explain it." The champagne was making me a little woozy. I felt my knees buckle a little and I giggled.

James was growing antsy as he looked back behind us and leaned in to put his face to my neck. I sucked in a quick breath and rolled my head back. He stopped just shy of my neck and I heard him sniffing.

"What are you doing?" It was getting hard to focus; the alcohol was definitely kicking in.

"Impossible," I heard him mumble and put one arm around my shoulders. Reaching out, he grabbed the handle on the door next to us and with a crack. In the next second, he swept me into a small closet.

Taking in the contents of the little room, I laughed at the cliché. "A broom closet, really? We have a great big room with a bed a few blocks away." I wrapped my arms around his neck, I was game if he was. Maybe we could even get back before dinner was over and dance a few together.

James' hands came up to take mine before they could wrap around his neck. "Claire, this isn't about sex," he kept his voice to a harsh whisper. As his hands held mine, I felt the fuzziness in my head clearing, leaving only the faint buzz from the champagne and the driving need to take off his clothes.

"Why *isn't* this about sex? It should be." I pushed myself at him, trying to reach his lips.

He caught me again and held my chin with a hand. "Claire this is serious. I need you to be still for a moment while I call Henry. Okay?"

Nodding, I leaned forward and lay my head against his chest. Touching such a large section of him helped and I remained still, inhaling his heady scent as he called Henry.

The hum of his voice was urgent. "I don't understand; she smells faintly vampire, her throat burns, her heart rate is dropping. She describes thirst and is completely disoriented when I'm not reinforcing her defenses physically." He paused, listening. "No, I haven't since before we left but that shouldn't be a problem. I've gone longer stretches between feedings." Another question, this one he answered sounding embarrassed. "No more than normal." He listened some more. I heard more mumbling but was starting to feel sleepy. I think I was dozing when the phone clicked shut, startling me awake.

James held me so that he could examine my face as I blinked lethargically at him. It had only been my third effort at drinking and I only had half a glass. I was ashamed to say I was feeling it. James was nearly frantic, that much I could see in his eyes though the "why" eluded my slow wits. He picked me up to set me on some boxes stacked behind me.

"Claire, I am going to do something to you that will help you to focus for a minute. I need to speak to you about something very serious." I nodded slowly, trying to understand what could be so critical. Maybe something had happened back home to one of the cats. I felt my stomach turn. Before I could worry more about that, I felt his hands on mine and he looked into my eyes. It was exactly how he looked at Stephen that day on the couch.

All of a sudden, my world shifted. It felt like a ride that jerks sideways, only it was inside my head while my body remained stationary. Then, my mind was completely clear. It was actually easier to focus on more than a few things at once. My eyes were even better than normal seeing farther in the dim space illuminated only by the one tiny fixture that had turned on when James had flicked the switch. The sounds of the reception had grown exponentially, it was as if they were suddenly all standing right outside this door. I could hear the glasses clinking and a familiar laugh.

"James, what did you do?" I was looking around grateful for the new clarity. Then I looked at him. Each wave in his hair was clearly defined. I could see the lines in his irises, his eyes were a dark midnight blue. They were magnificent.

"Love, please focus on me. We don't have long before this wears off and I don't want to do it again." I brought my mind to heel and stared at him, willing myself to pay attention. He saw that I was back in control and started again. "I am not sure what is happening or why, but you are thirsty." Shaking off the objection I was beginning to form, he continued. "No, I mean *thirsty.* Like one of us."

My throat constricted and I squeaked. "How?"

He shook his head frustrated, "I don't know and neither does Henry. We are away from home and all of my sources, which leaves us with few options. That is why I brought your mind back for a moment. We need to figure out what to do." Strong shoulders rounded in defeat. "I know I said I would never do it, but I cannot proceed without your consent. Think of it as sharing my perception for a few minutes."

"Is this how things look to you?" He nodded and I seriously contemplated changing in that moment. Someone was telling a story that sounded interesting.

"Claire, I know it is hard to focus right now. That is a side effect of our perception, lots of stimulation makes it hard to concentrate. It takes years to overcome that and we don't have that kind of time."

255

"Sorry. What do I need to decide again?" Now that I was trying to focus, I found I had lost the thread of our conversation.

He rolled his eyes and growled. "I'll make this quick. You are acting like a thirsty vampire and it is because of me. You are channeling my thirst and I can't keep it from happening. I don't have any sources for donor blood here so we have a few choices. I can excuse myself and go hunting, or," he struggled with the second option, "or I can take the edge off right now."

I wrestled with the choices, neither one was appealing. My mother would never forgive us leaving now and she would think James completely rude if he left me in the middle of the reception regardless of the reason I gave, and what if he was caught hunting in town? It was too risky. Making up my mind, I sat up tall on my pile of boxes and stuck out my arm offering him my wrist. "You can feed off of me. That seems to make the most sense." I figured he could hear my breath and pulse quicken so I didn't try to hide my anxiety as I asked, "Will it hurt?" Wincing at the break in my voice, I felt him tucking away his self-loathing.

Rethinking things he frowned at my wrist, both of us stared at the thin line of blue near the surface. "You don't have to do this. I can say an emergency came up and go hunt outside of town. It shouldn't take too long."

Shaking my head, I disagreed. "You can't go hunting on strange grounds. What if you get caught or go too far and now we have a body on our hands? This makes the most sense. I won't be weak will I?"

"No, with dinner on its way you will begin to feel better quickly. And, I have a theory that with us linked the way we are you will get stronger when I do." James was already regretting what he was about to do. "I know it is a lot to decide all at once and I am sorry. I will make this up to you, I promise." His expression was pained.

My vision wavered and I could feel the fog creeping back in. "Let's hurry up so we aren't missed. We are supposed to be getting Mom a drink, remember?" Never having seen someone bitten before, I was nervous about all the blood and how to hide the mark. I was trying to imagine what kind of neckerchief or wristband I could make out of duct tape or a napkin and chuckled to myself. I caught the queer look James shot my way.

"It's wearing off." He looked apprehensive again and reached back to tie the door shut with some cording, hooking it onto a steel rack nearby. As the fog crept in so did the fire in my throat and lower. I shifted in my seat. James stroked my cheek. "Love, I can make this so it doesn't hurt if you look at me first."

My thoughts were growing fuzzy again. I tried to focus on his eyes obediently. As I stared, I felt strangely floaty and light. He pushed me back on the boxes so I was lying down on my back and my legs were bared as he pushed my dress up. I moaned in anticipation. One hand came up to press against my chest as the other pulled my right leg aside. It was only in the second before he did it that I realized where he was going to bite me. He was right it was not painful as he bit down high on the inside of my thigh. The same liquid warmth that his voice washed me with was now coursing through my veins, making the experience sensual. My flesh tingled, accompanied by a warm wave every time he moved his mouth to draw more blood from the wound he'd created.

There was a sense of loss as James removed his mouth and gently licked his bite marks. Gasping, I felt my body tighten at the pleasantness of the sensation. He brought his hand up to wipe his palm against his mouth. Fortunately, I didn't see any blood on either of us. Holding out a hand for me he helped me up as his other smoothed my dress back into place.

Expecting to be lightheaded I carefully took his hand, shocked at the rush of strength that flowed through me instead. Tentatively, James asked, "Are you alright?"

Mentally taking inventory, I nodded. "I think so. My head is much clearer. Do I look okay? Not pale or anything? You're more pink."

He'd been appraising me since he took my hand, and he shook his head, looking relieved. "You look beautiful. Let's get back before we're missed."

I snorted. "Fat chance. My mom's probably given up on her drink by now."

James looked at his watch and shook his head. "No, we've only been gone ten minutes." With that, he lifted me down catching my eye. "What, is something wrong?"

"I'm okay with being your emergency donor when you need it as long as you don't change me or mark me or anything. Deal?"

Jaw tight, he ducked his eyes and agreed. "Deal."

Ch. 38

When we got back to the table everyone was still milling and standing just as we'd left them with the exception of the suspicious cast to my mother's features, demanding an explanation. James took the lead. "My apologies," he looked at my dad and then Mom. "My editor called about some last minute details and I had to take the call."

Dad looked at me with a raised eyebrow. "Did you need to speak to the editor as well?"

Seeing my stricken expression James answered for me. "Actually, she did." He squeezed my hand and smiled warmly. "I need a woman's perspective on my trip and I've invited Claire to go on my next travel assignment with me."

Squeezing his hand back, I voiced my objection. His shoulders came up and I saw an apology in his eyes. He was right of course, his explanation panned out and opened the door for everything else we wanted to say to my parents, just moving things forward a little faster than either of us preferred.

Taking up the torch, I chimed in. "Yes, James and I were talking about his trip to Scotland and I mentioned that I've always wanted to go there so he invited me. I hope that's okay with you two." I looked nervously from Mom to Dad.

Mom was concerned. "James, is that okay with your paper? Inviting someone else?"

Mentioning nothing about his argument with his office on that very subject, James lied flawlessly. "Actually yes, I am allowed to bring a companion on occasion." He caught my eyes. "This is a first for me, however."

I felt my heart give a flutter.

Dad floored me with his response. "Claire, I'm proud of you for stepping out of your comfort zone and going."

"Doug, what are you saying?" My mom gaped at him.

Dad serenely stared down my mother, challenging her to argue. Seeing she wasn't going to, he grinned at me. "It's true. Jeanette, we've talked about this for years. Claire you have always been so careful. Don't get me wrong, we are happy that you have always gotten good grades and grown up so well despite all of our moves and changes. I don't know what has gotten in to you," his eyes rested squarely on James and I crooked my neck to see James meeting my dad's gaze unflinching. "But I for one am happy to see you living your own life, finally."

My jaw dropped. I had never heard my father talk so much in my whole life. "Are you serious?"

Nodding, Dad assured me. "Honey, you are nineteen years old and intelligent enough to make your own decisions. You aren't traipsing across the world following a rock band. James, as a military man you have to make snap judgments about people's characters and you seem reasonably trustworthy." The look that passed between them was pure male. "Don't prove me wrong."

"Doug, I guarantee that I always have your daughter's safety in mind." I watched Dad accept his word and Mom drain her second glass of champagne.

Thankfully, someone tapped the microphone and the toasting began, halting our bizarre interplay for the time being. Finally, someone in a wait staff uniform walked to the father of the bride and whispered something. I was guessing they wanted to serve dinner since it was already seven and they could only hold chicken and fish for so long.

My instincts proved correct and we were all sitting and being served dinner shortly thereafter, which was good. My blood letting and champagne were beginning to take their collective toll. Our table got along really well, James was an excellent conversationalist and I enjoyed hearing him tell stories about his work for the paper and travels around the world. Again, he proved to be a great bridge builder and he got everyone talking about their own travels. I learned a lot about my parents' trips before I was born and Dad's transfers when I was much younger. Angie thought James' job was glamorous and I could tell it bothered Brad, but he was too good a guy to point it out in front of everyone. I was guessing there would be some discussion later when they were alone.

Both of my parents watched James like a hawk although Mom was more obvious. I actually caught her gaping at him with her fork hovering, forgotten by her mouth a few times. I had spent so much of my life pushing my mother away, I hadn't taken the time to see how clued in to me she was. Now that I could be near her, it touched me how well she knew me. She knew something was different, even if she could never have guessed what it was.

James hid the fact that he wasn't eating by cutting up his food and pushing it around his plate. Given the number of questions he was answering, I don't think anyone even noticed that nothing passed through his lips. The entertainment for the night was setting up as we were finishing our dry chicken and over poached fish. I saw cases for a guitar, bass and drums come out with microphones and amps and got excited.

When dinner was finished, the groom stood and took the microphone. His slurred words hinted at who was responsible for most of the empty champagne bottles at the head table. "Vanessa and I wanted to thank everyone for being here with us tonight and invite you to enjoy the rest of the night with some more friends of mine." With that, the

261

band kicked off into a short but enthusiastic wedding march. Travis laughed and returned to sit with his new wife while the rest of the plates were being cleared away. It wasn't long afterward that the wedding ritual moved to its next phase. The first dance between husband and wife flowed into one for the whole wedding party and then other couples began to trickle onto the floor, while some of the wedding party less into dancing wandered off.

The first song was a slow one and James stood, looking around the table before settling on my parents. "If you don't mind, I have been waiting patiently all night for this." When his eyes and smile rested on me, I took his hand and rose from the table.

Once we reached the dance floor James spun me effortlessly into his arms, poised to lead. The hand against the small of my back pressed me close to him. It didn't matter that a number of eyes followed us, mine were fixed.

"They seem to really like you."

His brow furrowed for a moment before he answered. "I'm not so sure about your parents. I think your dad is excited to see you doing well but your mother is very protective."

I nodded and answered thoughtfully. "I think she isn't sure how to take it all in. She sees you as the reason I'm different all of a sudden." I patted his arm. "We just need to convince her that's a good thing."

Grinning, he stepped into a more formal distance from me for emphasis. "I'm doing my best to be a gentleman."

Pulling myself back in to him, I teased. "How can anyone resist you?"

"I don't know. I've never met anyone who could." He sounded so sincere, I leaned back to study his eyes. He laughed with an unusual glint in his eye. "Maybe I could give a little suggestion to Jeannette. She'd never know what hit her and she would be our biggest supporter."

I sucked in my breath seeing my mother's glazed expression in my mind's eye. He could bespell her so easily.

"You wouldn't!" I gawked in shock to hear him say it.

James shook off his dark joke. "I would never do that to someone, I told you that." We both were quiet and I knew we were thinking about the same thing. He pulled me close, whispering in my ear, "You know I did that because I couldn't make the decision for you." Moving so that he could see my face, "It was that or have to explain to you after the fact that I'd taken your blood without asking." I saw the genuine concern on his face. "Are you still okay with it?" He referred to the decision more than my body's performance, though I found the latter easier to speak to.

"Yeah, I'm fine." I answered honestly. "I'm clear headed and can move around without holding on to you all the time. Not that I minded having you near me so much. It kept all those other girls off of you." I teased.

I saw him duck his head to hide his smirk and his arm tightened around my back, holding me close as we danced.

We were on our second song when I felt a tap on my shoulder. I looked up from James' shoulder and saw my father behind me. "Can I cut in?" We stopped dancing and I saw my mom beside him. I guessed she was waiting for James. I let go of James' hand and had a moment to catch his eye. He let one brow flick up speculatively, teasing just as he took my mom into a formal dance frame. I barely quelled my laughter as my dad pulled me into his arms.

Dad and I danced for a while without saying anything. He and I were both comfortable with silence and it wasn't awkward. He broke in first, "Claire honey, I've never seen you so happy. Is it him? Was it him at lunch that day?"

I thought back. It had been him, except even more than that, it had been everything. I felt like I had control over my life for the first time and it was empowering. "James is a big part of it, but I am just really finding my way at school, Dad. My studies are going well, I'm making friends and I think I have some direction for my future." I managed to tell him the important things without lying. "Does that bother you that I am happier out of the house?" I didn't want to hurt his feelings.

He shook his head, his smile fading only a little. "No, I understand that you didn't get a lot of say in your life up to now. It must feel pretty good to be your own boss, huh?" We shared a smile, and I rested my head on his shoulder. It felt good to do it pain free for once.

Dad and I danced for one more song and then it changed to a faster number. Dad and I walked back to the table and I saw James and Mom heading back as well. Mom looked happy. I hoped James had worked his non-vampy magic on her. I knew her well enough to know that once she saw that what we had was real, and that he was good to me, she would adore him. I think she considered me socially deficient before so this change was hard to justify against her mental picture of me.

As we arrived at the table, James asked if Dad would like to help him grab another round of drinks. Mom and Dad both wanted one. The others were on the dance floor now that the alcohol was flowing. I surprised myself asking to have a glass of champagne. James met my eyes before giving me a nod.

The men left and Mom and I were alone at the table. "So," I started. "Tell me what you think of him. Do you like him?" It frightened me how important her answer was to me.

"Claire, he is certainly a charmer and he seems to be well versed in most subjects. I can't find anything wrong with him."

Her tone hinted that there was more she wasn't saying. "What?"

She looked up at the ceiling formulating her thoughts. "I don't know. I can't put my finger on it, but he is *too* perfect. There's something not right, he doesn't talk about his parents or where he comes from. He only talks about now, and you. No past or future. What's he hiding?"

"Mom," I leapt to his defense. "James lost his parents when he was young. You can't hold it against him if he chooses not to focus on the past because it's painful. Living in the now has its advantages. You ought to understand that," I added, referring to my mom's perpetual search for a hobby, home or group of friends that would make her happy for the moment. It was something Dad and I usually avoided mentioning.

Mom was surprised at my boldness. "Claire, what would make you say that?"

I surprised me too. "I'm just saying that you aren't the only one who doesn't have it all figured out yet, Mom." Over her shoulder, I saw the men coming back with drinks. I stood to take mine from James and he slid his arm around my waist. Dad was well in James' corner. Mom would come around eventually, I hoped.

Dad, James and I talked about Europe. Apparently, Dad had been all over Western Europe during his military career. Before long, Mom was drawn in too and I saw her relaxing her guard. It was a pleasure to see her start to enjoy herself. A few times over the next hour, I actually saw her touch James' arm as she laughed with him. He had done it.

What a relief. I felt the weight lift off my shoulders and let out a big sigh. James glanced over curiously. My hand tightened on his in response and he impulsively leaned down to kiss my cheek.

We didn't stay much longer. I was getting tired and had drunk two glasses of champagne, which should have put me under the table, but thanks to the strength afforded me by James' consumption, I merely felt light. We were hugging my parents good night when my mother spoke quietly in my ear. "I hope you're being careful."

Nodding automatically I kissed her cheek and let James wheel me out of the room. The champagne in my stomach began to churn.

Dad shook James' hand and blinked a few times, sensing that things were changing. "Take care of her."

James replied with a firm handshake and a sober nod, "Above all else, Doug."

Ch. 39

When we got back to our room, I took off my shoes, threw my wrap over the back of the chair in the corner and flopped down backward on the bed. "Ow!" I forgot about my hair clip. Taking it out, I heard him snort from the edge of the bed.

James had lost his coat and loosened his tie, undoing the first button on his shirt as he made himself comfortable. Walking straight through the room he opened the balcony doors a crack for some fresh air. On his way back he sat down on the edge of the bed and situated himself beside me, stroking my hair back from my forehead. "They worry about you. You are lucky to have such good parents."

Startled, I turned to him. "Did you...?"

"No, I didn't have to use anything other than my eyes and ears to figure it out."

"James, you know before you I'd never, um."

"I know." He watched me, his expression untroubled.

"Well, um. Could it be possible that my mom could have reason to worry about us not using protection? I mean, I didn't really think about it. It was stupid, wasn't it?" I couldn't believe my thoughtlessness. My life had finally gotten to where I could manage it, enjoy it even and now I might have gone and thrown that all away. "That would explain my symptoms lately."

James had gotten up, pacing as I spoke, and came back to lean his knees on the edge of the bed. He shoved his hands in his pockets as he blinked down at me. Still not saying anything, he sighed and lowered himself to lie on his stomach beside me so that by turning his head we could see each other's faces.

When at last he spoke, my anxiety had reached critical.

"Despite the legends, vampires cannot have children."

At first I couldn't speak. The relief I would have expected at that news wasn't without a touch of sadness. "Really? Never? I heard there were situations where they did."

"Claire, think about it. I don't breathe for need, but out of habit. My heart does not beat. How can my body make living sperm? That would take a creation that an undead being is not capable of."

I found myself blushing at his mentioning the mechanics of the process and chastised myself for acting like a kid. I tried to get the nerve to ask him what I had been thinking about all night. "James."

He turned his head toward me, hair falling to the side and his eyes were grey blue. It was good to see him so relaxed, laying here with me. "Yes, Love?"

I couldn't look at him I was so dreading his answer. Avoiding his eyes, I watched my hands fidget with the clip I'd taken from my hair. "James, have you ever been married?"

He answered softly. "No, I have not."

My eyes sought his to gauge his reaction. "Have you ever wanted to be?"

I saw him struggle with himself and I wasn't sure he was going to answer me. He got up, hands in his pockets again, and walked up to the balcony doors to watch the boats on the bay. The lights at night were beautiful reflected on the water; I could see them from my perch on the bed. It was a long time before James finally answered me, and when he did, he spoke to the water, his voice drifted inside to me.

"Love, have you ever lost someone close to you?"

With a conscious effort, I dropped my shields and tried to reach out to him to find what he was feeling. They were so second nature to me, it took work to lower them all the way. "Yes, I've lost an uncle and my mom's parents." I felt nothing from him. He was blocking me.

"I have lost everyone I have ever known and loved. Henry is the only one in this world I call friend." His voice dropped to a whisper and I had to strain to hear it. "Do you know what that is like?"

Coming up behind him, I reached around his back to put my hands on his chest and lay my head against his back. His hands stayed in his pockets. "I couldn't know what that's like although I do know what it's like to be alone. I have to say, a month ago, I never would have even thought about sharing my life with someone. But now, I can't imagine not sharing every minute with you." I had said more than I meant to, realizing I wasn't sorry to have put it out there.

He shifted under my hands and turned, wrapping his arms around my waist. My head naturally fell into his chest and his chin rested on my head. I waited for him to respond, nervous he might find my neediness too much. After a minute I felt his hands start to rub my back and his lips slid down to run along my neck under my ear. I gave up on the discussion of long-term commitments tonight. I had said my piece and he knew my position on it; that was more than a lot of people could say for honesty in their relationships. The ball was now firmly in his court.

Ch. 40

Our flight wasn't actually until later which we confessed the next morning, agreeing to meet my parents for breakfast when they called to say good bye again. It was pleasant. Mom and Dad really seemed to be trying. For James' part, I have to say he was as effective at seducing the parents as he was the daughter. He seemed to find all of the right topics, from Dad's love of furniture and his travels across Europe before I was born, to Mom's unending desire to take a long trip to France.

I just watched and marveled at how smooth James was handling my parents, wishing I could know for sure we would be able to do this again. After a long good-bye at the restaurant with a particularly long conversation about quarter sawn wood that sent my mother and I to find sanctuary out of earshot, my dear vampire and I found ourselves wandering down the sidewalk, side by side.

The inside of my head was buzzing, I assumed as an aftereffect of the clattering of dishes so prominent in the open establishment where we'd had our meal. When we came to a crowd he reached out and, with one hand on the small of my back, maneuvered me automatically through until we reached a concrete planter that divided us for two store fronts. Coming back together, I saw his hand come out again as if to steer me and I prickled at the gesture.

"Do you handle me as intentionally as you handled them?" The insult came out before I could temper it. The idea that he was manipulating me took hold and held me fast.

Perplexed, his hand froze inches from my back and he waited for more. "What do you mean, 'handled'?"

"That's exactly what I mean. It seems so perfect, it's not possible for that to just happen. You fit what we all want you to be. You know what to say and when to say it. You've done this before." I didn't mean to keep poking at him, I couldn't help myself. My tongue had a mind of its own. The love I felt for him twisted and I heard my own doubts come back to me in my head. *James lived a life I didn't belong in. As soon as he was bored with me he would move on, not even hesitating to "clean up" the mess he'd made with a human.* My mother's statement joined in, *what's he hiding?*

His eyes took on a dark, angry glint. "Claire I honestly don't know what you mean. I have been nothing but honest with you." His eyes flicked up over my shoulder.

He couldn't look me in the eye. "James, you're a liar." I stopped walking. Turning on him, I pressed my fingers into his chest, my voice rising. "You're holding something back from me. Is it because you don't think I can handle it? Is someone here? Or is it something about Scotland? Or have you changed your mind and you don't want to bring me anymore? There's something you don't want to tell me and I know it." I accused him.

The flinch was barely perceptible and he tried to hide his face, turning it toward the street. Furious, I lowered my voice. "Why are you treating me like a child. Do you remember who asked who for help? How can you stand there and lie to my face about our situation? I'm not some helpless little girl who needs to be handled. I can take care of myself."

So enraged that my hands shook, I backed away from where James remained, bone white and unmoving, except for the muscles in his jaw twitching convulsively.

We were in the middle of the sidewalk on the main drag and I wheeled away from him in a huff. I could tell he didn't want to make a scene and took advantage. Spinning on my heel I took off jogging briskly in the opposite direction.

Jogging for about ten minutes, I ended up on the rocky shoreline. It was not as sunny and temperate as yesterday and I wished I had brought a raincoat.

Alone, I could think again. It was bizarre that I was still so angry when, less than an hour ago, I'd been more than pleased with James and my life. How could my views on the complications of our relationship suddenly be so offensive? It didn't matter. Still in a huff, I followed the path on the large boulders onto the point where the rocky ridge ended in the bay.

On the point, I was getting soaked from the cold spray coming off the lake as it struck the rocky outcropping and arced up into the air for the breeze to blow it onto me. With a sinking in my stomach, I realized what had happened. The realization sunk in, bringing with it a burning shame. James and I had been out of touch, physical touch at breakfast and had not resumed physical contact afterward except for a few chance brushes. The effects from last night's feeding must have worn off for me, possibly on James as well, and my hypersensitivity was me channeling James again.

It wasn't until I turned around to go back, to explain what had happened if James would hear me out, that I realized I wasn't alone anymore. Two pale figures stood about fifty yards away between the shore and me. I was trapped next to a foreboding lake that would alone bear witness to my end. I closed my eyes and tried to picture James as clearly as possible in my head so that I could say goodbye to him in spirit, if not in the flesh. With no one coming to help me this time, my fate was sealed.

Coming forward to meet my attackers I watched them mirror my advance. We met in the middle of the outcropping, their pale figures motionless in dark coats as I stood shivering in my sweater and jeans, soaking wet. The only things moving were their coats in the rising breeze. I didn't recognize the two vampires sent to kill me. One was a tall male; dark hair, dark eyes. He appeared to be in his late twenties. The other was a hauntingly beautiful female with bright blond hair. Her hair was soaked to her head like mine but instead of looking like a half drowned rat, she radiated a beauty a mortal woman would have sold her soul to possess. Together, they slowly advanced on me and I stood my ground, watching the waves crashing into the rocks beside me.

When we were within human hearing range, about twenty feet considering the roar of the surf, the female spoke. "We have been sent to find you. Our Master wishes to meet you."

"Who is your Master?" I assumed they worked for Bradley, though, the benefit of keeping them talking was that it could buy time. Time for someone to happen by or James to come find me. I felt a pang knowing this time he wasn't coming. How could he after the awful things I'd said?

The male spoke up. "It is nothing we need speak of here. Come with us, we can talk about it on the way to our Master. He is eager to meet you." He took a few more steps forward and I stepped back, my heels dipped precariously over the edge.

I noticed the way they were maneuvering me; I was being herded. In a few more feet they would be close enough to grab me without relying upon their speed. My stubborn streak flared and I bristled at the notion that I would go quietly with them anywhere.

I had options. I had been practicing. Maybe there was something I could do to help myself after all. Slowly I brought down my defenses, trying to feel both of them. Since we were alone on the rocks I didn't anticipate any interference.

Rapid flashes assailed me and I opened myself up to them. They *were* sent to find me that much was true. Except the

Master they served didn't want to meet me; he'd sent them to kill me. The why of it didn't matter and these two did not question the order. On the contrary, the male had some ideas about my death that turned my stomach. He liked to inflict pain, especially on women. His excitement was building. I could feel it; he was getting ready to lunge.

"No, I'm not going anywhere with you. There's no one with you who wants me anything but dead." They exchanged a look and I saw the truth of my accusation confirmed.

Panic took hold of me, clenching my insides within its iron grip. Again I pictured James and his kind smile, that generosity I had grown to love and his constant desire to do what was right. I choked back the emotion that threatened to erupt as I, again, glanced at the water and considered my choices.

Given my pick between the water and the vampires, I made my decision. If anyone were going to kill me, it would be me. With one big gulp of lung filling air, I jumped. It was sudden and sideways off the ridge, taking the vampires completely by surprise, enabling me to get in the water before they could stop me.

Unfortunately, courage couldn't overcome the shocking effect of the water engulfing my body and I took in a lungful of icy water as my head was pulled below the surface by the current. The good news was that I completely forgot about the vampires as my body struggled to survive the rocky shoreline, strong undertow and icy waters. At first I tried to fight the current while watching for someone at the surface to pluck me out. It was only at that moment that it hit me I had not given up hoping James would come for me. That he wasn't coming hurt more than the water forcing my muscles into a non-functioning frozen state.

Drifting in the current, I began to think about all that was being taken from me by dying here. I saw the life I could have had with James, laughing with Stephen and my parents coming to visit us in our home. Hosting my family for the holidays, finishing school and traveling to see some of the places my father said everyone should see before they die. That I should lose all of what could have been my life without a fight awakened my numb brain. Anger surged through me and I kicked hard, working with the current to bring me to the shore across the bay, away from the vampires.

I kicked and pushed my way through the water, my muscles becoming too painful to be effective, making my movements halting and uneven. Caught up in this last desperate fight to survive, I failed to notice movement in the water beside me until I felt hands grab my sweater and pull my head clear of the water. Unable to focus through the water in my eyes and confusion from lack of oxygen, I struck weakly at the hands pulling me along through the water toward the shore. Against the stronger grip holding me my feeble efforts were no match. The waves gave me a few more parting blows as I was brought up onto the shore and with my soaked skin exposed to the cold air, I quickly passed out.

Ch. 41

Upon waking, I thought I was floating before I realized it was the softness of the bedding I was enveloped in. I knew I wasn't dead. With regret, I remembered the iron hands that had pulled me from the icy waters of the lake. That I had survived the water was a miracle in and of itself, it was too bad I would now die at the hands of a monster.

Trying to pretend I was still sleeping, I peeked around and saw nothing personal to mark the place as a house. I wondered if vampires would bring me to a hotel to kill me. Then, I heard the sweetest sound in the world. "Claire, you're awake."

I struggled to find the source of the sound having a hard time finding my way out with all of the blankets and crinkling pillows around me. Why were the pillows crinkling?

"Let me help you, I have hot packing all around you. Your body temperature was so low I had to bring it up with what I could." Upon closer inspection, I could see the crinkling pillows were actually disposable heat pads that warm when you crack them. They were rolled up and shoved around my body so tightly I couldn't move. The down comforter covering the whole thing was so heavy I was willing to bet it was more than just one. "I raided housekeeping."

"James? How did you find me?" Batting the blankets down low enough to see over and spinning my head around, I finally located him and gaped at the sight. He was deathly pale, his eyes shadowed and black with his hair disheveled and all out of place. His clothes looked like he'd slept in them. James stood beside the bed, observing me with an exhausted slump to his shoulders and ran his hand through his hair.

"I was tracking you. It was hard with the wind switching around the buildings and I had to backtrack a couple of times. Then I felt this, I don't know, something in my head and I knew it was you and that you were in trouble. I even knew it was two vampires. I...I felt them." He rubbed his eyes. If he were human, I would say he needed sleep. "I've called Henry and talked through what I think has been happening with you and I. He agrees with me that you and I are bonded somehow; neither of us can explain it."

"Oh," I wasn't sure I could process what he was saying so soon after coming back from the dead. "It was you who pulled me out of the water? Where were the other two?"

His voice was tight. "Yes, I pulled you out. The others had left you for dead. They should have been right. No human could have survived that long in the water." James roughed his knuckled against his jaw, agitated. "You were in for almost ten minutes from the time you 'called me.'"

Mercifully, my mind shut down and I went back under while it all swam through my poor waterlogged brain.

I woke again with sunlight streaming in around the curtains in our room, the heat pads replaced by his cool body molded along my back, reminding me I was safe. He felt me move and pulled me tightly to him. It felt good to have him nuzzle my hair and neck as he breathed his spicy vanilla smell on me. I was certain I didn't smell nearly as good.

"Love, are you awake?" James murmured in my ear.

"Mmm."

He chuckled, chest rumbling against my back and it felt like this nightmare had never happened. We were back in bed where nothing could hurt us. I closed my eyes and pretended it was true for a few minutes longer.

"Love, we need to get you up and moving. We have a plane waiting." Reality came rushing back with a great big slap. A six o'clock flight to Edinburgh and the vampire Court awaited us. It was tomorrow. I rolled over and hid my face under the pillow with a groan.

His hand reached out and touched my forehead. "Are you in pain?"

"I don't want to go." It was hard not to sound like a spoiled child. My whining amused James and he laughed.

"You sound like you again."

I didn't see how he could be so happy about the same set of circumstances that had me wanting to burrow under the covers and pretend nothing existed outside this room. My head hurt, my lungs hurt; every muscle hurt. I was pretty sure my butt and legs were scuffed from the rocks and the last thing I wanted was to go see a bunch of vampires. Hiding, I threw my arms over my face and closed my eyes. "Let's worry about that tomorrow."

Undeterred, he put his arm around me. "We can't wait that long, our flight's in a few hours. Are you hungry? It has been more than a day since you've eaten."

Had it been a whole day since breakfast with my parents? "What time is it?" I grumbled, struggling to make my eyes work.

"It's two in the afternoon, on Sunday." He stroked my hair, which I was sure looked like a rat's nest.

"Oh no!" I struggled out of the blankets.

James put his hands on my shoulders to calm me. "Don't worry, we have hours before we have to be at the airport this evening. Since you're feeling better," he sniffed, "why don't you go take a shower and I'll order room service. Any requests?"

"Surprise me." I heard my stomach growl, "I think I could eat two of everything."

I battled my way out of the blanket cocoon to find the floor and worked my way to the bathroom. After a very long shower, I felt human again and came out to a full spread of food on the small table by the window. It looked like James had ordered the full menu. My stomach gave a growl as it woke up all the way.

When I had eaten my fill of a chicken sandwich and sweet potato fries chased by some wild rice soup, I sat back to breathe and put some order to my thoughts.

"Who were those two who followed me?" I asked with my eyes closed, digesting.

James leaned back in the chair across from me, his expression troubled. "I'm not sure; I didn't recognize their scents. They could have been sent by the Court to check you out, they have been known to do that before. Vampires don't like surprises."

"No, not unless the Court wants me dead." I was shaking my head. "I read them and that's what they were there for, not information. Plus they said their 'Master' and mentioned a male." I suggested an alternative. "Bradley or the other coven, do you think?"

James' white fingers swept a few crumbs off of the table and tossed them back onto the plate with the rest of my cooling fries. "It's possible, maybe we've underestimated Bradley's hatred of us and his focus on you."

"Why *does* he hate you two so much?" I couldn't believe I had never thought to ask him before, or maybe I had never believed he would answer before.

"Bradley blames us for the death of his 'brother' and his mate and he's a sociopath. He has a great capacity and desire to cause harm to others. Unfortunately, he has fixated his hatred on Henry, myself and your kind, and, now by association, on you."

Changing the subject to something less scary, I asked. "How did you find me? I get that you "saw" me, but how?"

"That's the part Henry and I don't understand. It seems you called me, psychically." He sounded as perplexed as I felt. "We're working on it."

All I could say was, "Huh."

He wasn't too concise either, "Huh, is right."

We got up and packed for the airport. When we went downstairs to check out, no one made mention of my recent "swim" and I had to ask James how he got me in without anyone noticing.

His expression was intentionally blank. "I carried you over the roof and down onto the balcony."

Putting my hand on his arm to stop him I looked up into his eyes nearly black from the strain of recent events and spoke softly. "I'm sorry. I'm sorry for what I said and for running off like that. It wasn't fair. Thank you for saving me, again."

He stopped breathing and ducked his head. "I'll be stronger next time, I promise."

James' head came back up and he growled. "I can't *not* help you, Claire." His black eyes bored into me, barely recognizable as his. "There is nothing you can say or do that would stop me from coming for you."

I wondered at the troubled expression he struggled to hide at his statement. Unwilling to consider it, I pushed away the obvious answer: *compulsion.*

Ch. 42

The long trip to the airport was of course shorter due to the fact that speed limits apparently don't apply to the immortal. Per post 9/11 regulations for international flights, we were there over two hours before our flight. As a matter of fact, we were there with almost three hours to spare, giving us plenty of time to check our bags and stop for a coffee; my choice for dinner considering I had just eaten my day's rations in one sitting only hours before.

Sipping on my plastic lidded meal, I watched James, concerned for his well being. I was too keyed up to sit in the gate area so we wandered. Normally, the Minneapolis airport is a great airport to have down time in with shops, restaurants, and tons of space to walk. It is *not* great when you are trying to find a place to talk privately.

So, we walked and tried to talk about what had happened and what we were about to do. I tried to find out what to expect, thinking it might help settle my nerves. It sounded like this "Court" was a small group of incredibly old vampires who kept tabs on the solitary natured vampires all over the world through a network of loyalists. They reinforced the rules necessary for keeping their existence hidden from humankind.

"What rules?" I asked, glad to learn more about their society.

"We are not to expose our true nature to a human unless the person proves trustworthy, and even then the bond must be for life." I gasped as it hit me how serious it was that he had opened up to me and so quickly.

"Why me?" I wondered aloud. "Why did you pick me to bond with?"

He met my brown eyes with his own midnight blues, the strain around his eyes adding an edge to his words. "When I met you I felt something within you that I had to have."

I tuned in to him; all of a sudden no one else existed. "What do you mean 'had to have'?"

"We are incredibly possessive creatures; you should know that by know. I met you and felt drawn to you at the very first. More than just your need for defenses; I felt something else in you, something I couldn't understand other than the fact that I knew I wanted you for myself. Stephen recognized it, which is why he forced me to swear an oath that no harm would come to you while you were in my care." James snorted shaking his head. "He's a lot smarter than he lets people know." Serious again, he went on, "It wasn't until I worked with you that first time that I felt the *need* to possess you. When you exposed your desire at the club, I was unable to stop myself. Does that sound strange to you? To want something terribly, though you don't fully understand why?" His eyes were an open window to the vulnerability within.

My hand touched his lightly. "I understand. The first moment I saw you, I couldn't think straight. It was like you pulled me to you; it was physical. I'd never felt that kind of attraction before. It was like I didn't have a conscious choice in the matter, I would have gone with you even without the clan's protection." My gaze met his, both of us bewildered. I had never put a lot of thought into fate and destiny but something bigger than us had brought us together; our joining was beyond our control. What was more, this bond we felt had gone beyond the mere physical, even our thoughts were becoming interconnected. "Is that what this bond is? Did it start back then, at the beginning? Does this kind of thing happen very often?"

He was silent considering the possibility, glancing around us at the fellow travelers coming and going as we walked through the terminals. When he finally spoke again he had lowered his voice. I took a step closer to hear, my nose filling with the scent of him and intoxicating my senses. James wrapped me into a bubble filled with only him and I stood rapt. "I was the last of five children. Did you know that?"

I nodded mutely.

"When my parents left England, they had nothing but hope for their new lives. They had no idea what was waiting for them on this side of the Atlantic." He looked down at me, the pain in his eyes still there after these many years. "My mother died of Tuberculosis before I was five. My father was lost without her. He tried to do what he could and managed to apprentice us out before we were in our teens. I was the last to go and watched the grief and drink devour him. There wasn't much left of him when he sent me away at twelve years old. I was apprenticed to a printer miles away where I remained until I was nineteen. Given the distance, it was impractical to visit and I never saw my father again. It was during my apprenticeship that I was turned." He took a long time to blink.

The memory pained him even now and I wanted to know more. "James," I prompted gently. "How did it happen?" I wanted to hear it, and I didn't.

When his eyes opened they were locked in a distant stare far away from here and now. "The printer I worked for was an older man. He and his wife never had children and we got on well. He asked me to stay on after my apprenticeship should have ended and I did. We had rooms above the print shop and one night I was awakened by a commotion downstairs and the smell of smoke. When I went down to investigate the shop was on fire. My master was dead, his head nearly torn from his body and a man stood over him covered in blood. His face was inhuman and terrifying. And in a moment of youthful stupidity, I grabbed the metal rod

284

we used to tighten the press, and rushed at him thinking to avenge my slain master and friend." His language took on the cadence of that time as he relived it. "Instead of being frightened, the beast's face changed to that of a human, and he smiled at me. It was not unkind and I remember forgetting why I was so angry. I put down my weapon and he held out a hand to me, inviting me closer. It was when I drew near that he changed again. His eyes were black and terrifying to behold, yes, but his teeth were what struck fear into my heart. They were long, like an animal. I thought he was the devil himself. He hissed and rushed at me; his attack was so violent I was nearly decapitated and close to losing my arm."

I gasped and he looked at me with a sardonic smile.

"Don't worry, I survived. It was to the arrival of our neighbors, come to put out the fire, that I owe my life. Their arrival and subsequent raising of the alarm scared off my attacker. From there I was put on a wagon and brought to the doctor's house where I was left for dead." His voice broke. "I rose while in his home. I was crazy with thirst and, I will never forgive myself, I slaughtered the doctor and his wife both. When they were discovered dead, the people I had lived among for years hunted me down like an animal and I could not blame them. They did not know what I had become. They thought that I had gone mad from the death of my master and the pain of my attack. I had no choice, I had to go into hiding. Except for Henry as my friend, it has been a lonely existence. No one has called to me until you."

I had no words for how I felt hearing his story, my very soul ached for him. I expressed my sorrow for his loss and promised to never let him be that lonely again in the only way that I could. My lips closed the distance between us, arms wrapping around his neck holding him close to me with the terrible image of James' wrecked body burned into my mind. I vowed silently to do everything in my power to protect him from ever experiencing that kind of pain again.

285

Ch. 43

The flight was just over six hours long. I was so grateful that James had arranged for first class seats. Being short, I normally didn't care about coach seating. But when we would be crushed together with complete strangers for over six hours inside a metal tube of recycled air and questionable meal options, I would take what luxury I could find. I had to remember to thank James properly for the upgrade.

We had both brought books to read for the flights, he tapped a finger questioningly on my choice currently lying idle in my hands.

"What? Consider it homework." I had chosen a popular book about vampires and humans coexisting peacefully in the world.

"You know that is pure fiction. Our kind will never be able to get along side by side in society. Not as a whole."

"Would you like to be 'out of the coffin' so to speak?" I'd never asked how he felt about having to hide who he was.

"I've thought about it." He admitted with a shrug. "There would be some benefits to it. Getting our nutritional needs met might be a little easier; there will always be a certain segment of the population who would jump at the chance to be donors. But I think the prejudices would be hard to overcome for the majority. We would be hunted as we have been in the past. Humans have too strong a fear of us."

"When were you hunted before? I thought nobody knew about you."

"Do you remember the war Henry and I spoke of before? The one that Bradley and his friends have already begun?"

I nodded. How could I forget; the thought of those vampires terrified me.

"We have been fighting humans for millennia, since the time of Lillith. You are familiar with the Bible?"

I nodded.

"It is a story among our kind that she was our first. God created her before Eve and then he cast her out for her rebellious nature." He picked absentmindedly at an imaginary piece of lint on his shirt. "Since the middle ages whenever covens are discovered, the humans have gone on witch hunts, please pardon the expression."

Looking around, I saw that most of the people in our area were sleeping. One woman had headphones on, listening to a movie she was watching on her laptop. We were essentially alone, our lights off, lending us a sense of privacy.

"One of the longest and bloodiest hunts took place near Jerusalem when a large coven was discovered under the city. The Catholic church, who by the way keeps our existence hidden as carefully as we do, proclaimed them infidels to prevent mass hysteria and waged a series of wars that lasted nearly two hundred years. The Crusades' true meaning has been lost to history but we remember. It was the same with the French Revolution. Why do you think they used a guillotine? It is one of the only effective methods of execution for our kind. Those are just some of the more famous large-scale wars. There have been countless others that were smaller and more easily hidden." He was matter of fact, lecturing without evidence of upset.

"Is there anything I learned about history that's real?" My whole view of the world was changing. It felt like my legs were being taken out from under me.

He looked down at me, one corner of his mouth twisted up in a derisive grin. "All of history is one sided, none of the stories are wholly true. We only hear the stories the victor wants told. The remaining stories, the plights, justifications and heroics of the losers are gone with time. Ours is such a history. We are stronger, yet rarely fight together because most of us prefer things as they are. Plus, humans have greater numbers and powerful weapons on their side. Too many of ours would be lost if we were to clash on a large scale."

"So why is anybody looking to start another war if they can't win?"

"That is what we have been working on for some time now. What our investigations have turned up is that there is something the instigators have in their possession that leads them to believe they can rally my kind and unite us under one banner for an uprising. That would enable them to finally achieve their goal of eradication of humankind."

Eyes growing wide, I gasped. If there was an army of vampires united against humankind, how could they not win? "James," I asked deliberately, "how many would they have? There aren't that many of you, are there? Not all of them would fight for Bradley's side, right?"

It took some time for him to answer, his brow furrowed in thought. "We aren't certain on either of your questions, our numbers are not clear. Our lifestyle of existing separately or in small groups keeps us largely disconnected from one another. We are like other top predators and must exist separately, not overlapping hunting territory. It is only those who choose to satisfy their appetites unconventionally that have been able to live successfully in groups like William's or Henry's."

"How big is Henry's group? Will I meet more of them?" I interrupted.

He held up a hand to stay my curiosity. "You will eventually meet them. The only reason that you haven't yet is because we have been keeping you under wraps for your own safety." My mouth gaped. "Because of the seriousness of this war we aren't certain who might be on which side, or if there are spies in our own coven. It wouldn't help us in our future ventures to be known allies with humans. Henry is doing me a great favor in helping to keep you alive."

Staring at him I could see how serious he was. I felt like I was going to hyperventilate. I knew they were keeping things from me, but this was incredible. "Would Henry's friends really kill me?"

James' mouth tightened. I watched his eyes darken again, his emotions were close to the surface today. I'd noticed he was having some trouble with control himself. "We are uncertain of any allegiances at this point, so only trust each other and the cats. Because they are bound to Henry, they cannot betray him. They're compelled to obey through their bond." He had been holding my hand, as we were now doing constantly, so that I wouldn't faint or zone out and I was starting to think it was draining him more than he let on. We would have to find a way for him to feed again before seeing the Court so that we could have some autonomy. He squeezed my hand and I flashed him a distracted smile; his corresponding effort felt forced.

There was too much to wrap my head around. A war was coming between my kind and his and because of Bradley's hatred of my lover and his mentor, my death could come from anywhere. What did being involved with me do to James' fate? Would a vampire looking to take me out have a moral problem killing James or Stephen as well? It didn't sound like it. The remainder of the plane ride, we spoke little.

I tried to sleep, unsuccessfully. My head was swimming and every time I started to drift off, I was haunted with visions of

James being beheaded or Sasha torturing Stephen or me being chased by an unseen monster. It was not with the usual sense of relief that I deplaned the next morning in Edinburgh. I wasn't so sure we weren't serving ourselves up to the very group we were trying to stop.

Ch. 44

In place of renting a car, we took a taxi to our hotel. James argued not having one set vehicle made our movements less predictable and harder to follow. Our taxi ride into New Town Edinburgh was chock full of new sights as it was my first visit. The isles, given their long, rich histories and lush scenery, had always held an allure. I loved how green it was and the rough, rocky terrain I had seen in pictures since I was a kid.

Our hotel, The Howard, was in New Town. From the street it didn't even look like a hotel. It was a discreet luxury hotel in the Georgian style. Famed for its privacy, it only had eighteen rooms, each decorated in rich traditional motifs. The limestone exterior was accented by one simple jade green door. Our taxi pulled up to the address and James escorted me into the building. The driver carried our bags into the lobby, where they were taken by a butler to our room while James checked us in.

With our travel now behind us, James turned to me and asked, grinning broadly, "Are you hungry or would you like to rest? It is your first time in this great city. What is your pleasure?"

It hit me that we were really here together. It was exhilarating to be in a foreign country with him. Not having done any traveling without my parents, I couldn't help feeling like we were doing something we shouldn't. Stealing glances around me, I soaked in the atmosphere and smiled. No matter what happened later, I was determined to enjoy my time with James now.

"If I don't look too gross, I would like to wander around the town. What do you think? What's our timeline? I mean, when are we expected?"

He was surprisingly untroubled, answering lightly. "We have all day today. Tomorrow evening is our appointment. So I ask you, Milady," he raised my hand to brush his lips along the backs of my knuckles looking up at me steadily. I couldn't be sure if it was the touch of his lips or his dark blue eyes as they looked up at me through his dark eyelashes that sent a delighted shiver tingling up my back. "What is your pleasure?"

The thrumming in my body at his touch made my first need clear. "Let's go see our room first."

***

It was nearly lunch when we were ready to go on my first foray into Edinburgh. James announced he'd spent significant time here and would gladly serve as my tour guide. He said that he did need me to eat at a few places specifically during our stay so that he could write up something for his article. Other than that, it was up to me what we saw. Even more exciting than the prospect of seeing the new city and culture, I anticipated seeing it through the filter of his eyes.

"What do you think is an absolute must see?" I wanted to know.

Enjoying his post as my entertainment director, James held up a finger. "First has to be Edinburgh Castle. We will go over the bridge into Old Town and head to the castle for the afternoon. If you would like, there is a romantic restaurant I had intended to spotlight in my article. We can stop there for a bite after."

That sounded great to me. Castles and romantic dinners were in keeping with my hopes for our time together while we were here. We took a taxi over to the castle and I was awed by its sheer size as I got out of the car. I had never seen a castle in real life and this one was in amazing shape.

It wasn't in ruins like the castles in pictures and postcards that I had seen from my Dad's trip across southern Spain years ago. This castle was grey limestone that had withstood the centuries with only some darkening streaks to mark its age.

We walked inside and I felt my jaw drop. The interior was breathtaking in its opulence. My head swam as I wrapped my head around the sheer size and age of the castle and the artifacts held within its walls. My hands touched walls kings and queens had touched centuries before my country was even a thought. The oldest section, a twelfth century building called St. Margaret's Chapel, was my favorite. James and I were the last to leave it. He watched me pass through, reading the plaques marking special sites and touching what I was allowed, smiling when I would make a new discovery. I spent the longest time of all in the chapel, even if it was the coldest.

We spent several hours at the castle and I realized when my stomach growled in the late afternoon, that I'd never had lunch. We strolled the Royal Mile and I got a coffee and pastry at the first café we crossed. There was so much to see and enjoy as we walked. I munched, taking it all in and enjoying my role as a tourist.

With my hands full and unable to clasp his, James had to put his arm around my back to keep me upright so I didn't have a fainting spell. Despite the fact that we seemed to be compensating for my malady quite well and I certainly didn't mind him touching me all the time, I couldn't ignore the effects of the strain on him. James was no longer bouncing back like he usually did.

"If this is where your kind is based can't you find somewhere to get something to eat?" I asked taking a nibble of pastry crust.

Stubbornly he shook his head. "If I go there to feed I have to announce our arrival formally and I don't want to do that."

"But you need to eat." I didn't understand his logic. "Who cares if they know we're here. Don't they anyway?"

Kissing my temple, he smiled. "An alarm doesn't go off when one of us sets foot in the city." My grouchy look warranted a smile. "Seriously, believe it or not we enjoy the same anonymity as anyone else."

"But, I thought you could smell each other."

James frowned and bobbed his head thoughtfully. "If someone who knows me crosses my scent or comes looking for me then yes, they will smell me." Brightening, he winked. "But why bring that upon ourselves prematurely? I brought you here so that I could have you to myself, at least for a little while, and I'm not giving that up so easily." His hand rubbed my back reassuringly. "I can make it one more day."

I tried to believe him, looking past his pale features and the tired lines in his face, new since this morning, as we continued on our stroll through the ancient city's newer quarter. Eventually, the city and being together cast its spell and, walking and talking, we watched the day change to evening. The architecture took on a different, more mysterious personality as it lit up for the night before us and our worries faded into the background.

Dinner was a romantic candlelit affair at a restaurant called The Witchery at the Castle. It was situated in the shadow of the castle as its name implied, granting it a cozy timelessness that enchanted me from the first glance of the faded stone walls and black painted wood trimwork on the outside. James had me describe each course to him in detail while he took notes. It made the tasting of each flavor more decadent, more sensual, to describe my reactions and sensations to every flavor and color. Though I was not as hungry as I should have been after such an active day, I enjoyed the tastes and experience.

I snuggled against him on the taxi ride home. My eyes barely stayed open as the effects of jet lag and a full day of walking caught up to me. He supported most of my weight on our way to the room, helped me into one of his t-shirts, my now preferred sleep attire, and into bed. I was sleeping before my head hit the pillow.

Ch. 45

With just over five hours of sleep under my belt, I was awake and refreshed before dawn and watched the sun rise, only to be obstructed by heavy cloud cover. That was probably preferable to James and I didn't care either way. It was always nice to see the sun, but unless I was in a bathing suit, I didn't need it to be all that hot and sunny to enjoy myself. Stretching, I felt his cool stomach against my back. It never failed to make me smile, beginning the day remembering my good fortune anew.

Reaching for his arm laying across my hip, I ran my fingers down his forearm and delighted in his contented sigh. "What would you like to do today Claire? Other than one quick errand, we don't have to be anywhere until after tea."

The realization that we had our meeting today slammed into me. Predictably, my chest seized up and breathing became a labor. I tried to calm myself with some deep breathing exercises to no avail. I tried to downplay my anxiety. "I had such a good time yesterday, I completely forgot about that."

"I must have been a good tour guide." He pulled me against his body and whispered in my ear, "You remember my promise. You will come to no harm."

He was trying to ease my mind despite both our nerves. I could tell from the tension in his smile and in his walk as we got ready to go down to breakfast that he was feeling it too. I wasn't all that hungry lately and settled for a coffee and pastry again as we wandered the neighborhood. It felt like we were locals strolling with the morning pedestrians on their way to work.

Leaning into his arm, I sighed, "I wish we could stay here. It's such a beautiful city."

"Yes," he agreed, "it's always been one of my favorites. We'll have to come back again when we have more time to spend, maybe when all this is over. You should see the Highlands in summertime."

"Hmm," I mulled that one over. I hadn't thought that far ahead. That we would still be together next summer, maybe taking a vacation together. It sounded wonderful. "You don't think you'll be tired of me by then?"

He squeezed me hard against him. "We could live forever and I wouldn't tire of you. I've been waiting a long time for you; I just didn't know it."

I smiled up at him. "Me too."
We found a café in a particularly well trafficked pedestrian area to watch the people go by. I had a coffee and he had one sitting in front of him for effect, as usual. Sitting across from him instead of walking beside him, I assessed his appearance. His color had me worried again. If he was human, I would have thought he was sick.

"James, we have to get you something to eat before we go see them." He hadn't eaten substantially for days and the small amount he took from me at the wedding was barely enough for the night. He could no longer convince me he could keep me insulated at no cost to him. He needed a full feeding soon or we would both be a mess for our meeting.

"You're very observant." He was grim. "Yes, it is getting more urgent. Don't worry, I will have access to what I need this afternoon. I'll make it until then if we take it easy."

He must have been weak with thirst by now and although traveling with a walking blood source, I was relieved he didn't want to exploit it unless in a dire emergency. Closing my eyes, I inhaled deeply. I pushed away the trepidation I felt and sat up straighter in my chair. "What fun things will we do with our second day in Edinburgh?"

He pointed with his chin to our east. "I thought with the time we have we could go down to the Ocean Terminal and see the yachts, maybe walk along the water."

"That sounds great. It feels like I'm really getting a feel for the romance of the city. It must be all of this strolling," I teased him.

He fidgeted absently with his coffee cup. "That's the spin I'm putting on the article, a romantic weekend. I'm thinking we could turn it into a whole series, romantic old cities."

"I'm not fishing for invitations or anything but I hope you aren't going to try to bring anyone else along on those excursions."

James flicked his eyes up to mine and I felt them burn into me. My stomach did cartwheels when he talked about love and me in the same sentence; combine that with the way he looked at me and I was ready to spend the rest of the day indoors. I knew it wouldn't fade for me, but wondered for the millionth time if it would for him along with my youth.

I had finished my coffee and stood up to throw away my napkin when I looked across the street and saw them. I froze and felt the blood drain from my face.

"What is it?" He whispered, concern clouding his handsome features and standing up to draw tight to my side.

Without speaking, I wasn't sure I could find my voice if I tried. I nodded my chin toward the man and woman standing across the street. They were not a romantic couple. They were a couple of killers. The last time I had seen them, they had left me to die in Lake Superior. Their return sent a spasm of fear through me, only it wasn't just for me this time. A sideways glance reminded me how desperate James was for blood and I was scared to lose him if he had to fight now. Two to one were not good odds, especially today.

His growl was low, I could feel it vibrating my body as he focused on them. Sliding his arm down from my back and resting it over my hand, James surprised me by making a request as he stared at the couple. "Claire, can you get a feel from them?"

"Yes, I did it at the lake." I felt him look down at me and I met his eyes, enjoying the pleased surprise I saw there. "That's how I knew they weren't there to talk." I saw his eyes tighten and his growl rumbled again; he pulled me back into his side in a defensive gesture.

From my safe position, I tried to appear nonchalant to any casual observers as I brought my focus to the woman. James' touch helped me to filter out the "buzz" of the humans around us while he kept himself closed off to avoid any "contamination." Bringing down my shields enough to feel her, I sucked in my breath through my teeth. I knew we were in trouble. Hearing my reaction, James flicked his eyes down to me.

"What did you get?" He asked urgently.

I gulped. "She got in trouble after they failed last time. Their boss, the one they call their Master, punished them severely for it." Dropping my voice, I whispered. "He used a knife and it hurt. The blade was some sort of stone; why?"

Brow furrowed, James explained why. "It takes a lot of damage, but we can go into something like human shock," he mumbled under his breath. "Wooden stakes can paralyze us, silver can kill if it enters our blood stream. He probably used something else to maximize his results."

James looked around us, assessing our options, and turned west toward the bridge and Old Town. Looking back, I confirmed they were indeed following us. We didn't have to hurry, there were enough humans around and it was daylight; they had to be careful not to be visible.

We walked briskly, trying to appear unhurried as we gave wide berth to alleys and deserted areas. James was clearly trying to avoid a conflict with the two trailing vampires. I followed along, waiting for a chance to ask him what his plan was, but the streets had gotten crowded and we couldn't stop.

My strength was flagging after several miles at a good clip. My experience hiking gave me no advantage. It had been at human pace, not vampire, and I was spent. "James, can we slow down just for a minute? I'm human, remember?" He rumbled in his chest, cutting me a warning glare. Virtually running these last few miles, I hadn't seen his face before; now I could see how close the vampire was to the surface. The effect of days of stress and hunger were reflected in his eyes. "We have to figure something out soon or I'm worried the city's going to see a vampire showdown in broad daylight." He made no indication that he heard me. "And then we're all dead." He blinked.

Distracted, James nodded. "I don't know what to do. If I could hide you, I could handle them, but I am going to have limited control during a fight." He turned his tormented face to mine. "I don't want you anywhere near me if that happens."

"If?" I snorted. "You mean when. They aren't backing off and you don't have much left in your reserves. You've used them up taking care of me." The flash in his eyes, before he carefully tucked it away, confirmed my suspicions. "If you think you can take them, then let's find the best place for it. Have you ever had to fight in a city before?" Gauging from the "duh" look he gave me, I was guessing he had. "Well, then what's your best bet?"

Back to thinking in terms of strategy he had answers for me right away. "I need privacy, firm footing and open space. An abandoned building is perfect."

Feeling like I finally had a purpose and means by which I could help, I began to walk again. This time, I scanned the area and quickly saw a small black brick faced pub closed for renovation. Better still, there was plastic sheeting over the inside of the windows providing a total blackout on the inside. I spoke his name quietly and gestured with my chin and eyes. He immediately understood and I saw his face set grimly as he readied himself for battle.

"Claire, I am going to need your help luring them into the pub. They are after you, not me. After we have them in there, you will need to find cover, preferably something that locks so that I can be free to move and not worry about leaving you open to an attack. We'll see what they've left in there during their construction."

Bravely, I agreed, carefully guarding my reservations about being front and center in a fight between three vampires. The only one I could call an ally was so blood starved even he couldn't guarantee my safety once he was in the heat of battle.

Hand in hand, we walked past the front door of the pub and made an exaggerated right turn on the sidewalk. Following the walk, we came upon a standard sized metal door painted red. The lock on the door was probably a good idea unless your intruder was a determined vampire. I heard metal squeal before the lock gave way and the door opened. We left it cracked to make it obvious where we had gone, hoping they wouldn't resist the chance to capture their prey even if they did sense the trap.

Once inside, James pulled me close enough to grab my shoulders and clamped down so tightly it hurt. He was always so careful with me I knew he was more scared than he was letting on, his tenuous hold on himself slipping in the building tension. The terrain the building provided was sparse. They had gutted it entirely. We were looking at concrete floors and glass windows with plastic sheeting hung to protect the glass, reducing the light inside to a hazy gray glow. The cherry wood bar and the big mirror behind it were the only things inside.

He looked at me, face tight with nerves and fear. "We have no other choices. You need to hide behind the bar. Don't come out; don't move, whatever you hear. Okay?" Nodding, I started to walk away to take my position behind the bar and his vice like hold on my arm yanked me back. I snapped into his chest with a force that would leave a bruise. His lips found mine, his kiss was hard and desperate. When I withdrew, I saw his fear and felt my stomach plummet. I told myself he would be okay, he was virtually indestructible, and I hurried behind the bar.

I hadn't been hiding ten seconds when the side door creaked open and closed. They were inside and, by their stealth, we could assume they were there to kill. My fear for James was stifling and I was having a hard time breathing, trying by sheer force of will to keep my human heart and breath from giving away my position. They would only serve to make James' job harder than it was already. I was left to do the only thing I could, be still and stay out of the way. As I settled into a nook behind the bar, I saw a small crack in the wood. It allowed me to see a narrow section of the dimly lit pub in front of me; at least I wouldn't be completely blind to the action.

They were all so quiet I couldn't hear any hints of movement at all. Then something broke the light when it passed in front of one of the windows. Within a moment, I saw a pair of legs directly in front of the bar. I held my breath as the legs paused and turned away from me. I recognized the long, thin legs as the pair belonging to the blond female. They had started to walk away from my position when she dropped into a crouch and I could make out the outline of her shoulders, relieved to see her back was to me. Then, I jumped and hurried to cover my mouth when I heard it a second later. James and the male were facing off. Their growls reached me from the front area of the pub, the area blocked from my sight by the blond. I felt my heart begin to pound as my fear rose to new heights.

Ch. 46

Too late, I remembered the hearing of the female directly in front of me. In my defense, I don't think I could have controlled my heart rate anyway. She whirled toward me and in one stride, had jumped up onto the bar. Dropping down, she landed crouched in my face with her fangs bared and eyes dark with hatred.

Her smile filled me with sickening dread. It wasn't a happy smile. "I won't make the mistake of assuming you died again. This time I will kill you with my own hands."

When she grabbed me, I felt by her touch that she did not have any sort of psychic shielding. It had never occurred to me that like people, not all vampires have special abilities beyond what their nature and age granted them. I couldn't believe my luck. I had an advantage in that she couldn't block anything from me. I'd thought I could read her before because she wasn't trying to block me out, that she hadn't been consciously shielding, but it was with a surge of elation that I realized she didn't block because she couldn't. Facing my imminent death, I thought this would be an opportune time for me to test something I had been working on with Tara.

After the attempted attack on campus, I had meant it when I told James the next time I would be stronger. In our down time at the house, I had been working with Tara on the sly to project like Stephen did instead of just receiving signals. It was like throwing the reverse switch on my channeling ability and, if things went well, flooding the other party to distract them.

Looking into the blonde's hate filled eyes, I decided there was no better time to test it out than right now. First, I needed to find something in her head to use. Maybe since she didn't know how to block people out, she wouldn't recognize my intrusion and would let me dig around in her head. When I had felt her in the cafe I had gotten a strong sense of jealousy and anger toward her partner due to the fact that he had the ear of their leader and she did not. Grabbing onto that combustible combination, I mixed it with a taste of my own anger toward them. They had terrified me, caused my family to exhaust themselves protecting me and now were trying to kill me a second time in a week as well as my lover now fighting for both our lives only feet away. My fury rose up inside me and I visualized my hands grabbing onto it and pushing it toward her.

I saw it in her eyes when my emotional cocktail flooded into her and, as I had hoped, her eyes broke from mine. Letting go of me, she rose and I watched her transfer her glare to the men in the corner. My concentration was taxed as I continued to focus on her, to flood her with anger toward her partner. I didn't think I was strong enough to calm her down enough to avoid a confrontation; her hatred was too powerful. I could only twist what she already had and hope that I could try to control it.

I knew that if I watched her go toward James, I would panic and lose focus. Not wanting to lose my tentative control over what I was doing and have her attack him as well, I stayed where I was and concentrated with every fiber of my being on making her attack her partner.

I carefully fed her rage with my own and funneled it down the connection I had built to her mind, tying rapidly into the feeling in my head that was her. I flashed pictures only of her partner, supplementing hers with my own images of his dark eyes and hair and his small, powerful build. His image was burned into both our minds and I made sure that his was the only face I saw in my head as I took over her mind, twisting it through our connection.

The growls inside the pub changed. There were three now instead of two and the female's grew to a snarl. Seconds

305

later, I heard the crash as two bodies collided and a high-pitched scream before the female's snarl abruptly ended. I felt the connection I'd shared with her suddenly snap back, broken, and I was shocked as the power of the fury I'd been feeding her recoiled, slamming itself headlong into my mind.

Too fast for me to have a chance at deflecting it, I felt it flood into me taking me over at once. I wanted to kill the male. My anger toward him was her anger. It was a jealous anger and had nothing to do with his current desire to kill James or me. Rising up, I threw myself bodily on top of the bar and rolled over to drop to my feet on the other side. As I faced the men I saw James in a half crouch, arms out defensively toward the smaller male making ready to leap at the first opening. The male had stepped over the headless body of the female and his own form was tensed to spring at James.

My words were not my own as I shouted to get his attention. Because I was channeling the last of her thoughts, I had the same lack of fear for my own safety. At the sound of my cry both men turned toward me, their reactions polar opposites. James' was one of horror and the small male's was pleasure. When I saw him, the fury raged inside me and propelled me forward. I needed to sink my fangs into him.

Mid-stride, another connection screamed at me to stop. Temporarily stunned, I stumbled to a halt and blinked in confusion. The thick veil of the blonde's killing rage lifted enough for me to feel the anguish coming at me through my mysterious bond with James. My eyes sought his and found his jet black and wide as he stared from me to the male, gauging whether or not he could reach the male first before I did. As I tried to shake down the fog of the dead blonde's anger, the tiny piece of my human mind, crushing under the power of the invading psychic energy, told me that I had just put James in the exact position he had feared. My heart twisted.

Movement from my periphery brought me back to the male on my right. I saw him make his lunge and the rest was so fast, it didn't make sense until after it was all over. The male took a run and launched himself at me. James leapt over the legs of the fallen blonde and with both hands out, hit the male from the side, deflecting him and sending him flying. James' momentum carried him to land next to the male, who had staggered to a stop just before going through the exterior window. Fortunately for us, no one passing by could see us through the sheeting and the noise on the street covered any sounds of the scuffle within. I could only hope we wouldn't draw more vampire attention before we could get away from here.

The smaller male twisted, grabbing James' arm and tried to pull him in toward his teeth. James proved elusive and spun himself away. In a move that turned my stomach, James chambered a leg and brought it down on the male's knee, which gave with a snap and dropped him to his knees. James lunged forward and with a quick movement of his hands, efficiently decapitated the male.

The body had barely hit the ground when James turned to me. I held my breath as he panted, breathing me in. For what felt an interminable period he waged a different battle, this one internal. Lowering his lips over his fangs, I saw his desire to have me as mate win over his desire for my blood.

Placing his hand against my cheek, he turned my face up into his own. Stepping back he scanned for any sign of injury. Seeing nothing but shock in my frightened eyes staring back, he closed his eyes briefly and calmed himself so that when he reopened them, he was James again. Almost.

Though he had hidden his fangs and the flesh on his face regained some of its human softness, the darker color to his irises gave him away. Leaving me no time to process all that I had seen, he put his arm around my shoulders, pulled me into his side protectively and commanded, "We have to leave, now." He steered me through the pub and out the metal door we had come through just minutes before, fearing for our lives. Now, as we left, it dawned on me that we had lived and James had just torn the head off of a vampire right in front of me. And here I was, strolling down the streets of Edinburgh with his arm around me, feeling nothing but comfort at his touch. There had to be something wrong with me.

We had walked nearly a mile before James felt safe stopping. With his arm still cradling me, he halted my progress as well and I let him bring me around to face him. The sunglasses were back in place leaving me blind.

"Claire," his voice was warm on my skin cool from the brisk air, starting to bring me back to myself. "We need to get you back to the hotel. I think you need to lie down." I saw his brow furrowed with concern and I reached up to push back his hair off his cheek, needing to touch his skin and feel the cool hardness of his body. It wasn't a sexual need. I had come to depend upon him so much to regulate myself, that it frightened me. He was a part of me, our connection made us two parts of a whole, no longer easily distinguished from one another mentally.

"Me? What about you? You need to feed soon or you're going to lose it."

He waved me off. "I will have what I need in a few hours." Seeing the worry in my eyes, James pulled me close stroking my back soothingly. He spoke quietly. "I didn't want you to see that. Why didn't you stay hidden?" I watched the concern flash to anger as the details of the altercation came back to him. "What the hell did you think you were doing throwing yourself into a fight between two vampires? You could have gotten yourself killed."

I pulled away, mad I couldn't see his eyes behind the dark shades, my own anger flaring. "She found me and was going to kill me. Sorry I didn't just sit there; I used her anger to make her go after her partner." A little embarrassed, I had to admit I had gone off half-cocked in there and almost ruined the whole thing. "I wasn't expecting the recoil. But you have to admit it helped."

His struggle was evident as he warred between his anger over my putting myself in danger and conceding that I had been able to effectively equalize the fight. "You've been holding out on me."

Suddenly self-conscious, I couldn't meet his eyes. "Tara's been helping me; she's really good at projecting. I didn't want to be completely helpless the next time there was a fight, and I didn't think learning to throw a punch would work with your crowd."

He snorted. "Well, you're right about that." His tone grew serious and there was something new in his voice. "I'm proud of you, Claire. It took a lot of self-control to do that and to keep it together when you saw," James' brow darkened, "when you saw what you did. It had to be difficult. I wish I could tell you that you won't see that again, but that would be a lie. We don't know how all of this is going to come out or how much more fighting we will all see before this ends."

I leaned into his chest. I just wanted to be touching him right now and not thinking about Bradley or the Court or the bond I had with James. Whether it was love with a vampire or magic that was causing it I didn't know, but it didn't seem to be hurting us so I wasn't going to fear it for now. I mumbled into his chest, "How much time do we have before we have to go to our meeting? Can we still see the marina? If you're up to it."

309

"We have time." He kissed me gently, "It's one of my favorite parts of the city."

"Show me." I tugged his arm and began to lead him away. Laughing he lowered his head so that I could see his eyes behind his sunglasses. "The marina is the other way, Love."

I smiled and shrugged my shoulders, letting him redirect me as I clung to his arm. As long as he was leading, I didn't care where we went.

Ch. 47

We headed back to the hotel at three so that we could clean up and present ourselves to the Court on time.

I put my hair up in a bun with chopsticks in keeping with my Chinese theme and put on heavier makeup than usual to make my eyes dramatic. As I was putting on my lipstick, an understated shade of red, James came into the bathroom. "What is taking you so long?" He broke off as he came around to lean on the doorframe and saw me.

Dubious of the wisdom of the ensemble chosen for me my hand froze, lipstick halted mid swipe.

"What? Is it too much?" His reaction made me question Tonya's choices. *She* could pull off exotic, not me.

He was shaking his head, an odd expression on his face. "It's so...I've just never seen you look so, dramatic. It's perfect, they'll be very impressed." Pushing off the doorframe, he came up behind me and wrapped his arms around my waist, lowering his head to my neck. James rubbed his lips along my neck and down to my collarbone. My insides fluttered and my breath caught; he chuckled at my reaction and the vibration had me biting my lip.

I had to swallow a couple of times first, but managed to warn him off. "If you want me to walk out that door, you are going to need to take two very large steps back." Slowly he pulled back and I missed his cool touch as soon as it was gone. In a blink, I thought of something I hadn't before. "James, are we going to have to hold onto each other the whole night? Are they going to let us stay together? Or do you think your eating will be enough?"

There was a flash of the dread on his face I knew he'd been attempting to hide from me. With our connection, I had been feeling more and more from him. I knew he was nervous about this meeting as much as he tried to deny it. Our bond also let me in on something he hadn't vocalized, the fact that he did not fear the Court. There was someone there he trusted. Someone he didn't want to tell me about. The knowledge hurt and I reminded myself I didn't want to know about his former lives, or lovers. "I don't know what it will be like," he said carefully. "I've never gone before them with a human."

Fighting the trepidation I felt at meeting them was the simple-minded giddiness of what it meant that he had never brought a human to the Court. I was a first for him and it felt good since he was a first for so many things for me. "Do we have time to call Henry? Maybe he has some advice." Really I wanted to ask about Stephen and find out if they were okay. "We need to tell him about the two earlier, don't we?"

Shaking his head, he looked at his watch. "No, he's tied up right now."

"How do you know what he's doing?" I studied him. "Do you have some sort of psychic link or something?" Nothing was beyond my belief at this point.

James patted his pants pocket. "Cell phone. We've been in regular contact while you and I have been here. He's monitoring the situation here as well as stateside. Sasha has been handled," he added almost as an afterthought.

Relief coursed through me at the confirmation that my friend and his family were okay. Then I hesitated. "When have you had time to call him? I haven't heard you make one call." Curious, I sought clarification. "Did they kill her?"

He gave me a look like I was missing something. "You *do* sleep, and yes, she and one of her females is dead. The other ran off. They will try to find her before they have to come home but if they don't it doesn't matter, one young vampire won't attack a clan of weres."

My temporary relief was quashed knowing the clan was still seeking out vampires. I nodded at him, "Okay."

He understood my sudden lack of pursuit of the subject and kissed my head. Stepping away, he rubbed the tops of my arms, whispering quietly. "We should go."

Mutely, I nodded again and we walked back into the main bedroom, gathering the last of our things before we left together to face a very scary group of very scary vampires, asking them if I could keep breathing. I wondered whether it mattered if we asked them to consider helping to stop Bradley from bringing a war before or after we asked for my approval, or if they were more likely to do something to one of us if they were displeased by either request. My imagination kept feeding me images of James' head torn from his body or a silver stake being plunged through his heart. Goose bumps covered my arms as we stepped out our door.

Ch. 48

We sat with our sides touching in the taxi. He held my hand loosely in his own. The ride was short and before I knew it, he was helping me out of the car in front of a pub on the George IV Bridge. When I saw the shingle out front, I gawked in disbelief.

"Really? The Frankenstein Pub?"

Amused, he grinned. "Sometimes the best place to hide is in plain sight. People come here expecting monsters. They don't *see* the real ones. We aren't flashy enough."

I stood rooted to the spot when he tried to maneuver me toward the doors.

"What?"

"I...I'm afraid they won't like me." Feeling a coward for admitting my fear, I watched him closely for his disapproval. James had dressed for the occasion, his extra pale skin served to set off his black suit and white shirt. He had broken his monochromatic appearance with a silk tie perfectly matched to my dress' green embroidered accents. He took his necessary daytime eye protection off for just a moment and I saw him wince as his eyes felt the fading sun directly.

Raising my hand to his lips in his act of long dead chivalry, he kissed it. "No harm will come to you. I made you a promise."

Managing only a weak smile and willing my legs forward I didn't argue. We continued to hold hands as we walked into the pub.

The interior was a gaudy tourist trap heavy on the macabre. It was probably great fun when one wasn't afraid for one's life. James stowed his shades in his jacket and started scanning the room. To anyone who didn't know him he was the picture of calm and cool, but I could see the tension in his face. He was on high alert.

I looked around, seeing nothing that screamed vampire. All of the tourists were busy goggling the staff dressed as various sorts of monsters The locals were visible in their ready acceptance of the bizarre, some were even playing along.

I didn't see anything genuine until my eyes landed on the large, brutish male bartender. He stood behind the counter about fifteen feet away directly across from us. He probably weighed in close to three hundred pounds, his curly black hair and deeply tanned Polynesian skin making further details hard to make out in this dim light. The dark eyes looked black to me, no white in them at all. I was curious if he was some new non-human creature. James' hand tightened around mine and I heard him growl under his breath. He stepped forward and I jumped a step to keep up with him as we crossed the narrow distance to the bar.

The bartender spoke to James, his scratchy voice insanely deep. It rumbled straight out of his barrel chest. "Anything I can get you?"

James held up his index finger, indicating he would like one. The bartender nodded his large head slowly. I guessed that everything he did was slow; it was inherent to his massive size. James turned to me and raised his eyebrows. Nodding, I answered for my dry throat, "water." Turning back to the bartender, James already had a bill out of his pocket and on the counter.

His drink looked like red wine in a very large goblet, though I knew it was something he would find significantly more

315

palatable. It didn't even strike me as twisted that I was pleased he was getting to feed. It had been too long and he needed it if we were going to have a chance at presenting a strong front to the Court.

We brought our glasses to a private corner booth with high sides upholstered in black leather and brass buttons. I was watching James intently and noticed a slight tremor in his hand as he lifted his glass and drained half in one long gulp. He held his eyes closed for a long moment and when he opened them again, I saw with a sigh of relief that his face was far more relaxed. It was too dark to see if his color was changing yet. I sipped at my water, unsure whether my stomach would reject it. My nerves were stretched tight.

We sat at our table speaking very little and James ordered another glass, drinking this one more leisurely. Shortly, a stocky redhead came over to our table. As she came closer, I could tell that she was a vampire. She was physically older than any I had seen so far. It appeared that she had been turned in her mid to late forties. When she spoke, her voice was raspy like an old smoker.

"Come with me, we have a private room for you." As we stood, she motioned to the table, "You can bring your drinks."

I looked to James for direction and saw that he grabbed his with his free hand, while keeping his left hand firmly on my waist. It would appear a casual gesture, but I had the feeling he would be keeping me very close during our visit. At least now he would be strong since he'd fed. I didn't know how much blood he would need because it had been so long; hopefully two glasses were enough for what lay ahead.

Our guide led us to a door to the right side of the long, narrow bar. We walked through it and down a long hallway. The bar's owners must have shared space with the building behind it because I could tell we had walked too far to still be in the same building. We turned and had to walk down a dimly lit stairwell with ancient looking stone steps, grooves worn into them from feet over who knew how many years. James' arm slid off my waist, down my arm and over my hand never breaking contact. I felt stronger. It had to be coming from him. There was definitely more there than I'd felt since we'd been in Scotland. I wanted to talk to him about it but thought it best to do so when we left here.

At the bottom of the stairs, I could see that we were in a large room about the size of the entire bar above. The ceiling and walls were all pale limestone and worn smooth. The floor was constructed of large pavers of the same stone pushed tightly together, no spaces between them. On the walls were lit torches acting as our only sources of light. I was guessing they were not for effect, but that there was no electricity down here. It was, nonetheless, dramatic and more than a little unnerving. Shivering, I noticed there was also no heat down here.

Our guide held up her hand for us to stop, "Wait here, please. You will be received shortly." Her plain blue dress rustled against her tights as she retreated up the stairs.

I didn't know what to do so I just stood there, not speaking. James looked at me, his features and body gone still and unblinking. Here, away from human eyes, he was dropping his disguise giving me a clue that our audience with the Court would be more like time with Bradley than Henry. I swallowed hard, preparing for what was coming. He drained the rest of his glass and set it down on a step.

We waited several long minutes. I could see from the set of his unmoving shoulders and jaw that he was as tense as I was. The unknown was what was most nerve wracking of all. This room with its plain, monochromatic stone walls, ceiling and floor was bare of furnishings, sound or any other stimulus. It felt like some sort of gigantic sensory deprivation chamber and was having the same effect on me.

317

My senses were growing hyperaware, reaching for something to hear or see; anything at all. I was just about to ask James if he could sense anything when a door in the wall to our right, that had blended so well it escaped my notice, opened smoothly and without sound.

In through the door stepped a delicate pale woman. Her skin held no pigment that I could see and her pure white hair hung straight down to her slender waist. Her rose-colored dress hearkened to a time with knights and kings. I had seen its likeness in tapestries during my visit to Edinburgh castle. The sleeves were fitted, a square topped bodice opening low revealed a small amount of delicate cleavage and its plain skirt lay smooth on her legs. Her matching slippers covered tiny feet, fitting for a woman her size. She was smaller than me, which was unusual. She might be five feet in her slippers. Not many people made me feel big, yet next to this one I felt positively clumsy.

When she spoke, it was so quiet I had to strain to hear. "They will receive you now."

We followed her into the interior room beyond. She backed into it, blocking my view until she moved aside. As we entered, my eyes searched all around trying to take in my new surroundings, rapidly determining the danger waiting to befall us. My pulse raced yet my mind remained quiet. It was as though everything slowed down enough for me to take my time evaluating all that I was seeing. My death grip on James' hand didn't loosen once. I was glad for his lack of body heat because it kept our hands from sweating and slipping. Instead, our hands were locked firmly together.

The room itself was large, as tall as a two-story home and wider than my high school gymnasium. The décor reminded me of the castle I'd seen yesterday. I felt like I had been transported back in time several hundred years. Beautiful, richly colored tapestries hung from the walls breaking up the monotony of the cold stone, iron sconces held torches between them and several large roughly hewn wood and metal candelabras hung from the ceiling. Milling about the room were not less than a hundred people, no, vampires. Many were dressed like they were going to a costume party themed for the court of King Louis XIV, others in various other period fashions including our own. All were formal of course. Several of the men wore hose and those short pants I had seen in paintings, coats that buttoned down the front and some had hats with feathers in them, three who stared boldly at me when we passed wore tuxes with tails complete with white gloves and top hats. At the front of the room were several high backed chairs and three vampires standing nearby exuding the type of power and confidence befitting kings and queens. This must be the heads of the Court we were here to see.

The albino woman who had walked us in continued to lead us across the long room and through the crowd to halt mere feet before the three members of the Court. She curtsied low to the ground, her head nearly brushing the stone floor. I stood in awe of her grace, noticing she didn't wobble once. Standing, she announced in a voice as miniscule as when she spoke to us outside, only now I could hear it easily by some miracle of acoustics.

"James Thomas and Consort, if it please the Court." With that simple introduction, she backed away and left us to face them. I actually felt a little more alone after she left, silly as that was.

The three of the Court were equally focused upon us as we studied each other. The leader, I was guessing since he was in the center and had that air about him, was the shortest and fattest. Dressed all in pale blue silks, he had long, wavy brown hair that hung loose over his shoulders. He couldn't have been over five and a half feet without his heeled shoes. His face was doughy and bore no facial hair. I had never heard of an obese vampire before so seeing his fleshy face and matched protruding belly took me by surprise. When he waved a hand at our escort I caught sight of the lace edge of his handkerchief hanging from his cuff.

To the left of the fat man was a man quite different in dark blue. His style of dress was of the same period, but he was the complete opposite of the doughy man next to him. He had to be over six feet tall and built whip thin. His thin blond moustaches and goatee reminded me of one of the musketeers.

To the far right of the men stood the most beautiful woman I had ever seen. In life she must have been of Spanish blood, judging by her darker coloring and the dress she favored. Her black hair was swept up in a loose plait, partially hidden under a small round black hat with a short black lace veil ending at the bridge of her nose. Her red silk dress was trimmed similarly in black lace.

The three stood, watching us expectantly as James and I held hands facing them. I had no clue what to do and waited for someone to give me a direction. James spoke first, bowing low at the waist. "It is a distinct honor to be in your presence once again. Thank you for accepting my request for an audience." Indicating me with a nod of his head, I simultaneously felt a squeeze to my hand and knew I should try to curtsy. Working very hard not to fall, I tried the never before attempted maneuver as low as I dared and held it a few long seconds before coming back up. James introduced me. "Please allow me to introduce to you my human companion, Claire Martin."

The man in light blue spoke first, inclining his head slightly toward James. "It has been far too long James. Henry has spoken highly of you in our discussions of late; he finds you to be a great asset. It is unfortunate he could not be with you today, he is still my favorite opponent to face over a chessboard." His voice was high pitched, like that of a child.

Nodding back, James agreed. "Henry wished to be here with us and sends his regards. He had urgent business in the states that demanded his full attention." Unflinchingly, he added, "I'm sure you're aware of the anarchy in Milwaukee. Given its close proximity to our coven, we are most anxious about it ourselves."

At the mention of Milwaukee, the three exchanged a glance and I heard rumbling from the audience. The man in dark blue spoke up, his voice resonating through the stone around us. "Charles welcomes you on our behalf and you waste no time in bringing up unpleasantness. There are consequences for such insolence." Fangs flashed as he spoke.

James stood straight, staring unafraid at the man. "I mean no offense Anton. My apologies if it causes any undue discomfort." James continued bravely on, "I have come here to discuss these very matters with the Court. As well as the actions of an old adversary."

The man in dark blue growled. "How dare…"

Charles interrupted the tall vampire. "Anton, please. Let us welcome our guests. The mention of unpleasantness is necessary, albeit unfortunate. I understand Henry's coven and allies have been seeking tirelessly to find the responsible parties involved in the difficulties in Milwaukee. It only makes sense that the matter would be at the forefront of his associate's mind."

"He forgets himself." Anton glared at James without giving Charles a glance. "He no longer carries favor with this Court and we will not discuss *our* investigations with him. Court business is no longer his concern," he said decidedly.

Ignoring his intended insults, Charles turned away from Anton to face us, looking mildly amused and changed the subject. "This is not the only purpose for your audience today James. I understand you have come to us to request permission for a human's admission into our society. Is that correct?"

I felt myself blushing when Charles directed his attention to me. James answered clearly. "I have indeed and I request your approval."

Charles approached me, smirking at my discomfort. "James, I believed you were uninterested in anything so permanent." He waved a hand dismissively, speaking to no one in particular. "Not that it really matters. Some take them so seriously, as if it weren't possible to get out of it if you choose." He tipped his head, black eyes boring into mine. "Miranda, do you see how she flushes? How enchanting." He studied me from less than three feet away, so close I could nearly touch him. "Tell me, human, do you flush for shame to lie with a vampire or because I speak of your death so casually?"

Wishing I could look to James for guidance, not wanting to offend Charles by looking away, I answered the best I knew how. "No Sir, I am blushing because my relationship is private and your mention of it publicly embarrasses me."

At my answer, Charles laughed airily. Turning to James, he asked, "You took an innocent, James? I'm impressed." He aimed his explanation at me. "That is a challenge for our kind due to your natural fear of being hunted. It is instinctive and stronger for the pure than the more experienced, let us say, who might enjoy the pursuit a bit more."

I couldn't help but peek at James as I wondered at that. How could I be afraid of James? I couldn't resist him if I tried, not that the thought had ever crossed my mind. I considered briefly the Glamour Stephen had mentioned at our first meeting, then brushed away so quickly. Even with his eyes black and body unmoving, more vampire than human, he was still the man I loved and trusted.

322

He sensed my curiosity and blinked at me, letting blue bleed back into his irises, clearly aware how unlike himself he must look to me. "I can compel someone to come to me, but I cannot take away their fear entirely. Your lack of fear was one of the things that drew me to you." It astonished me that he spoke so freely in front of the Court. It had been nothing but formal to this point yet he showed no hesitation in addressing me while Charles looked on with a vaguely pleasant expression on his face.

Charles glanced back at me and then at James, his disinterested mask slipping away. As he examined us, a puzzled expression set in. "Miranda, would you come here please? I need your expertise."

My heartbeat went into overdrive and sweat sprung up on my lip. Could he sense my ability? I had tried to block it through my shielding. I didn't want to call attention to myself any more than necessary. Charles turned back to face me and stepped in toward me, close enough to kiss. His face was right next to mine as if he was going to whisper in my ear. Leaning in, he sniffed my neck. Why did everyone do that lately? Irritation prickled me.

Charles startled backward a step, his eyes opening wide and I watched Anton stiffen expectantly. Miranda continued her graceful steps toward us without hesitation at Charles' reaction. As Miranda drew near, Charles pointed a stubby finger in my face. "Smell that."

Without hesitation, Miranda approached and leaned in between James and I, sniffing my neck. It had been frightening when Charles did it, yet this was different. Miranda's slow, deliberate movements were mesmerizing; her raw sensuality made her inspection intimate. Her seductive nature was agonizingly uncomfortable and I held James' hand tighter since I couldn't look at him without turning my face even closer to Miranda.

She withdrew slightly, staring into my eyes from only inches away. Her black eyes were hard. "James, you are too bold. Marking a human before gaining the Court's permission carries a hefty penalty. This one has not been admitted to our society and yet you have taken the liberty to bind her to it? We do not have many rules, but we do require strict adherence lest we have anarchy. Have you forgotten so much since leaving us?" Her voice was deadly calm and I didn't like the cold fury I saw in her eyes. Nor did I like the words coming out of her mouth.

"Marked?" I sputtered, forgetting myself and furiously turning to face James. That explained this connection and why no one would tell me more about it. It wasn't so mysterious after all. He had promised me he would never do such a thing without my permission, something I wasn't sure I would ever have given, and I had believed him. Feeling a fool, resentment began to build within me.

The accusations forming on my tongue froze as I registered the astonishment written plainly on his face. James' dismay was not feigned. He appeared equally shocked and taken aback at Miranda's words.

James was shaking his head in denial. "I did not mark her. I have only bitten her once and it was to feed." I knew he was not lying and out of habit, I opened myself up for only a second to confirm that I could still count him as trustworthy down here among these creatures.

Anton moved closer and I now had the very uncomfortable pleasure of three ancient vampires, pissed off at my boyfriend for something he didn't do and more than likely me by association. Trying to smooth over the situation, I sent as much confidence as I could through my shields. As I projected, Anton stepped in and struck me so fast I was on the floor without even seeing his hand fly.

James moved nearly as fast, a growl ripping from his chest as he hovered protectively over me, cradling me, dazed as I was, in one arm, the other held in front to stay any advances. The mood in the room switched from politely tense to outright violent. I tried to project calm again, despite the fact that my head was ringing and distracting me, making my efforts shaky. The audience in the hall grew hungry and it was hard to control their images in the face of the onslaught. Their hunger beat on my shielding with an almost physical, primal force. Within me, the burning thirst began to build.

Anton looked at me, hatred burning in his inhuman cerulean blue eyes. "Stop!" It was a command ringing with authority. Refusal was not an option.

Spitting out the blood in my mouth, I knew I had made a stupid mistake and hoped I hadn't signed our death warrants. I shook my muddled head in an effort to clear it.

Miranda alone was reasonable. "James, you have much to explain. Your mate is marked, she smells of you, and she has special abilities you have not disclosed to us." Her flat stare settled on James' face. I did not allow her unperturbed demeanor to give me false hope.

James still held me protectively while he waited for my head to clear. "I swear to you that I have never marked her. If there is a physical link, it is equally shocking to me. She is a gifted human with a strong ability, but I was not aware until today that she could project as well." He looked down at me and the blank expression on his face was more frightening to me than Anton's explosion. I was blind. He was blocking me and I couldn't read what he was thinking. My disorientation was total.

Miranda directed her attention to Charles and spoke carefully, "There is a possibility that their connection is a *psychic* mark. We have not seen such a thing in centuries. It has happened only very rarely in the past."

Anton spoke up, anger still evident in his posturing, though he had mastered his features back into a mask of boredom. "It is easy to confirm whether or not they tell the truth. Miranda, would you please?"

While I didn't want her to touch me, I was willing to do almost anything to prove we weren't lying to them.

Miranda bowed her head to her companions and moved over to James first. Crouching down, she held her hand out to him nearly touching his forehead with her fingers. When she was inches from his face, she stopped. "You must let go of the human. I need to touch you separately."

My physical reaction was visceral, panic shooting through my entire being. Trying to hide his own anxiety, he shot me a tight smile that did nothing but heighten my stress. James helped me to my feet and with a final squeeze, he let go of my hand. I felt the loss sharply. Fighting my body to stay up and not wobble was difficult, my head was still spinning from Anton's wallop. *I must have a concussion* I thought. This was the second time this week I had gotten hit in the head by a vampire. A body could only take so many of those, I mused lightheaded.

I had no idea what Miranda was seeing as she "read" James for the truth, her elegant hand resting lightly on his chest. Standing there, I could see Charles and Anton watching me. Anton glared at me so darkly I feared he would hit me again. I thought if I tried to look meek and stare at my shoes they might lose interest. When my eyes broke from theirs my sense of balance left me, I felt my battle with my body turn. Knees buckling, I fell to the floor like a ragdoll and everything went black.

Ch. 49

I don't know how much time passed before I became aware of a cool hand on my head and noticed the ground I was laying on was soft instead of hard stone. Giving a silent prayer that we were back at the hotel, I opened my eyes gradually. We were not. However, I felt physically lighter from the relief of seeing James unharmed in front of me. He smiled and, though not completely at ease, I noted the tension around his eyes had disappeared. Miranda must have approved of what she had "read."

"Claire, you're all right. Charles had a chaise brought out for you to lie on. Do you think you could stand?"

I wasn't sure how to answer that with our current audience. Did we want them to know how weak I was or was it too late to hide that since I had fainted like an idiot? Casting my eyes around us, I saw that the three stood within human earshot and a number of those milling about had gathered to watch not bothering to hide their interest in our private drama unfolding off to the side of the thrones. I didn't doubt they could hear everything I said. Nodding, I mouthed "yes" and held my hand out to him. He reached for me and helped me to my feet, keeping hold of my hand, sensing I needed him for stability.

Once I was up, the members of the Court looked me over. Miranda walked toward me. It was my turn, but I couldn't stand without James, that much I knew. Would they let me sit back down? She surprised me by speaking kindly. "Claire," my name sounded exotic with her accent. I wasn't sure I liked it, or her. "I have seen both your thoughts."

She had touched me while I was out and unguarded? The thought of it left me feeling violated.

"James has told us the truth, he did not knowingly mark you. However, the fact remains that it has been done." I glanced imploringly at James. I didn't understand how he could mark me without either of our knowledge.

"His mark on you is not physical. It is rare, but some vampires can mark a human mentally. It is a mark on your mind, not your body, that he has given you."

I wondered if it was from our sessions together or our relationship.

"Please think carefully," she continued, "have you experienced physical symptoms that you cannot control?"

My eyes widened in surprise and I felt James' hand squeeze mine. Of course, it explained all of my symptoms lately. Personally, I'd believed it was my own weakness that I couldn't guard myself sufficiently when I was with him; that I was too distracted by him. Strangely enough, knowing I was wrong was reassuring. Unable to form a cohesive sentence I gaped, and Miranda seemed to take that as my response.

Mouth tight, Miranda nodded once and turned to Charles and Anton. "They are linked totally. She has physical effects through him and I would assume he has the same."

James disagreed. "That is not true. I have not felt physical symptoms as Claire has, and hers have been apparent only when I am thirsty."

Miranda turned back and considered us for a moment. One long delicate finger rested on the tip of her aquiline nose. "We have no choice but to honor your request for approval James. Yours by its very nature is a life bond and one I have not seen for three centuries."

I wondered at her deciding for the Court without discussing it with the other two. I must have missed something while I was out. Surprisingly though, she seemed pleased.

"Because your mate is an empath she is able to bridge your emotional minds. Am I correct in assuming you have spent a significant amount of time together recently?" Seeing James nod, she went on to explain. "Your gifts compliment each other well. Hers has linked you and she together psychically. And your own sensitivities have given her a bridge to your physical being. Do not be foolish enough to believe that bridge is one directional. You might have to look harder but I assure you it is there for you both. When you are weak so is she and when you are strong she is as well." Miranda's eyes sparkled for the first time in her excitement as she looked to me. "I must be honest, this development does intrigue me." Turning abruptly back toward the other two, Miranda swished away in her dress, skirts whispering on the stones. Anton and Charles fell in behind her and strode out a door someone had opened in the wall behind the chairs, and they were gone.

As they left the large hall, James and I were left holding hands in front of the chairs I had decided were thrones for their royals. We didn't feel free to speak with so many witnesses in the room, leaving us plenty of time to think quietly amongst ourselves.

I wondered if it was good or bad to be linked like this to James. Yes, I loved him and felt that we were two halves of a whole, but I had meant that metaphorically, not literally. And what did it mean for us mentally in the long term? Would I become more vampire or would he weaken through my human frailty? I tried to connect my symptoms to Miranda's explanation. Was this why I was not as hungry or tired? Did that mean his nature was stronger than mine and was pushing mine aside already? My mind wrestled with all of the possibilities as we stood staring at the closed door.

"Excuse me," I heard a familiar voice at my side. I looked over and saw the pale woman waiting calmly for us. I was surprised I hadn't heard her approach. She motioned for us to follow as she led us out of the receiving room and into the antechamber where she indicated we were free to leave.

As we walked back into the disorienting noise and garishness of the monstrous bar, James went to the bartender and surprised me by asking for another glass. I gave him a curious look and he was apologetic. "I am sorry Claire, I need this. We will leave as soon as we can." In rare form, he gulped down two more glasses in rapid succession before indicating with a gesture that we could leave.

It didn't matter what Miranda said, I didn't feel safe again until we were back in our room with our doors locked. For good measure I tucked a chair under the doorknob. James didn't make a single teasing comment.

Once we were locked in for the night I took down my hair and kicked off my heels. James got comfortable as well, taking off his jacket and tie and loosening his collar. I had a sense of déjà vu as we went through the same motions as the night of the wedding. But this time my relief was due to us still being alive, not just accepted. The stakes were much higher for disapproval in his world.

James was standing next to me as I examined myself in the mirror over the desk. "Where did he hit you?" He asked curiously, eyeing my reflection.

That was what I had been standing here wondering as well. The last time a vampire hit me, she had given me a concussion, knocked out a tooth and nearly broken my jaw. This was a similar blow yet I didn't see any residual marking on my face. "Do you think I'm getting stronger, like you?"

He stood, watching my eyes in the mirror. I don't think either of us knew how we should feel about this new twist in our relationship. He shrugged noncommittally. "You must be. That was a hard enough hit to knock you down. It should have raised a bruise by now, maybe even cracked a bone. There isn't even a hint of color."

"Well," I finally sighed, "it's not all bad then if it makes me a better healer, since vampires seem to want to hit me or kill me a lot. But what about you? Why don't you show any signs?"

He appeared thoughtful, his eyes had returned to their smoky hue now that he was well nourished. "I have been thinking about that since Miranda voiced her observation. My signs have been here all along as well."

Fascinated, I waited.

"My humanity. I have struggled with it since my change. It is hard for my kind to maintain our humanity and to experience our human emotions for very long after changing. They begin to fade almost immediately. But, ever since we have grown closer," he smiled making me blush at his reference to our intimacy, "I have experienced more human emotions than I have in over a hundred years."

Not certain if that was good or bad, I watched his face closely in the mirror. "Is that hard for you?"

"No," he sighed, "it is probably the single most thing I miss about being human. That, and chocolate." He grinned and ducked his head. I tried to picture him as a human enjoying a simple meal. Smiling a little uncertainly, James turned and kissed my cheek still facing the mirror. "Are you sorry to have met me?"

"That is the one thing I'm not sorry about in this whole thing. I'm so much happier having you in my life and I don't see that changing no matter how this turns out. We can work through everything else." And I knew we would. It felt natural to be with him. I could no sooner cut off an arm than be without him, James was literally a part of me now. Hearing it from Miranda had only proven what I already knew to be true. "You know, I don't think I've eaten a real meal all day." I thought about my stomach for the first time all afternoon.

His brow furrowed. "Yes, I noticed that. I think that's something we should watch."

Shrugging, I explained, "I've noticed I eat and sleep less. Honestly, I thought it was because of all the weird stuff going on and our schedules being messed up. But right now, I would love to eat." He was more than willing to call down and have food sent up. I felt like a lab rat as he watched me eat. "Do you mind?" I laughed, a little annoyed. "You can't constantly watch me for signs that I am turning into you, okay?"

Properly chastised, he grinned sheepishly. "Sorry. For the record though, I do like to watch you no matter what you're doing. I will endeavor not to bother you by staring constantly; I can't make any guarantees, though."

I ate, though not my usual amount, I noticed. *That still made me human,* I thought, suddenly fiercely protective of that fact. Love James as I might, I was not prepared to make any long-term decisions about changing my mortality status. I held out hope that we would find a way to control the bleed between our natures, to put a gate on the bridge, so to speak.

After my belly was full we were sitting on the bed, me in my dress with my legs pulled up underneath me. He lay on his back, feet hanging over the edge, body propped up on an elbow. We spoke quietly about family and love and what it meant to us.

"What do you want in life?" James asked me, genuinely curious. "Have you ever thought about it?"

"You know, up until a few weeks ago I just wanted a quiet little life. A job that let me use my brain without having to be around too many people and enough money to take a vacation once in a while. Maybe I would get a cat or something, but I had never really thought that hard about it." I shrugged. "Now that I can enjoy being around people, it opens up my options. It *is* still a strong possibility that I will work with books but maybe now I'll open my own bookstore instead of hiding in the back of a library." I went on boldly, wanting to reiterate my point even with the questions Miranda's discovery raised. "I know that I have to have you with me. It just isn't me anymore unless you're here."

His expression was guarded. "Did you feel that way before the marks? Do you think you have a choice or is it the connection between us influencing your decision?"

"I chose it when I first met you." Smiling, I tried to reassure him. "That won't change no matter how strange or complicated this gets."

He tipped his face as I leaned in making it easier to kiss him. Pulling back, James looked at me. "I have something for you." I was confused as I watched him reach under the pillow and his hand emerged with a small box wrapped in light green paper and a white bow.

"I love green." I teased. He put the box in my hands.

His eyes warmed as he smiled boyishly. "I know." It struck me how human he really did seem now that I had some perspective. I hadn't noticed before due to my lack of exposure to other, more typical, creatures of his kind. The difference was night and day.

Leaning forward, I kissed him again, touched by his thoughtfulness. "You have no idea what you already give me, what having you in my life means..." I couldn't finish. I felt the tears welling up at the thought of the years of loneliness I had anticipated.

James touched my hand, stroking the back with one finger. "You've almost died several times since I've known you. It might be that this isn't the life you should be living. Wouldn't you rather have some nice suburban life with a dog and 2.5 kids?" He wouldn't let on what I could feel coming from him. He really did worry that I might change my mind. That the danger of his world would prove too great and I would run and that he wouldn't blame me or stop me.

I shook my head wiping at the tears blurring my eyes before they could fall. "This is the *only* life I want to be living. Ever."

He tapped the package. "Open it." I heard his voice grow rough and I redirected my attention to the small box in my hand.

Carefully, I untied the bow and unwrapped the paper to reveal what was inside. It was a small black box and I sat looking at it for a moment spellbound.

Impatient, James reached over and clicked the box open. Inside was a beautiful opal necklace; the large oval stone was surrounded by small, delicate diamonds. I was breathless holding my hand to my mouth, admiring its elegance. As I held it, my hand shook and the light touched the stone at different angles, changing the face. The light green and golden brown veins ran through several shades of blues and gray changing in the light. I was transfixed.

"Do you like it?" He prodded curiously, anxious that I wouldn't.

I answered with the first thing that came to mind, watching the colors change and dance, "It's us, isn't it?"

He nodded. "It seemed right before when I bought it, even more so now."

I was speechless. The tremor in my hand caused the colors to shift, blurring the definition between the two, so much like we found ourselves now.

Reaching over, he took the necklace from the box and fastened it in place. My eyes were wet as the moment and the past few days washed over me in an emotional wave.

James' hands slid up to draw me in, finishing his gift with a kiss. When he released me, I felt a bubble expanding in my chest.

"James, I don't know what to say. It's beautiful. I love it."

His blue eyes held mine. "I bought it when I decided to bring you here. This seemed like the right time and place to let you know I was serious when I said, 'I love you,'"

"Are you going to write this into your article on romantic Scottish getaways? Because girls love jewelry," I teased, loving the smile it brought. He was still sitting from putting on my necklace. Sensing something was afoot, his brows peaked just a split second before I jumped at him and he let me roll him over to give him a proper thank you.

Ch. 50

The next morning, again before dawn, my eyes opened and rested on my hand lying in front of me. It was clasped loosely within a pale one. I studied the way they looked together before stretching into the body behind me. It seemed strange that when we went home I would be settling back into college life again. I wanted to finish school and liked it a lot, although after the few weeks I'd just had, it seemed anti-climactic to go back to books and a degree I wasn't sure I'd live to use. I sighed. Maybe we could go abroad while I studied in another country. Being overseas with James had reawakened a travel bug I'd buried when dad had retired. Initially, I had thought England or France would be good candidates for study, but now Scotland held the most interest for me. I wondered if James was tied to Minneapolis with work.

His chest rumbled with a playful growl. "Are you *trying* to get my attention?"

"No," I realized that was only partially true and blushed. "I was just thinking about school. It's going to be kind of boring after this. Have you ever thought of going abroad?"

We were interrupted by a knock at the door. James untangled himself from me and got up. Sitting up and clutching the sheet over my bare body, I watched tensely as he grabbed a bathrobe off a hanger in the closet. I couldn't help but stare at his figure as he strode away. Sensing it, he shot me a look over his shoulder, I saw the hint of a smile before he turned back to answer the door. It was out of my sightline so I listened closely.

A thick Scottish accent spoke first, "A message was left for you sir." I heard paper rustle and the door closed.

James walked slowly back into my view as he came down the hallway from the door, staring at the elegant cream stationary in his hands with a gold "M" emblazoned on the front. Looking up at me, I saw the tension in his face. "It's from Miranda."

Brow furrowed, he came over and sat next to me on the bed. With a smooth, practiced motion, his finger slid under the envelope flap and he steadily withdrew the note card. We both studied the script for a moment. It was on my third time reading it that the words finally registered.

James-

We enjoyed meeting your Claire. Keep us apprised of any developments, we are watching the situation with great interest. We look forward to meeting with the two of you again.

Regards,
Miranda

"Developments?" I mumbled, confused, as I started to breathe again. "What does that mean?"

James was unconcerned. "The Court knows we're looking into Milwaukee, which has led us to Bradley. And now Bradley's coven knows we're watching them, the Court as well. Henry wanted to fire a warning shot, if nothing else to let Bradley know he has an audience and to be careful not to overstep." Frowning he added, "And I would assume we have an audience now as well."

Realizing we'd done what we needed and were really in the clear for now, I offered him a grin. "We still have a few hours before we have to leave. Let's go out and say good-bye to my new favorite city."

Ch. 51

The flight home was long but pleasant and I was still basking in the afterglow of a glorious last day in Edinburgh with James. My hand kept going to my throat and moving my necklace so that I could look at it. It was "us" I had said. And now, we were going to be "us" for a lot longer thanks to Miranda's interest.

We deplaned and walked to our car. As soon as we were inside, the phone buzzed and James snapped it open. "Henry, yes we're on the ground. Have you had any luck finding anything?"

At the mention of Henry's name, my ears pricked and I sat up. I guessed we were going to hit the ground running. Of course. We just needed to avoid a war between humankind and vampires, *then* we could relax. No problem.

James listened quietly, occasionally making a noise into the phone. His face was expressionless as his thoughts ran elsewhere. After a moment, he hung up his phone and started the car. He snapped his sunglasses into place and I felt the familiar irk. I wanted to be able to see his eyes and get a better read for what was really happening.

Caught up in his own thoughts, James still hadn't spoken by the time we were driving rapidly up the freeway toward home. "I would assume we are going to your house?" I prompted somewhat crossly.

Without taking his eyes off the road, he answered tightly. "Claire, things have changed here while we've been gone. You are in danger as long as they are in the area." We both knew who "they" were. Settling back into my seat, I sighed and crossed my arms. So much for my afterglow.

He glanced at me as he exited the freeway. We were already in his neighborhood. That hadn't taken long. "Henry said that there has been increased traffic at Glamour, you remember the club." It wasn't a question and I didn't feel inclined to interrupt. "There are some new vampires in from out of town and Bradley owns the club so we've been watching it. The newcomers have been keeping to themselves and Henry's man says they look like pretty rough customers. They might be the ones we've been waiting for. I'm going to have to put you under lock and key for the time being."

"No," I blurted, hating the idea of being a prisoner even if it was for my protection.

His free hand reached over and stroked mine, sitting on my knee. "I know you don't like being kept hidden, but what else can I do? You might get hurt out walking around and even if it weren't for how much I love you, I am still sworn to protect you."

Fearing something had changed to raise the threat level, I stared straight ahead and tried to keep my voice even. "Has anything, uh, happened? Is everyone okay?"

We had pulled up to James' house and I opened my door. James put a hand on my arm to stop me shaking his head. "No one is here. Henry asked me to stop and grab some files on the way to Tara's where they are all waiting for us."

James scanned the area, frowning. "Stay here, I'll just be a moment." In a flash, he was gone and his front door was closing. It felt eerily quiet without him and I turned up the radio.

He had been gone less than a minute when a movement to my right caught my eye. I knew without a doubt that I was in trouble. Just like in Edinburgh at the Court, I was able to think through my options quickly, yet thoroughly, and without distraction. My guess, knowing what I did now, was that it was an effect of the marks allowing me to be calm under pressure. Like him.

I was reaching over to honk the horn to get James' attention, when my door whipped open and a pale hand locked on my arm at the wrist. Looking back, I saw the face that haunted my nightmares. Gina's eyes were black with hatred, lips curled up to show her fangs fully extended for attack. With a force and swiftness that took us both by surprise, my free hand flew across my body palm first to smash up into her nose. I felt the crunching of bone as it broke. Her hands flew to her face and I was free. My left hand flew back to honk the car horn and I was successful in giving it one push before her clawlike hands were locked around my arms, pulling me out of the car and down the driveway.

With my hypersensitivity, I could see several things at once. I saw a curtain move upstairs in the house when I honked the horn. The blue Mercedes I had seen before pulled up with a screech at the end of the short driveway and the half crazy vampire carried me toward the now open rear passenger door of the blue car. The small Asian man flew out of the front passenger door with a knife held in front of him. I was only relieved for a moment when he passed me to stick the knife into the back tires of the Audi, instantly disabling the car.

"Claire!" I heard James shout in anguish through the glass as the woman pushed me in, slid in beside me and slammed the door. James had made it to the front door as we pulled away from the curb, only to be intercepted by a blur of something rushing across his lawn and colliding with him, knocking him back into the house. I saw the frustration on his face as he wrestled only for a few seconds with the vampire before casting the limp body into the interior of his house.

My attention was brought back to my immediate danger as the woman next to me hissed, "You're stronger than you look, human. I'm going to make you pay for that when he gives you to me." My mouth fell open and I watched her lips curl into a cruel smile around her fangs. The blood had already stopped and she was wiping at her face with her sleeve. "He promised I don't have to give you back this time."

I tried to clear my head, to think things through, except all I could think about was the pain she was clearly excited to inflict upon me. Death was frightening enough, but she was going to make it hurt and I already had a small taste of her methods. Being better equipped to physically handle damage gave me no comfort. I wondered just how much more I could take before it was too much. I started breathing faster until eventually my mind shut down from the lack of oxygen, and I faded out.

Ch. 52

When I woke, I was once again tied to a chair. I was in a house; I couldn't hear well enough to tell if it was in the city or country. My eyes couldn't make sense of what they were seeing. I heard the buzzing of nearby voices, fuzzy and difficult to discern. I was reminded of previous episodes becoming all to frequent. Fortunately, the confusion was limited to external stimuli, leaving me with internal clarity of mind. Why was that?

It had happened the first time at the wedding in a crowd of people I knew; the rest of the times were in Scotland. All of those times were in crowds of people and the last was with vampires, so I knew type of being didn't matter. Thirst! James was thirsty when I had all of my episodes. When he was weak, I was weak and when he was strong, I was strong. That was what Miranda had said. I couldn't help but smile as I thought of breaking the brunette's nose. That had to be from him, as had been the ability to think clearly even when my life was in danger.

That was it. I had to think clearly right now. James was probably going to need to feed to get his strength up, however, he wouldn't take the time because he would be looking for me. I remembered what he'd said about when I'd "called him" in Duluth and I wondered if I could do it again.

Forgetting everything outside my head, I went into my mind and concentrated only on James. Not just his appearance or voice, but *him*. Everyone has an essence or feel to them and James was no different. I focused my mind completely on who he was and I felt that fuzzy dizziness like before only it was different than the other times because this was controlled. It felt like the back of my head had expanded, reminding me of a painkiller I was given once for a sprained wrist. It was trippy and I considered it progress. Hell, I was trying to exploit a psychic link with a vampire I was bonded with for life. It didn't get any trippier than that.

Digging down deeper, I refocused my energy and concentrated on James until I felt like I could smell him. I saw him pacing in his living room. Henry and Troy were standing nearby speaking to Stephen. They all looked tense and upset, I could almost hear their voices rumbling as they argued. I thought as hard as I could about eating. Not like a human thinks of hunger where the belly growls and maybe there's a side pain or two; I thought of the feeling I had at the wedding, the burning in my throat, the intensity of it. I combined it with my own human sense of hunger and thirst, hoping it would be enough to convey my message to him. It was exhausting and the image faded after a while. Stopping for a few minutes, I brought it up again, faster this time and I continued trying to send the message through my marks.

I had lost track of time when I heard someone shout from the other room. An angry reply came, muffled, through the wall to my left. I glanced up as the doorknob turned and my fear wiped away all of my focus in a flash. Bradley himself stood looking down at me, flawless in a dark, double-breasted suit complete with handkerchief in the breast pocket. His short, slicked back blonde hair was perfectly groomed, his neatness contrasted with the haphazard appearance of the well-muscled, hairy individual standing beside him.

His companion looked to be about five foot nine, stocky and barrel chested with spiky, black hair that came from a bottle. His black cargo pants were tucked into gouged and worn combat boots, dark chest hair stuck out through his open flannel shirt that had lost its sleeves at some point in its lifetime. The face looking at me was handsome in a vampire way, but the nose was a bit too bulbous and lips too thick for true beauty. In his human life, he had most likely been an unattractive bruiser. Maybe it was my time around soldiers, but I knew without question he was just that by the way he

343

entered the room and automatically scanned it. I knew this was the one we had been searching for, the one from Chicago who had massacred William's coven in Milwaukee. Henry was right; they were here.

"Gaston," Bradley addressed the bruiser in his clipped, manner of speech. "Have you met Claire yet? She belongs to James and Henry. You remember Henry, don't you? He is the bastard you've come here to help me kill."

My blood ran cold and I tried to fight the impulse to scream. From somewhere in my racing thoughts came the realization that I could focus again. Had my efforts worked? Had I gotten through to James? If I had, that meant I could send them what I could of Bradley's plan to kill Henry. I had to get them to talk, to find out what I could before I fled.

"Why would you want to kill Henry? He's not dangerous, he doesn't even hunt humans." Though I no longer saw Henry as the gentle fatherly type, he was far from being lumped into the same level of depravity as Gina or Bradley. It didn't make sense that they were so intent upon his destruction.

Bradley snorted at my remark. "Not dangerous? How well do you know Henry? I have known him for over two hundred years. I have seen your dear Henry, awash in blood, remove a woman's head from her body while she screamed for mercy. You should ask him about it sometime; it is a fascinating story." The sarcasm dripped from Bradley's tongue. James said Bradley blamed Henry for the death of his mate. Could that be the woman he was talking about?

"What woman Bradley?" I asked hoping to keep him talking.

He stared right through me. "Gaston, would you let the others know it is time to move the weapon? I won't be long here." The brute nodded and opened the door, turning to leave when Bradley spoke quietly, "Oh, and let Gina know she can have her prize as soon as I am done."

My stomach twisted, anticipating what was coming. I had less than no time left. I was hoping he would want to gloat or maybe I could delay him with some good information. Maybe buy freedom. If the marks had proved effective, I'd like to think I could call for James, though I wasn't sure. Because of the fact that my head cleared from my earlier efforts, I was willing to gamble everything I had on it. "Bradley," I tried again, "my hands are numb, I wonder if you could come loosen them just a little."

Bradley didn't even blink, it was clear that he was ignoring my requests. Then, when he did turn his attention on me I felt my heart stop. "What were you doing in Edinburgh, little pet?" His voice slid over me like a snake, leaving me feeling unclean in its wake. My tongue felt too thick for my mouth. I couldn't have answered him if I wanted to. "Were you meeting with the Court? Are those bleeding hearts trying to rally support against me again?"

When Gaston had opened the door to leave, I had a clear view down a long hallway and through a window. I was in an upper floor room of what had to be an older farmhouse. Turning to my right, I saw a wooden desk, an older computer on it with a neat stack of papers piled on top. Judging from the sounds I was hearing now, we were out of the city. There was some machinery running somewhere nearby, men speaking outside the window behind me. Nothing gave me any indication of location, though. My eyes desperately searched the window, the walls, anything to tie this house to an address.

Gaston walked out and when he closed the door, a piece of paper fluttered off the desk landing beside it facing me. Squinting, I noticed my eyesight was much improved. The address at the top of the letter was legible if I concentrated really hard. As soon as I memorized it, I snapped my eyes

345

shut and, using my meditation experience, I calmed myself enough to focus and tune Bradley out.

I pulled up my ability and the marks like they were tangible objects from my mind. Picturing the house and address, I closed out everything else and projected as clearly as I could. A nuisance, a sound like a buzzing fly; I heard my name at the periphery of my awareness and ignored it. The buzzing annoyance continued, growing more insistent and finally grew impatient enough that I felt my eye explode in searing pain and my chair sailed backward.

"When I speak to you, I expect an answer." He looked at his hand and I saw his brow furrow in consternation as he righted my chair and studied my face. "You should be bleeding." Just a few seconds more and I watched it dawn on him. "He marked you, that bastard." A fury I was soon to understand flooded his face and he raised his voice. "Yet another weak, pathetic human to distract us from our true destiny. It's becoming an epidemic." He directed his tirade at me. Once again the master of his demeanor, he ran his hand over his hair to smooth it. "Do you have any idea what Henry is doing to our society, keeping you humans around? It's unconscionable."

The longer I kept him talking the better my chances of living and finding out more about what he was going to have Gaston do to Henry. "Henry said you hate humans and you want to start a war to get rid of us. But you killed other vampires, others of your kind. Why would you do that if you want to save your kind?"

He smiled and sighed as though he were speaking to a child. "Humans have caused more damage to mine than you could ever fully understand, Claire. And sadly, some of our kind are unwilling to see that, they are sympathetic to humans. If we are to unite, these sympathizers need to be eradicated. They are as much a barrier to our success as the humans themselves. Social cleansing is a necessary part of any well conducted coup." Shaking his head and putting his hands out as though to encompass the room, he looked out the window behind me. "What I would like to know is if you understand your *specific* involvement."

Deliberately, I shook my head no. There was no way I was going to mention that I knew Henry had killed Bradley's mate. A trickle of doubt entered my head asking *why* Henry had killed his mate. What if Bradley had a point? Not that it justified ethnic cleansing, but it would go a long way toward explaining why he hated my family and me.

"Henry is a sympathizer like William. He has a weakness for your kind; I heard it has something to do with making amends. I don't care. It is a weakness he shares with his associate, James." My body stiffened automatically at the mention of his name. Bradley noticed and smiled coldly. "Yes, I know you are his pet and that is why you are here, my dear. You see, where I come from, we believe that turnabout is fair play."

My instincts were correct. That cleared up that little piece of the puzzle.

"Let me share with you something you do *not* know about Henry. It might change how you feel about his 'peaceful tendencies'. Your friend Henry and I have always disagreed about the role of humans in this world. Time and again, he has gone to the Court about my methods and each time I have been able to argue the merits of my case. But he has no valid justifications for his requests for censure and he knows it." Bradley waved a hand and shrugged, the picture of persecuted innocent. Again, his mood shifted and hate flowed back into his eyes. "Where he went beyond the point of no return was when his associate was changed. Have you heard the story of when your Master became a vampire?"

I sat frozen, afraid to speak.

Grinning shrewdly, Bradley gave a small shake of his head. "Certainly not the whole of it. James was never supposed to be turned, he was attacked by an associate of mine and my associate got sloppy. Sometimes that happens to the very old among us. They go a bit mad; no matter." Smiling absently he waved a hand. "A dead human is not a loss but a victory for our side. This is war and it has been going on for millennia."

I realized then that Bradley was not starting a war, he thought we were already in one and that justified everything he did to destroy humankind.

"Coincidentally, Henry had been in the area spying on my ally and myself, once again trying to convince the Court of our wrongdoing, when he heard about the humans being attacked and he interfered. He pretended to help at the scene so that he could check for survivors and saw them drag James out of the building, put him on a wagon and take him away. Apparently, there was still a faint heartbeat and the boy who had been pronounced dead was left unattended on the doctor's doorstep, while the town fought the fire before it could burn down their village." He snorted, putting a hand to his nose as if he were coyly hiding his smirk. "That would have been a real tragedy."

My jaw was clenched tight as I fought the urge to kill this crazy monster as he spoke so dismissively of James' harrowing death. These were the kind of vampires James meant when he said that they could lose their humanity. I was instantly glad of our bond if it would keep him from ever being this cruel, though I doubted he had the capacity.

"No surprise to you," Bradley continued on, drawing me back, "the boy did not die because your dear Henry found him and turned him. He fed him a small amount of his own blood, but he was discovered and had to abandon the boy. He was not there when he rose. By the time he arrived, young James had already drained the good doctor and his wife. From there, he had no choice but to guide the boy. Henry took James away, helping him to elude his pursuers who declared him guilty of all three murders."

Bradley paced up and down the room, becoming agitated. "Henry was able to keep James from the humans, but not my associate. You see, my friend enlisted my help and that of my mate to take care of the boy. He had taken offense at Henry's interference and we did not want the fool corrupting a young vampire with his ideals. When we caught up with them, your dear peaceful Henry killed my friend," he paused and I saw the blank facade crack for a second, "and my mate." His black eyes raised and I saw the tips of fangs beginning to stick out, "And as I said, I believe in an eye for an eye. Henry has not taken a mate for some time, but I have been waiting patiently and now James finally has. To my way of thinking, you owe me no less than *two* eyes, one for my associate and one for my mate."

My stomach flipped over and I tasted the bile at the back of my throat. I sat there, staring at the loathing in Bradley's eyes and knew there was nothing I could say or do that might help me. I had nothing. Bradley watched the color fade from my face and smiled, calling over his shoulder, "Gina, you may come in now."

She had been waiting outside the door and her long stride swept her to his side in two steps. Gina rested her white hand on my shoulder and I looked over and saw purple polish on her short nails. It matched the color streaks in her hair. Funny what catches your eye when you know you're going to die.

Speaking to Gina, Bradley continued to look at me and calmly gave his instruction. "Do what you want to the rest of her, but I want the eyes." Turning to her he asked, "Have they readied the weapon? We are moving on Minneapolis tonight. We can take the entire coven as peacefully as we did in Milwaukee." He turned to face me and explained with an infuriating smirk. "It is a wonderful thing to understand one's political system. No matter his suspicions, by the laws of our kind he cannot refuse my request to meet. To sweeten the pot I will tell him I will bring you. James will be sure to attend as well. The rest are of no real interest, I've been able to deter most of the locals from siding with what are soon to be enemies of the Court."

Gina's enthusiastic smile sickened me. They were talking about wiping out two people whom I cared for like it was nothing. And my friends would go like lambs to the slaughter with no acceptable means of refusing. What about the Andrews clan, would they be bound to follow Henry into this trap?

His business with me finished, Bradley left and closed the door behind him leaving just Gina and I in the room, which now felt infinitely more restrictive.

Thinking fast, I remembered why James said Gina hated humans and tried to reason with her. "Gina," I struggled to make my voice soothing like James did. "I know what it's like to feel like you're going crazy; I know what you're hearing all the time. It's a special ability you have, it isn't madness. James and Henry can help you to control it. They can teach you to block people from getting into your head. They helped me. If you can help me get to them, we can teach you. You don't have to suffer." I hoped James had heard my call for help and was coming although I didn't know how far away I was or even if my call had been successful.

Her eyes were black and eager, fangs out. Gina didn't even flinch at the sound of my voice. "You would say anything to save your skin, humans never speak the truth. Bradley showed me that."

He had poisoned her against my kind. That explained the direction for the hatred; how many others had he turned and

350

twisted for his own purposes, creating his own band of supporters.

"Humans don't have any control over their minds, you're too simple. But we can. Those who have abilities can serve our cause, that is the only way to redeem the evils your kind has done to us in the past. Like the boy. He is a weapon, and once enough vampires see what he can do, they will flock to the cause and finally put humans in their place forever." Her eyes held all the fever of a religious fanatic.

"What boy?" I felt the fear coiling into a cold ball in my chest.

Proud to know something and enjoying her power, she gloated. "Gaston found the boy living on the streets. He has an ability that works on vampires, but not special ones like me. He can make vampires do anything we tell him to do. Did you hear what happened in Milwaukee? We did that with him." She smiled, showing off now. "He turned them against each other while we just watched. We didn't have to do a thing. He will do the same tonight with your beloved Henry. Who do you think will win, Henry or your James? Which one will have the honor of being executed by my Master?"

My head was spinning and I could barely hear over the blood in my ears. James had an ability, that they knew, but not Henry; at least not one they knew about, or me either for that matter. The boy wouldn't affect James but he would be able to manipulate Henry into going after James and, guessing from Henry's age, I was assuming he was very powerful. My heart was in my throat.

Trying to distract Gina and buy time, I tried to throw her a curve. "What about Henry's werecats? Can your boy turn *them* against each other? They are neither human nor vampire. Maybe *they* will kill your boy. Or you." I hoped I was doing the right thing mentioning the clan.

351

As I had hoped, doubt flowed across Gina's face casting it in shadows. She aimed a nasty look at me. "Bradley has thought of that; he thinks of everything."

I wondered what Bradley's relationship with Gina was. She was clearly enamored with him. Even though she professed complete confidence in her idolized leader, I saw the doubt flicker again in her eyes. Without another word she strode from the room. I presumed she went to speak to Bradley. That didn't give me much time.

As soon as she left, I started working my wrists, only they were bound too tight to budge. I hadn't been kidding about not being able to feel my hands. If I could get a hand free, I figured there had to be scissors or something in there I could use. My legs were tied at the ankles to the chair legs, but I could hop the chair, I bet. Giving it a test, I hopped a tiny bit and the chair moved, noisily, a few inches toward the desk. I only had to move it a few feet, and I decided sound was less important than speed, hopping hurriedly over to the desk. It was less than a minute and I held my tied right hand to the drawer. I could reach if I balanced on my feet and held the chair cocked with my hips turned. It was awkward but it allowed me to use my hands at the right level.

Luck was with me and I found scissors in the top drawer. Working the blades against the rope, I was concentrating on my task so intently that when she came back in the room and slammed the door behind her, I jumped. And dropped the scissors.

I watched her face change when she saw the scissors on the floor. She crossed the room in less than a second and her hand flew to strike me, as promised, across the nose. It brought tears to my eyes and I felt a few drops run down my lip, then it stopped.

Judging from the look on her face, Gina wasn't getting the desired response. She had been hoping for more of a human reaction. Maybe she remembered how much I'd bled the last time. Bradley must not have told her I was marked. She roared with rage and grabbed the scissors from the floor. Before I could register what was happening, she stuck them into my left thigh.

I felt the metal scrape bone and I screamed. The pain was intense. I wished I could pass out, although I could feel it wasn't going to happen. The blood was pouring out of my leg and I wondered if she'd struck something vital. Now that she got what she was looking for, her lips pulled back from her fangs, smiling with sick pleasure. She liked to see blood. She pulled the scissors out, licking them languidly and I saw her raise them again. I screamed before they went in my left shoulder.

My mind didn't let me pass out until she had stabbed me for the third time; the scissors were still sticking out of the last one, low on my left side. She had nicked an artery somewhere given the amount of blood pouring out onto the floor. The last thing I saw before fainting was Gina dragging her fingers across the steady trickle and sucking my blood from her fingers.

While I was out, I dreamed of James. He was driving on a country road in the late afternoon, the sun low on the horizon. I was frustrated that I couldn't see the blue of his eyes one last time behind his black shades. I wished I had the strength to send him a warning about Bradley's trap. We were both going to die today. I heard his engine rev higher as I thought of our impending deaths.

I was still dreaming of James when a bone jarring blow struck the back of my neck, sending my chair crashing forward. My head and left side hit the wood floor hard, knocking my shoulder out of socket again and smearing my face and side in the blood on the floor. I'd regained consciousness, I noted sadly. I would rather dream of better things as I bled to death.

Gina pulled my chair up as if it weighed nothing and righted it. As she reached down and pulled at the scissors again, apparently her weapon of choice today, I heard a commotion outside in the yard. Gina did as well and glided over to the window to see. She roared and opened the window to yell out.

I was lightheaded from pain and blood loss, wondering vaguely what she had seen as I sat in the chair, blood dripping from my body and adding to the growing pool on the floor.

Their weapon maybe? I wondered how old he was or if he knew what he was doing when he made vampires kill each other for Bradley's amusement. The noise from below floated up through the open window and I listened to it as I faded into unconsciousness.

There was a fight between two barn cats, I could hear them hissing and growling. The other sounds weren't as easily recognized. Tearing fabric maybe, metal bending and wood breaking. Once or twice I thought I heard yelling or screaming. Then, it was quiet.

All of a sudden my hands were loose and I was floating. My left arm hung uselessly at my side. I heard myself whimper as I was shifted gently into a seated position. Hearing an engine, I tried to focus. Who was moving me and to where? "Can't you just let me die in peace?" I grumbled at my captor. I knew it was going to happen, and then I thought about the family I'd come to love and how I had failed them. I felt the fight go out of me as I acknowledged my family was going to die. It made it easier to bear, knowing that I was going to die too. Faintly, I was aware of a car's engine revving higher as I mumbled about death and traps and weapons, and somewhere in the car, something growled over the engine.

I can't say I was awake during my trip to the hospital, although I never completely passed out. During the drive, I was aware of cool hands stroking my face as I lay against the seat. Upon arriving at the hospital, I was picked up again and carried into the building. The bright lights above me were disorienting, then I saw a flash of the side of James' face as he carried me. Trying to speak wasn't working, but I made enough of a squeak that he looked down at me. He didn't look very much like himself though, I wasn't sure why. Maybe he was sick. Could vampires get sick? That was when I finally faded out.

Ch. 53

I woke up in the hospital, an IV was in my arm, and I could tell they had doped me up because nothing hurt. I would have to kiss my nurse for that. I could hear voices outside the room and recognized James' voice speaking with someone else. Trying to see out the door, I shifted.

There was no stopping the scream that erupted from my mouth. The pain in my side was incredible. Seconds after I screamed, I saw James and my doctor. That must have been who he was talking to outside. My eyes remained on James' face the entire time I listened to the doctor. He said something about a nicked artery, transfusion, dislocated something and concussion. He also mentioned some older cracked skull bones and jaw that were recent, but fully healed. James said something about a hiking accident and I mumbled in agreement. I just wanted the doctor to leave.

Finally he did and James reached to hold my hand. Smiling weakly at him, I tried to match the gesture and failed. He picked mine up. "You came for me." It sounded thick coming from my dry throat. Looking around, James found a glass of water with a straw and held it for me while I took a small sip. I waited a moment while I decided if that one would stay down, when it appeared it would indeed, I took a longer one.

"I was nearly too late. I've failed in my oath again," he whispered, his voice so hoarse that I could barely hear him.

Blinking slowly, I gave a small headshake. "Some things are beyond your control James." Then, for his benefit, I changed the subject. "How did you find me? Did it work?" I knew he would understand what I meant.

He nodded, his face lighting, "It was much clearer this time."

I was proud of myself. "Did you hear both times?"

He looked confused. "Both?"

Crinkling my brow, I clarified, "Yes, the first time I told you you had to eat something."

His mouth formed a little "o." "That was you telling me to feed? I was unable to think of anything but feeding; I was frustrated that I was thinking of my comfort while you were missing." His faced tightened. "That was smart, the address. How did you get it?"

I told him about the letter from the desk. "What happened? I'm a little foggy but trying to put it all together." I watched his face as he told me. He took a deep breath and his eyes turned inward as he remembered.

"The Andrews, Henry and I left immediately when we got the address that you gave me. While we were in transit, Henry received a call from Bradley asking us all to come discuss Court business that night. In our society, we are compelled to hear all Court business on neutral ground. It isn't an option to decline. It is their way of passing their messages along." His eyes clouded. "While Henry was on the phone, I felt you with me and I heard you tell me we were going to die."

He stopped when I gasped at that last. "Are you in pain?" He asked, looking around at my IV to see that it was still dripping its numbing agent into my vein.

Shaking my head, I spoke quietly. "I thought I was dreaming of you driving on a country road. I was imagining you one last time and I said good-bye. I was mad I couldn't warn you about his trap. I thought I'd failed you."

Speaking was difficult for him, his emotions were threatening to get the better of him. "When we got to the farm where they were holed up we found some new recruits. I'm guessing they were the ones we were waiting for, providing our information about military training was true. The two males we found there were very proficient fighters. The cats took them out while Henry and I got past the guard and some others." I heard his growl at the memory. "We had surprise on our side thanks to you and took care of them quickly. Inside the barn was a bit more confusing. Bradley had been there with a human; we could smell them but they had gone by the time we arrived."

I sucked air in quickly through my teeth at the mention of Bradley's secret weapon, the one that was capable of turning Henry on James.

He touched my face and whispered roughly. "Did he do this to you?"

"No, it was Gina."

"Then I am glad to tell you she won't bother you again." James' expression darkened in confusion as he continued, "I don't understand why he had a human with him. He hates humans. Did you hear anything?"

"The boy is like us, he can do things others can't. He can manipulate your kind." I saw his shock. "They used him to turn William's coven against each other in Milwaukee and Bradley executed the last one standing. They were going to do the same thing to you. The boy's talent doesn't affect others with abilities, so it wouldn't have worked on you but he was going to turn Henry against you and watch you kill each other." I was grateful for the mind numbing effects of the drugs, it made it easier to talk about James dying.

So much had happened; it was too much to absorb all at once. I didn't know I was crying until I felt him wipe my cheek with his thumb. His touching me broke what little control I had of myself and my shoulders shook painfully as

I let go of the pain and fear I'd been holding onto for the past twenty-four hours. James slid his hands into my bed to pick me up and move me over so smoothly, I didn't feel any discomfort with the shifting this time. He lay next to me and I put my head against his chest. We stayed like that for a long time until I was cried out. At one point I heard someone approach, tell him visiting hours were over, and felt the rumble of his harsh response followed by a quick retreat of feet.

It was a while before I thought of my parents. "Do my parents know I'm here?" I didn't want them to worry, plus how would I explain what had happened?

"With you being an adult they don't need to contact your parents. I was able to convince your doctors to speak to me until you regained consciousness."

"Thanks for thinking of that, I don't want them to know I'm in here." Pulling back to see his face, I added, "I like you telling people we're together. Did I ever tell you that when Beth stopped by the house and saw us I knew she was going to spread it at the office? Secretly, I was glad because I wanted people to know. About us."

He was mockingly serious. "You have created quite a stir at the office with your scantily clad appearance at my door. I hear a few of the male interns have volunteered to deliver my packages next time I can't make it in." He nuzzled my ear as he added, "I hope you'll do it again soon."

"I'd love to." I raised my head. He knew what I wanted and kissed me gently.

Ch. 54

I was released from the hospital a few days later with James instructed to stay with me so that he could watch for any complications. He swore not to let me out of his sight. With a bubbling fullness in my chest, I knew that was true.

My teachers allowed me through the end of the week to heal up since they were still under the impression I was recovering from my first abduction. It would be pushing my luck to ask for more time than that. Given my new capacity for rapid healing, I didn't really need any more time anyway.

Stephen was healing from his fight with Sasha. He was apparently stronger than I had thought. He'd taken down a vampire by himself, which was hard to do as he continually pointed out, and Troy and Tonya had taken the other female down. No one had heard anything about the third and we were assuming she was on her own and no longer a threat.

Since returning to school, Stephen and I had lunch every day on campus and often walked to class together whenever the opportunity presented itself. Because no one knew where Bradley, Gaston and the boy had gone, I was still guarded about as well as any crowned princess. As a result, when I wasn't with James or Henry, I was visiting Stephen or Tara. I liked visiting her now because the rest of the clan hung out there a lot and I was able to see them all quite frequently. Tara and I were also continuing with our practice sessions. James had told Henry what I had been able to do with the marks and projecting, and he was intrigued with my potential.

Moving back into the dorm was not as hard as I had thought. Probably because I wasn't there much. I felt slightly guilty for not getting my money's worth out of the accommodations; however, James' house felt more like home. And, as he'd said, I was welcome for as long as I wanted to be there.

Our relationship had grown slightly more complicated. We were in love, but also were exploring the possibility that our need to be together might be more than a little tied to the psychic connection we shared. Henry and James were using their contacts within the supernatural community to learn more about psychic marks and their effects without giving too much of the "why's" away, it wasn't in any of our best interests to have it be common knowledge that a human and a vampire were tied together. In the meantime, I had to work to balance romance with academics.

Mom and Dad started coming for lunch once a week and James often joined us. At first it had been a bit awkward, but my parents seemed to be genuinely fond of James. And James was excited about my dad teaching him about woodworking. *That* I couldn't wait to see.

It was still a very tempting idea to go abroad for a while, although for now I was busy playing catch up before finals. I had lost a few weeks of studying with all of my near death experiences. Also, James did confirm he would accompany me anywhere in the world I wanted to go. For now I was living only for today, because who knew what the future would bring.

Acknowledgements

This is the third edition of this series and, even though I'm sure my editors are tired of it, I still love these characters and have to thank them most of all for coming to me and letting me tell their story.

I would like to thank, as always, my family and friends for acting as sounding boards and for giving me their honest opinions when I needed them most. Leslie and Dawn for being more than patient test readers and keeping my ego intact while doing so. Of course, my husband for being my biggest supporter and best friend, and my mom for encouraging me to keep trying.

Also, to my editors, Sean, Sarawho tirelessly read and re-read each book, challenging me to make sure they're perfect. And helping me laugh when they aren't. The wonderful cleanup artists, Katie and Brittany who make extra extra sure it all makes sense and help us all look good.

And lastly, to Grace without whom I never would have taken the chance.

CPSIA information can be obtained at www.ICGtesting.com
Printed in the USA
BVOW072034020613

322194BV00001B/7/P